150

THUNDEROUS ACCLAIM FOR
THE CANFIELD DECISION
SPIRO T. AGNEW'S
SIZZLING SUPERSELLER OF INTERNATIONAL BE-
TRAYAL, SEXUAL SCANDAL AND HIGH-LEVEL
POLITICAL CRIME—" . . . INTRIGUES INVOLVING
MURDER, MILITARY BRINKSMANSHIP AND, YES,
VICE-PRESIDENTIAL TAPES."
—*The Chicago Literary Review*

"THE WRITING IS CONCISE, COLORFUL AND COM-
PELLING . . . IMMENSELY EXCITING . . ."
—*The Seattle Times*

"THE STORY IS EXCITING AND SHOCKING, THE
SETTING DRAMATIC AND REALISTIC."
—*The Columbus Dispatch*

". . . INTERESTING . . . TENSE . . . WELL CON-
STRUCTED."
—*Harper's*

"FASCINATING AND EXCITING. IT'S ONE OF THOSE
BOOKS YOU DON'T WANT TO PUT DOWN."
—*MERV GRIFFIN*

THE CANFIELD DECISION

SPIRO T. AGNEW

A BERKLEY MEDALLION BOOK
published by
BERKLEY PUBLISHING CORPORATION

Playboy Press
747 Third Avenue
New York, N.Y. 10017

Library of Congress Catalog Card Number 76-3475

SBN 425-03338-4

BERKLEY MEDALLION BOOKS are published by
Berkley Publishing Corporation
200 Madison Avenue
New York, N.Y. 10016

BERKLEY MEDALLION BOOK ® TM 757,375

Printed in the United States of America

Berkley Medallion Edition, MARCH, 1977

To Judy

1

STEVE GALDARI put down the newspaper and looked out the double glass window. The brightness of the sky struck his eyes with a near physical impact. Far off to the west, the Sierra Nevadas made the horizon a jagged blue-gray pencil line. It reminded Galdari of a sales graph, with Mount Whitney being a very good week. Twenty-six thousand feet down, the barren, rugged Great Basin slid by, looking colorless and undefined in the summer heat.

The 727-E cruised quietly and effortlessly. Galdari preferred it to all other planes. He considered himself somewhat of an expert, having logged over three million miles in air force transports. The 727, he reflected, always had been the ideal plane for in-country missions. It was fast, quick-climbing and comfortable. It could go anywhere the smaller Jet Star could, and it could get into small city airports that a 707 had never seen. And now the engine modifications and increased fuel capacity of the E model gave it enough range for intercontinental missions. He was glad they hadn't gone supersonic. There was little enough time between countries on international visits.

The thing he liked best about this bird was its quietness. You didn't have to crawl right up into somebody's ear to have a conversation. Talk was never an idle social exercise with Galdari. For the Special Agent in Charge of the U.S. Secret Service vice-presidential protective detail, there was always plenty of work to discuss between stops—work that wouldn't wait until some convenient time.

In about twenty minutes, they would be near the Grand Canyon, but passing too far west to see it. Then it wouldn't be long before he felt that slight jolt as Col. Ridge Potter disengaged *Air Force Two*'s autopilot and began to let down into Phoenix.

He glanced at the flight card copilot Joe Roper had dropped on the adjoining seat shortly after they left Oregon. It told the SAIC that their estimated time of arrival was 1710, 5:10 P.M. PDT. He looked at his Seiko watch, a souvenir of his first Far East trip and still performing well in spite of having been dropped carelessly on hundreds of hotel night stands. It was 4:25 P.M., and they'd be on the blocks in forty-five minutes. *Air Force Two* was never early, and almost never late. It was a point of personal pride with Potter, who could stretch five minutes of taxiing time to twelve minutes or cut it to two, as the occasion demanded.

He shifted his 205 pounds to a more comfortable position. He wasn't quite in the shape he used to maintain during his basketball days at Columbia, but the muscle tone was a lot better than that of most forty-two-year-olds.

"Coffee, Steve?" It was Joe Hentz, one of the affable, hard-working stewards.

"Thanks, Joe. I need something to wake me up. We've got a nut warning for Phoenix." He worriedly ran his hand through short-cropped, thinning black hair. "Who'd ever think a nice, peaceful place like Phoenix would have so many weirdos running around?"

Hentz smiled confidently. "You'll handle them, Steve." He handed the steaming mug of black coffee to the agent. "I've got my own troubles this trip," he laughed. "Having the press aboard is no picnic. I guess I'll never learn to move fast enough to run booze to those newsies. Man, they really scarf it up, especially the writers. Of course, there are exceptions; but none of them seems to travel with us." Hentz's expression showed his distaste. "Just because their papers pay a first-class fare, some of them think they're entitled to special treatment, including a private consultation with the veep every time they get itchy."

"Yes," agreed Galdari, "I liked it better when the old man was around. He wasn't always kissing their butts."

He was referring to former Vice President Alan French, who had been stricken with a fatal stroke four years before while presiding over the Senate. At sixty-four, the former governor of Montana hadn't been consumed by the presidential ambitions that gnawed at his successor. He had been a quiet, pragmatic, considerate man.

"Well, I guess we'll see a lot of newsies from now on," said Joe. "We're only a year from the nineteen eighty-four convention and our man is starting to sniff the air already."

2

"Oh, yes, I've noticed. He's got the professor and the illustrious senator from California up there with him right now, and I suspect they aren't talking about girls."

Suddenly a raucous voice from back on the other side of the aisle exploded, "Hey! Steward! How about another gin and tonic?"

"Atherton," whispered Joe. "What a fourteen-carat pain he is. He's looking for his fifth gin since we left Portland. See you later."

Joe moved away easily. "Coming right up, Mr. Atherton," he said, and no one could have detected his irritation. He was a pro, and courtesy to everyone aboard *Air Force Two* was automatic.

As Joe moved down the aisle, Galdari stretched, turned around and took a quick inventory of the other passengers. There were two shifts of Secret Service, twelve agents in all, including the drivers; the four-man Transworld Broadcasting System crew with the ambitious young Douglas Drake presiding; peripatetic, blustering, officious Sid Winehart of United Press International; and Joe Hentz's present tormentor, crusty Bruce Atherton of the Washington Bureau, dean of the Associated Press workhorses, whose drinking habits and refusal to create sensational copy were responsible for his having been passed over for an executive assignment at the main office. Needless to say, this did not improve Atherton's normally dour disposition.

In a miraculously short time, Galdari saw Joe hand Atherton a fresh gin and tonic, at least a quarter of which disappeared before the glass hit the tray. "Let's see," said the reporter to no one in particular, "this is my third. Guess it'll have to hold me until after dinner."

Joe smiled patiently and moved away.

Galdari mused briefly about Atherton, whom he had known for several years. The AP man was well aware that it wasn't his third, just as he knew it wouldn't be his last before dinner. But even if he was a fool about the health of Bruce Atherton, no one could dispute that he was a sharp and experienced reporter. He had a tremendous backlog of political information accumulated over the years by hard work and a questing, perceptive intellect. His writing style was clean and incisive. Atherton got to the point quickly because he did what was necessary to find out what the point was before he began writing.

During Galdari's early days in the Service the press had been much more professional and objective. In the mid-sixties, they had been just as tough, but seldom ready to jump into print without verification. Accusations then were the raw material for quiet investigation. Now they were bombs to be used against political

3

enemies or defused for political friends.

The trend toward advocacy journalism did not please Atherton either. A reporter was supposed to get the facts, and a good reporter never came to a conclusion until he had filled in all the blanks. Atherton admitted that digging it all out had a tendency to make you cynical; that it permitted no heroes. But men were fallible, so what was the good of trying to convince his readers that some were saints and others were sinners. Everyone he'd come across had a liberal portion of the devil in him, including some past presidents whom the revisionists were now sanctifying.

Bruce Atherton tipped his glass again and turned to the UPI man in the seat next to him. "What the hell are you so busy writing, Sid?" he asked.

The tired writer glanced up impatiently. "I'm doing an analysis of Vice President Porter Canfield's future plans," he snapped. "UPI doesn't pay me to rewrite the garbage that press secretaries hand out every day. Canfield's Portland speech was just the same old crap. Everybody knows Israel's a great country and we've got to keep our eye on the rest of the Middle East. It's no secret that the Hurley administration favors the Israelis over the Arabs, and it's certainly no secret that Porter Canfield gets a pretty good slice of the Jewish vote and can be depended on to court the pro-Israel sentiment in the American Jewish community. What the hell's new about that? Yet Pete Rosen hands out the speech like it's diamond encrusted. Well, I know Canfield likes to get good ink, but I'm tired of falling for the same old baloney just because it's wrapped up to look like porterhouse."

Atherton winced at the pun, then smiled. "You missed the whole thing, Sid," he said. "You really did."

"What whole thing?" demanded Winehart with the anxiety of a reporter who has been beat too many times.

"Well, since my story is already on the wire, I'll tell you. Hurley can't run again. He's had two full terms. Canfield's just given the first signal that he's made up his mind to run for President in nineteen eighty-four. His Portland speech went beyond the administration line on Israel. Now you can say I'm leaping to conclusions, but I've been around this political track a good many miles, and I can tell when a politician is getting ready to spring out of the starting gate."

"Bull! Canfield's only been elected Vice President once. He had one year before that by courtesy of presidential appointment after French's death. That means he can still run for reelection. He doesn't have the base in the party that the speaker of the House has, and he certainly isn't as popular among his peers as the senator from Arizona, who has been majority leader for years. Canfield's practically guaranteed another four years if he behaves himself and doesn't step on anybody's toes. He can do this by contenting himself with the second spot again. Besides, the senator from Arizona has the speaker on his side; and President Hurley is certainly no rabid fan of the Vice President.''

"Canfield's not going to forfeit the only chance to be President he'll have in years just to be veep again. Remember, the guy in the forward cabin has some things going for him, too. The veep's got the big media, the intellectual community and the college kids. He's got the money and the looks. Women think he's wonderful. Add to that the fact that he'll do anything to get a vote. Don't count him out.''

"Crap,'' said Winehart flatly. "He hasn't got any more chance of being nominated than Rockefeller had against Goldwater.''

"Please, gentlemen,'' interrupted a deep, well-modulated voice from the seat behind them. "Do not become too quarrelsome. Your favorite television commentator is trying to take a nap.''

"Go back to sleep, Drake,'' growled Winehart. "You wouldn't understand this intellectual discussion. All you have to do is satisfy the viewer's eyeballs. We print people can't get by with just a nice smile and a pretty face. We have to *say* something.''

Atherton concurred. God, how he despised the aggressive young men of the electronic media. They learned nothing from day to day. They just flitted from flower to flower, intoning resonant banalities.

Air Force Two was configured to provide three independent cabin areas in addition to the cockpit. The front section was for off-duty crew. It included a small but well-stocked executive kitchen.

The center section provided both working and sleeping accommodations for the Vice President and was known as the Executive Cabin.

The large rear portion of the airplane contained two tables similar to restaurant booths. Behind the booths were rows of adjustable passenger chairs, similar to the first-class section of a commercial airliner.

The Executive Cabin housed two bunks in the forward portion and a small conference table seating six on the starboard side of the aft portion. On the port side aft was the Vice President's chair and table with another chair opposite it. The communications console was to the left of the Vice President's chair. At the moment the chair was occupied by Porter Newton Canfield, incumbent in that high office.

At forty-eight, Canfield was a likely Vice President. Handsome, with aristocratic features and a compact, trim appearance, he had a full head of light brown hair, a high forehead and large blue eyes that seemed even more prominent because of the contact lenses he wore. Always impeccably dressed, he carried himself with an intense, assured manner.

He had had the best of everything from the start. He was graduated cum laude from Princeton in 1957, entered the University of Virginia Law School that same year and graduated in 1960.

Commissioned an ensign in the navy, he was assigned to Portsmouth Naval Base as an aide to Vice Admiral Thomas, an old friend of his father. He was released from active duty in 1962 and married Philadelphia socialite Amy DeVrees Webster the following year.

He then entered his father's law firm—Canfield, Rodeman, Adams and Preller (a combination that made a delightful acronym for struggling young attorneys without connections). This was a society firm with an estate and business practice.

He was elected to Congress in 1968 from a nonbluestocking district and surprised everyone by getting the labor vote. He was reelected to the House of Representatives in 1970 and elected to the Senate in 1972. After being reelected to the Senate in 1978, he was appointed Vice President the following year to succeed Alan French, deceased.

In 1980, running with President Walter Hurley, Canfield was elected to a full term as Vice President.

Despite the Princeton cum laude, some did not consider him too bright. His enemies claimed that the honor came more from the heavy Canfield endowments than from his ability. However, it was conceded that he was personable and a quick study. He had a trendy familiarity with current causes and code expressions, but was sometimes criticized as a self-convincer and an oversimplifier.

The Canfields were one of America's oldest and wealthiest families. Their resources originated with Great-Grandfather Porter Starrat Canfield, who made it all in the department-store business in Philadelphia. It was said that sharp practices and ruthless competition were the bases of the Canfield millions and that old Porter fleeced both his partner and the public, but the years had long since rinsed the dirt from the Canfield money, and now the family name was associated only with philanthropic and social activities. For his part, young Porter never touched the principal, being content to live on his share of the income, which amounted to the not inconsiderable sum of about $200,000 annually.

Vaguely uneasy, Porter Newton Canfield now drummed his fingers on the arm of the vice-presidential chair. Directly across from him sat Stanley Bedson, California's junior senator, and his closest confidant in that august body. Bedson was idly flipping the pages of *Twiceweek,* but his attention was directed more to Canfield than the magazine.

"What's eating you, Newt?" Bedson finally asked, as the vice-presidential discomfort became increasingly difficult to ignore.

"Probably nothing worth worrying about, Stan," replied Canfield. "It's just that the White House makes me nervous sometimes. This morning my press secretary was awakened at six A.M. to take a call from the President's assistant press secretary. Now those people are aware of the three-hour time difference, so getting Pete out of bed was no accident."

"Well, hell, you can't get upset because your staff and the President's like to use the Chinese water torture on each other," said Bedson with a smile.

Canfield frowned. "It isn't that," he replied. "I'm used to the staff interplay—although it does give me a lot of grief. What really bothers me is what the fellow said. Pete's pretty careful, and he wrote it down. The exact words were: 'Did the Vice President really say in his Oregon speech that intermediate range ballistic missiles may soon become a necessity for Israel's continued existence?' Now, Stan, that's a rather pointed and unusual question. Makes me think that Hurley or somebody like Josh Devers or maybe the secretary of state didn't appreciate my ideas on Middle East policy."

The senator nodded understandingly. "I see what you mean, Newt. To be candid, I did get the impression that you stripped some of the safety fuzz off the administration position. If you want to avoid controversy in this business, you don't dare use language that tells people exactly where you are. I think Hurley wants the Israelis to believe he feels exactly the way you do, and I think he also wants the Arabs to get a different impression. As long as he speaks equivocally, he has a chance of being in two places at the same time."

The Vice President leaned forward slightly and lowered his voice. He could see Peter Rosen pretending to write but perceptibly straining to hear from his seat across the aisle at the other end of the conference table. "My dear senator, you and I have known each

7

other for a long time, and some things are best left unsaid, particularly when other ears are obviously interested. I have great confidence in Pete's knowledge of the media, but he is inclined to drop them a tidbit occasionally. I'm not yet ready for him to make any assumptions.''

Bedson threw up his hands disarmingly. ''I understand completely, Mr. Vice President. All I'm saying is that you must expect that some of the old hands in the back are going to get the idea pretty quickly that you may be about to stake out an independent position. Perhaps you should have selected a subject more subtle than IRBM's. You know how direct the Israeli hints have been that we should help them with such installations.''

The Vice President shrugged. ''Well, you have to take a chance now and then. Frankly, I thought our known shipments to Israel of the more sophisticated offensive weapons made IRBM's a logical and natural request. Anyhow, it's not worth worrying about at this stage, unless I hear from someone at a higher level than an assistant press secretary.''

The aft door to the Executive Cabin opened and Steve Galdari entered. He stood in the doorway awaiting recognition by Canfield.

''One of your people wants to talk with you, Mr. Vice President,'' said Senator Bedson.

Canfield turned in his chair. ''Yes, Steve. You want me?''

''Yes, sir,'' said Steve, squatting quickly beside the Vice President's chair. ''I wanted a chance to go over the Phoenix itinerary. It's important that we plan your airport movements. We had a telex in Portland about a possible troublemaker. Probably nothing to worry about, but we shouldn't take any chances.''

''Okay, get Bill over to the conference table, and we'll do that right now. You might also ask Professor Miller to sit in. He's going over the final speech draft with one of the girls.''

''Fine,'' said Galdari, heading for the door.

''Wait a minute,'' called Canfield. ''While you're back there, ask Kathy to come up in about fifteen minutes. I want to check over the political briefing and give her a list of acknowledgments for tonight's speech.''

As Galdari went to summon the others, he felt a slight alteration in the plane's motion, a gentle throttling back which signaled that the descent into Phoenix was about to begin.

At the port table just inside the rear compartment four of his agents were playing gin rummy. Trent Gilbert, a ten-year agent from Denver, glanced up. "Need anything, Steve?"

"Not right now, but I will want to brief all of you shortly about the Phoenix routine. Meanwhile you could check with Bob Bright to see if we have any further information out of Phoenix or Portland on the warning."

"Okay, boss." Gilbert put down his hand. "You were dead, Billy Joe," he proclaimed to Agent Jestes. "It was strictly schneider day minus two minutes. You owe Mr. Galdari two dollars for saving your reputation and tomorrow's groceries."

Billy Joe laughed softly. "Hell, Trent. Ya'll know ah've got contacts in Phoenix. Never had to worry 'bout buying gorceries or any other of life's goodies in a warm climate. The people take care of me. They just natcherly appreciate mah warm Southern blood."

Disengaging himself from the good-natured banter that greeted this announcement, Galdari turned to the opposite table, where Prof. Zack Miller was dictating a last-minute speech insert to Maxine, a highly efficient but strikingly unattractive secretary. Galdari waited politely until Miller had completed his thought and then relayed the vice-presidential summons.

"Be there in a minute," snapped Miller, more irritated at the messenger than the message. "Rough out what you've got so far, Maxine, and let me have it immediately," he said, shoving a sheaf of notes into a battered black briefcase and eyeing the agent with obvious impatience.

Steve Galdari nodded coldly and moved away. Why, he wondered, did this hyperactive college professor harbor such dislike for the agents and permanent staff? It was just a week ago that the Vice President had dropped him among them like a wrench in the machinery. Chief of Staff Bill Shelby had suddenly found his heretofore unquestioned authority challenged and frequently short-circuited by this quick-thinking, rapid-talking new arrival who obviously had the Vice President's ear.

The result was a lowering of staff morale, which had never been too high. It was not easy to compete with a college roommate of the boss, especially one who had been a campus hero and a personal idol. Galdari, an excellent athlete himself at Columbia, was aware of the brilliant college career of the great Zack Miller. All-star halfback, captain of the tennis team, president of his class, graduated from Princeton magna cum laude, Ph.D. from New York University in only two years, associate professor there in six years. It was an enviable record to combine with a strong, yet sensitively handsome face and a powerful, graceful body. Miller's large, dark, magnetic eyes were capable of cruelty or tenderness—truly a window to his emotions. Girls had always sighed over Zack Miller, and they still did, if and when he had the time for them. They were oddly understanding about his casual acceptance or dismissal of the favors they offered.

Miller's only serious handicap was cyclothymia, a mild manic-depressive tendency. He could be sky high or down in the dumps, depending on his emotional curve.

As the years passed, the always intense Miller had become more and more committed to civil libertarianism and even more impatient of those who favored conservative approaches to the great problems of society. What Galdari saw as personal hostility was a strengthening conviction on the part of Miller that most people entrenched in the system's organizations could never accept the radical reforms necessary for true progress toward what he saw as the ultimate goal of a free society—complete control by each individual of his own destiny. Paramilitary personnel such as Secret Service agents he held in special contempt.

As Zack Miller walked to the Executive Cabin, Maxine heaved her lumpy self from behind the table and proceeded awkwardly to the typing desk.

"Thar go one of the all-time great bodies," Billy Joe said, pulling slowly on his cigar and winking at Gilbert. "That's real earthquake material."

Gathered around the conference table in the Executive Cabin, Vice President Canfield, Bill Shelby, Zack Miller and Peter Rosen listened with varied reactions to SAIC Galdari's suggestion that Canfield limit his exposure to the minimum at the Phoenix airport because of a warning that there might be a troublemaker in the crowd.

"Mr. Vice President," said Galdari, "it is up to you; but I recommend that you not work the fence today."

"Hell, Steve," said Peter Rosen, "that'll kill the coverage. All they'll write is that the boss stiffed a friendly crowd and went to rest in his hotel room."

Galdari nodded seriously. "I know all that, Pete, but we can't afford the chance that there is a homicidal nut down there."

"I'd have to go with Steve's recommendation, Mr. Vice President," said Shelby flatly. "A bad story isn't that important this early in the game, or any time for that matter."

"Hold it, everybody." The commanding voice left no room for discussion. "Let's not panic over a nut warning. We've got enough protection to move quickly if anything looks suspicious. Not only that, but we have local riflemen on the roof of the terminal building. There's no real danger," Zack Miller continued with a forced smile. "This may be early on in the campaign, but these first heavily covered events will set the whole media tone for the future. Newt, I think you should go ahead as usual."

Canfield hesitated for a moment, then said, "Unless there is something more after we land, Steve, I'll go as usual."

Galdari's jaw tightened, but his voice gave no sign of his feelings as he said, "Yes, sir. We'll go as usual unless we get more information."

The plane was leaning over into its final approach course when Kathy Dryden, Canfield's personal secretary, entered the cabin, shorthand pad ready. How cool and fresh she looks, though Galdari. Sexy, but more heavenly sexy than earthy sexy. She glanced at Steve and her eyes held the question, "What's wrong?" Galdari shook his head slightly and smiled, reassuring her that nothing was seriously amiss. She was, he said to himself, a very sensitive lady.

Kathy sat down quickly and began to take a list of acknowledgments from the Vice President. In a few minutes they would be on the ground.

A respectable crowd of three to four hundred waited behind the temporary barricades at the Phoenix airport. Tomorrow's news reports would estimate it anywhere from one hundred to seven hundred, depending upon the way the reporter felt about Vice President Canfield. In the front ranks most stood patiently, the young marrieds with tots in arms and tykes firmly in hand, and the elderly displaying the stolid stamina that always surprises their juniors. At the rear there was sporadic movement, with late arrivals jockeying for position and roving youths strutting for mutual approval. To one side were the organized groups, ready to wave their homemade signs and banners at the proper moment.

Off to the flank was the consolidated high school band, whose members maintained good position discipline and were chatting among themselves.

Tall and lean, his brown face the ropy texture that comes from many years' exposure to the hot, dry Arizona air, the majority leader of the U.S. Senate towered over the small group of VIP's awaiting the arrival of *Air Force Two*. It wasn't so much Roland Gray's height that made him stand out, nor was it the shock of white hair that was always a bit tousled but never untidy. There was something else—a magnetism, an air of quiet command drawn from years of experience in the Senate. He turned with a smile to the plump young man in the houndstooth sport jacket next to him. "Mayor Sam," he opined, "you are about to give the key to the city to a man who may try to open Sixteen Hundred Pennsylvania Avenue with it. From the look of what he said in Portland, this trip is not to sell Hurley policy, but to sell Porter Newton Canfield." The smile faded. "It's too damned early for that!"

"Senator Gray, you're the one who decides what door this key fits and what door every key in this state fits," said the mayor diplomatically. He glanced quickly behind him at the casually dressed people, patient in the still hot but not unpleasant afternoon sun. "There isn't ten percent of that crowd that won't follow your lead, sir." He shifted his weight uncomfortably. Friction between the big boys of his party was always dangerous to his own congressional ambitions for the future.

The majority leader grunted. "Guess I'd better hold more keys than Arizona if I want to slow this fellow down."

Then came the moment, always exciting no matter how often repeated, no matter how jaded the viewer. There was a flash of silver, low against the blue sky. Those who were alert and blessed with good eyesight shielded their eyes and pointed, and a murmur of excitement ran through the crowd. A few moments later, the blue and white 727, coming in hot in the light, dry air, settled with a puff of tire smoke on the long runway.

Political advance men and Secret Service agents on the ground moved rapidly into position, mouths or ears never far from their walkie-talkies. In their roped-off area, the local press, radio and television people readied their note pads and equipment, cursing each other without real rancor as they fought for preferred positions. On the roof of the airport, local constabulary tightened their grips on rifles and looked more intently at the suddenly vibrant crowd.

Ridge Potter reversed the thrust of the engines and braked *Air Force Two* to a manageable speed, preparing to turn off into the nearest taxi lane.

"Welcome to Las Vegas," said Canfield to those in the Executive Cabin. "We come in the belief that we best promote the interests of our party by promoting the interests of our country, and getting away with that in Senator Gray's bailiwick is strictly a gamble."

"How about advance copies of the speech for the press, Mr. Vice President?" asked Peter Rosen. "The traveling press is asking. They say they never get the stuff early enough to do a decent story."

Bill Shelby cut in testily, "Damn it, Pete, don't bother the boss with that. I'll let you know when we get to the hotel."

"But, Bill, I get all the—"

"Bill, you and Pete check with me when we get in. I've a few ideas to lessen the friction," Miller interrupted authoritatively. "That is, if it's okay with you, Mr. Vice President," he added, looking to Canfield.

"By all means," said Canfield. "A few ideas might help. I get tired of hearing about this."

Shelby flushed and said nothing.

By now *Air Force Two* was approaching the blocks. Those aboard could see members of the nearby greeting party holding their ears against the scream of the jet engines.

The door between the Executive Cabin and the rear of the plane opened to admit Galdari. He spoke quietly to Canfield.

"Mr. Vice President, will you go from the welcoming committee to the press to the crowd, as you usually do?"

Canfield nodded.

"Then, sir, please be aware that we may have to ask you to move quickly if we detect any trouble in the crowd. I will be right alongside you. If I place my hand on your back, please move in the direction I indicate. There will be agents all around, so we don't expect a problem; however, if one develops, we will need your cooperation. We just can't afford to ignore the warning we received earlier, even though our people on the ground don't see any obvious difficulty."

"Okay, Steve, but probably the biggest danger is that the mayor will drop the key to the city on my foot or that Atherton will breathe on me and pickle me forever," said Canfield wryly.

Peter Rosen jumped in. "Speaking of Atherton, Mr. Vice President, would you please give the traveling press time to get off and in with the locals before you disembark? They have trouble getting in position, and sometimes they miss something important."

"Oh Lord," said Bill Shelby, shaking his head. "What a bunch of prima donnas. Those characters never give the locals a chance to get a word in edgewise. Instead of local press coverage, all we get is a running interview with the traveling press, each one trying to develop his own angle for an exclusive story."

"Bill, that's not quite fair," said the Vice President patiently. "Most of those fellows are giving us pretty good coverage," he continued. "I'll wait for them to get set, Pete."

As the plane eased into its resting place, Canfield looked out to check the greeting committee against the list which had been given to him by his chief of staff. "Bill, I don't see Congressman Donnert. We're supposed to be here to help his campaign. The least he could do is be here to meet us." There was irritation in his voice. Donnert, a first-term congressman, was totally controlled by Senator Gray and was not likely to be drawn into orbit by Canfield.

"Here he comes now, sir," said Shelby. "He's been over in the bullpen charming the rinky-dinks," he added sourly, still smarting from being overruled by Zack Miller. Moreover, he lost no opportunity to zing the press, which was often critical of the caliber of the Canfield staff. The gentlemen of the media sensed his disaffection and missed no chance to criticize him.

"Come on, Bill, knock off biting the press. We have to live with them. Besides, they're just like everyone else. They prefer a friendly approach to a hostile one." He smiled to take the edge off his words. Shelby was hardworking and loyal. He was also very sensitive to anything that could be construed as criticism in front of other people.

"Yes, sir," said the chief of staff, but the tightness in his manner made it evident that he remained unconvinced about the press's being like everyone else.

Although Canfield shifted his attention back to the waiting greeting committee, his mind was still on Shelby. He would have to have a long talk with him. He was concerned about Bill's fighting with the media. It made nothing but trouble for him because sometimes they lashed back at Canfield himself. And even if they contented themselves with criticizing the operation, people blamed him, not Shelby, for the problems. If he was going to carry through with an effective presidential campaign, he needed the media. Good ink and honeyed commentary about Porter Newton Canfield were a must. They were possible if he made his people use basic intelligence in dealing with the press, because ideologically they were with him. They were fed up with lackluster Hurley and his conservatism. They wanted the party to revert to the excitement of years gone by—years when big, bold decisions championed the little guys, the oppressed minorities and the unrecognized young. Porter Canfield would bring back those days.

Galdari roused him from his reflections. "Ready, sir? We can move now."

"Let's go," said Canfield, swinging his chair out and slipping his arms through the coat being held by the steward. "Zack, you and Steve follow me down; and the rest delay a minute, then come. I don't want the news shot to show too many people. Then all they write about is security and how many there are in the vice-presidential party."

• • •

Canfield appeared at the doorway of the airplane and stepped out onto the ladder platform. Cameras whirred, the band struck up a bright tune and the people cheered. He paused, waving for a moment, then descended to the applauding greeting committee. As he spoke cordially to Senator Gray, the mayor and other dignitaries, the last of the traveling press was scrambling under the ropes into the bullpen and frantically setting up equipment. Secret Service men were unobtrusively fanning out in the waiting crowd.

"Good to have you here, Mr. Vice President," said the Congressman Phil Donnert. "I appreciate your making the stop and particularly want to thank you for agreeing to attend the reception before the dinner. That keeps the big givers happy."

"Don't tie up the Vice President too long with your fat cats, Phil," cautioned the majority leader. "That makes poor press and alienates a lot of people who are giving all they can afford just to attend the dinner. Besides, a lot of those big givers are giving just as big to your opponent. They don't care who wins just so they can brag about electing him and get in to ask for impossible favors."

"I think I know how to handle it, Roland," said Canfield, choosing to see an overbearing attitude in what was meant as a sincere attempt to be helpful. It was an indication of the lack of rapport between the Vice President and Gray that they seldom spent more than a few minutes together without some misunderstanding or unpleasantness occurring.

Gray nodded and turned away coldly as the mayor began his mini-speech that went with the presentation of the key to the city. There was no way, he thought, to be nice to this pompous big shot.

Amenities concluded, Canfield, followed by Zack Miller and agents, headed for the roped-off area where the media eagerly awaited him. He linked his arm in Donnert's, saying, "Come on, Phil, let's brave the bullpen together. I know you've been over there already, but the most dangerous bulls have just arrived with me."

As the two politicians approached, there was a great deal of pushing and shoving. Cameras banged against bodies amid such angry cries as "Don't block me, damn it!" and the omnipresent entreaty, "Over here, please, Mr. Vice President." The officials stopped at the approximate center of the group of newsmen, and the Vice President allowed that he was delighted to be in Phoenix and to report to the discerning voters of this great city that Phil Donnert was doing an outstanding job in Congress and was a vital member of the Hurley team. He went on to say that it was rather early to talk about next year's election, but that this was a big country and he

15

might not get back to Phoenix, so he wanted to endorse Donnert for reelection right now.

While Donnert beamed modestly and the local press was dutifully writing it all down, the national reporters traveling with the Vice President fidgeted impatiently, looking for the opening that would let them resume their serial interrogation of this possible candidate. Finally it came, hard on the heels of Canfield's first pause for breath. Winehart was the first into the breech.

"Mr. Vice President, your recommendation in Portland that Israel be given IRBM's seemed to go beyond the prior administration statements on arms for that country. Were you announcing a new administration policy in that respect?"

Canfield smiled disarmingly. "That's a loaded question, Sid, but I won't duck it." Positioning himself for the best camera angle and allowing the friendly smile to fade into an expression of statesmanlike gravity, he went on, "Only the President of the United States makes foreign policy. As a member of the Hurley administration, I support that policy. I believe that what I said in my Portland speech is a logical construction of what is inherent in that policy."

"But, Mr. Vice President, at this morning's news briefing at the White House, the presidential press secretary was asked whether President Hurley approved your recommendation of IRBM's for Israel, and he said that the administration policy regarding Israel is as it has been enunciated by the President in the past. And he refused to respond to repeated questions as to whether the President supported what you said in your speech. Does that mean that you went beyond administration policy?"

"Sid, I support administration policy. As I said before, my remarks are simply a logical extension—I mean of what is inherent in administration policy." The Vice President appeared slightly flustered at the mistake, but quickly recovered.

"Now, I'm not going to fence with you on that anymore today," he said with a laugh. "How about another subject?" Inside, he was far from relaxed. He knew that the media would not let the thing rest for long. Both the press secretary's and his responses were transparently evasive. Sooner or later Hurley would have to face the issue, and then things would hum. Separating a President from his Vice President was an ancient and favorite media sport. Tons of news articles—analytic, speculative and largely inaccurate—would result.

But in this case the basic proposition would be correct. Vice President Porter Canfield was going his separate way and carving out his own position on an important foreign policy issue. Therefore, he was a presidential candidate.

"Wait a minute, sir—"

"Mr. Vice President, would you comment on the lack of funding for the Gila River Basin Reclamation Project?"

Canfield ignored the effort to resume discussion of the caveated subject and graciously allayed the fears of the local reporters with respect to the conservation project. Then he abruptly disengaged from the press and walked briskly toward the crowd. Galdari moved quickly to his side as the handshaking began. Another agent kept the eager cameramen from underfoot. Reporters with pads jotted down parts of the conversation between the Vice President and the people, and the inevitable directional microphone reported the stereotyped exchanges, in position to intercept any insult or gaffe.

About midway along the barricades Canfield stopped for a moment to comfort a frightened child who had burst into tears when ordered by her father to shake hands with the Vice President. He was about to move on, when a gaunt, wild-eyed man near the rear of the crowd suddenly pushed toward the front. He got to the barricade at the point Canfield had just passed and called out, "Here, Mr. Vice President. I have something for you," at the same time reaching with his left hand into the inside pocket of his rumpled blue jacket.

Almost instantly Steve Galdari said, "This way, sir!" and stepped between the Vice President and the man, placing his hand firmly against Canfield's back, thus preventing him from finishing his automatic turn toward the voice and propelling him away from possible danger.

Simultaneously, a strong hand closed over the petitioner's arm before he could remove his hand from his jacket, and a tense voice in his ear ordered him to freeze.

The man's mouth flew open in astonishment. He made no effort to resist. There was no scuffle; only the people near him were aware of the incident. As directed, he removed his hand slowly from his jacket to reveal a worn New Testament.

"This was my grandmother's. Her name was Porter, same as his first name. I just wanted to give it to him for luck." The man was bewildered and frightened.

"All right, sir," said the agent, releasing him. "We'll take it for him. Sorry to grab you, but we have to be careful, you know. Here's a pair of vice-presidential cufflinks. I know that the Vice President would thank you personally if he had the time, and he would want you to have these."

The man's eyes glistened with emotion, and he broke into a

17

smile. "Wonderful! Thank you, young fellow. I'll never forget this day. Imagine. Me having cuff links from the Vice President of the United States! Thank you, and thank him for me."

As Galdari deftly had spun the Vice President out of potential harm's way, Winehart had turned back toward the scuffle, ever alert for something different. Now he vaulted over the barricades and rushed up to the still bewildered citizen.

"What happened, sir? Why did they rough you up?" Still influenced by the Chicago Syndrome, those unforgettable conditions that he encountered on his first big assignment, Winehart already had the broad dimensions of a story in mind. Since the Democratic National Convention in 1968, all law enforcement people were bullies who "roughed up" innocent citizens.

The man smiled uncertainly. "It was just a mistake," he said tentatively. "I guess they thought I had a gun or something."

"What is your name, sir?"

"Henry Weldon."

"And your occupation, Mr. Weldon?"

"I'm pastor of The Church of the Healing Light in Phoenix." The man began to take interest in the reporter's flying pen and brightened as the prospect of getting his name in the newspaper dawned on him.

"I was just going to give the Vice President the Word of God to guide him," he continued. "These gentlemen thought I had something dangerous in my pocket, and they grabbed my arm." Weldon demonstrated by clamping his right hand over his left forearm.

"Did they hurt your arm?" asked Winehart.

"Not really. It just startled me. My pocket was torn a little more, but that was already started."

"Okay, Mr. Weldon, you were shocked by the sudden assault and your pocket was ripped. What did the agents say to you?"

"I don't remember exactly. It happened pretty fast." Weldon looked hopefully at Winehart. "Could you mention the church in your story? We're just beginning, you see. Actually, there is no church yet. Just a tent on a vacant lot." He smiled at the reporter. "The publicity could attract new worshipers."

Winehart nodded. "Sure, Pastor. Now you are going to register a complaint about this, of course."

"I hadn't thought about it. There really was no harm done." Weldon nervously rubbed his forearm. This wasn't going the way he had hoped. "I don't think I'll make any complaint," he said. "The men who stopped me were very courteous."

The reporter appeared not to hear him. "Okay, sir. Thanks very much. Sorry you had the problem.''

"Wait—wait a second! How about the church?" said Weldon. But Sid Winehart was already gone.

To the obvious disappointment of that segment of the crowd he had not yet reached, Canfield was ushered directly to his car. Others in the vice-presidential party hurried to their vehicles. A few moments later the motorcade began to leave.

"Wait for Senator Gray," said Canfield, observing the majority leader rushing up on the left side. The driver flipped up the automatic lock and Roland Gray jumped in.

"Damn it, Mr. Vice President, there are a lot of people out there still waiting to greet you—including the kids in the rally group and the band. You aren't going to leave them standing there and just drive off, are you?"

"Sorry, Roland. There's some sort of security problem," said Canfield. "What was it all about, Steve?"

"No problem, sir, but it could have been. A man ran toward you, reaching into his pocket. He had a book to give you. Our men didn't know what he was reaching for, so they grabbed him. He wasn't too upset—very decent about it."

"Well, then. Let's go back to the crowd," said Gray. "We'll make some people very angry if we ignore them and leave."

Galdari looked at the Vice President. "We'll do whatever you want, sir, but I suggest that we'll create chaos if we reverse the signals again. Besides, it's getting late and a lot of the people have already started for their cars."

Canfield said, "I think we'd better head for the hotel, Roland," and with that the driver pulled away. The Vice President waved and smiled, seeming not to hear the cries of disappointment. Gray sank into his seat, a black look on his face.

Canfield was aware of Gray's continuing anger. He would have liked to joke him into a better mood, but their relationship was not close enough to permit that. Finally, as the big armored limousine flown in that morning from Washington sped down the highway, he said, "I'm sorry, Senator. Perhaps I can try to make it up to the rally group and the band by sending a letter of thanks and apology. These inadvertent snafus happen sometimes. They're part of politics."

Gray looked at him levelly, masking the distaste that had built up over the years. "The congressman has a tough race next year. It doesn't make sense to alienate people without good reason," he said.

"They won't be mad at Donnert," said Canfield with a short laugh. "They'll be mad at me, if anyone."

Gray looked away without responding.

Several cars back of the vice-presidential limousine, Zack Miller held on grimly while the onrushing motorcade sped through the streets of Phoenix. It was nearing five-thirty and the rush-hour traffic, startled by the escort siren, splayed itself into a weird obstacle pattern. For the staff car in which he was riding, and the other vehicles to the rear of the column, keeping up was a hair-raising game of crack-the-whip. *Why,* he thought, *doesn't the escort ever remember that those in the back have to drive twice as fast to cope with traffic interruptions?*

Between him and the driver, Kathy Dryden sat quietly, firmly grasping her bulging handbag. Her skirt had ridden up to expose her thighs, and Miller's eyes from time to time were drawn in that direction. She's a cool one, he thought. I don't think she likes me. Every time I have to straighten Shelby out, she gives me a dirty look. And most of her smiles are reserved for that overconfident bodyguard, Galdari. Well, she isn't all that attractive anyhow.

His eyes involuntarily again rested on Kathy's legs. Admit it, Miller, he thought, you've been through a long dry spell, and she's cute—besides, she's right here.

"Kathy," he said, "could you do a couple of sensitive memos for me after the dinner tonight?" Maybe if he could just get her alone for a while.

"Sorry, Dr. Miller. I've got things for the Vice President that I must get done. But I'll arrange for Maxine to do them for you as soon as we get to the hotel." Her voice was completely neutral, but he knew she really wanted to tell him that she worked for one man only, and that his current position of preferred advisor and old friend of the boss made no difference.

"Okay, thanks," he said, retreating from a losing situation. He glumly envisaged Maxine. It was certain the memos would be brief. He always seemed to wind up with Maxine, who was referred to among the agents and male staff as Miss Saltpeter of 1983.

For Porter Canfield, the ride from the airport to the newly built Vista Hotel was not a stimulating experience. Several times he attempted to make pleasant conversation with the taciturn majority leader. Each effort was stalled by grunts or at best monosyllabic replies. The senator was still very ticked off about the sudden disengagement from the welcoming crowd and he wanted the Vice President to understand that his visit had started poorly. However, Canfield was inclined to accept the situation philosophically. Gray never would be helpful to him. The best he could hope for was temporary neutrality because they were on an inevitable collision course, both edging out on the tightrope they hoped would lead to their party's nomination and then to the White House. So if neutrality had to vanish earlier than expected—no great loss to Canfield.

Now, as the limousine entered the downtown area of the city, the Vice President leaned back and closed his eyes. He was on track to the ultimate objective—the presidency. It had always been in his mind as a sort of pot of gold at the end of the rainbow, but that was the dream of many a boy. After he had entered politics, it had been nice to hear a friend or relative predict that ''Newt might be President some day.'' Such remarks were not to be taken seriously. But then he had been able to engineer his appointment to the vice-presidential vacancy. Yes, engineer it. It came through smart politics and hard work—not because Walter Hurley liked him. As a matter of fact, Hurley had wanted Roland Gray. All the pros knew that.

Canfield permitted himself a small smile. Yes, Hurley had wanted Gray, but the party liberals had put great pressure on for good old Porter, and the slowdown in the Congress of certain crucial legislation and appointments finally had persuaded the President. So now the presidency was an attainable objective—thanks to the hard work of Meredith Lord, now secretary of Health, Education, and Welfare, Zack Miller and a host of other friends. Beautiful Meredith. Quite a campaign diversion. He could have and should have taken her to bed that night in Minneapolis. Well, if Amy didn't act more like a wife, it might not be too late. Why was Amy so obstinate about shunning the Washington people? She wasn't asocial—heaven knew that. All that gadding about in Philadelphia society. But as far as being on court politically, she just wasn't in the game. They just kept drifting farther apart, and he had little real feeling left for her.

Galdari brought him abruptly out of his reverie.

''Dr. Miller would like you to remain in the limo until the traveling press has set up in the lobby to film you coming in, sir. Is that okay?''

''Ridiculous!'' interjected Roland Gray. ''What news is there in walking through a hotel lobby?''

''It's okay, Steve. Tell Professor Miller to pull in front of us. We'll move on his signal.''

''Good Lord,'' muttered the disgusted majority leader. Then he sighed heavily and hunched down deeper into his seat, his mouth working nervously.

Canfield addressed him blandly. ''Roland, we are public officials, and the public has a right to observe our actions. The only way the public can know what we are doing is through the news media.''

This patronizing remark drew only a frigid, blue-eyed stare from the senator, and the Vice President uncomfortably looked away.

The driver swung the heavy Cadillac into the hotel entranceway. Agents leaped from the follow-up car, frightening off the hopeful doorman, who was about to officiate at the most memorable occasion in his life—the arrival of a Vice President of the United States.

The small group of spectators clustered around the entrance craned and peered, trying to get a good look at the arriving dignitaries. After a five-minute wait in the car, the word was passed by Miller, and Canfield walked through the lobby to the elevator, smiling and waving for the cameras and occasionally stopping to shake a hand or make a light remark. The Douglas Drake television crew slowly gave way before him, backing clumsily in their ritualistic dance, hand-held camera and glaring light straight in the eyes.

''Good Lord,'' muttered the blinded majority leader again, this time more fervently; he had tripped and almost fallen down the single step leading to the elevator.

After a nonstop ride to the next-to-the-highest floor in a commandeered elevator, during which the Vice President was inspected with clinical unabashedness by the operator, at long last they were at their doors. Almost immediately Gray took his leave of the Vice President, informing him that he would return in time to escort him to the reception. Canfield posed for the unavoidable picture with the hotel manager and gratefully closed the door to his suite. Miller was there with Shelby, who had a V.O. and water all ready for the Vice President. As they settled into easy chairs, two agents completed their final check of the suite and departed. Canfield swirled his drink over the ice cubes and shook his head.

''What a rat race,'' he said.

''It'll get no better—never has,'' said Shelby.

Miller was unimpressed by their sacrifices. ''Too bad about the goof-up at the airport,'' he said. ''The Service shouldn't have moved you to the car so fast. Made Gray mad and disappointed people who were waiting to shake your hand. The Service handled it like a bunch of amateurs.''

''They had no option. I think they handled it rather well,'' said Shelby.

''They probably overreacted a little,'' Canfield observed. ''Roland Gray had a fit about my leaving. The old goat would have found something else if that hadn't happened.''

''Well, the press will kill you tomorrow,'' said Miller. ''Forget about your speech tonight. You won't see any of it, except in the Phoenix papers.'' He rose suddenly and paced the room, almost catlike in his movements.

"I can see it now," he predicted. " 'Security tight as V.P. arrives.' Then four or five paragraphs about how many agents are with you and perhaps a photo of a local cop with a rifle silhouetted against the sky. Then a hint that such goings-on are more reminiscent of a military junta than a government of the people, by the people, for the people. Then, of course, an interview with a disappointed child who waited for hours to shake the Vice President's hand. None of which is good for the causes of Porter Canfield.''

"Well, damn it, we can't jeopardize the boss's safety!" Bill Shelby exploded. The events of the afternoon had built up a full head of steam, and it was all he could do to avoid telling off this smug amateur who thought he had all the answers. He fought for control and went on in a calmer tone. "Steve and the Secret Service people have a very large responsibility by congressional directive. It doesn't leave any room for mistakes.''

Canfield said nothing—just quietly sipped his drink. The argument was ageless. Miller, however, was not ready to quit.

"If a man can't be elected, it's no skin off the Service. They keep on drawing pay and just transfer over to the guy who convinced the people he cared about them. Hell, Bill, they're more worried about the forms they'd have to fill out if someone shot the protectee than about the man himself, and you know that.''

Shelby's blood pressure rose again. He liked and respected the protective detail.

"Dr. Miller—'' he spaced out and emphasized each word "—you just happen to be very wrong about that.''

As Zack was about to continue the dispute, Canfield raised his hand wearily. "Come on now. Cut it out. We don't have time to waste on such matters. Zack, I'll speak to Galdari and try to get them aware of the problem. What we need is a compromise.''

The Vice President finished his drink and stood up. "Guess I'll shave and clean up for the big walk-through of the fat-cat reception. Bill, have Kathy leave the speech where I can check it over before the dinner. We move in about twenty minutes.''

"Yes, sir, and if you care to say a few words at the reception, there'll be a hidden mike available. Just let the advance man know a few minutes ahead.''

"If it's all right with you, Newt, I'll skip the reception so I can try to patch up our problem with the press. Pete needs some help,'' said

Zack. Upon receiving the okay, he left immediately, followed closely by the chief of staff.

The day was ending as a spruced-up and refreshed Porter Canfield appeared at the door of the Apache Room to mingle briefly— as briefly as decently possible—with the two hundred people, most by now well lubricated, therein assembled. As the Vice President stepped into the rather dimly lighted room, Congressman Donnert descended on him.

"Hel-lo there, Mr. Vice President. It's so nice of you to attend the reception," he gushed. "We have scads of wonderful people who are dying to shake your hand, sir. Come right in and— Here is an old friend of mine, Herman Poparch. Shake hands with the next President of the United States, Herman. Herman's big in the cattle business, Mr. V.P. Operates ten thousand acres and has been very helpful to me, sir."

Canfield smiled benignly at Mr. Poparch, who looked as though he wanted to make a speech. "Delighted to meet you," he said, "and thanks for being so helpful to Phil."

Before Poparch could get a word out, he moved on, smiling and saying, "Wonderful to see you here," and "What a pleasure to meet you," to the people who crowded in on him. Most were considerate and courteous but not all.

Uh oh, though Canfield. Here she comes. There was one at every reception.

With a viselike grip on a martini that was sloshing over at each step, she forced her way through the crowd. She was about forty-five, he judged, dressed to the teeth in a metallic gold evening gown. Her eyes were lost under several coats of green eye shadow, and her sun-speckled arms had the color and texture of freshly cut salami. She had a cruel slash of a mouth, and her lipstick had stained one upper front tooth. She was bombed out of her mind, a self-propelled mess, an accident waiting to happen.

There was no escape. Canfield attempted to move away, but this battlewagon cut across his path and intercepted him as easily as the *Arizona* catching a slow freighter. She fired her opening salvo across his bow.

"Vice President Canfield. How are you?" By now she had him by the arm, her martini sprinkling the unfortunates alongside. "I'm Royton Kelly's sister. You remember Royton, I'm sure."

Canfield had never heard of Royton, but he nodded and said, "Oh, yes indeed. Very well."

24

"Well, Royton wants me to get a picture of us together, and my husband, Harry, can take it," she said, firmly seizing his arm and treading heavily on his instep. There was a flash as she quickly kissed the Vice President on the cheek, smearing him with lipstick. Canfield's face set in a rigid smile while agents quickly and expertly blocked her out and steered him away. As he walked toward the spot where the mike was hidden, wiping his face with his handkerchief, she was still talking: "Wait a minute! Wait a minute! I'm not through! Let's get one more picture for insurance."

The Vice President and his entourage inched their way through the pack of people that had quickly formed around the reception chairman, who was calling, "Your attention, please," over and over again through the powerful public address system. The scuttling movements of his escort in such congested areas always gave Canfield the impression that he was being carried along by a giant crab.

While the chairman turned the microphone over to Congressman Donnert, Canfield glanced quickly at the note Bill Shelby had handed him. It read, "Gray not here—acknowledge Gary Root, reception chairman, and Congressman Phil Donnert. Also mention Herman Poparch—big giver."

Donnert didn't appear eager to relinquish the spotlight. He seemed infatuated with the sound of his own voice and was mentioning far too many names. Worse, the lavish praise he bestowed on those he did recognize was certain to alienate those he forgot. Canfield wondered why fledgling politicians were so slow to learn the cardinal rules of brevity and simplicity.

Now the advance man was whispering to Donnert that time was a factor and the congressman was stumbling to a weak close. Then, at last, the mike was Canfield's. He began with a smile.

"Thank you, Congressman Phil Donnert, for your kind words. And thank you for the excellent job you are doing for the people of Arizona in the House of Representatives. President Hurley, ladies and gentlemen, relies on team players like Phil to implement the progressive policies of his administration—" Applause and cheers.

That's enough, thought Canfield, for Roland Gray's man Donnert.

He paused until the room quieted and then went on, his face becoming serious and earnest. "It's easy and natural for those of us who do our best to represent our party in Washington to thank each other, and in a battlefield like Washington, we are grateful for the mutual support. But, ladies and gentlemen, too often we forget, or accept as automatic, the day-to-day grass roots work that is done by

25

the people who make it possible for us to be in Washington. The people in this room—people who give their time and their money, people who fight the opposition at the precinct level—are the real infantry soldiers who carry us forward. People like Herman Poparch and your dynamic chairman, Gary Root, and all the members of his committee, are the ones who carry the party's banner into action. Members of the committee, please raise your hands so we can show our appreciation.''

There was a burst of applause as the blushing committee members, goaded by friends and relatives, modestly raised their hands. Herman Poparch swelled with pride and a vision of the famous Iwo Jima statue crossed his mind. There in the center was Herman, impervious to the danger, planting the flag.

The Vice President continued, ''To all of you here—for your loyalty, for your sacrifices, for your participation and, most of all, for your patriotism—we in Washington say 'thank you' and 'God bless our free system that produces citizens like you.' ''

He smiled and waved to enthusiastic applause, shook a few more hands and unobtrusively slipped through a rear door to return to his suite.

''Great job, boss,'' said Shelby as they hurried into the sitting room, where a worried-looking Miller was pacing back and forth.

''Thank God, you're back. We have an emergency of sorts,'' he said, biting off the words in his staccato style. ''Senator Gray is waiting in my suite to see you about what he calls 'a grave message from the President.' He doesn't look happy. I tried to tell him that you only have a half-hour to change and review your speech, but he insists it's urgent. Says it may affect what you say tonight.''

''He says he has a message from the President?'' asked Canfield. ''Since when does the President communicate with his Vice President through a senator?'' A flush crept up his neck. He had had enough of this game of hints and messages. If Hurley had something to say to him, why didn't he pick up the phone and call? It would only take a minute. White House communications were known to be the best in the world.

Miller looked challengingly at Shelby as if to cut off an anticipated objection. ''I think you should see him right away, Newt,'' he counseled.

Shelby remained silent, watching the Vice President for a reaction.

''Okay, bring him in, Bill,'' said Canfield wearily, ''but please, on the way down the hall, suggest to him that I have a serious time problem, so he should make it fast.''

"Yes, sir. I'll get the senator right away," said Shelby, hurrying out.

Canfield motioned Zack to a chair. "Stay here. I'd prefer to have a witness to this conversation rather than have Gray tell another story later, knowing that any challenge of its accuracy will be just my recollection against his."

Zack smiled. "Okay, Newt, but I doubt that President Hurley would consider me an unbiased witness if the senator disputes your version of the conversation."

"Well, I want to have your advice on this anyhow; and you should hear it all."

There was a knock and the door opened. Shelby led Senator Gray into the room. The majority leader looked like a man who had a job to do that he wanted to get done as quickly as possible.

"Sit down, Senator," said Canfield, and the warmth that was usually in his voice when addressing important personages was noticeably absent. "I understand that you have a message for me?"

Gray ignored the invitation and remained standing. He said solemnly, "Yes, Mr. Vice President. While you were at the reception, Josh Devers called me. He had just come from the Oval Office and had a message for you from the President. Because of the sensitivity of the matter, he asked that I deliver it personally as soon as you returned."

Gray paused a moment to clear his throat. It was obvious that he did not relish the execution of the assignment, even though its probable impact on his rival no doubt pleased him.

Canfield remained calm and cold. "What did the counselor say, Senator? I don't have a lot of time."

"The President would like you to avoid any further remarks about our policy in the Middle East—especially about arms to Israel," Gray said.

"Mr. Devers said to emphasize that the President considers your compliance with this instruction vital to the integrity of administration policy. If you have any questions, Mr. Devers suggested you call him. He will be at his office until eleven P.M.—that is eight, our time."

Zack could tell that the Vice President was steaming. To a casual observer, he might appear calm, but Zack knew the signs from long observation. The small muscle near the jaw hinge was working. It was a sure sign that Canfield was close to the boil-over point. Zack recalled vividly seeing that muscle in action for the first time during their freshman year in Princeton. It had been just before mid-year exams. Canfield had been having real trouble with a basic calculus

27

course and was leaning heavily on him for assistance. During a particularly frustrating coaching session which had exhausted them both, a classmate not very well liked by Canfield had strolled into their room and turned on the radio. Canfield had asked him to turn it off and had been told by the visitor that anyone who couldn't concentrate with music playing was suffering from a basic learning deficiency. Zack had watched that jaw muscle go into motion. Minutes later, the visitor had made another remark to the effect that people who had to cram were not really Princeton material. There had been then a moment of silence, followed by a furious assault as Porter Canfield, arms flailing and cursing wildly, had launched himself at his astonished tormentor. Zack recalled he had had to use all his strength to pull them apart and that it had been several minutes before Canfield regained control of himself. During the years he had known Newt there had been only two other times he had lost his temper, but each time that twitch of the jaw muscle was the precursor of violence.

Zack moved quickly to prevent catastrophe.

"Before you discuss this any further, Mr. Vice President," he said, "I have some very important information to give you." Then, looking pointedly at the senator, he added, "Since time is short, perhaps now would be the best time."

Roland Gray, looking for a convenient escape, said immediately, "Well, I'll get out of your hair, sir. Sorry to bother you at such an inconvenient time, but there was no alternative." And he departed with unusual alacrity for a man of his age and dignity.

Zack said, "Now Newt, relax. Don't let those bastards upset you."

Canfield clenched his fists, but the moment of uncontrolled anger was over, and he now felt only cold fury.

"Goddamn Hurley and his insults," he said. "Imagine having that pipsqueak Devers relay an order through Gray. What utter gall. Well, we're not going to comply. We're not going to roll over and play dead for old Walter. We've got to chart our own course."

"Right you are, Newt. You're certainly not going to get any help from a hostile, lame-duck President who's already committed to your competition."

"Let's think this through, Zack. It needs delicate handling. Certainly, we won't respond to Devers. You go along now while I dress and check Kathy's final speech copy. We'll talk later tonight."

With that the Vice President walked into the bedroom and closed the door behind him.

He showered, brushed his teeth, touched up his face with the electric shaver and dressed in a white shirt, conservative tie and dark suit. All this was done with surprising speed and the unusual efficiency of movement that comes after much practice to actors, politicians, military men and others whose routine activities require many clothing changes. He was combing his hair and nearly ready to go back into the sitting room, where Kathy and Peter Rosen were waiting for his final okay on the speech before distributing it to the press, when the intercom buzzed. Canfield slipped the comb into his pocket, walked to the night stand and picked up the phone.

"Yes?" he said crisply.

"Mr. Vice President, it's Mr. Devers calling from the White House," said Trent Gilbert, the Secret Service shift leader down the hall in the Command Post. "He's on line one."

"Hold on just a minute," Canfield said to the agent, whose voice he did not recognize. He thought a few moments, then said, "Who's this?" Then, after the agent identified himself: "Okay, Trent, tell Mr. Devers to hold. I'll get Professor Miller to take the call, but don't indicate to Devers that I'm not coming on."

Canfield quickly depressed the connection button and, as soon as the intercom light went out, let it up and dialed Zack's room. The phone rang several times before an irritated voice said, "Miller. What is it?"

"Sorry to bother you, Zack," Canfield said.

"Oh, no bother, sir," said Miller with a laugh. "I'm used to jumping out of the shower and dripping all over the place while answering the phone. Remember, we used to do it at Princeton all the time, but then the odds were that it would be a girl rather than a Vice President. But seriously, Newt, what's up?"

"Josh Devers is up, Zack. He's holding on line one. He thinks he's going to talk to me, but he's going to talk to you."

"What do I tell him?"

"Tell him nothing. Just listen. Play it by ear. You don't have to make any decisions. Say you'll get to me as soon as you can, but that I've left word not to be disturbed by anyone until the speech is over."

"What if he wants to know about the meeting with Gray?"

"Be factual, but volunteer no observations about how I reacted. Got it? When you're through, come down here and brief me."

"Okay, Mr. VeePee, here I go into the battle and *au naturel* at that."

Canfield hung up the phone and went immediately to the sitting room, where he looked over the speech while Kathy Dryden and

Rosen waited. After making a few minor changes in his reading copy, he said, "It's a go, Pete. Make distribution so the TV people can flag in advance what they want to film. The repeat on IRBM's will make headlines in the Washington and New York papers, and the nets will play it heavy on their morning news shows."

"Yes, sir," said Rosen, delighted to have some red meat for the voracious traveling media. "This'll get Winehart and Drake off my back. They've been bugging me about whether you're going to pull in your horns on that one." And he left quickly. As always, the area where he had been waiting looked like a microcosm of Woodstock after the 1969 invasion—grape seeds, cigarette butts, empty glass and Coke bottle, dirty napkins, plus a few balls of crumpled paper.

There was a discreet knock at the door, and Steve Galdari entered.

"All set, sir. They're ready for you downstairs. Usual routine—ruffles and flourishes, then enter with spot to 'Hail Columbia.' "

"Let's hold for about five minutes, Steve. I'm going to wait for a report from Dr. Miller." Canfield turned to his secretary and said, "Would you get him to come right away please, Kathy?"

A minute later Zack Miller dashed into the room. "Sorry, Mr. Vice President," he said. "I was just hanging up from talking to Devers when Kathy came to get me."

Canfield held up his hand. "No apologies needed, Zack. Just give me the bare bones as quickly as you can. No need for you to leave, Steve," he added as Galdari diplomatically started for the door.

Zack took a few deep breaths and said, "Okay. Here's the distillate of the waters of wisdom that flowed from the great Josh Devers. First, he wanted to know whether you had received the message from Senator Gray, and I told him you had. Then, he wanted to know whether you understood. He was sure, he said, that you would honor the President's decisions on foreign policy—you always had been a strong, steady influence in that respect. However, he was worried that you might not regard this request as really being a mandate, so he was calling to make certain you fully understood the importance of abandoning the subject of Israel. Oh yes, and would I please let you know he would be home by midnight Washington time and would welcome the chance to speak to you personally regardless of the hour."

Canfield grimaced. "That changes nothing," he said. "There's no time to talk about it now. We're already late for the dinner."

"Two minutes more, please, Mr. Vice President. You haven't heard the most important part. You've had the stick, now here's the carrot.'' He paused dramatically. Canfield paced impatiently, not in the mood for theater.

"Here's the grease, sir,'' Zack continued. "The President would like the Vice President to handle a delicate international matter of great urgency. It involves a trip to the Far East and the Vice President should be prepared to leave within two weeks. You will be briefed by the President personally on return to Washington. How do you like—''

Canfield cut him off in mid-sentence. "Stay available to the phones please, Zack. No time to talk now. I'll see you after the event.'' He hastened down the hall, following his Secret Service detail. Galdari raised his walkie-talkie and said, "Three minutes,'' to the agent posted just outside the banquet hall. Then they were in the waiting elevator. One of the agents keyed it to nonstop and they rode it to the basement. A minute's walk through the service area brought them to a flight of fire stairs that led directly to a side entrance of the hall. There they met another agent, who, by prearranged signal, let the advance man standing by the orchestra know of the Vice President's arrival and readiness to enter.

Inside the room the capacity crowd was becoming restless. Some of the local luminaries had left their places at the head table to circulate among the guests, and here and there adventuresome extroverts, activated by a long cocktail hour, were jamming the space between the tables and making nuisances of themselves.

The Vice President nodded his readiness to enter, and a second later the band struck up the three ruffles and flourishes traditionally used to announce the nation's second-ranking officer. Porter Canfield stepped through the open door and paused in the spotlight. Then to the vigorous notes of "Hail Columbia'' he walked briskly through the cheering audience and bounded up the steps to the table. As he made his way down the dais, he greeted the other honored guests with smiles and handshakes. Here and there he stopped to exchange a few words with those he knew. The ebbing applause swelled again as he reached his place and waved a greeting to the crowd. The dinner chairman stepped to the microphone. In a few moments the opening ceremonies were concluded and the dinner began.

Canfield took a look around the busy room, his appraisal as skilled and as quick as that of a professional quarterback looking over a defensive formation. Immediately he spotted two things he liked and two things he did not like. He was happy that the room was very well filled with an enthusiastic audience and that the dinner chairman, seated to his left next to the lectern, was obviously apprehensive about his duties. Nervous chairmen did not chatter too much. He was unhappy about the position of the television cameras. They were to the right of center at middle depth, just opposite him. Therefore, the camera stand blocked the view of at least six tables of guests. That was poor planning and revealed inexperience on the part of the committee, which had probably been browbeaten and sold a bill of goods by the network people. Result—a lot of supporters out there who would go home angry and not likely to plunk down a hundred bucks again very soon. The other item that bothered Canfield was the microphone. It was positioned poorly on the small lectern and had emitted periodic yowls and high-pitched whistles during the invocations. He hoped this was due to the inexpertness of the minister, but he was afraid it revealed a technical flaw in the system. Nothing was more destructive of a good speech than a lousy mike, and Porter Canfield worked best when he could use his fine voice subtly.

"Good crowd for you, Mr. Vice President." The speaker leaned over Canfield's shoulder and blew a blast of cigar smoke in his ear. "Yes sir, this is really Hurley country. Good old Roland Gray sees to that."

The Vice President held his breath until the pollution subsided, then turned toward the speaker—none other than Herman Poparch, the big giver.

"Thank you, Mr. Poparch, but neither the senator nor I nor the President can take credit for the tremendous job you and the members of the committee have done. I meant what I said earlier today. You are the real heroes."

"Well, we just know how to handle things in Phoenix, Mr. VeePee," Herman said, reaching a new individual high for modesty. "Incidentally, you can call me Herman. Shake my hand, will you, Porter? That's my company photographer out there, and he'd like to get sort of an intimate shot of us together. Perhaps after the speech you could stop up to my suite—it's fourteen hundred—and he could take a few more informal shots."

"I'm terribly sorry, Mr. Poparch—I mean Herman—but I have to meet with my staff about an important matter as soon as the dinner is over," Canfield said, looking disappointed. "However, if you send the picture he just snapped to me, I'll be glad to inscribe it personally for you."

Mr. Poparch was not ready to leave the arena.

"How about breakfast in the morning? We could get it done over some real Arizona ham and eggs."

"Not possible, Herman. I'll take a rain check for some other time. Nice to talk to you and keep up the good work.'' Canfield swung around and engaged Mrs. Gray, who was at his right, in conversation. Mr. Poparch departed, impervious to the abrupt dismissal bordering on rudeness. Later he would tell Mrs. Poparch that "Porter" had asked his advice on a variety of important matters.

The surprisingly good dinner progressed smoothly, notwithstanding that from time to time the bright television lights were turned on the head table in the hope that the zoom lens might catch some bit of gaucherie such as open-mouth mastication or an errant dribble of gravy down a distinguished chin. And then it was time for the speeches—when you found out whether your advance man had done the hard-nosed job he was supposed to do.

If there were no more than five people who came to the microphone before the principal speaker and if they took no more than fifteen minutes in total, he had done very well. But if the audience was exhausted by a steady stream of windbags before the main event, then forget about good attention and audience reaction.

This night, thought Porter Canfield, was going quite well. Two minor hopefuls as well as Congressman Donnert and the governor had spoken. Now Roland Gray was standing at the lectern, acknowledging a standing ovation in the flawless underplayed style that served him so well. The room quieted as the tall, distinguished majority leader raised his hand.

"Now I want you to know that the last thing the President said to me after the leadership breakfast yesterday was 'Tell our Arizona friends we rely on them. They're the shock troops, the cadre for our training program. Give them my thanks and my best wishes.' That's what your President said, Arizona.'' More applause.

Canfield stirred restlessly. Such messages from the President, whether real or fictitious, were traditionally left for the Vice President to deliver.

Roland Gray continued for two more minutes, giving a brief report on the work of the Senate and the status of measures important to his listeners. Finished with the nuts and bolts, he straightened his note cards, tapping them gently on the ancient lectern, and looked directly into the news cameras.

"You all know I have worked diligently with the speaker of the House and the congressional leaders of the other party to keep the President's brilliant foreign policy free of political interference. Peace in the world is too important to us all to risk destroying it for a temporary partisan advantage. The leaders of the opposition party realize this, and they have been very cooperative, especially in regard to the touchy situation in the Middle East. Nonetheless, some

33

highly visible leaders in politics, the academic community and business don't seem to recognize the danger of inflaming the emotions of those who have ties with a contesting foreign nation." Here Gray paused for a long moment.

"It is to your interest, my friends, to discourage such recklessness by indicating disapproval of it wherever you encounter it."

Then he concluded by saying simply, "Ladies and gentlemen, the Vice President of the United States."

Canfield was momentarily stunned by the audacity of the attack. It was cleverly done, probably the work of Josh Devers. It was unthinkable that cautious Roland Gray would deliberately confront the Vice President of the United States, a member of his party, without warning. So it had to be Hurley's decision. What it amounted to was an ultimatum: Either retreat from the messing with Israel as an issue or face open battle with your President. And here I am, he thought, standing here with a prepared speech, already distributed to the press, that throws down the gauntlet.

The applause was subsiding, and thoughts raced through Canfield's mind. He knew he had to make a decision either to delete the offending paragraphs and face national embarrassment or move to a posture of open hostility with Hurley. There didn't seem to be much choice. He could not survive the ridicule that the media would subject him to if he waved the white flag—that would end any serious chance for the nomination. Well, to hell with Gray—and Devers. Yes, and Hurley too. He was going to be his own man and fight for what served the political aspirations of Porter Newton Canfield—particularly, said his conscience, since it's right.

The quiet audience seemed somehow to sense the drama of the moment. Canfield began quietly.

"Governor McCabe, distinguished guests, ladies and gentlemen." There was no thank you for Roland Gray, but that was no problem since it is entirely proper to acknowledge only the senior guest. Governors are always first at events within their own states.

Canfield looked down at the staff table to his left with the barest hint of a smile. Bill, Kathy and Pete were probably the most nervous people in the room, except maybe for that contemptible fink, Roland Gray. Canfield smiled again, this time more openly. Well, he would show them all—the whole world—that he had guts. The American people admired guts, and they hadn't seen any large demonstration of courage since Harry Truman.

Without so much as a word for Gray or even for Phil Donnert, who was the raison d'être of the entire event, and who, under normal circumstances, would be buttered up for at least three minutes, Canfield jumped into his prepared text. As he progressed toward the paragraphs on foreign policy, which were near the conclusion, his voice became more expressive and emotional. The audience sensed that this was no ordinary stump speech. The head-table guests were unusually attentive and the media men were not walking around, knocking over equipment and talking rudely among themselves as they so frequently did.

Additional television lights were suddenly turned on when the Vice President reached the paragraphs of his text that dealt with Israel. All four network commentators signaled their crews not to miss this part.

Gaining confidence, the Vice President looked up from his text. "I am aware that what I am about to say will be very controversial," he said. "But I consider it urgent and vital to the interests of the United States and to our ability to continue to function as a great nation in the world community."

The hushed hall radiated excitement. Esurience satisfied, the audience waited to slake a different hunger. All eyes were glued on the gladiator about to enter the arena. Canfield lifted his chin in challenge.

"Our young nation, hardly into its third century, did not become the superpower it is by following a course of compromise and conciliation. No, we became great because we faced the great issues squarely. We did not equivocate when our separation from the British became necessary to preserve our self-respect. We did not equivocate when war was the only way to save the free world from aggression—we did not hesitate in France, nor in the Pacific to make great sacrifices for principle. We did not hesitate to admit error in Vietnam because freedom is our trademark—it is more important to us than infallibility. Some say we have too much of it, and at times they may be right, but that is endurable because nothing is worse than having too little of it."

Here there was generous applause, and the Vice President paused to take a sip of water. Leaning forward slightly, he continued, "From its beginning, the tiny nation of Israel has had a very special relationship with the United States of America. Americans listened in agreement when the idea of a Jewish national home was proposed by the distinguished British foreign secretary, Arthur James Balfour, in nineteen seventeen; Americans cheered on May fourteenth, nineteen forty-eight, when the state of Israel was created in Palestine; Americans have watched with great approval and sympathy the struggles of Israel; yes, and where necessary Americans have intervened to keep Israel from being swallowed up by an unfair coalition of forces.''

The applause was courteous, but hardly thunderous. After all, less than 15 percent of the crowd was Jewish. Down at the press table, where less than 15 percent was not Jewish, the reaction was ecstatic.

Canfield continued, undismayed by the relatively tame reaction. This was Phoenix, not New York, and he was playing to the national audience.

"This is nineteen eighty-three, and we have become used to seeing the Israelis overcome the odds and successfully defend themselves time after time. It's our way to become slightly bored with champions. If you don't believe me just remember that people grew to dislike them because they won too much. And need I remind you of the moon landings? The first one was watched breathlessly by hundreds of millions. Today nobody pays any attention to the explorers we have had there for four months. The point is that the Israelis have become—''

There was a loud crash near the rear of the room as the chair a drunk had been balancing precariously on two legs tipped over. The man's contact with the carpeted floor would not have made much noise, but unfortunately he seized the edge of the tablecloth on the way down and pulled all the dishes down on top of him. Covered with leftovers, he stumbled to his feet, and the crowd roared its approval of the diversion.

Canfield said, "That proves my point, ladies and gentlemen. The unexpected always gets attention. If the gentleman fell every night, no one would even turn around.''

In the back someone yelled, "Charlie *does* fall every night!'' and the audience howled again.

Not wanting to turn a serious matter into a joke, the Vice President quickly said, "Thank God we Americans can laugh at ourselves and thank God we know when to be very serious. And nothing is more serious than the point I was about to make—the fact that we take Israel's ability to survive against all odds for granted, and we shouldn't. We must not,'' he said, pounding his fist on the shaky lectern, "because external forces have quietly and efficiently upset the balance of power in the Middle East. Israel is vulnerable to attack with new sophisticated weapons, and she needs the weaponry to defend herself against this probable attack. Israel has asked the United States for help—not men, only weapons. Last night in Oregon, I recommended that we give Israel an intermediate range ballistic missile capability. Tonight I repeat that recommendation and urge that those Americans who feel they have a stake in the survival of our tiny ally write to their congressman on this issue. For my part, I pledge to work untiringly until Israel is no longer threatened.''

Again there was polite applause, but little excitement in the press section, where reporters were leaving the table to rush for the exits, and camera personnel were feverishly packing their equipment.

The Vice President closed his remarks with a few amenities about Arizona, but again avoided any mention of Gray or Donnert. Then, after acknowledging the ovation, he left the hall.

Zack Miller turned off the local television station that had carried the Vice President's speech live and stood for a moment looking thoughtfully at the darkened screen. Tomorrow morning the nets would flash excerpts of the speech across the nation and Porter Canfield's popularity would rise in the big eastern cities and in the big universities all over the country. A new hero would be hailed by the liberal community. The militant group, Israel Now and Forever, a Zionist group Miller had found politically useful when handled discreetly, would undoubtedly demonstrate its approval. A course had been charted by his protégé and they were off and running toward, if not yet for, the presidency. Smiling at his reflection in the mirror, Miller moved to the well-stocked bar and mixed himself another Scotch and water. Yes sir, he thought, the only thing Newt had needed was a social conscience. Now he had one. If he could just keep him on the straight and narrow, Zack Miller could become the new power behind the President. And there was so much that needed doing for the country. The timid policies of Hurley had provided no new exciting social program, and the people were hungry for bold leadership—leadership that would deprive big money of its vested and corrupt interests, so long entrenched in a stagnant bureaucracy. Miller, through Canfield, would change all that if, he reminded himself, he could keep Newt on the straight and narrow.

At college Canfield had always been involved with one girl or another. Several times Daddy had had to bail him out of a heap of trouble. There was that Wellesley girl who slept all around, got in trouble and elected Newt father of the child. That cost a bundle. Then there were a few hustlers whose pimps had gotten ideas watching ''Candid Camera.'' From the looks of their girls, they were contemporaries of the original program. But always, the good old Canfield money provided a convenient escape. However, now was different, very different. Political careers could disappear as the harsh result of clinical scrutiny by the media. Newt must be controlled, even if he had to be locked in the male version of a chastity belt.

Maybe he needed monitoring, too, Zack though ruefully. The image of Kathy Dryden's legs crossed his mind and he registered a physical twinge. The plain fact is that I'm lonely, he admitted to himself. From a hyperactive love life at Princeton and during his graduate days he had gradually sublimated his drives in academic achievements and peer approval.

The intercom buzzed suddenly, recalling him abruptly to the present.

"I'm in the suite, Zack. Come over. We need to talk about things, especially your conversation with the great Devers."

The Vice President sounded elated, pumped up. Zack could always tell when Canfield was happy with his performance. It showed in his voice and attitude.

When he entered the Vice President's sitting room, Zack found Canfield sprawled in an easy chair with an ecstatic Peter Rosen dancing around him.

"They've got a million questions, Mr. Vice President. What shall I tell them?" the press secretary asked, his voice doing acoustic entrechats. "Principally, they want to know whether the President cleared your speech or whether you've broken with administration policy." He pleaded, "Can't you give me a short clarifying statement on the Israel thing?"

"Clarifying statements always become weapons to attack the speech, Peter," said Canfield. "Just tell them that the speech speaks for itself. Volunteer nothing more than that."

"All right, but this thing is big, really big! It's going to make the A wires and all the nets. Drake says Bradley Barton himself is going to do an analysis on it tomorrow, and everybody is going to jump the President at his news conference next week."

Canfield smiled benignly. "Don't worry, Peter. We'll survive. Now be sure not to get trapped into speculating about things. Just tell them they have the speech and that's it. Be especially careful of Atherton. He's good at piecing things together."

"Well, okay, Mr. Vice President, but it's not going to satisfy them." With the air of an important man on an important mission, he rushed by the Secret Service agent at the door.

"Now, Zack, suppose we begin by your bringing me up to date regarding Devers," said Canfield. He waved his arm toward the bar. "Get yourself something if you want."

"No thanks. I just finished a couple while watching you on the tube. Incidentally, that was a great delivery to a tough audience. I liked the way you shafted that sanctimonious bastard, Gray."

Canfield sighed. "Well he asked for it; but I felt a little sorry about Donnert. He was an innocent victim."

"Don't feel that way. He's Gray's man, and he'd cut your throat in a minute."

"Perhaps that's true, but he really didn't do anything to justify my castrating him tonight." He threw a leg over the chair and dangled it back and forth. "Okay, let's hear more about Josh's call."

Miller threw himself into the chair facing Canfield's. "Well," he said, "for starters, you're being banished from the Kingdom. The President wants you to visit Singapore and Malaysia to reassure them that the United States is not complacent about last year's overthrow of Thailand by the communists. He wants you to inform them that he shares their concern that the coup was masterminded by North Vietnam and that the North Viets have ambitions to establish communist governments all the way down the Malay Peninsula. You can fill in the trip with stops in Japan and Korea. Furthermore, relates Josh, your presence will be a signal to the Russians that, although we did not interfere about Laos, Cambodia or Thailand, we are not willing to let the whole damn southeast Pacific fall under their influence. After all, says Josh, we were satisfied with restoring a republic in Cuba in nineteen eighty. We didn't try to swallow the whole Caribbean."

As Miller paused to light a cigarette, Canfield frowned, then asked, "What do you think is behind it, Zack?"

"I get the idea the purpose is threefold. First, to bribe you with an allegedly important mission into abandoning the confrontation; second, to get you as far away as possible from the Washington press for a while; and, third, to throw you in the cage with that wily old devil, the prime minister of Singapore. Devers says it will be publicized as an important mission. State will draw the usual briefing papers, and the President will see you off in a wave of glory."

Canfield picked up the phone and called the Command Post.

"Get Kathy in for a minute. I want to dictate a memo for research," he said.

"She isn't in her room right now, Mr. Vice President," said the shift leader. "I think she may be in the hotel lounge. Shall I get her?"

"No. Don't bother now. I'll do it in the morning."

"Kathy not around?" said Zack casually.

"No, they think she's in the lounge."

"Probably with Galdari again."

"Well, she's got to have some personal life," replied the Vice President. "She's as good a secretary as I'll ever find. I'd hate to lose her."

Zack smiled wolfishly. "I'd rather think of her as a well-stacked girl than as a secretary. When you've been confined to Maxine the glutinous one, you get a different perspective. I had Maxine in for memos tonight, and believe me, memos is all I'll ever have her in for."

Canfield frowned. "Knock off the levity, Zack. Finish up the Devers briefing."

Unintimidated, Zack sighed loudly. "You just don't appreciate my condition, Newt. Being a political principal might dim your lights but staff work puts me on high beam."

He snubbed out his cigarette and refocused on Devers.

"There really isn't much more to relate about my talk with Josh, except for one thing. After he had finished about the trip to the Far East, he very casually in an oh-by-the-way fashion asked whether you had agreed with the President that it was best not to give the press an opportunity to confuse the foreign policy picture. I told him I had no idea what you thought because I had not talked to you since Senator Gray relayed the message."

Canfield pulled thoughfully at his ear. "I think your diagnosis is correct, Dr. Miller," he said slowly. "They want me far away and busy with the worried Asian leaders until they can figure out what to do about the problem. Also, they hope that a little flattery and attention will soothe me. But when they find I've bitten the bullet tonight, things will probably change. I may be sent away, but I doubt if it will be with such fanfare as Josh suggests."

"Hang in there, Newt. You're on the right course. Remember, you can only be President by separating yourself from Hurley. Otherwise, he'll nudge Gray right into the nomination."

"Or the speaker, Zack. But you're certainly correct in saying it wouldn't be me."

Canfield rose and stretched. He loosened his tie and unbuttoned his collar. "Think I'll turn in," he said. "We have an early start tomorrow—ten A.M. wheels up, I believe—and I want to be fresh for the queries of the Fourth Estate at the airport."

Miller looked keenly at his friend. "Don't let the pressure get you, Newt," he said. "You've suddenly become the most visible and incandescent political personality in the United States. My suggestion is to say as little as possible for a few days. They've got plenty to chew on already.''

"Well, I have to play it my way, Zack,'' Canfield looked mildly reproving. ''I think I know how to handle things.''

For midnight, the hotel lounge was unusually busy. Steve Galdari walked past the crowded bar and sat down at the table where Kathy Dryden was having a drink with Shelby, Rosen and one of the research girls. To a man, the traveling newsmen were clustered around Bruce Atherton, Sid Winehart and young Douglas Drake. They had just finished their supplementary filings and were seeking reassurance from the big three that they were on target.

"The Vice President made a lot of sense tonight,'' said Drake, solemnly stirring his drink. ''He sounded like the kind of leader TBS respects.''

Winehart nodded thoughtfully. ''For one of the few times in your life, you're right, Mr. Dranitz,'' he said. It pleased him to refer to the television reporter by his original surname because he resented people who changed their names for professional reasons.

There was an immediate chorus of agreement from the lesser lights. Then Bruce Atherton summarized his disagreement and contempt with a snorted obscenity, delivered with such emphasis that it hung in the sudden hush like a physical presence. Peter Rosen heard the sibilant expletive clearly and went at once to the source of the controversy.

Galdari smiled at Kathy. ''Sounds like a disagreement over the red meat.''

"Yes, and Peter's going to get bit for sure if he tries to separate them.''

"At least he's gone and Barbara's gone. I need to talk, and it's so hard to get a moment alone with you.''

The girl returned his warm smile. ''You need advice on security for the Man?'' she asked teasingly. Galdari covered her hand with his and gave a squeeze. She made no effort to draw away.

"I need advice on me, Kathy. I get very nervous when we're on the road and not able to spend any time together without the whole world knowing it. That guy Miller dislikes me; and he has long antennae. He'd be the first to complain to the boss about our breaking the unwritten rule against Secret Service dating the staff.''

Kathy nodded sympathetically. ''I know, Steve. We were just beginning to know each other. But we'll be back to a regular schedule in Washington soon. Then you can take me to that great Chinese restaurant in Arlington.''

''Wrong, unfortunately, Kath. I have a feeling that we'll be on the road for the Far East in a week or so.'' He frowned bitterly and gestured toward the bar. ''And with the whole traveling circus.''

Her eyes widened in surprise. ''I hadn't heard a hint of that! It must be brand new.''

''Right off the wire tonight. Relayed by Josh Devers to Zack Miller to Number Two.''

''He's making the President angry again, isn't he?'' she said.

''Yes, and he's making me mad when he complicates my seeing you.'' He scowled darkly in feigned rage. ''Never make your watchdog mad. He may turn on you.''

''Oh, Steve. You're impossible,'' she said. Then, catching a glimpse of Rosen returning, she whispered, ''I'm going up and get some sleep. The hyper Dr. Miller will make the day tough enough without starting off with Peter's paranoid fears. Good night, Steve.''

''Good night, Kathy. Drop into the C.P. for coffee in the morning.''

Galdari reluctantly turned his attention to Peter Rosen, who slid into the chair next to him, looking worried. Rosen scooped up a full hand of peanuts and popped a few into his ever-restless mouth.

''The traveling press is going to make plenty of trouble between the President and the Vice President,'' he said through a filter of half-chewed peanut particles. Galdari instinctively drew back to avoid being decorated, but Rosen seemed not to notice. He expertly refueled his masticating machine and continued. ''They approve of the boss's position on Israel. Hell, most of them are left-wing liberals who work for left-wing liberals. But regardless of that, they're out to make a big story of this speech tonight. They've reported it as a palace revolution, and Hurley will have to spank the boss or be accused of losing control of his own administration.''

''But they're not unanimous,'' said Galdari. ''I heard Atherton disagree in no uncertain terms.''

''He's all by himself,'' said Rosen sadly. He washed down the nuts with a gulp of beer. ''There was a time when they would have listened to him, but no more. They consider him a derelict waiting for the graveyard. Besides, he regards Canfield as a lightweight. He really doesn't admire any pol, but between our man and Hurley, I think he prefers the President.''

Galdari shrugged. ''That's not my specialty, nor my responsibility. I'm paid to protect the man, not worry about his political problems." It was the standard disclaimer, the retreat into the insulation of noninvolvement. Galdari knew it wasn't really that way, however. You couldn't be with a person day and night—sharing victories and vulnerabilities—without caring more than you should. He stood up to leave.

"Wait, Steve. I need your help," said Rosen, rising with him. They walked toward the door together. Galdari noticed that all the press had left, except Atherton, who sat hunched over a dry martini, a mournful expression on his face.

"What kind of help?"

"Tomorrow morning, the Vice President is going to answer some questions at the airport before getting on the plane to go home."

"So?"

"Well . . ." Rosen hesitated, fumbling for the right words. "Well, the professor thinks all this controversy is just great. He'll want the boss to really give it to the President and Gray. Now the last thing our man needs, when he's puffed up anyhow, is lots of applause from the wings."

"Just what do you mean, Pete?"

"I mean that Miller will be telling him how great he is, and he won't want to leave the stage. If he answers questions long enough, they'll get him for sure. They'll tape all his answers and spend the whole flight back cutting and pasting and misconstruing what he said until they develop a sensational new angle to start an open fight within the party. Believe me, Steve, I know how they work."

The little press secretary was puffing in his effort to talk and at the same time keep up with the agent's long strides.

Galdari paused at the elevators. "What does that have to do with me?"

"Try to get him aboard as quickly as you can. Try to move him as though there is a security problem the first time he pauses between answers."

"I can't do that," said Galdari firmly. "That's not my job, Peter. Why don't you try to convince Miller to help?"

Rosen's face sagged with disappointment. "Are you kidding? Miller thinks he's the consummate political pro. He won't help. He never consults me or anyone else, for that matter." He placed a hand on Galdari's arm. "Please, Steve. It's important."

"Can't do it, Pete."

"Okay, Mr. SAIC, but remember, you just put your protectee into a heap of trouble."

• • •

The glare of morning sun, unsoftened by cloud cover or pollution, reflected brutally from the concrete taxiway to the eyes of the small clusters of people standing near the waiting jet. Besides the air crew at the nose ramp, there were two Secret Service agents near the tail of the blue and white 727 and about twelve newsmen in a cordoned area to the side. Sitting in a parked car nearby were the mayor of Phoenix and the party chairman.

Suddenly, there was a roar of motorcycle exhaust and the motorcade swung around the edge of the terminal building. The bikemen peeled off, dismounted and lined up for the expected vice-presidential handshake as the black limousine pulled to a stop near the front of the plane. It was as though sodium had been dropped into still water. There was instantaneous turmoil. People piled out of cars on the run, the traveling press dashing for the cordoned area and the staff for the aft entryway of the jet, where agents checked their hand luggage as they boarded. Glutinous Maxine tripped on the steps and the contents of her large shoulder bag flew everywhere. She turned a bright red as Agent Jestes retrieved her *Playgirl* magazine, which had perversely fallen open at a nude photo. He presented it to her with a leer. "Please put it away, Maxine. It makes me feel so inadequate."

Unaffected by the frantic scurrying, Porter Canfield sat coolly in the limousine. Miller was making last-minute, rapid-fire suggestions, but he was only half-listening. He had pretty well in mind what he wanted to say to the press. Galdari, in the front seat, was watching the media people set up. Finally, he gestured to the agent standing outside to open the door. "They're all in position, sir," he said, jumping out of the car and signaling the other agents.

Canfield pulled himself out of the deep rear seat, waved to a few people at the distant fence and shook hands with the mayor, who had come hurrying up to the car.

"Senator Gray and Congressman Donnert asked me to convey their apologies, Mr. Vice President. They wanted to be here to see you off, sir, but they had an emergency in Washington and were forced to take a very early flight back." The city official was obviously nervous, hoping that Canfield would not request any details of the fictional early flight.

"I understand, Sam." He was not deceived, but saw no reason to press the matter. "Thank you for coming. Would you like to stand with me while I talk with the press?"

"You're very kind, sir, but I think I'd better get back to the office. If you'll excuse me, Mr. Vice President . . ." The mayor had read the morning papers and watched the local television news. He had no doubt where his political future lay, and it wasn't with Porter Canfield. Senator Gray could end his career with the wave of a hand, so the mayor didn't consider pictorial togetherness with Canfield an asset at the moment.

"Suit yourself," said Canfield disinterestedly. He walked toward the waiting reporters.

"All right, gentlemen," said Peter Rosen to the unheeding press in the bullpen, but he might as well have been speaking Swahili. "Gentlemen! Gentlemen—please!" he yelled, trying to be heard above their talking and movement. Things quieted a little, and he tried again. "All right, gentlemen. The Vice President will take your questions, but please remember that we have to get back to Washington, so don't keep him out here all day. When I raise my hand, that means he'll take one more question. Is that understood?"

The newsmen were paying absolutely no attention to the press secretary. They strained toward the front of the roped-in area. The electronic-media people stretched hands holding microphones toward the approaching Canfield. He was still twenty feet away when they began their litany.

"Mr. Vice President, over here, please, sir."

"Mr. Vice President, are you splitting with administration policy?"

"Why isn't Senator Gray here to see you off?"

"Have you heard from the President yet this morning?"

Smiling and nodding good-naturedly, Canfield stopped in front of the center of the group. He made no effort to respond to the welter of questions that cascaded over him. Expertly scanning the group, he noted the positions of the network cameras and the reporters from the most prestigious organs. He waited patiently until he thought they were all in position, then took the best stance for a good camera angle.

"Good morning, gentlemen. May I say before I leave this beautiful city of Phoenix how much I have enjoyed being with you and how I wish I could stay longer. In the brief time I have been here, it has been a pleasure to meet so many interesting people and to enjoy the wonderful sense of well-being that goes with this desert climate. Had I been lucky enough to grow up in Arizona, I doubt that anyone would have been able to persuade me to go to Washington."

While the local television cameramen dutifully filmed this tribute, the national media men shifted uneasily. Douglas Drake had shut down his cameramen with the cut sign, moving his finger across his throat as soon as it became clear that the statement was simply self-serving filler. The Vice President went on with a few

45

more amenities and then said, "All right, I'll take your questions."

There was a cacophony of eager voices, which Canfield finally subdued by designating suave Douglas Drake for the first question.

"Mr. Vice President, this morning the official Soviet newspaper, *Izvestia,* criticized you for inflaming an already tense situation in the Middle East and dangerously interfering with the progress of serious negotiations under way among the various governments involved. What is your response to that?"

"I never respond to accusations or provocations from communist nations. When they are ready to give my statements and viewpoints fair exposure to the millions of oppressed people who suffer under their domination, then I will consider reversing that policy."

"Mr. Vice President"—this time it was a reporter from a Midwestern daily newspaper with large circulation—"do you feel that your speech last night put you in the position of breaking with the administration policy on the Middle East?"

The Vice President smiled patiently. "I have already said, sir, that I believe my position on IRBM's is a logical construction of what is inherent in administration policy. It is the President's policy to maintain the balance of power in the Middle East. If it takes IRBM's to do that, and I believe it does, then I don't think they are outside administration policy just because they were not specifically mentioned when the policy was set."

The reporter was not convinced. "But, sir, surely there are limitations to how far we should go to maintain the balance. By your definition, we could be called on to do anything, including sending American troops and installing MIRV's, ICBM's. Is that what you mean?"

"That is not what I mean. Those steps would be contingent on a degree of strength opposed to Israel that is neither existent nor likely ever to become existent. I cannot answer such speculative questions nor approve of such illogical extensions of a perfectly clear situation. My view is that the Israelis need IRBM's to offset existing sophisticated weaponry that is already in place against them."

At this point Peter Rosen announced, "This is it, gentlemen." He raised his hand to signify the last question. His words were drowned by a chorus of excited voices, each attempting to be recognized next.

Canfield held up his hand to quiet them. "Now, gentlemen, I'll answer a few more questions, but if we're going to get this job done, you'll have to maintain a semblance of order." His tone was no longer cordial, for he had been annoyed by the last question. He felt that his answer would be lost in the speculative brush fire that the question would ignite among editorialists, columnists and other foreign policy amateurs. Doing his best to conceal his irritation, he next designated Atherton, who stood calmly in the front rank, ignoring the commotion around him.

The veteran reporter had a small notebook open, in which he had made several entries in shorthand. He fixed his cold blue eyes on Canfield and said in a flat, weary voice, "Mr. Vice President, the Soviet ambassador made an early visit to the White House this morning. He was not on the regular schedule of visitors, and he looked very grim, according to my informants. Now, in view of the *Izvestia* criticism, does that worry you?"

To Porter Canfield's credit, his face did not reflect the sinking feeling in his stomach. Well, this is probably it, he thought. You wanted to break with Hurley, and it looks like you're getting your wish.

He lifted his chin slightly, and looked directly at the camera. "No, it does not. First of all, we don't know why the ambassador was there. It could have been for an unrelated reason. Second, whatever the reason he was there, I am answerable to the people of the United States, not the Soviet Union. I owe my national constituency my best judgments and my honest opinions, and my primary obligation is to my constitutional office."

For a moment, it was very quiet while the reporters jotted down his exact words. Then Atherton said softly, "How about your obligation to the President?"

Caught in the drama of the moment, Canfield did not retreat. In a voice that was even, yet somehow revealed strong emotions, he said, "I am loyal to my party and my President, but my primary obligation is to the American people. I see no conflict in that, but if there ever should be a conflict, the obligations of my constitutional office supersede those to any special group or individual."

"Even if that individual is the President of the United States?" pressed Atherton.

"No matter who," said Canfield. "But the question is really academic," he added quickly, "because no President would ever expect his Vice President to agree with him on every point in the name of loyalty."

"Has President Hurley asked you to shut up?" This insolent question came from Sid Winehart.

Canfield looked at him distastefully, as though he were a drunk at a garden party. "President Hurley is a courteous gentleman, Mr. Winehart. Since you are assigned to cover the White House, you have an unusual opportunity to learn good manners. I suggest you

47

avail yourself of that opportunity."

Walking quickly away, the Vice President smiled to himself when he overheard Atherton say in the background, "Winehart, you are a real stupid ass. You broke our pick. You really blew it."

As the plane climbed to cruising altitude, he settled back in his seat and looked at the news summary that had just been telexed from Washington. Three full pages were devoted to Porter Canfield—a Porter Canfield of stature that the media had apparently just discovered. A feeling of power surged through him. It will be very interesting, he thought. Very interesting.

2

FEDOR GREGOR ANTONEV, firmly wedged between two plastic suitcases in the back seat of the small car, was far too happy with himself to be at all uncomfortable. The Iranian-built Citroën, called a Jyane, was neither easyriding nor attractive, but it was taking him to what he fully expected to be an exciting two days in Tehran. He remembered Nicholas Bretov's description of the dancer at Shokoufeh Now, the famous nightclub in the Old City. Bretov had done well in Tehran, and if the Persian girls liked ugly Nicholas, they would fall all over him. Antonev tried to mask an involuntary chuckle with a cough as he caught a glimpse of the driver watching him through the rear-view mirror. Quickly, in the practiced way of Soviet bureaucrats under observation, he cleared his face of expression and let the results of his recent visit to Afghanistan run leisurely through his mind again.

Just a few hours ago there had been the stop at Rasht and the deposit of a large amount of money at the Bank Melli branch there—not his money, unfortunately, but because of the transaction a comfortable commission in untraceable and spendable Iranian rials rested in the inside pocket of his jacket. He wondered if his sister, Teresa, and her husband, who had paid him to take their money out of Afghanistan, would get safely to Iran to enjoy the fruits of their long labor. He had not wanted to frighten them, but there were certainly indications that should alarm the visibly well-to-do in Kabul—signs familiar to him because of his instinctive recognition of the progress of totalitarianism. Everywhere the poor were becoming restless and angry, and the rich were showing a furtiveness that bespoke a gnawing anxiety about the future. That was progress. That was what made the Soviet Union great: the rising of the oppressed from the yoke of materialistic tyranny.

When Teresa and her dashing Afghan husband left Moscow to open the fashionable restaurant in Kabul, Antonev had been somewhat envious. His squat frame would never move with Arro Etalini's easy grace. The polish and confidence of generations of aristocracy were reflected in his brother-in-law's every gesture, every word. Antonev, however, had no feeling of inferiority. He frequently joked about Arro's fancy manners and elegant clothes; he thought them decadent. Antonev was satisfied that he had accomplished much with the solid and dependable qualities instilled in him by his own heritage of hardship and frugality. He had worked hard and made the most of what society offered him. After all, being director of the Caspian Fisheries Administration, a department of the Soviet Ministry of Natural Resources, was no small achievement for a farm boy raised more than two thousand kilometers from the sea. And the future looked even brighter. He had been so right to learn English and specialize in United States history. Soon he would be transferred to a more important post, where his knowledge of the adversary would be put to good use.

The little Jyane, its two cylinders violently protesting the strain placed on them by the Elburz Mountains, struggled through the Sefid Rud area. Antonev twisted around and glanced back down the mountain at the strikingly beautiful view. Behind them, the lush greenery surrounding the Caspian Sea unfolded like an endless blanket. The strong, clear summer sunlight accentuated the contrast between the blue sky and the green earth. But the peace and beauty of the pastoral scene was marred by the ugly duckling Jyane and hundreds of other vehicles that snorted and coughed across the mountains. It was Thursday, the end of the Moslem work week, and the traffic from Tehran was becoming heavy. By afternoon, it would be much worse; the sides of the road would be littered with cars of every description disabled by the dual assault of heat and altitude.

Antonev shifted his weight again and shoved against the larger suitcase, which kept sliding over against his leg. He glanced at his driver with a mixture of amusement and contempt, remembering the man's impotent fist-shaking and shouting when an arrant bus loaded with vacationers nearly collided with them in the recently passed village of Manjil. Chairman Dradovov was right in his judgment that Iran would never assume her role of major world power that the Shah had envisaged for her. The Persian personality was far too volatile. Iranians did not possess the discipline nor the patience required to create an integrated and mutually supportive society. Only Russian determination, thought Antonev, was capable of competing with the depersonalized technology of the Western overlords.

Suddenly there was a muffled report and the awkward little car began to fishtail wildly. Antonev hung on to the front seat while the driver frantically maneuvered to avoid oncoming traffic. Finally the Jyane was brought to a stop on the shoulder of the road. The Iranian climbed out, cursing effortlessly in Farsi. His serenity destroyed, the Russian felt a wave of irritation. The blowout would delay them, and the weather was getting too hot for daydreaming. Laboriously, he extracted himself from the cramped back seat and walked back to join the driver. When he saw the right rear tire was beyond repair, he sighed and shook his head.

"Do you have another tire?" he asked in English. The driver looked at him blankly.

When he tried again, this time with gestures, he was rewarded with that classic lifting of the shoulders and palms that can signify anything from truculence to an inability to cope with the monstrous forces of nature.

Antonev wrestled his suitcase out of the back seat and reached into his pants pocket. He separated a thousand-rial note from an unimpressive roll of cash and tendered it to the driver, whose expression left no doubt that he considered it an inadequate amount for his services. When Antonev pressed it on him, the man kept backing away and shaking his head from side to side. After some more argument in pantomime, the Russian impatiently added another five hundred rials, picked up the two heavy suitcases and moved away from the disabled vehicle and its still dissatisfied owner.

What a way to begin a vacation, Antonev thought. Here I am, afoot in the Elburz Mountains in a heavy suit on a hot summer day. There are no means of transportation, and, unless I can prevail on somebody to stop and pick me up, I'll be sleeping in a field instead of sharing a comfortable hotel bed with a beautiful Persian girl.

But his luck was better than he would have dared hope. It wasn't longer than fifteen minutes before a well-kept Hillman-Peykan braked sharply, pulled off the paved surface and backed toward him. The driver, a dark-complexioned, prosperous-looking middle-aged man, hailed him in Farsi and then, seeing that he did not understand, tried English.

"Had some trouble," he observed.

"Yes, sir, my car broke down."

"Just put your bags in the back and climb in here. This is no day to be standing on the main road. In another hour, the traffic will be fierce, and when an Iranian is delayed on his way to the Caspian Sea on a Thursday, trouble is inevitable. You may be just run down without a second thought!"

"Thank you," said Antonev, climbing in and gratefully easing his bulk into the front seat. "I'm Fedor Antonev. I'm going to Tehran for a visit."

"My name is Zardeh," said the Iranian. "Welcome to Iran. Have you been to Tehran before?"

"No, this is my first visit to the city. I do get to the Caspian sometimes."

"Where will you be staying?"

"I have a reservation at the Hotel Naderi. Have you heard of it?"

"Oh, yes. I know it well. It's an old hotel, but very comfortable —just remodeled, in fact. It's near the Russian Embassy. Are you Russian?"

"I am a Soviet Fisheries official," Antonev responded with some pride. "I have just finished negotiating an antipollution agreement at Bandar-e Pahlavi."

The man glanced at him with new interest. "I'm an ecologist. I work for His Imperial Majesty. My primary field is birds and other warm-blooded animals. Fish I don't know much about, but I hope you're working hard to make sure we don't lose our famous caviar. You people have industrialized the north Caspian so intensely."

"Oh, I don't think there's any worry about that. We have the latest equipment installed in our factories. We are even working on thermal pollution, and you don't get to that stage until you've conquered the problem of inorganic impurities."

Zardeh nodded in acceptance, but not necessarily agreement. "Actually," he said, "the Americans seem to have made better progress in these areas than the rest of the world. They have a constant struggle between productivity and environmental cleanliness. Wouldn't you say that your country is more oriented toward productivity?"

The Russian sensed a point of contention and, in the guarded, ritualistic way he had been taught, avoided a direct answer. "The Americans are doing all right," he said, "but sometimes their propaganda exceeds their performance. They are a declining power because they haven't learned to discipline the individual for the benefit of the group."

This time the Iranian nodded in agreement. "The history of mankind shows a never-ending struggle between efficiency and freedom," he observed. "In this country, our Shahanshah, through his wide experience, has been able to achieve a great deal without an undue restraint on individual liberties; yet, he is our ruler, and everyone recognizes his absolute authority. Perhaps we have the best system."

The Russian took the offensive quickly. "Your system depends on the integrity of one individual and his continued adherence to policies which benefit the people. We in Russia will never again trust one individual to that extent. That is why we now have a true democracy, one in which the people speak through their party and maintain eternal vigilance over those in authority."

Zardeh smiled. "But you have only one party, and your Mr. Dradavov's hold on it is absolute. Surely you don't believe that Mr. Dradovov concerns himself with what the ordinary people think?"

"Oh, yes! A great deal! Chairman Dradavov knows that he must be responsive to the voice of the Soviet people as enunciated through their Central Committee leaders."

"I see," said the Iranian, choosing to break off the conversation rather than pursue this blind alley.

They drove on in silence. Antonev noticed that the green grass had given way to brownish rock and was struck by the suddenness of the transformation. The descent to the high barren plain that stretched to Tehran had begun. From the junglelike Caspian area they had moved into a hard, brittle desert of sand and rock.

They were headed now down the more gradual southeastern slope of the Elburz Mountains, and, despite the increasingly heavy northbound traffic from Tehran, their rate of progress for a time improved. Zardeh was an excellent driver and expertly maneuvered the little Persian Hillman around the slower traffic when straight sections of road permitted passing. However, as the afternoon wore on and the northbound vacationers from Tehran became more numerous, opportunities to pass safely came less and less frequently, and the Peykan was restricted to a much slower pace.

The minutes seems to drag by. Antonev succumbed to the over-powering drowsiness that affects automobile travelers on warm summer afternoons. His companion no longer seemed eager for conversation. The Peykan rode more smoothly than the Jyane, and he allowed himself to doze in relative comfort until he eventually slipped off completely. When he awakened, several hours had passed, and the two-lane road had been replaced by a six-lane dual highway.

"Where are we now?"

"About five kilometers past Karaj," said Zardeh. "We should be in Tehran within a half-hour."

"This is a very good road. It reminds me of Moscow."

"Yes, His Majesty has many new programs, and he is giving great priority to improving our road system."

"My government could help a great deal. We have done some very advanced construction for Afghanistan, for example. Have you ever seen the excellent roads in Kabul?"

"No, I haven't been to Kabul."

"Well, the roads there are extremely good, thanks to Soviet planners and builders. We have given Afghanistan a great amount of aid."

"I know you have," Zardeh said, "and the A-ghans are following in your political footsteps. They have made many changes. They seem to be adopting the Russian way of doing things, though for a while it was a standoff as to whether you or the Americans would have the greater influence."

Antonev laughed easily. "I think we are more expert at persuading people," he said.

A cynical smile crossed the Iranian's face, but he did not say anything.

"When the Americans want to get something done outside the United States," continued Antonev, "they have to convince too many people in their own country that it is the right thing to do. Even worse, the way to become important there is to disagree and demonstrate your dissatisfaction in the most irresponsible way possible. That brings the news media immediately. In our country, the leaders decide. There is no confusion. You see, we are much more efficient."

The driver smiled. "I guess we are back on the subject of efficiency versus freedom. I'm not sure that I agree with you fully, but I have to admit that in the last twenty years your foreign policy has been much more successful than that of the Americans."

Antonev was eager to brag about his country. "Yes, much more successful! Other nations want to identify with strong leadership. Even your Shah is changing his viewpoint to some extent. He used to be very pro-American, but he is more evenhanded now. He sees that the new American leaders have not been as reliable friends as he might have expected. The intellectuals in America will not permit strong leadership to develop."

"We Iranians have sincere admiration for the United States," Zardeh said. "They have given us a great deal at a time when we needed it desperately, and they have asked very little in return."

Antonev nodded solemnly. "But that was when they were a great nation. Most international observers agree that America is now on the wane. The country is under attack by professional critics with an unlimited supply of ink and microphones. That is why your Shah has adopted a more international point of view—just as it is why Afghanistan seeks to model itself after its strong friend to the northwest."

Zardeh, sensing that he had struck another stone wall, tried to turn the conversation to things more trivial. "Have you heard of our Shahyad Monument?" he asked. "That's it there, just ahead. It was dedicated in nineteen seventy-one as a memorial to all the Shahs of Iran. The occasion was the twenty-five-hundredth birthday of our country."

As they swung into the circle around the towering monument, Antonev leaned down to look up at its graceful blue and white symmetry. "What does it do?" he asked.

"Do?" Zardeh laughed. "Why, nothing, I suppose. There is a restaurant on top, and down below there is a theater and a film library where tourists are shown some of Persia's history, but the monument itself? It does nothing." He paused and looked quizzically at his guest. "What would you expect it to do? What does the Eiffel Tower do? What does Lenin's Tomb do?"

"Well," said the practical Russian, ignoring the comparisons, "I mean what is it used for. A structure with that much concrete and steel in it should have some use. It seems a waste that more of it was not made in the form of a building, with more useful space to educate people."

Zardeh smiled. Forgetting that his English was far too polished and advanced for the Russian, he continued, "Perhaps life has to be a compromise between things that are beautiful and things that are useful. In a country as young as yours, usefulness seems everything, but in a country with over twenty-five hundred years of turbulent history, the people need to be reminded of the legacies of the past. Iran has never been dismembered or separated by her conquerors. The integrity of the Person personality remains intact, and, to us, that is something more important than a transitory usefulness. The word 'useful' too often relates to man's comfort and too frequently connotes the sacrifice of beauty for something new. I am not certain that change is always in the interest of humanity."

Antonev did not respond. As a matter of fact, he had heard little of the Iranian's reply because his attention was distracted by the sudden appearance of hundreds of vehicle-borne maniacs who seemed to have come from nowhere onto Eisenhower Avenue. It was the incredible Tehran Thursday traffic. All about them was chaos. Tempers flared in the late afternoon heat. Drivers screamed imprecations and obscenities. Fundamental traffic rules were totally ignored. Oblivious to their vehicles' fragility, people glided bicycles and wheeled carts obliquely through the swerving cars. Jaywalkers stepped serenely into the traffic, averting their eyes from the cursing motorists. There was an old theory in Tehran that, so long as you did not look at a driver, he would not hit you, but once you made eye contact, you were lost.

It was Antonev's first trip to Tehran, and he sat bolt upright in his seat, rigid with apprehension. What a bunch of crazy people, he thought. Rather than wait five seconds, they will risk a collision. The lines that divide the lanes are apparently for straddling, the police stand about ignoring all violations, traffic lights are considered optional, and insanities that would land you in jail in Moscow in two minutes are routine!

Finally, unable to contain himself any longer, he said, "These people drive like lunatics!"

Zardeh gave way to the left to avoid a swerving cab. "You should have seen Tehran fifteen years ago," he said. "Actually, the police have become much stricter. Now, if there is a serious collision, they give a ticket."

"But don't you get angry when someone cuts you off like that?"

"No, that's just the way we drive here. I don't take it personally when someone wants to take advantage of an open space. After all, I do the same thing myself."

"Well, it's just crazy. The dangers are too great for the benefits of getting there a few minutes sooner."

"It's just our way," repeated Zardeh. "It does upset foreigners at first, but they get used to it. An Englishman once observed to me that every Iranian behind the wheel of a car thinks he's Xerxes headed for Thermopylae. An American I know put it more crudely. He said that the Iranian driver considers his car a phallic extension —part of his manhood."

They drove around the diamond of Cinema Center and on to Shahreza Street.

"On your left is Tehran University Stadium, and up further are the university buildings. There are many interesting places to visit in Tehran, but above all, you should see the crown jewels and the Peacock Throne."

"Thank you, but I don't really expect to do too much daytime touring," Antonev said with a slight smile. "I have been working very hard, and I have come here for a little night life and relaxation. One of my friends in Moscow tells me that there are some good shows here. He mentioned in particular a nightclub called Shokoufeh Now. Do you know it?"

"Of course. N-o-w is pronounced 'no'—it means 'new.' Every Persian knows Shokoufeh Now. But be careful if you go down there. That's a pretty rough section of town."

"Oh, I can take care of myself," laughed the Russian.

"Nevertheless, be very cautious. If they see you have money, they will try to relieve you of it as quickly as possible. Not the management of Shokoufeh Now, you understand, but the professional ladies and the criminal types that hang out in the area of Shahre Now."

"What is Shahre Now?"

"That's the red-light district. Shokoufeh Now is right on the edge of it. The whole area down there can get pretty bad. The Old City area is difficult to police—narrow streets and old buildings."

Zardeh cut off an encroaching Datsun. A moment later he resumed, "Over there on the right is Pahlavi Park, and here, where we are turning, is police headquarters. Down on your left is the Russian Embassy. We are almost at Hotel Naderi now."

"Well, I thank you very much for bringing me here," said the Russian. "I hope that you will allow me to pay part of the expense. Without your kindness I might have been stranded overnight up on the mountain."

"No thanks are necessary. Consider it part of our traditional Iranian hospitality, and certainly I would not allow you to pay for the ride. Besides," Zardeh said with a sly smile, "you'll probably need every cent you have for Shokoufeh Now."

At Hotel Naderi the Russian again profusely thanked Zardeh, and the doorman removed the bags from the car. The Peykan pulled smoothly away, and Antonev went to the registration desk. At last, he thought, I am in Tehran. I have no responsibilities, and I have some money. These are going to be two very fine days.

Just as Fedor Gregor Antonev was throwing himself across his hotel bed for a nap in anticipation of a big night, a man who was quite familiar with the part of Tehran that so interested Antonev left another bed after a very active and amusing afternoon with a beautiful woman.

Sirana Amiri frowned at the man's back as she watched him

dress. She was strikingly beautiful by any standards. She enjoyed her involvement with Assad Izadi because it was satisfyingly exciting and demanded little discipline. The drudgery of sustained effort was distasteful to her.

Now she was irritated because this handsome, lithe man had disengaged so casually from their lovemaking and obviously had dismissed her from his thoughts. She reached out to touch his muscular back. "Why do you have to get up, Assad? Stay with me a little while," she said.

Assad Izadi moved away from her touch and turned to look impersonally at the beautiful body which gave him such easily forgotten pleasure. His dark eyes dominated the chiseled features of a face that could qualify for the stage or screen. At the moment, they were cruelly empty of affection. "I can't lie around all day, Sirana," he said. "There's too much to do."

Behind the thin plywood partition that separated the two rooms of his apartment he splashed water from the basin on his face and body. The early evening heat was oppressive, but he was used to it. He toweled off with a slightly soiled piece of cotton cloth and thought of Sirana. She didn't like the heat and perspiration of summer lovemaking, but once he got her started, surroundings meant nothing. She was a wonderful bed partner, and he liked her very much, but she would not leave him alone. He remembered what she had said to him earlier in the afternoon: "You know, Assad, I know your body intimately, but I don't know you. The only glimpse I've ever had of what's inside you was one night when you woke up suddenly and held me very close. For a moment you seemed to be frightened and vulnerable. But even that lasted only a few seconds, and then you turned away."

He had had a nightmare that time—the same one he'd had since the age of twelve, when they killed his grandfather. He wondered how things would have turned out if his grandfather had not been shot down in front of him. His mother died when he was three, and he had loved his grandfather more than anyone, even his father. Although a very important man, his grandfather always had time for him—more than his father ever had. He used to take him to the legislature to listen to the speeches and to learn debating.

He could still hear his grandfather telling him that you learned the truth about yourself from intelligent adversaries, not friends. It was his wish that Assad become a legislator and follow him into the Majlis, or that he even become a minister.

Those bastards. What a man Grandfather had been. Notwithstanding his loyalty to the Shah, he had by no means been a rubber stamp. Sometimes he had been forced to extreme positions that were not entirely compatible with Imperial ideas, but he was never an obstructionist. Once the Shah decided a matter, he did not actively continue to oppose established policy. Grandfather had been against all social programs except free education. He had been for free enterprise and minimum government interference in private business. It was his hatred of communism that made him such a strong supporter of the Western world. As is usually the case, his conciliatory pragmatism and humanitarian qualities were overlooked because of his frequently fiery oratory against what he perceived as the Russian threat to his country. He became famous or infamous—depending on how far right or left his evaluator stood. But above all, he had been influential, a recognized leader in the Majlis. His speeches were followed fervently throughout the country, and he had had a decided impact on important legislation.

Inevitably, he came to the attention of the highest levels of the KGB, and it was a tribute to his effectiveness that the Soviets initially sought to transmogrify him. Legislator Izadi was invited to Moscow for the alleged purpose of clarifying some of his misconceptions about Soviet society. After a two-week visit, he returned home unconvinced, despite the most flattering attention and high-level effort of his Soviet hosts.

From that time on they ignored him, hoping, perhaps, that his age would diminish his influence in the Majlis or that he would tire of the game. They had miscalculated entirely. The dedication of the old man burned ever brighter, and with each passing year he converted additional thousands of followers to his point of view.

Then one day, according to popular belief (there was no doubt at all in Assad's mind) his antagonists turned to the ultimate solution. They decided to liquidate their tormentor. Although the killers were never apprehended, the fact remained that an assassination did take place. For young Assad, it occurred under the most unforgettable circumstances.

As was their habit on a quiet afternoon in late fall, Assad and his grandfather had been walking on the grounds of the nearly deserted Imperial Club, not far from the Hilton Hotel in northwest Tehran. The brisk, thin air tired the old man. He had stood for a moment to catch his breath while Assad ran ahead. When the boy was about eighty yards away, he had turned his head. "Grandfather, time me while I run to you."

"Get ready, Assad," his grandfather had said, pulling out his pocket watch. "Now go!"

He had dashed forward toward the old man, who waited with

open arms. Assad had traversed about half the distance between them when it happened. He would never forget the moment. How often it had replayed itself in his dreams. He was about thirty yards away, his eyes fixed on his grandfather's face, when suddenly he heard an indistinct report and he saw a black hole open over the old man's right eye. The watch flying from his grasp, Grandfather fell at his feet, blood pouring from the gaping hole that used to be the back of his head.

Even now it was very strange to Assad that every detail of that scene was etched with such startling clarity in his mind, even though the immediate events that followed were totally lost to his recollection.

He had told Sirana about the nightmare. It was usually in slow motion. He would see the old man slowly bending, arms open in anticipated embrace. Then that sudden, ugly little black hole in his forehead—his grandfather's head snapping momentarily backward, the watch falling, then the legs collapsing and the slow tumbling of the body to the ground.

Later they told him that he had run to the country club screaming and sobbing. After guiding help to the spot where his grandfather lay dead, he had become completely hysterical and had to be kept under powerful sedatives for two days. They could not get the watch from his clenched hand until they knocked him out with the drugs.

During the months that followed he sat for hours, impassive and withdrawn. In school the former honor student just managed to pass his courses.

Then, suddenly, after a year's time, he snapped out of his lethargy. His detachment disappeared and he became intensely aware of the social aspects of his environment. He became a leader, effortlessly controlling his peers in both academic subjects and athletics. He led his high school class by a wide margin, and had later been sent to college in California. In his late teens at the university, he had had an opinion on everything. Stubbornly he resisted any modification of his ideas by others; however, he would change his mind later if those ideas were demonstrably untenable.

He provided dynamic leadership to all who came in touch with him. He had read avidly all of his late grandfather's speeches and writings, but he construed them in a rather simplistic and extreme manner—sometimes reaching conclusions never intended by the old man. He was not alone in his conviction that the communists were responsible for the assassination. Thousands of others felt the same way, and right-wing journalists were not timid about their accusations.

He returned to the bedroom to find Sirana nearly dressed.

"God, it's hot," she said. "Can't we put an air conditioner in this place?"

"Sirana, you know we can't. The League needs every cent we can scrape together. They would not understand spending money on air conditioning when they can't be reimbursed for simple expenses."

She sighed hopelessly. "Next time you come to my apartment. It's cool there—and clean—not like this pigsty. I'll cook you *chelokebab* and we'll make love all night."

"When I get some time," he said, moving toward the door. "See you later. Ali has a message from one of our people in the Caspian area. I must meet him at the bazaar."

He walked purposefully down the narrow alley and out onto Mowlavi Street. Turning north off Khayyam Avenue, he quickly covered the six blocks to the center of the old bazaar. The streets were steaming hot, and here and there small puddles of tar stuck to his sandals.

His thoughts returned to his grandfather. He wondered if the old man would approve of what he had done with his life. He had no doubt that he would be comfortable with the ultimate purpose of the PPL—the protection of Iran from communism—but he sometimes doubted that his grandfather would approve the means to that end. Izadi tried at first to enlist the aid of the well educated and affluent among whom he had been raised, but the dangers inherent in the undertaking put them off and he was forced to look elsewhere.

He'd worked hard to put together his organization. The PPL now numbered about one hundred soldiers—they were proud to be called soliders—and these hundred, although mostly poor and uneducated, had proven far more effective than his indolent former associates. In addition, many of the soldiers had a personal reason for membership over and above pure patriotism and their belief that Iran must be protected from communist domination. Like Ali, who had lost a hand to communist terrorists; like Boldar, who enjoyed hurting people and who had found that League activities offered many opportunities for violence; like Assad himself, who was avenging his grandfather; and like Sirana, who seemed to be in love or infatuated with him. "I wonder what will happen when she tires of this filthy work," he thought.

He entered the bazaar, and the dank cellarlike coolness was a relief from the oppressive heat outside. The old market was packed with Thursday shoppers. Rich and poor, young and old, native and tourist mingled in the skylighted tunnels. Everything imaginable was sold here, from a bowl of soup to a diamond bracelet.

The mosaic of sounds and smells so noticeable to the stranger from the West made no impression on Izadi's senses. He hurried through the crowd, nimbly dodging the aggressive merchants and their haggling customers.

Turning down a narrow and little-used alleyway, he came to a small stand selling cheap cotton products. An unshaven, middle-aged man with a scarred stump of a forearm protruding from a dirty T-shirt smiled at him.

"Well, if it isn't our great leader," he said irreverently. "Before I am swamped with customers, let me give you my report from the Caspian."

Izadi glanced quickly around, assuring himself that they were, in fact, alone. "Okay, Ali. What have you got?"

"Mohammed called. There was interesting information." He paused to savor the moment.

"Get on with it. I've many things to do yet today."

"Well, this may change your plans. There was a Russian official up in Bandar-e Pahlavi negotiating some kind of contract on pollution with the Shilat. Mohammed found that he did not come with the rest of his group, but came independently, all the way from Kabul by small airplane. Mohammed followed him as far as Rasht this morning. The Russian went into the Bank Melli carrying a briefcase and came out without it. I think we can assume he deposited money there. Then he hired a car and headed for Tehran. Mohammed went back to Bandar-e Pahlavi. There he found out from the concierge at the hotel that the Russian will stay in Tehran at the Naderi for a couple of days. Our people seem pretty sure that he is up to no good, so we should make plans to intercept him and get him talking."

"Leave the planning to me, Ali," said Izadi flatly. "Is there any more information?"

"That's all he gave me."

"Have you checked the Naderi? Do you have his name? Is he using an alias?"

"His name is Fedor Antonev. I can't think of any reason why he wouldn't use that name at the hotel, but I haven't had a chance to leave here to check."

An old woman stopped at the counter near them and began fingering some cheap cotton blouses. Izadi gave no sign that he noticed her, but easily changed the subject.

"Ali, I have your order for the napkins, but it may take two weeks to fill it. I'll do the best I can, but labor is short, and it's hard to hold to the prices we quoted you."

The old woman looked up at Assad, then moved away when Ali turned to approach her.

"Your prices are too high," she muttered over her shoulder.

Ali turned back to Izadi. "She gave you a look. Do you think the Savak is on to us?"

"Why should the secret police worry about us. Their real work is to keep tabs on the communists. Besides we have no record of unlawful conduct."

"Things are changing, Assad. The left is getting stronger. They executed the devil who cut off my hand, but today I doubt if they'd even search hard to find him."

"My grandfather had some friends in the Savak. There are some of them who sympathize with what we are doing," Assad said. "Anyhow, we have our work, regardless of danger. I believe in it. I wouldn't have left the university six months short of my doctorate in political science if I didn't. Now, back to business. Do you have a description?"

"Yes, he's medium height, heavyset, blond hair, about forty-five years old. Oh, yes, and in the short stay of two days at the Pahlavi Hotel, he made passes at at least three waitresses. That will give you some idea of his vulnerabilities."

Izadi's face relaxed, and he laughed. "Good, Ali. It shouldn't be very difficult to get him talking. He's obviously here to break Tehran night life wide open, and we'll give him an assist. I'll send someone to the hotel to keep an eye on him if he's there. See you later, and thanks."

On his way back to the house on Mowlavi Street, Izadi began to map his plans for the evening.

What a piece of luck, he thought. The Russian was obviously on a mission apart from the negotiations with the Shilat about fish conservation. It involved Afghanistan and Iran. Izadi had grave suspicions about Soviet intentions in Afghanistan. Afghanistan was the key to Iran, and Iran was the key to the whole Persian Gulf—the assurance of energy for Russian war machines.

The young Iranian looked up at the darkening sky and increased his pace. His thoughts raced. This Russian official, obviously important because he is traveling alone, may reveal the latest communist trickery. He is either corrupt himself or is paying off some corrupt Iranian with that satchel full of money he deposited in Rasht. But best of all, exulted Izadi, his conduct at the hotel on the Caspian indicates that he is a *khanoumbaz*, a woman chaser, who sees an opportunity to make his visit to Tehran a memorable sexual adventure. Since the communist had the inclination, Assad would provide the opportunity.

The heat was abating. A small breeze had sprung up, and the people on the street seemed less irritable. In the Old City, however, the breeze was not entirely a blessing, because it wafted about the fetid odor of human waste that flowed down the troughs in the centers of the cobblestone streets. The smells were no longer noticed by Izadi. They were a part of the Old City, and a part of his life for the past five years. At first it had been disgusting to live in such surroundings, but he soon learned that it was infinitely safer and more convenient for the nondescript group of dissidents in the PPL.

As he turned into his street, he noticed that Sirana's Volkswagen was no longer on the curb. He shrugged off the fleeting feeling of disappointment. She had probably returned to her apartment. Short of a direct summons, about the only thing that brought her to the miserable hovel off Mowlavi Street was an intense physical need for him. Once that was slaked, she couldn't wait to get out of the dirt and poverty. It was not difficult to understand her revulsion, thought Izadi, going up the narrow entranceway.

He stepped out of the shadows into the open courtyard just as a giant of a man emerged from one of the rooms, carrying a large chunk of cheese in one hand and a heel of bread in the other.

"Hello, Boldar. I'm glad you're here. We have something important to do tonight."

The fierce-looking Persian took large bites of the cheese and bread and chewed thoughtfully for a moment. "Good," he said, spraying minute particles of food in front of him, "I hope there's some action for a change."

"Boldar, if you don't beat up someone at least every other day, you're unhappy. Your fists have nearly caused us trouble several times. Get it through your head that fighting causes arrests, and arrests bring the Savak. So if you have to have action, find some dirty bar on the other side of town and do your fighting there. We have more important work."

The big man grinned without resentment. He flexed his enormous arms and made a mock assault on Izadi. "Careful what you say to Boldar," he growled. "I could tear you in half."

Izadi quickly stepped inside the lunging giant and brought his knee up to within an inch of his crotch. "Boldar, I know your weakness," he said. "The target is unmistakable. I would suggest that you buy a steel cup before you go hell-raising again."

Boldar laughed loughly and thumped Izadi on the shoulders with his forearms, spraying more cheese and bread randomly about. "That is your department, little Assad," he bellowed. "Leave the fighting to me. You take care of the ladies." His face took on a look of mock sadness. "You take care of Sirana. She was just pulling away from the curb when I came in. She didn't look too happy."

"Boldar, when women look too happy, men are in trouble. Now go and find Little Man and Mahmoud. Tell them to be here at ten o'clock and to stand by for further instructions. Explain that they may have to wait some time before they hear from me, but that they should under no circumstances leave until released. Understand?"

"Okay, Assad. Shall I wait with them?"

"Yes, I'd like you to be on hand at the same time. We have a Russian in the area, and this may turn out to be a very busy night."

The big man wolfed down the last of his bread and cheese and disappeared into the entranceway on his way to the street. Izadi went into the bedroom and threw himself down on the pallet, where he could still detect the faint odor of Sirana's perfume on the pillow. Rolling toward the phone, he dialed her apartment number.

"This is Assad, the Lion and the Light of your life," he said after a sleepy voice finally answered.

"Oh, Assad. I had just gone to sleep. Why did you waken me so that I have to remember what a beast you are?"

"What do you mean, beast, darling Sirana? You're the only one who bites holes in the pillow."

There was a pause at the other end of the line, followed by a few choice expletives. "Stop treating me like a Shahre Now slut, Assad. I won't stand for it."

"Calm down, angel, I was merely paying tribute to your passion."

"There has to be some reason for this call," she said, somewhat mollified. "What is going on?"

"We have an important subject in town tonight, and I may need your help."

"Damn it, Assad. Can't you call me once when you don't need something? I'm not going out of here tonight. I'm tired and I have to do some stills tomorrow. I need to take care of myself and get some rest."

"Now, don't be upset. It shouldn't take very long. Just keep yourself ready to move on a half-hour's notice."

"You're inhuman," she said savagely. "You don't care about anything except your personal revenge. It's eating you up inside, and I don't like what it's turning you into."

He broke in quickly. "Please, now, Sirana. This is my life, and if you're going to share part of it, you might as well get used to the devil inside of me.''

"No, I won't do it," she said flatly. "Not tonight."

"I haven't asked you to do anything yet."

"But I know you will. I also know I probably won't like it."

His voice suddenly turned colder. "Since I've serviced you this afternoon, you're pretty damned independent, aren't you—" he began. There was a loud bang and a disconnecting click in his ear. Izadi laughed to himself. "She'll be ready," he thought, "and she'll do what I want her to do, just as she always has."

He wandered into the small kitchen and opened the tiny refrigerator, pulling out a can of beer and a large salami. Opening a drawer, he took out a knife and hacked about five inches off the loaf of bread Boldar had left on the counter. Then, carrying the food into the next room, he pulled a rickety wooden chair up to the piece of plywood between two sawhorses that served as a table and sat down.

Methodically, he began to eat as he considered the task for the evening ahead. It would be best to start with the Naderi Bar, he decided. The Russian would probably sleep for a few hours before starting out on the town. Chances were that he would begin his carousing with a drink at the hotel bar. In any event, they had the hotel covered. Reza Farzaneh was already there to follow the communist in the event that he made an earlier-than-expected departure. Izadi chewed thoughtfully. At some point, preferably early in the evening, he would have to make a friendly overture to Antonev. If all went well, he would offer to show the Russian the night life in Tehran. And the earlier the better. Once he had the Russian moving with him, he would be able to control the situation much better. Eventually, he would be able to get him drunk and turn him over to Sirana for more private and exhaustive interrogation.

Izadi shook his head in mild irritation. There was something that bothered him about Sirana with another man, even this oaf of a Russian who was no threat to him. She was exceptionally beautiful—a mixture of firm slenderness and soft curves, the athletic body of a dancer, which she had been, but with plenty up top to avoid the little-boy look that most dancers had. Her eyes were large and luminous and the planes of her face were typically Iranian, projecting a sultry beauty that recalled a poet's description of Cleopatra. She was all woman, and she was his woman if he wanted her. He picked up the beer can again and frowned. That was what he had trouble figuring out. He really didn't want to be burdened with responsibilities. There was no place for marriage in his hectic life.

Besides, she would probably begin to nag him about the work of the PPL and the demeaning way that it forced him to live. Both of them had money. He had been left a comfortable amount by his grandfather, and she had her own inheritance from a wealthy family as well as the accumulation from three years' successful modeling in the United States. But they could never live up to their means, because the other members of his organization were poor and expected every penny to be put to the important work of the League.

Exasperated, he tossed the remaining crust into the courtyard, threw the beer can into a wastebasket and went to get an hour's rest.

The jarring jangle of the phone startled Antonev into wakefulness. Disoriented for a moment, he reached to his right for the familiar night stand, then, suddenly aware that he was not at home, jumped from the bed. He had drawn the curtains, and the room was in total darkness. He had no idea what time it was. Feeling blindly in the dark, he at last touched a lamp and found the switch. Meanwhile, the phone rang ever more urgently—the way in which hotel operators usually communicate their annoyance at not being answered immediately. Finally reaching the receiver, he was rewarded with a dial tone. He jiggled the cradle in irritation but without result. Next he found and searched the list of instructions to see how to get the operator back. Just as he was about to dial, the phone rang again. "What is it?" he asked acrimoniously.

"Mr. Antonev? You had a call from Moscow, but the long-distance operator could not wait." The operator spoke in English, in an impersonal, mildly reproving voice.

"Damn it," roared Antonev. "You rang only a few times. Why couldn't you wait? Was there a message?"

"No, the party left no message."

"All right, at least try to get a message next time."

"We take messages when the party wishes to leave one," said the operator coldly and abruptly hung up.

By now fully awake, Antonev turned on all the lights in the room and found his watch. It was 9:00 P.M. He drew the curtain aside and looked out. It was getting dark, and the incessant traffic continued to move relentlessly, headlights blinking on and off like fireflies. The din was mercifully muted by the closed window. Antonev pulled on his robe and went into the bathroom.

An appetite for the evening ahead was beginning to grow in him, and he found his spirits improving with every passing minute. There was, however, a gnawing worry about that phone call. He hoped the chief was not ordering him home early. No one would deny he deserved some rest; he had been working on fishery matters for nine months straight without a break. Maybe the best thing would be to get out of the hotel before the phone call came again.

He was in the middle of shaving when the phone rang again. He hurried into the bedroom and picked up the receiver. "Mr. Antonev, the international operator thought you would like to know that the lines to Moscow are out and we do not know when they will be available. We are sorry for the inconvenience."

"Oh, that's all right," said Antonev. "I'm sure they'll get me by telex if it's really important."

"The telex lines are out also."

"Well," the Russian said philosophically, "there's nothing we can do about it, is there?" He hung up, happy that he probably would not be disturbed in his revels.

Some twenty minutes later, scrubbed, refreshed and happy, he stepped from the hotel elevator into the busy lobby. Everywhere around him pulsed the mass of frenetic humanity endemic to Tehran's hotels. American, European and Asian businessmen, each carrying the inescapable briefcase and wearing the same look of fierce determination, hurried to important appointments. Iran was booming, and they were part of the great Persian gold rush. Next week, they would be gone, and others would take their place. Wealthy Iranian merchants held court on the worn sofas, dropping names of government dignitaries to impress the naive foreigners who would soon enlist them as agents because of their supposed influence with ministers they had never met. Children played among the crowd, drawing disapproving looks from the serious-minded adults.

Antonev paused for a moment to orient himself, then headed for the concierge. He paid no notice to the man in the dark suit cut in the flared Iranian style who followed him to the desk and stood beside him addressing an envelope. "Any messages for Antonev—five-o-seven?" inquired the Russian.

The clerk checked the cubbyhole. "Nothing, sir."

"Is there a lounge or bar in the hotel?"

"Yes, sir. A new lounge. Go right through that door at the far end of the lobby. The Naderi Bar."

Antonev made his way toward the bar, and Reza immediately stopped writing, put the envelope in his pocket and went to a phone near the hotel entrance.

• • •

Izadi put on his last clean shirt and rummaged through the rusty metal trunk that served as a dresser. It took him several minutes to find a tie that looked respectable—ties were not normal to his wardrobe. "Sirana is right," he thought. "I must get some decent clothes and pay more attention to how I dress."

He knotted the tie awkwardly, shrugged into a jacket which could have stood a pressing and ran a comb through his dark, unruly hair. The phone call was very good news. Already the pigeon had roosted in a vulnerable position. Now, if the Russian would just stay there long enough, Izadi would see that the evening met his expectations and more. The chances of Antonev's staying put for a while were quite good, because the Naderi Bar would be very busy on a Thursday night. It would, Izadi estimated, take him at least an hour to make up his mind whether any of the attractive women who were bound to be there were possible pickups. But there was no real problem even if he left early, because Reza was watching and would follow him to the next watering place.

Izadi was starting out the door when a sudden thought brought him up short. Why not get Sirana to the Naderi right away? The Russian should feel that he is making a conquest. He should meet Sirana in a respectable place—not at Shokoufeh Now or some other nightclub. And, he thought, as he developed the scene in his mind, she should be escorted. She should flirt with Antonev, and he should take her away from her escort. Antonev should believe that she cannot resist him. Nothing would loosen the Russian's tongue more than the desire to impress a beautiful woman who found him fascinating. It would be natural for her to be curious about his life, and she could ask very probing questions without arousing his suspicions.

He picked up the phone and dialed her number. Halfway through the first ring the familiar voice came on. "Hello, Assad. I'm glad you called again. I didn't mean to be nasty to you, but I was very tired."

Izadi was surprised that she didn't wait for him to identify himself. It was a very confident attitude, but at least it showed she wasn't expecting a call from another man.

"That sounds more like my girl," he said. "We have a chance to get some critical information tonight. Are you ready to help?"

"Of course, Assad darling. I want to help you in any way I can. Besides, I want to see you. I miss you already."

"Listen carefully, Sirana. How fast can you get dressed to go nightclubbing this evening?"

"If I don't have to wear a long dress, I can be ready in twenty minutes." She laughed in the musical, husky way that never failed to stir him. "You see, my love, I was expecting your call."

"I want you in a short dress. Don't cover up those beautiful legs. Meet me in the lobby of the Hotel Naderi in half an hour. Don't be late. This is very important. I'll brief you later."

"I'll do my best, Assad. Unless the traffic is very bad, I should be there on time."

"I'll meet you just inside the doorway." He started to hang up, then hesitated, hearing her voice again. "Of course I love you," he said. He gently put down the phone and thought, Things are going just perfectly! The communist will think he's irresistible, a real lady-killer, before the evening is over; and he'll do flips trying to impress Sirana by telling her everything he knows.

He turned off the light, locked the bedroom door and walked confidently through the dark passageway to the alley. As he turned the corner toward the main street, he happily hummed a popular Iranian tune.

The night people of Tehran were just beginning to stir on Mow-lavi Street. Groups of young men lounged nonchalantly against the steel storefronts, ready for excitement. Late-working merchants locked their doors and ran to catch the buses that would take them home to dinner, a few hours of relaxation and whatever problems had entered their lives during their absence. A pair of adventurous prostitutes, far from the protected area of Shahre Now, strolled with studied sensuality, eyes alert for the most subtle acceptance of their implied invitation.

Across the street, Persian music came from the doorway of a bar, and shouts of raucous laughter proved that Bacchus was already in control of some of the inhabitants.

Izadi hailed a passing taxi and went directly to the Naderi. He passed Reza in the lobby without giving any sign of recognition, went to the newsstand and bought a paper. Then he found a seat on a divan that was somewhat away from the flow of people and sat down. In a few moments Reza took a seat next to him. Holding the newspaper so that his mouth was concealed from direct view, Izadi said quietly, "If our man is still in the bar, don't say anything, just nod once and listen." Out of the corner of his eye, he saw the expressionless Reza, looking all the time straight ahead, move his head up and then down.

Izadi turned the page of the paper and continued. "Sirana is on the way here and should arrive any minute. I'm going to take her

nto the bar. We'll try to get the pigeon in a conversation with us
nd, if possible, latch onto him for the evening. You call Boldar at
he house. Have him go with Mahmoud and Little Man to
hokoufeh Now, get a table close to the show and reserve one next
o it for us at midnight. Understand?''

Again Reza moved his head. It was more of a neck stretch than a
od. He leaned forward as if to get up.

"Wait," said Izadi. "In case we can't get the Russian to go with
s and he leaves independently, you tail him and page me here as
oon as he lights again. If we do leave with him, try to get into his
oom and go through his things. Don't take any chances, and don't
eave a mess. It would be best if he thinks he's lost whatever you
night take. Lift anything that looks like instructions or official
apers, but no money or jewelry. Check his passport to see how
nany times he's been to Afghanistan, but don't lift it. When you're
inished, join Boldar and the others at Shokoufeh Now.''

Izadi for the first time looked at Reza.

"Now if you understand, get góing. If you're confused, wait here
nd I'll have Sirana come and go over it again when she arrives.''

Reza got up immediately and strolled toward the bar, where he
vould nurse a beer until things developed one way or the other. He
vould have no trouble entering the Russian's room. He was an
xpert lock picker.

Izadi glanced at his watch. Where was Sirana? She should have
een here fifteen minutes ago. He dropped his paper on the divan
nd walked toward the hotel entrance. "We just can't afford to muff
his one," he thought. "All the indicators point to Afghanistan.
Something must be going on there, and this Russian could be the
key to the communist planning. Why can't His Majesty see that all
his Russian sweet talk is the traditional softening up process used to
get you off guard, and then, when you least expect it, they hit you
and you're gone.''

He reached the door just as Sirana hurried through. He looked at
his watch and frowned. "Oh, Assad, I'm sorry," she said. "I had
rouble getting a cab, and the traffic was awful. I hope you haven't
een waiting too long.''

"Luckily, no harm has been done," said Izadi, "but we don't
ave a great deal of time to waste." He drew her away from a
well-dressed Asian who obviously was trying to hear every word
and escorted her to the still unoccupied divan. Following her across
he marble floor of the lobby, he observed her trim figure with
oride. The tailored skirt ended just above the knee, as current
ashion dictated. It was a length that ill suited most women, because

71

it covered the first curve of thigh, but revealed the entire knee. There weren't many kneecaps that could stand being the center of attraction. Legs had to be superior to look good under such circumstances, and Sirana's were certainly that. As she turned toward him, he was conscious of the provocative swell of her breasts against her low-cut white blouse. That would not go unnoticed by the amorous Russian. All in all, Sirana was a complete package of high-class sensuality, and it would be a cold man who would not respond to her allure. "You look exceptionally beautiful tonight," he said, "and your beauty will allow you to perform a great service for the League and your country."

"Don't tell me I have to sit and listen to some boorish Russian peasant all night," she answered. "I remember the last time all too well. We were turned away from three places because of that dolt's appearance. Finally we got into some horrible little bar, and he spent the night swilling cheap vodka with beer chasers and telling me about tractors and how many hectares of grain a cooperative could harvest. Then when I was about to go completely out of my head from boredom, he fell right off the chair and passed out. Please Assad," she begged, "don't make me go through another night like that. It was worthless; and if you remember, Boldar and Reza got into three fights just getting me out of that place."

Izadi smiled sympathetically. "No, Sirana, this will be nothing like that. There is a high-level Russian staying at this hotel. He speaks fluent English, so you will not have to struggle with your pidgin Russian. He will not be gross or rude."

Seeing her immediate disappointment, he quickly continued, "Besides, love, I'll be with you. You and I are going together to the bar, and he will know that you are my date. We'll try to get him into a conversation, relax him with plenty of drinks and take him to Shokoufeh Now. We have information that he likes floor shows and pretty girls. Your job will be to make him feel that he is the most handsome and attractive man you have ever met. Then you can get him talking and find out what he's been up to, why he's traveling in Afghanistan and Iran. Understand?"

"And you'll be with me the whole time?" she asked anxiously. "I won't have to fight him off when he decides he wants to take me to bed?"

"There's no reason to cope with that at the moment. We'll be able to find out whether he has any worthwhile information by the way that he handles himself during the evening. There isn't any use crossing that bridge until we come to it, is there? Besides, you might like him."

72

"Assad, you are absolutely amoral," said Sirana hotly. "If you think that this man can be helpful, you won't hesitate to roll him into bed with me. Well, I just want to warn you, I'll not have any of that! I promised to help you, and I will, up to a point, but let it be clearly understood that it doesn't include sharing his bed."

Assad kissed her lightly on the forehead. "Whatever you say, darling. Now let's go to the bar and find this handsome blond official of the Soviet Union."

As they went arm in arm through the lobby, heads turned to watch the attractive couple. Male eyes were automatically drawn to the girl's body. Sirana's movements had a graceful, innocent sensuousness. In the minds of men, she somehow was both the girl next door and a flagrantly provocative stripper all rolled into one.

The Naderi Bar was very busy. It was a new installation and had become one of the "in" places for the new cosmopolitan Iranian middle class and foreigners who were knowledgeable about Tehran. On Thursday night, the night before the Islamic sabbath, it jumped with holiday celebrants.

Sirana and Izadi entered the crowded room and were instantly engulfed in its warmth and excitement. One could sense the electricity that flows between the sexes when they turn every effort to being attractive to each other. The muted music encouraged conversation, so that people talked to each other rather than drowning passively in waves of amplified noise.

Some couples were at the bar, but most were seated around the well-filled room at small cocktail tables. Here and there, single men twisted on the high, swivel barstools and openly stared at unescorted women at the tables. No one seemed intoxicated yet, but there were some who gave every indication by their rate of consumption that they would not finish the evening upright.

Izadi stopped just inside the door to allow his eyes to become accustomed to the diminished lighting. It took him but a few moments to spot in a row of brunette heads the heavyset blond man near the far end of the bar. To the man's right was a thickly made-up, not particularly attractive fiftyish woman. To his left was an empty barstool, and then a young couple who were obviously engrossed in each other.

Izadi directed the girl to the empty seat and squeezed in next to the young man alongside her. The Russian's head swung about when Sirana moved into his line of vision, and he apparently liked what he saw.

"Good evening," he said with a smile, courteously moving his stool down to give her more room. He spoke in English, aware that the language was widely spoken among educated Iranians.

"Good evening, sir," responded Izadi, choosing to include himself in a greeting addressed only to Sirana. "Thank you for making room for us."

Antonev nodded at the young Iranian. "You are most welcome," he said, again showing his even, white teeth of which he was particularly proud.

Sirana shot the Russian a brief smile and half-turned to Izadi. "I'll have a whiskey and water, please," she said.

Izadi ordered it and a Smirnoff with soda and a twist of lemon for himself. He leaned close to her ear and said in Farsi, "Turn your stool around. How can we start a conversation with your back to him?"

"He's fat," she replied, injecting into the words not only disapproval, but a judgment of final disqualification.

Izadi was about to respond sharply when he saw the bartender coming with the drinks. He looked neutrally around the bar as the man put the napkins and glasses in front of them. The Russian was guardedly sideglancing at Sirana and ignoring the obviously accessible woman to his right. The bartender moved away, and Izadi again leaned close to Sirana. "He's clean, he's well mannered and he's got information we need, darling. We are not trying to marry you. Now for heaven's sake, stop acting like a spoiled child. Turn around and be pleasant."

She gave him a sulky look, but said nothing. "I'm not kidding, Sirana," he said sternly. "This man is important to us. You promised you would help. Let's get to work." His eyes looked past her toward Antonev. The Russian was very interested, but becoming discouraged by Sirana's back. It was time for stronger medicine.

Face impassive, Izadi took her arm just above the elbow. "Goddamnit, Sirana, you're going to wreck the whole thing." He squeezed her arm. "Now either get with it or get out!"

An expression of pain crossed her face. "Assad, you're hurting me," she said.

He ignored the complaint. "Well, what's it going to be?"

Tears came to her eyes. Suddenly she capitulated. "Please, Assad," she pleaded. "You're really hurting me. Let go and I'll do what you wish."

He eased his grip on her arm, and his voice relaxed. "Then turn around, my dear, and make yourself available so that we can get a conversation started."

The girl swiveled her stool to the front. She took a tentative sip of the whiskey and water which had been placed before her and glanced toward Reza at the far end of the bar, for the first time favoring the Russian with a clear view of her beauty.

Antonev was obviously enthralled, but just as obviously at a loss as to how to break the ice. How would the man with her react if a stranger spoke to her? He took a long pull at his vodka and soda, looking vacantly in her general direction, but not directly at her.

Izadi saw that he was going to have to take the bull by the horns. Leaning a little forward to look around Sirana, he addressed Antonev directly, "You're sure we're not crowding you too much? I suppose I shouldn't have squeezed in here like this."

The Russian smiled, delighted that his problem had been solved for him. "Not at all," he said.

"Are you a stranger to our city?"

"First trip to Tehran. I came in today from Bandar-e-Pahlavi. I'm a fisheries official from Moscow, and I've been working with your people at the Caspian on an antipollution agreement."

"Most important to everyone's future. My friend here"— indicating Sirana—"reads everything she can find about environmental protection. Oh, excuse me," he continued, "may I introduce myself? I am Assad Ali Izadi, and this is Miss Sirana Amiri."

"Fedor Antonev," replied the Russian, extending his hand to Izadi. "Delighted to meet you and this lovely young lady."

Feeling the heat of Izadi's eyes upon her, Sirana for the first time looked directly at the Russian and favored him with a dazzling smile. Actually, she thought, he's not all that gross. He's more than a little overweight, but not flabby; and he has a face that would be handsome except for the heaviness around the jowls. He seems friendly and cultured, and since I'm stuck with talking with him for the evening, I may as well make the best of it. "You are in a fascinating field," she said, extending her hand. "The average person doesn't appreciate the many difficulties faced by people who have dedicated their lives to the preservation of our natural resources. As Assad said I'm somewhat of a conservation buff. I'm sure you've earned some relaxation, and I hope you enjoy your visit to our city."

Antonev was overwhelmed by the warmth of this opening exchange. "You are both very kind. I am looking forward to an enjoyable evening and your hospitable interest has started me off in the most pleasant manner imaginable." Then, glancing at their nearly empty glasses, he asked: "May I show my appreciation by offering you a drink?"

Izadi declined. "You are a guest in our hometown, and it would be an unthinkable violation of Iranian hospitality if we did not entertain you.'' He snapped his fingers at the bartender. "Another round for the three of us, please.''

After the second drink Izadi suggested that they move to a table. Antonev was openly enchanted with Sirana, who, once she had decided to be delightful, pulled out all the stops. She flirted with him and flattered him, aware that under such circumstances it was difficult to overplay to his ego. Izadi helped out when the conversation lagged and once left the table to speak to a friend so that they could explore more frankly their newfound, apparent attraction to one another. As he passed Reza, Izadi winked encouragingly at him.

The vodka warmed the Russian, and he became more expansive. He talked at great length about his work and the interesting ideas being explored in the Soviet Union to protect the environment. As though celebrity-struck, Sirana hung on his every word. At times she leaned close to him in breathless fascination at some wise revelation of technology. The scent of her perfume combined with the alcohol circulating in his blood gave Antonev a feeling of vitality and power.

Izadi played the part of good friend admirably, making it clear in a variety of ways that he was not seriously involved with Sirana and did not look with disfavor on the fact that the Russian found her highly desirable. As the evening wore on, Antonev's fundamental objective of fun and girls began to show through the veneer of affability. He guided the conversation to subjects peripheral to sex, feeling his companions out on contemporary mores, the erosion of taboos, the diminution of parental and religious supervision of the young and the emerging liberal attitude toward censorship. From there, it was but a short step to discussing nightclubs and shows.

"Tehran has some excellent nightspots," said Izadi. "The Persian nature is to enjoy life, and His Majesty, although very straitlaced personally, has never been repressive about personal liberties. Actually, in the last ten years Tehran has become the cultural center of the Middle East. This pleases our government greatly; and our leaders realize that, if the arts are to flourish, they must have the freedom to develop.''

"Interesting," remarked the Russian, who had less noble things on his mind. "It is good to have a place to come to let one's hair down. Back in Moscow, we are very strict.''

Izadi caught the waiter's attention and ordered more drinks. "I have heard that you are very strict, yet Russia is a great cultural center, too," he said. "You have excellent ballet, music, and you are strong in the literary arts. Your government, I understand, actually subsidizes these undertakings."

"That is true, but there is very little fun in our culture. The development of the arts is a serious business, and the government participates because accomplishments in this area are expected of a great nation."

What a smug, ponderous ass, Izadi thought. He thinks his nation is great and serious, but he'll come here to play in our sewer. He lifted his glass, as if the motion itself would terminate the serious direction that the conversation was taking. *"Na zdorovye,"* he said. "Here's to culture—No, here's to fun and laughter and beauty. There are enough toasts to culture already."

The Russian raised his fourth vodka of the night. He held the liquor well, but it was beginning to show just a little. "And so long as we are drinking to beauty, let us be more specific and drink to the lovely Sirana, who is warm and alive, not just a cold canvas or a series of musical notes."

"You are a poet yourself, Mr. Antonev. Thank you very much," replied the girl, turning her multiwatt eyes upon him.

"Please call me Fedor. I feel as though you and Assad are old friends."

"All right, I will—Fedor." She looked down demurely, then impulsively put her hand on his. "You seem like an old friend, too." Then, as though suddenly realizing what she had done, she quickly drew her hand away and picked up her drink.

The Russian was very pleased. "Let's make a night of it. Such good company should not go to waste. But I insist on being host. You have entertained me enough, and I must now show my appreciation by reciprocating your hospitality." He gave Izadi a broad smile. "Will you be the tour director, Assad?" Then, winking with mock solemnity, he said, "I'll leave it to you as to what kind of culture we should pursue. But I have to tell you that I am behind in my research on pretty girls."

Sirana clapped her hands delightedly. "Let's show Fedor Shokoufeh Now."

"I have heard of it from a friend at home who visits Tehran frequently. He said it was very interesting."

"It's a landmark in the Old City and an institution so far as the night life of Tehran is concerned," Izadi said. "Some think it a little risqué, but by the standards of Copenhagen or Paris, it's quite tame. Nevertheless, it has an authentic Persian atmosphere, and the girls are very beautiful. Would you like to go?"

77

"Oh, please say yes, Fedor," broke in Sirana. "It's so much fun."

"Of course we'll go. Can you make the arrangements, Assad?"

"Thursday night is difficult, but I just happen to have a few good friends who may be able to work out a ringside table. Let me go make a phone call. I'll just be a few minutes."

Moving past Reza, Izadi signaled him to follow with a slight nod of the head. In the men's room, they stood silently at adjacent stalls until the only other person in the room had departed. "We'll be leaving in a few minutes, Reza. We're taking him to Shokoufeh Now. You know what to do from here."

"I've already checked a couple of doors. My key works perfectly," said Reza. "It shouldn't take too long."

The men's room door opened, and two men entered, obviously feeling no pain. Izadi quickly washed his hands and returned to the table. "We're in luck," he said. "It's almost show time, and I've been able to get a very good table. Let's finish our drinks, and then we'll go."

As the Russian drained his glass and they stood to go, he ogled the lovely Iranian girl appreciatively. Fedor, he said to himself, you are a very lucky man. I would guess that she likes you very much. The drinks are thawing out her natural reserve. With any kind of break, you'll have an interesting experience to relate to Nicholas Bretov when you get back to Moscow!

Outside the Naderi they got a cab and climbed in. There was still considerable traffic, but it was moving freely. The taxicab circled the Maidan-e Qasvan, passed Farab Hospital and a few minutes later drew up in front of Tehran's oldest nightclub.

"So this is the famous Shokoufeh Now," Fedor Antonev said, peering out of the dirty cab window at the old walled building.

"Don't worry, it's better inside," said Sirana with a laugh. "This is one of the oldest sections of Tehran, and it shows it. We're right on the edge of Shahre Now, the red-light district, but Shokoufeh Now is not part of it. You'll see entire families here. It's an institution."

"It has atmosphere," added Izadi. Then he instructed the driver, "Wait, please. We may be a good while, so don't think we're not coming back."

Seeing the expression of doubt on the man's face, he continued, "I don't mind if you go to get something to eat as long as you're back here in an hour."

The driver was satisfied with the arrangement, so the three of them climbed out to be greeted by the hovering doorman, who ushered them inside the venerable gates to a brown and beige tiled courtyard packed with small tables—some grouped and some separate. There were large potted plants at the fringe of the open courtyard. Beyond them in three separate covered sections were more tables. At the center of the wall to the left was a good-sized stage that at the moment was serving as a drum for the heels of several flamenco dancers. All the tables were occupied except the ones in the covered areas farthest from the stage and a few at ringside which had large "Reserved" signs. The high walls were cut with niches that held stark white statues intended to look Athenian.

Most of the area was uncovered. The high altitude of the Iranian Plain caused the hot daytime temperatures of June to drop to a comfortable level with amazing speed after dark.

As they were being led to the front table that Boldar had reserved for them earlier, Antonev breathed deeply. It was very pleasant, and there was the faint smell of jasmine in the fresh, dry evening air. Suddenly, the roar of a jet inbound to Mehrabad Airport overwhelmed the sounds from the performers. It seemed out of place, as if from another age.

They were seated at the small stageside table by the headwaiter, who exacted from Izadi the traditional tribute and registered the traditional expression of disappointment upon inspecting the amount. Izadi seated the girl next to the stage with the Russian on her left. As he sat down opposite Antonev, he waved to Boldar, Mahmoud and Little Man. Then he noticed there was an unexpected addition to that table—a girl who gave every indication of being a hustler. Izadi frowned. Boldar had a tendency to show off in front of such women by drinking too much. He would have to keep a close eye on that situation.

"Now, right here, my Iranian friends, I become the host," said Antonev. He shushed their objections and ordered a bottle of Russian vodka and a bottle of whiskey. "Would you like something to eat?" he asked.

Sirana, who was beginning to get hungry, was just about to accept when Izadi said, "Thank you, but no, Fedor. We have already eaten."

She gave him a private frown, but he paid no attention. He wanted the intoxication of the Russian to progress without interruption. "Besides, drinking is much more fun; and we have a lot of celebrating to do, don't we, Fedor?"

"Yes, indeed. We can eat later. Right now, I intend to drink again and again to my new friends, Assad and the beautiful Sirana.''

The flamenco dancers departed, to be replaced by a knife-throwing act, distinguished chiefly by the female target's brief costume. Then came a singing quartet—a group of young but slightly overweight chorus girls exhibiting the usual bruises from the night before—and a fairly good girl vocalist, who kept mistaking the generous applause for a request to stay on.

The vodka level fell steadily as the big, blond man warmed up. Izadi made a pretext of keeping up with him, but found ways to dump part of his glass. Soon the vodka was gone, and another bottle replaced it.

"Are you enjoying the show, Fedor?" asked Sirana. The vocalist was beginning what Antonev sincerely hoped was her last selection.

"Yes, it's quite good. This is a very interesting club, and being outdoors like this in the summer is so much better than being cooped up in a hot, smoky room. But what do they do in the wintertime? Doesn't Tehran get too cold to sit outside?"

Izadi laughed. "The girls in the chorus would turn blue in the wintertime out here. They just move the entire operation indoors. There is a room about the size of this courtyard beyond that wall."

Sirana said, "Assad is right. Tehran can get very cold. It's much nicer here in the summertime."

Although pretending to be satisfied, Antonev was actually disappointed by what he had seen so far. His friend Bretov had painted a delightfully wicked picture, and all he had seen up to this point could have been shown in a cabaret at home. Becoming mildly bored, he concentrated on the girl. "Let me pour you another drink. You've hardly dented that bottle of whiskey. You must relax and have a good time with Assad and me."

Sirana held out her glass. "I'm having a fine time. I guess I'm not much of a drinker, but I do so much enjoy being with you and hearing about all the interesting things you are doing." The nightclub noise made it hard for the Russian to hear, and he leaned closer to her. "This is hardly a good place for conversation," he said. "I hope you and I will get a chance to talk later." Sirana chose to ignore the unmistakable allusion.

The girl singer had finally exited triumphantly, after three bows and what amounted to a flat refusal by the orchestra to begin a new song. Suddenly, most of the room lights went off and a single spot focused on a corner of the stage. The featured performer, a voluptuously beautiful brunette in a dress that fit like a wet suit, appeared dramatically in the blue light, and the orchestra began a slow lament with a heavy beat. An immediate hush came over the audience, and all heads turned to the dancer. At the next table Boldar rudely jabbed an elbow in the ribs of one of his loquacious companions. "Shut up," he said as though noise affected his eyes. "I want to see this."

Antonev turned his chair slightly and casually laid an arm across the back of Sirana's. "Maybe Bretov was right," he thought. "At least things are improving."

The girl began to move through the ritual of the striptease with grace and assurance. She was exceptionally beautiful and very well endowed. While she stripped, Boldar stage-whispered suggestive remarks to his friends, occasionally tousling the hair of the small man seated across from him and offering to assist in solving any engineering problems that might arise should he be able to seduce the dancer. Little Man sat rigid, staring at the disrobing girl with an intensity that would have been frightening in a less public place.

Had it not been for Sirana's presence, Antonev also would have been absorbed in fantasy. As it was, he found himself curiously divided, part of his attention going to the sensual display on the stage and the rest to the lovely woman so close to him.

Izadi kept a close watch on the Russian's reactions and made sure the glasses were never empty.

The stripper was now down to a fraction of a bra and a bikini. She did not prolong the moment of near nudity, and the audience was unprepared when she exited without further revelation.

There was a gasp of disappointment and disbelief as the lights came back up. Then came the applause, far longer than for any previous performer. Antonev turned to Izadi.

"That was faster than I expected," he said.

"Don't worry, Fedor, she's not through yet. Now she goes to the Eastern side of her act."

The applause was just beginning to die when the lights again dimmed and the girl returned to center stage, this time in the filmy costume of the belly dancer. Again, that unnatural hush descended as the Eastern music began and the mystery of untold years of seductive Persian dancing was focused in the writhing body on the stage. The movements were so provocative and the message so personal that Antonev found it difficult to sit still. It was as though there were an electrified wire between him and the dancer, and the wire was connected to the most intimate parts of his body. For ten minutes, while the nearly nude dancer practiced her abandoned sexual sorcery, every other woman in the room was an outcast.

Cigarettes burned unnoticed in ashtrays, drinks sat ignored on tables.

Then the illusion ended, as all illusions must, leaving the voyeurs with a vague sense of disquietude. The lights came up and Antonev expelled his breath sharply. "She's not a dancer, she's a hypnotist," he said.

Sirana looked around at the Russian with that amused, tolerant expression that women reserve for the sole purpose of letting a man know his vulnerabilities are visible. "I think you liked that, Fedor. She certainly had your undivided attention. For a moment I thought Assad and I had lost our new friend."

He acknowledged her teasing with a smile that fell just short of open embarrassment. "I wasn't alone in my appreciation, was I, Assad?"

"Not by any means. She is an exceptional performer. Lonely men come back here night after night and sit the entire evening for just twenty minutes of fantasy with Nina."

"Well, we certainly don't have anything like that in Moscow," said Fedor. "It would be destructive to the national purpose. Workers have enough distractions on a day-to-day basis. If one wants to see such things, one can always go outside the country." His face had a defensive and almost guilty expression.

Out of the corner of his eye, Izadi saw Reza enter the courtyard and make his way toward Boldar's table. Reza sat down, caught Izadi's eye and smiled briefly to signify that his mission had been successful.

The vodka was beginning to get to Antonev, who was reaching the stage where a natural boorishness was beginning to show through the studied charm he affected in more sober moments. "Assad, you're a good fellow, and it's fascinating to be here in Tehran. This is a city for play, just as my friend, Bretov, said it was. You Persians have spent ages in a search for personal pleasure. You are experts at it."

The Russian raised his glass to Sirana. "I hope that you, my dear, will always be as carefree and as interested in your own femininity as you are now. What a waste it would be for you to wrinkle your beautiful forehead with worry over some serious matter."

The girl found it hard to keep the contempt out of her eyes. This fish custodian thinks that he and all of his robot countrymen are the master race, she thought. He actually believes that Iranians are children. Remembering Izadi's admonition, she merely said, "We Iranians are serious about life, Fedor. We work to feed and educate our families, to build our country. The most important thing a woman can do is to make some man happy and productive. That doesn't mean that she can't have a job or interests of her own. It does mean that her fundamental purpose is the perpetuation of her heritage."

"Of course, dear Sirana," said Antonev condescendingly. "But let's forget about people in the individual sense for a moment and talk about nations. Iran is not equipped to survive the current dog fight among the three superpowers. Your Shah's current policy of nonalignment will turn out poorly, I predict. I'm afraid the Yankee capitalists have made their deal with the Yellow Plague to the south. Small nations such as yours should more actively identify with the Soviet Union. Your own survival is at stake."

The Russian took another long drink from his glass. "Take, for example, Afghanistan," he said. "I happen to know a little bit about that country because I have visited it several times. The Afghans went through a long period of indecision. They did not know who to believe—us or the Americans—but now things are changing. They have decided definitely that ours is the more intelligent way of life. They are inviting, openly inviting, an increased Russian presence in their country."

Izadi's attention was riveted on every word. "But the Afghans need to preserve their own national identity," he said. "Their culture is quite different from yours. They are much more nomadic and not adaptable to the stringent disciplines of the communist way of life."

Antonev shook his head in disagreement. "The best thing that ever happened to the Afghans was their acceptance of our instruction and assistance. I'll tell you something, Assad. It's not beyond the realm of possibility that they will vote for annexation before the year is out. That's something that Iran, too, may have to consider on down the road."

"My God," thought Izadi, "my suspicions are being confirmed. There is some sort of plot to overthrow the present government in Afghanistan. Iran is in grave danger."

"Tell me more about it, Fedor," he said. "It's very interesting."

"Well, obviously, I can't discuss matters of foreign policy with authority, nor should I. These are just my personal observations."

Sensing that he had overstepped security rules and might soon be treading on quicksand, the Russian quickly changed the subject.

"We have gone from appreciation of the charm of one woman, to infatuation with the physical beauty of another, to politics," he said. "I didn't come to Tehran to think heavy thoughts. I came to enjoy myself, and that I have been doing beyond my highest expectations, due to your generosity and kindness. Let's keep it on that level, Assad, and you'll send a very happy Russian back to the seriousness of Moscow relaxed and refreshed."

Sirana smiled. "That's exactly what we intend to do, Fedor. Please excuse Assad. Sometimes he gets too serious." Then, looking at Antonev with a frank invitation in her eyes, she added, "I'm having a lot of fun being with you because you're Fedor, not because you're an important official in the Soviet Union."

This ended the discussion, which was beginning to interfere with the pleasant ambiance of the evening, and Izadi sensed that now was an excellent time for him to leave Antonev alone with Sirana for a while. "They're getting on toward closing time," he said. "If you will please excuse me, I haven't seen my friends at the next table for quite some time. I'll go and talk with them for a few moments."

At the other table, Izadi shook hands all around and, noting with satisfaction that the B-girl had departed for more fertile fields, slipped into the empty chair next to Reza. Looking back, he also saw that Antonev had wasted no time in turning his complete attention to Sirana. The Russian leaned closer to the girl to resume their conversation. It obviously would be no problem for her to hold his interest for the remainder of the evening.

"What's the situation, Assad? Am I going to have a chance to break our communist friend's back?" Boldar was hoping, as always, for violence.

Izadi laughed sardonically. "Sirana will find out more by arching her back than you will by breaking his."

Boldar grinned lasciviously and tossed off a straight vodka, the shot glass looking ridiculously tiny in his great hand. "I'd like to arch that belly dancer's back. What a body, eh, Little Man?" The giant jabbed the small man with unrestrained enthusiasm, nearly knocking him off his chair. Little Man, who had been engaged in another carnal fantasy and was paying no attention to the conversation, reacted instinctively. There was a short, quick jerk of his right arm, almost too fast for the eye to follow, and a vicious-looking switch-blade materialized in his hand.

"Keep your hands to yourself, Boldar," he snarled, "or I'll have to cut you."

The giant's eyes widened. "My, aren't we touchy," he said, but he made no further move.

"Put that knife away, Little Man." The authority in Izadi's voice was unmistakable. He looked directly at the offender, who hesitated only a moment before meekly replacing the weapon.

"Now, Reza," Izadi said, turning back to his lieutenant, "tell

84

me whether you found anything interesting."

"Maybe," said Reza, reaching for his pocket.

"Not here. He might turn around. Just tell me what."

"I'm not certain—couldn't take the time to look everywhere, and some of it was in Russian. I was afraid the maid might come in to check the room. One thing was a deposit slip dated today from the Bank Melli branch in Rasht for—get this—fifteen million rials. I was afraid to take that. Then there's a letter in Russian from Afghanistan. I took a chance and lifted that."

"What did his passport show about Afghanistan?"

"There was only one entry stamp, just a few days ago."

"So he was lying about frequent visits to Afghanistan— Good work, Reza. Get Anwar to translate the letter first thing in the morning. Then bring it to the house. And notify all squad leaders to be there at seven A.M. tomorrow." Reza rose to go, but Izadi stopped him. "Stick around," he said. "I want you to keep an eye on our communist friend until he's tucked in bed at the Naderi. Then you can go."

Izadi slid out of his chair. "I'm going back with them. Sirana and I will be leaving shortly. We'll try to drop him off at the Naderi. If he goes with us, follow by car and don't leave him until you're sure he isn't going out again. If he doesn't go with us, stay with him until he gets home. I want to be sure he doesn't have any meetings. If he does, tail his contacts. Remember, all squad leaders at the house at seven tomorrow. Don't be late.

"Reza, I want you to stop at my table in a few moments to see Sirana. I'll tell the Russian you have a message from a mutual friend. Then you tell her in Farsi that she need not spend the rest of the night with that pig. I'll take her home. But she should keep him hopeful about tomorrow night—tell him she came with me and feels obligated to leave with me—leave the impression that she'd rather be going with him. Get it?"

Reza nodded that he understood, and Izadi continued. "Now, I don't know what he'll do when he finds out that there's no chance with her tonight. Apparently he's got his heart set on a big time, but that may be only a ruse to cover a meeting. I want him covered until he goes back to the Naderi, and I don't want anything unpleasant to happen to him—not yet." Reza nodded again. "And, Reza, make sure that I have that translation as early as possible in the morning."

With that, he rejoined the girl and the Russian, who tried very hard to conceal his disappointment that they were again a threesome. He gave Izadi a warm smile and said, "I have had a wonderful time talking with Sirana. She has told me about modeling and films, and I have told her about Russia and our dream of a better world." He favored her with an intimate smile. "I'm afraid that I talked much more than you did, my dear."

Sirana touched his mouth lightly with her fingertips. "Not so, Fedor," she said. "You are a very good listener. And once you get a woman talking to someone who is really interested in her, it's hard to stop her. Besides, what little bit I gave you a chance to tell me about your country was fascinating." She flashed him one of her most devastating smiles.

"Sounds like a mutual-admiration contest," said Izadi, with just a hint of jealousy in his voice.

"Fedor is a charming conversationalist. I could spend hours talking with him," she said sweetly.

Izadi watched the Russian rise to the bait. "Let's all go have a bite to eat," he suggested, angling for more time to figure out how to get rid of Assad Izadi.

They were interrupted at this point by the arrival of Reza. Izadi made the introduction, and, after a few words of Farsi from Reza, said to the Russian, "Reza has no English. He is delighted to meet you. He apologizes for intruding, but he has a message for Sirana from one of her friends."

"No apology is necessary," said Fedor.

Reza then relayed Izadi's instructions to the girl. When he had finished, Assad said to her in Farsi, "I'm going to refuse the invitation to eat for both of us. Give him your phone number so that he can call you tomorrow. Keep him on the hook."

After Reza departed, Izadi said, "Thank you so much for your kind invitation, Fedor, but Sirana and I both have early appointments in the morning. We really must get home, so we'll drop you at the Naderi on the way. Perhaps we will see you tomorrow?"

Antonev's face revealed his disappointment, but he brightened a little when the girl quickly broke in, "I'm very sorry, Fedor. I only wish I had known that I would meet you tonight. I would have made other plans." She looked earnestly at him. "And I do want to see you tomorrow. Let me give you my number." She quickly wrote it and handed it to him.

"I wish you didn't have to go," said Antonev thickly, taking the paper from Sirana and holding on to her hand for an awkward extra moment. "This has been such a wonderful evening that I hate to see it end. But perhaps this telephone number will make it the beginning of something very beautiful." Izadi suppressed a laugh as the Russian rose heavily to his feet and stood unsteadily. It was clear that the liquor had hold of him; yet he battled to preserve his dignity.

He gave what was meant to be a courtly bow. "I will certainly call you tomorrow afternoon, my dear, and I thank you and Assad for such a pleasant introduction to your city."

He extended his hand to Izadi. "Assad, I am very grateful for all you—" Here a single, explosive hiccup threatened to destroy his serious demeanor, but he somehow recovered. "—Excuse me, kindness, but I think I will stay for a while. For some reason, I am not yet sleepy." Struck by another gastric repercussion, he added lamely, "There is still good vodka to be drunk, and it's the best cure for hiccups."

The Iranian couple barely won the struggle not to laugh.

"We'll leave the car for you, Fedor. I'll instruct the driver to take you back to the Naderi when you are ready. And thank you for the drinks. Incidentally, I checked your bill, so they won't try to take advantage of you."

"Call me if you get a chance, Fedor," said Sirana invitingly.

Antonev waved goodbye, then sat down and poured himself another drink. The vodka was finally taking over, and everything round him was a pleasant blur. He chuckled to himself and thought of Sirana Amiri and how he would make love to her. He would fondle her beautiful body until she screamed for relief. Such thoughts brought him warm feelings in his groin, and the alcohol prevented any uncomfortable tumescence.

Fedor, my lad, he said to himself, you have learned something. You are obviously irresistible to women! You are a strong man, and there is enough of you to go around, so you may as well investigate the Shahre Now before you rest up for Sirana. He then called for his check, paid it with a five-thousand-rial note, left a handsome tip and started for the door. The courtyard was nearly empty. A heavily made-up girl in a very tight dress got up from a rear table and walked provocatively in front of him. Near the door, she looked back and smiled the ancient invitation, and they went out into the street together.

"Damn it all," whispered Boldar to Reza. They were seated in a car parked across from the waiting cab. "He's picked up a whore. We may never get to bed." The two Iranians watched the girl and Antonev engage in an unsatisfactory attempt to communicate and then, suddenly, reach agreement. The girl said something to the cabdriver, and there was a furious exchange between them. Antonev then produced a bill and gave it to the driver, who indicated his displeasure by leaving with a squeal of tires. The girl and her Russian client then strolled off toward the center of Shahre Now. A few moments later, they were followed by Boldar and Little Man on foot, with Reza and Mahmoud moving a safe distance behind in the car, headlights off.

It was nearly noon, and the squad leaders of the Persian Protective League were gathering in the house of Mowlavi Street. The ten leaders, each responsible for nine other soldiers, came from all over Tehran. The motley crew ranged from a lawyer to a street cleaner, but they shared a dedication to Iranian nationalism and a fear that their rich country was in grave danger of attack by foreign powers. They were well disciplined in the important respects, even if lacking the outward signs of organization and routine. There was no question of their allegiance to the League or of their acceptance of Assad Ali Izadi as its commander.

In the bedroom Izadi was reviewing the previous night with Reza, Boldar and Little Man. He did not look pleased, and his brow furrowed while he read for the second time the translation of the paper that Anwar Maadi had brought him earlier. Marked "General Directive No. 245" and signed by Dradavov, it contained a prohibition against distribution below Class III department heads and a classification of "Secret." Anwar had made a summary translation in Farsi:

Department heads who travel to other countries on government business should be mindful at all times that they represent the Communist Party as well as the Government of the U.S.S.R. In dealing with the business of their particular agency, they must be cautious of revealing technical details which might hasten the development of competing technologies, bearing in mind that preserving the superiority of our nation is essential to the carrying out of the Party mandate.

It is urgent that department heads should use every opportunity to encourage the spirit of revolution in the oppressed, wherever it is encountered, because the liberation of others from the autocratic or capitalist yoke will expand our brotherhood throughout the world.

It is especially important to the security of the U.S.S.R. to remain aware of these Party responsibilities when in contact with unstable, non-Communist governments within our immediate geographical sphere of influence. Chairman Dradavov

Izadi looked up from his reading. "Now, Reza, tell me exactly what happened after I left Shokoufeh Now."

"Well, I'll give it to you the best I can. I wasn't there for everything. You'll have to get Boldar and Little Man to fill in." Reza shifted his weight uncomfortably. He knew that Izadi was worried and had a vague feeling that somehow he was responsible. Nervously he described what happened when Antonev left the nightclub—the pickup, the incident with the cabdriver and how they followed the girl and the Russian into Shahre Now.

Boldar picked up the narrative: "The girl took him into an all-night place, where they had a cup of tea. We watched through the window and saw her signal to a couple of rough-looking characters at the counter. The two guys left immediately, and I figured that either they were getting ready to set him up for a mugging or else there was going to be a meeting, so I got Little Man to follow them while I waited for the Russian and the girl. It wasn't five minutes before Little Man came back and told me that they were hiding in a doorway in the alley, so I figured that she was going to lead him into a trap. When the girl and the Russian finished their tea and left, we tagged along behind. We couldn't get too close to them because there weren't a lot of people around and it would have been obvious that we were following them. Anyhow, they turned into an alley, and, just as we figured, these two guys jumped him. The floozie got lost quick. Little Man and I plowed right in. I got in some good punches, but we were too late to stop the Russian from getting rapped on the head pretty hard. One of the hoods had the Russian's wallet. Little Man carved up this fellow's arm and took the wallet away from him, and then the two guys took off like scared rabbits.

"We kept the wallet and his watch. There were some papers in the wallet and over five hundred thousand rials in his inside coat pocket—quite a haul for our treasury. Later we gave the papers to Anwar, so he could check them. He translated one—the one he gave you when he came in this morning. I see you have it there in your lap. Anyhow, after we relieved him of his money, we went to a pay phone in the little place we had just left. Little Man, Mahmoud and I talked loud so no one would be able to listen while Reza called the police and told them where to pick up the Russian. We figured they would take him home after he filed his complaint against the whore. Then I called Avengeh in my squad and told him to get his ass over to the Naderi first thing in the morning. We hung around until the cops came. Everybody ran out to see where they were going, and we did too. They picked him up, all right. After that blow on the head, he'll not be ready for any meetings too early today."

Izadi picked up the other paper, the letter that Reza had taken from Antonev's room. "Okay, Boldar," he said. His face relaxed as he glanced from the big man to Reza. "You did the only thing you could under the circumstances." He looked at the translated letter. It had been written a month ago.

Dear Fedor:

Come to Kabul as you can. We will be ready to discuss our plans for Iran. Things are coming to a head here, and the change is imminent. Please stop here before you go to the Caspian. It is urgent.

Etalini

Izadi's head snapped up. He took the phone and dialed Sirana's number. "Get the squad leaders into the big room right away, Reza. I want to talk to them."

He remembered Sirana's account last night of what the Russian had told her when he was alone with her and his tongue was loosened by alcohol. It all fit in. Antonev had boasted that the communists would change Afghanistan from a backward country to one belonging to the people and hinted at governmental changes to come soon. He claimed that capitalism was on the wane as a way of life in the world, that the United States would no longer be able to exploit monarchies as a front for it. Antonev would naturally have restrained himself from criticizing Iran to Sirana, but he did say that the Iranian people were too bright to go on forever without any say in their own destinies. Sirana had reminded Assad that the Russian was more interested in her than in discussing politics. Nevertheless she recalled some other things, such as Antonev saying that his country had an obligation to make certain the people of the world understood the advantages of communism. At one point he rambled on about Indochina and how his country had stood on the side of the masses who were willing to fight to overcome oppression—and that was why Indochina had been reunited under communism. The Russian admitted that this willingness to help the oppressed sometimes placed his country in danger by provoking confrontations.

Sirana's number began to ring. After six, then seven, then eight rings had brought no answer, Izadi felt a stab of fear. Perhaps he had dialed wrong. He was about to hang up and try again when the phone clicked and a cheerful voice said hello.

"It's Assad. Are you all right?"

"Of course! I'm sorry I took so long to answer, but I was in the tub. You know how long it takes to get ready for photographs."

"Well, it gave me a bit of a scare. I thought your new lover had decided to make an early call on you."

She laughed lightly. "Don't be silly, Assad. I was relieved when I didn't have to bring him back here." Her voice became stern. "But that didn't mean that you had to leave right away after bringing me home. I can remember when having to get up early wouldn't diminish your passion."

"We'll see how much it's diminished when I see you this evening," he said. "But now I have a meeting here and just wanted to tell you this. There isn't any need for you to see this Russian any more. We have everything we need. If he calls, make some excuse, but under no circumstances should you see him again. Understand?"

"I not only understand, I'm delighted! Frankly, I expected him to call earlier. Maybe even in the middle of the night. He seemed so eager."

"I'll tell you about it later, love. Actually, he got himself in a little trouble and was not able to call. I hate to hurt your pride, but he found another girl."

"What? I don't believe it! Tell me!"

"Later. Now get ready for your pictures. I'll see you this evening. I have to go into the meeting. Goodbye."

"Goodbye," she said, the note of incredulity lingering in her voice.

Izadi sat for a moment on the bed, piecing it all together. It certainly made sense. His theory about Afghanistan was confirmed. The letter, the directive and the deposit slip, reinforced by Antonev's remarks the evening before, led to an inescapable conclusion that the Soviet Union was attempting to take over Afghanistan. This Russian was not too important, he judged. Probably only a courier to make deposits at Rasht; he wouldn't have been fooling around Shahre Now if he had other important business. But the large sum of money left at the bank in Rasht was certainly an indication that the Soviets were about to expand their operations in Iran. The observations about monarchies and the people of Iran being too bright to continue under the present system were probable indications that Russian financial assistance would be available for any left-wing group that would promote civil discord.

He got up and went into the large room where the squad leaders were crowded around the table. The hum of conversation subsided quickly as the intense young Iranian strode to the open space between Boldar and Reza. He looked around the room very seriously, making maximum eye contact with his audience. Then, in a voice that was quiet, yet charged with emotion, he said, "Gentlemen, our country is in grave danger." The silence in the room was nearly absolute. He paused for a long moment, then continued. "Thank you very much for being here on such short notice. I would not have called you had it not been urgent." He paused again, his eyes sweeping the room. "Most of you have been with our organization for some time. You know that our work has produced little information to make us feel secure. Time after time we have gathered intelligence that could only be interpreted as a threat against the security of our country. Our national preoccupation with internal development has led our government to lose its sensitivity to the danger signals around us." Although still well controlled, his voice became louder. "That is why the Persian Protective League was begun. It was formed because the Russians are undermining our country in the most invidious ways—political assassination, discrediting our religion, encouraging license and immorality in the name of personal freedom and encouraging complaints about defense spending. Our Shahanshah is too trusting when they tell him they want peace and friendship. We know he is being deceived by the communists and that they will turn on him in a moment when they feel they have Iran isolated."

All around the room, eyes were riveted on the young Iranian. They did not understand all of the words or the implications of everything he said, but they were convinced that he was correct in whatever he concluded.

Izadi dramatically tossed the papers on the table. "We now have unmistakable evidence that the Russians are preparing a political coup in Afghanistan. That is not new to us, of course, because we have had many reports of the subversive activities of the left in that country over the past few years. However, for the first time, we know the coup is to be very soon, and we are certain that there is a connection between the takeover in Afghanistan and the weakening of Iran. A Russian agent whom we have had under observation has provided us with the link. We know that fifteen million rials have been put in a bank in Rasht to the account of an Afghan leftist for use of the communists here in Iran."

There was an audible gasp around the room, and the squad leaders bristled with indignation. "I have information to substantiate that," continued Izadi. "This paper, taken from the Russian spy"—he picked up the translation of the Dradavov directive—"is absolute evidence that they are acting under the express instructions

92

of the highest officials in the Communist party. Gentlemen, I tell you that Iran's future is dim unless we move quickly to upset Moscow's plans."

Down the table to the left, a voice said, "Commander, I have total faith in your sincerity and your conclusions, but what can a small organization like ours do to stop a superpower?" It was Anwar, who had been with the PPL only a year but had been made a squad leader because he was the best educated among them.

"Your question is a very good one, Anwar, and the answer is that we can do nothing by confronting our enemy directly."

"Then what can we do—go to the government with the evidence we have accumulated? I remember we tried that once. Not only did we get laughed out of the Ministry of War, but two of our best people wound up in the Savak 'unstable persons' file and are no longer of any use to us because they are watched continually."

"Your memory is good, Anwar," said Izadi. "No, we can't complain to the government. They would probably say that the Dradavov paper is nothing new. Even if they decided to look into the matter, it would be stuck in red tape until it was too late."

"Then what can we do?" repeated Anwar. "We're too small to do anything ourselves, and going to the government would be useless. Does that mean that we just sit back and wait for the Russians to move in?"

"Be patient, Anwar. All this does not come as a surprise to me. I have suspected it for months—ever since the left wing took over in Afghanistan and implemented a total change of policy." He allowed himself a brief smile. "I have the beginnings of a plan," he said.

Around the room, worried faces brightened. The squad leaders had come to expect solutions of their commander. His tactical planning had always been good: the disappearance of the stock of a subversive bookshop in an unexplained fire; the sudden disruptions of communist meetings. All had been beautifully planned and there had been no hitches—no arrests, no finger pointed at any of them. So far as they knew, the Savak did not know there was a Persian Protective League.

Izadi continued. "Our enemy is a superpower with a plan of aggression and the capability of carrying out that plan. A superpower cannot be stopped by ordinary means." He paused dramatically. "It can only be stopped by another superpower."

"That makes sense," said Reza, edging in to challenge Anwar's monopoly of the dialogue.

"It makes sense, but we do not control another superpower, unfortunately," said Anwar.

"Patience," Izadi said quietly. "If you'll just let me finish, then I'll listen to your comments."

He lit a cigarette, marshaling his thoughts. It wasn't going to be easy to explain because he didn't have all the details filled in yet, but they needed to know that the situation was serious and that something was being done. He rubbed the stubble of beard on his chin. "Here's how I see it," he began. "The Soviets have not had to worry too much about their defenses for the past fifteen years. Prior to that time, they were frightened to death of the nuclear superiority of the United States. They were behind in technology, so they tried to keep up by producing overwhelming quantities of the weapons they were able to build. As you know, they have a magnificent propaganda machine, and they scared the world by advertising their numerical and size superiority in missiles." He paused to take a drag on his cigarette.

"What the Russians really wanted was to get off the expensive treadmill of the arms race with the West, but they were afraid to let up the pressure without some limiting agreement. So they kept the pressure on, kept building, at the same time crying to the international community that they were only balancing the threat from the United States. They let it be known through their pawns in the United Nations that they would like nothing better than an agreement limiting nuclear weapons." He paused a moment, listening to a noise in the yard. "Are we secure here?" he asked Reza.

"Yes, we have the place covered, both outside and inside," the lieutenant replied.

"Okay. Well, the liberals in the We fell for it. They put immense pressure on the United States fense establishment, complaining bitterly about the budget and how the high costs were preventing better education and more help for the poor. The most influential of the United States media, who usually follow a few left-leaning intellectuals, began their own campaign. It was no contest. The President gave in, and the Strategic Arms Limitation Talks began." Izadi shook his head sadly.

"It was quite a victory for the Soviets," he continued. "They capitalized on being tough negotiators, knowing that the Western media would not stand for an impasse and would kick the United States until they gave in to the most ridiculous conditions. That's exactly what happened. The arms limitation agreements made it possible for the Russians to retain their nuclear warhead throw-weight superiority without installing more missiles. That let them spend their resources to catch up technologically.'' Feet were beginning to shuffle uncomfortably for much of the monologue was going over the heads of the squad leaders.

''I'll try to make it as clear-cut and simple as possible,'' said Izadi. ''The Russians obtained the right to catch their breath in a race they were about to lose. They found it very profitable to talk to the United States. Détente was good business for them, so they extended it in every trade, space, international law—the whole business.''

Izadi paused again to snub his cigarette in the cheap metal ashtray. ''You know what happened. The Chinese didn't like the Soviets and the United States playing footsie, so they got into the peace propaganda act. It should have scared the United Nations to death when the three giants began to talk among themselves about settling international disputes that did not respond to UN solutions, but those idiots just continued romping in their New York playpen. They didn't understand what was happening to them.''

Somewhere outside a door banged—the lookouts were being changed. With hardly a pause, Izadi continued: ''With the confrontation with the United States averted, our Russian friends have revived their expansionist ideas in this area. The Americans, the Chinese and the Soviets have been gobbling up pieces of the world under the excuse of solving disputes the United Nations can't handle. As a result, Indochina is communist—sort of a Russian-Chinese compromise—and Cuba is a West-leaning republic again.'' Izadi's face became grim, and he hammered his hand on the table angrily.

''We are the prime target of the Russians. We are next. They want our oil. Who knows what they will concede to the Americans and the Chinese to look the other way. Gentlemen, they will outflank us in Afghanistan and move on us when ready. Maybe they'll give the United States the entire Caribbean and give the Chinese Malaysia. Thailand was the first pawn for the Chinese communists. Who is to say Malaysia and Singapore won't follow?''

The room again was perfectly quiet as the Iranian leader paused for dramatic emphasis. ''All right, I'll get to the point—but it was important for you to understand the background. A while back we agreed that you can only stop a superpower with another superpower. That's what we must do.''

An exclamation of disbelief exploded from Anwar. ''But how?'' he asked. ''We don't influence the Americans or the Chinese.''

''No, that's true, and we can never influence them directly. But we can set forces in motion that will destroy the détente and provoke a confrontation between the Soviet Union and the United States."

"Assad, you must be dreaming! How?"

Izadi chose to take no offense at this breach of discipline. "By irritating the most sensitive nerve of the United States—the Jewish community."

Anwar shook his head, incredulously. "But the American Jews love the détente. They are liberals for the most part. They helped drive the United States out of Asia in the name of peace at the same time that Israel was attacking the Arabs, and they are all out for heavy social spending."

"True, Anwar, but don't forget their respect for individual freedom and their disapproval of the lack of it in the Soviet Union."

"I still don't see how you will use a small minority of the American population to destroy the détente."

"You must understand the structure of American politics to see that, Anwar. American Jews exert an influence on American opinion that is far heavier than their numbers would indicate. They are the strongest single influence in the big media—the media with worldwide impact. They control much of the financial community, and through it, large segments of the academic community. Therefore, they heavily affect, through propaganda, the majority of the Congress. Oh, they scream anti-Semitism whenever anyone mentions their power, but it's true. Look at the tortured differentiations that the intellectuals tried to create between aid to Israel and aid to Vietnam. The Viet Cong were oppressed patriots, but the Palestinians were anarchists."

Reza posed a question for the first time. "But how do you get the American Jewish community to change directions and oppose the détente?"

"By exposing the nerve. By causing trouble over Israel," responded Izadi. "We're going to use terrorism to reopen the Arab-Israeli wounds. We're going to force the Americans to react strongly for Israel. That will alienate the Arab nations friendly to the United States and make the Russians come out strongly for their Arab friends."

Izadi was pleased by the expressions of approval on the faces around him. He didn't want to go too far in this meeting. There were too many people involved. All he needed was an endorsement to go ahead.

"What I want is the League's approval to move on this," he said. "It's a matter for the planning committee to work on. Then we'll advise you of the details. Do I have your agreement to go ahead?"

There was a strong murmur of assent.

"Then we'll break up now. I want you to continue with your coverage of foreign nationals in Tehran and with disruption of the local communists wherever possible. There is no need at the moment to brief your squads on the matter we have been discussing. The meeting is adjourned."

As the men moved out of the room, Izadi motioned to Reza and Anwar to remain. "The planning committee will meet right now in my room," he said.

Ten minutes later Reza and Anwar sat leaning against the bedroom wall, stirring the mugs of sweet tea they had just brought from the kitchen. Izadi had flung himself across the bed, fingers laced behind his head. Already, the summer heat was beginning to make itself felt in the small house. "It's going to be one hell of a hot day," ventured Reza. "I'm glad you got the meeting over early."

Assad Izadi, as usual, was unaffected by such mundane considerations as temperature and personal comfort. "I think it went well," he said. "The squad leaders needed something to cheer them up. It's a pretty frustrating job they have, and sometimes it gets very boring. They need to know that there is a larger purpose to our local activities."

Anwar sipped his tea thoughtfully. "I think you were right in not getting into any more specifics in that meeting," he observed. "The details of what we are going to do, if I understand your intentions correctly, should be closely held."

"Speaking of details, what about them?" asked Reza.

"Well, I don't have it all mapped out at the moment. I wanted to kick it around a little bit with you both." Izadi sat up and leaned forward. "It's not a simple idea," he continued, "but I think it's fundamentally sound. We've got a few things going for us. First, there are already anticommunist Zionist organizations in the United States. One of them I happen to know is called INAF and it's led by a man who hates the Russians as much as we do. A fellow named Yoram Halevy."

"What does INAF mean?" asked Anwar.

"Israel Now and Forever." Izadi laughed. "That should give you some idea of where their sentiments are. In any event," he resumed, "I know this Halevy and we have exchanged information in the past. If you think our troops are strong for action, you should see this INAF group. They are all out for Israel." He preempted Reza's mug and took a long swallow of tea, then grimaced. "Damn it, Reza, you are going to create a sugar shortage all by yourself."

Reza laughed. "It's my only vice. I follow the Islamic doctrine

97

and don't use tobacco or alcohol. Women find me repulsive. Sugar is small solace."

Izadi became serious again. "You know, I keep an eye on the foreign newspapers, especially the big ones in the United States. A few weeks ago, I saw a report that Mr. Halevy was complaining bitterly about a visit to America being considered by Soviet Chairman Dradavov. Halevy said that if Dradavov came to Washington, INAF would protest his presence because of the unconscionable repression of Russian Jews, especially the Russian policy on Jewish emigration from the Soviet Union. INAF seems to be a good starting point for us if we want to stir trouble between American Jews and the Soviet Union."

"Maybe," said Anwar, "but I would imagine that this INAF outfit has been popping off for years. Why would they suddenly have an effect on American opinion?"

"That's what we have to figure out," said Izadi. "In some way we have to use INAF to cause terrorism that the Arabs or the Russians will be blamed for in the United States. That will enrage the American public."

"Maybe we could get INAF into a gang war with some Arab group," suggested Reza.

"No, the Americans are insensitive to extremist crimes as long as the victims are confined to the extremist organizations," said Izadi. "For example, they couldn't care less if two Mafia families exterminate each other. But wait, maybe you do have something. We could stir up trouble and cause terrorism outside the extremist groups. That would open the eyes of the American media. The time is right, because there is an election coming up next year, and there is always some politician who needs a vehicle to attract attention." Izadi leaped to his feet. "That just might work. Somehow we've got to convince INAF that some group of respected Americans is accepting oil money to destroy American support for Israel. Now, how do we do that?"

Anwar rubbed his nose thoughtfully. Already his alert mind was racing through the possibilities.

"Fill us in on Halevy as much as you can, Assad. What do you know about him personally?"

"We met at a mutual friend's apartment in New York, Anwar. I had heard of INAF's anti-Soviet activities, and I thought we might benefit by exchanging intelligence. The PPL and INAF both hate the Russians, even if for unrelated reasons. Personally, I don't give a damn about Israel, and I'm sure Halevy cares even less what happens to Iran—but we do share a concern about the Russian accumulation of power."

Izadi paused to light another cigarette and blew smoke at the low ceiling. "We got along well," he went on, "because we both saw our organizations could be useful to each other. He is a zealot—a not-too-bright zealot, although he has a college degree in the humanities area somewhere—I'm not sure of the exact field. He would run through a closed door for Israel. Zionism is his life, and he has good connections to the American power structure through Zionist activities. INAF is full of real activists, the kind who take pleasure in being arrested for nonviolent but unlawful protesting every week. They are always released without a conviction by some leftist judge."

Izadi flicked the ash off his cigarette and waved away the pall of smoke that was clouding the stale air in the little room before he continued. "Halevy keeps me up to date on American politics as they affect the Russians and the Israelis. He's very close to a professor who works sometimes for the United States Vice President. He's supposed to be brilliant—name of Isaac Miller."

"He must be the fellow who is advising Vice President Canfield to call for more aid to Israel," said Reza. "I read in the *Tehran News* about a speech Canfield made recently—said Israel should have United States nuclear weapons for protection against her enemies."

"Yes. Halevy said Canfield may run for President next year and that INAF would support him if he did."

Reza laughed. "Sounds like he's already running on the Zionist ticket. Maybe he can raise enough hell to provoke the confrontation we need."

During this exchange between Izadi and Reza, Anwar sat staring at nothing. Suddenly he jumped up. "Wait, wait!" he said excitedly. Izadi and Reza looked at him curiously.

"If we can figure out how to get the American liberal power structure really mad at the Russians, Canfield will grab the issue and capitalize on it. That will give it national dimensions. The media won't be able to get enough of it." Anwar fairly danced with excitement, but Izadi and Reza were not impressed.

"Sure, that's fine, but how do we get the liberal power structure really mad, and mad about some substantial grievance that arouses the support of the rest of America?" inquired Izadi. "You know," he added, "there are many Americans who are not altogether sympathetic to the constant involvement of their country in the problems of Israel."

Anwar's face fell. "There must be a way," he said lamely.

For a long two minutes the three members of the PPL planning committee sat silently staring into space. The answer eluded them.

Anwar dejectedly sat down again. "If we could just get a bunch of radical Arabs to terrorize some prominent supporters of Israel," he said softly, "that would give Canfield and the media something to yell about."

"Maybe we should go over there and do it ourselves, then blame it on the Arabs," said Reza.

Izadi frowned. "No, that won't work. We don't know the country or its customs well enough. We'd surely be caught, and Iran would suffer for our stupidity."

"INAF could do the job. They're Americans. They could get away with it," said Reza.

Izadi laughed contemptuously. "INAF terrorizing Zionist sympathizers—not likely." He picked up the international *Herald Tribune* of the day before from the pile of newspapers on the floor. "Let's see if this can give us an idea," he said and started to skim through the pages. A few minutes later he tossed the newspaper aside in disgust. "Nothing," he said. "Nothing on the subject except an article on how the Arabs made an offer to the estate of some rich man to buy a lot of stock in a television network and were refused. The network owners found out about it and raised hell. I don't see how that can help us."

"Well, we might as well break up for now and think about it for a few days," said Reza.

"When do you want us again, Assad?" asked Anwar, after Izadi had nodded his assent to the adjournment.

"Oh, better check with me by phone tomorrow. Of course, if you get an idea, call me right away."

As the lieutenants prepared to leave, Izadi picked up the newspaper again. Suddenly, he grabbed Anwar by the arm. "Hold it, hold it!" he yelled. "I think I've got it! What do you think of this? It may be crazy, but then what is sane in this insane world?" He pointed to the article in the *Herald Tribune*. "Suppose we persuaded INAF that important liberal media—for example, the two big newspapers that publish this overseas edition—were about to sell out to the Arabs . . . sell the Zionist cause down the river for that filthy oil money. Imagine the hatreds that could be fanned if Halevy believed that someone like Mark O'Mara, an important publisher, who has been chairman of several big Israeli bond drives, is going to sell his soul to the Arabs—just to make a financial killing—or that Karen Rankin, who holds a decoration personally presented to her by Golda Meir, would let her publication, *Twiceweek,* fall into enemy hands. One thing the Jews understand is the power of money. INAF would believe that such defections were possible. They know how much money the Arabs have. Halevy would be mad enough to liquidate the traitors."

"Come on, Assad. You must be joking! INAF is a militant group, but murder is a very dangerous undertaking."

"No, Anwar. I know Halevy, and I think I understand that type of personality. He would kill without a qualm and would consider it a patriotic act to protect his beloved Israel."

"So what good would it do," interjected Reza. "They would be caught and convicted. And the American liberal community would agonize over their aberration, write hundreds of columns on why they cracked under the strain and blame the reactionary Hurley administration. It wouldn't change anything regarding the United States policy in the Middle East."

"I disagree," said Izadi. "You're a pessimist, Reza. First of all, it would have to be planned perfectly so they wouldn't get caught. We'd leave clues to hook the killings to the Arabs and blame them on the victims' support of Israel. Some Arab terrorist group would probably rush to take credit for them anyhow. Don't you see—it's beautiful—the Arabs can't buy the heroic and free American press, so they murder in frustration. God! What wonderful clay we have to work with. The American Jews are ultrasensitive to persecution. The Anti-Defamation League goes berserk at the slightest criticism of Jews. What do you think they'll do with murders? I'll tell you what—there'll be screams of genocide, and every liberal in the Western world will predict that Israel is in grave danger of attack and needs nuclear defenses. The politicians who like an adoring press will make speeches and the Congress will act to help tiny, courageous Israel endure."

"I think Assad has something," began Anwar.

He got no further. Feverish excitement in his eyes, Izadi interrupted: "And the militant Arab nations will be enraged! They will call the whole affair United States propaganda for the Israeli war machine and will turn to the Soviet Union for protection against an Israel with nuclear capability. The Soviets will have to save face. *Voilà—la confrontation! Voilà*—Iran is saved!"

Anwar shook his head in wonderment, and said, almost reverently, "Assad, you crazy, brilliant man—with anyone else saying what you just said, I would recommend the straitjacket—but you— you might just pull it off. It all depends on how well you can handle

Halevy and how well the details can be orchestrated. I'll go along with you."

Reza simply smiled and said, "I vote aye."

"Good," said Izadi. "Now get me all the information you can on Vice President Porter Canfield and Isaac Miller. I need it as soon as possible—before I leave for the States. I think I know how to approach Mr. Halevy."

3

ALL DAY the innocuous white clouds had been gathering. But their innocence proved ephemeral. By late afternoon they had become an ominous gray and had built rolling thunderheads over the Catskills. Then, pushed by a freshening northwest wind, the cumulonimbus drifted across the Jersey flats, drenching the dusty earth amid fearsome pyrotechnics. By early evening the storm had snarled the rush-hour traffic in Manhattan and crossed the East River to torment the last populous areas in its path. The low-pressure system would eventually dissipate somewhere over the Atlantic.

To Yoram Halevy, it seemed that this thunderstorm had saved its maximum fury for the Williamsburg section of Brooklyn. A few moments ago he had stood at the immense second-floor window of the old building looking down at the people as they ran for shelter from the sudden deluge. It took only a minute before Broadway, the main street, became a giant parking lot. From everywhere had come the discordant blare of horns as motorists sought exculpation from causing the chaos by blaming one another. Halevy had peered through the huge letters I N A F, which were imperfectly painted in dark green on the window, and smiled at the spectacle.

Now he leaned forward tensely in the creaky old swivel chair. His eyes, focused on nothing, shifted their gaze from place to place on the cluttered desk while he concentrated on the voice in his ear. Behind him, a small window air conditioner throbbed heavily. For several days it had been engaged in an unsuccessful effort to wring moisture from the stale, recirculated air. The storm had come on the heels of an unusually hot and muggy week.

A brilliant flash of lightning daylit the shoddy office, and Halevy winced. Neither the lightning nor the attendant thunderclap frightened him, but his eardrum was numbed by the sharp crackle in the telephone receiver.

"Yes, yes, I can hear you, Rabbi," he said, changing to his other ear. He toyed with a Zippo lighter, flipping the hinged cover up and down with his thumb while he listened to his caller complain about the connection.

"There's a terrible storm going on here, Rabbi. I'm going to get off the phone before I get electrocuted. I'll talk with you again tomorrow morning about final plans for the demonstration down there. Meanwhile, I assume you have arranged for any D.C. permits we may need?—Good."

He hunched his left shoulder to hold the instrument steady against his jaw while he shook a cigarette from the crumpled pack and touched flame to it. The phone ground the stubble of his heavy beard into his neck, making it itch. Halevy needed two shaves a day, but seldom made the effort.

"Yes, we make final plans tonight. The people should start arriving for the meeting within an hour. I'll call you tomorrow with the full story. Good night, Rabbi."

He hung up and wiped his perspiring forehead with the back of his hand. Outside, the storm raged unabated. Christ, it's hot, he thought, wishing they had decent headquarters in one of those modern skyscrapers in Manhattan instead of this cheap walk-up over a Brooklyn deli.

He stood and stretched his powerful body. The jeans clung tightly to his muscular legs except in the baggy places vacated by his knees. The fit in the crotch would have made a ballet dancer blush, but Yoram Halevy found the uniform of the young essential for recruiting the youthful zealots that INAF needed in its work. What had that writer for the *Village Clarion* said? If Israel had to depend on those limousine liberals, she would be in real trouble. The only thing they did was buy bonds to outdo one another. They weren't really involved in the fight to save ghetto Jews around the world from genocide. That took guts, activism—facing the Man where street activity was necessary to attract the jaded news media. How else would the American people know of the problems? He laughed. Hooray for *Village Clarion*!

He looked at his watch. In about forty-five minutes his troops would begin to arrive. They would come, rain or shine. Meanwhile, where was that Iranian, Izadi? He had phoned from Kennedy more than an hour and a half ago. Halevy wanted to hear the important information that he had said he had, and he wanted to hear it before the meeting. It might affect the planning of the Dradavov demonstration.

The phone rang in the outer office and he heard Bea Bernstein say, "Good evening, INAF." There was a pause and then Bea's voice again: "INAF"—she pronounced it "eenaff"—"this is INAF, the office of an organization called 'Israel Now and Forever.' " Then another moment of silence. "You're a smart son of a bitch, aren't you?" she said bitterly.

He heard her slam the phone down and he went into the outer room. "What was that all about, Bea?"

The girl's anger quickly faded, and she gave him a bright smile. "Just another smart alec, Yorie. He said we should change INAF to ENOUGH because he's had enough of Israel and pushy Jews to last him forever. One of those heavy WASP conservatives, I guess." She made an obscene gesture. "Well, up his!"

Halevy's face became stern. "Don't let an ignorant clown lead you into such a cheap exchange, Bea. When you get that kind of garbage, just hang up—say nothing, and hang up. Understand?"

"Yes, sir." Bea's plain face colored at the reprimand, and she swung her gawky body back to the old typewriter, squeezing back the tears that her hero's harsh words had brought to her eyes.

Halevy stared at the back of her head. "Make sure the chairs are all set up in the meeting room, and ask Sam to check on the coffee and cold cuts from downstairs. And I'm expecting a Mr. Assad Izadi from Iran. Let me know the minute he arrives." He issued the orders coldly, aware of her erubescent neck but cruelly ignoring her discomfort, then strode quickly into his office and closed the door behind him. He looked out the window. He could imagine the foul smell of the steamy street, of excrement from city pets, and garbage recklessly tossed from the windows of passing cars.

Over the noise of the air conditioner he thought he heard a muffled sob. Dumb broad, he thought. I ought to can her. But then, where else could I get someone to type and watch the phone for seventy-five bucks a week?

Dismissing the idea from his mind, he sat down at the desk and lost himself in a lengthy *Times* article on Alexander Dradavov. In the article the Soviet chairman was lauded by an adoring *Times* man, who the week before had called President Hurley a "dim bulb in a dark room."

So complete was Yoram Halevy's concentration on the annoying article that he did not hear the office door open. He looked up with a start at old man Hackenschmidt, the third and only other full-time employee of INAF. Hackenschmidt was an active, wiry seventy, with thick, snow-white hair and piercing blue eyes set deep in a seamy face that was always cheerful. He had more energy than most seventy-year-olds. He had been to Israel twice and would have stayed to fight except for the fact that they wouldn't let him enlist because of his age.

"Sorry to break in, Yorie, but I have to know how many buses we need for Washington," he said.

"Oh, hi, Hack. I'll let you know within two hours."

"I've got to give 'em an estimate now and a final figure early tomorrow."

"Well, we have a hundred and eighty paid now. I'd guess we'll get another thirty tonight. Better tell them five buses for now. And Hack—" The old man, who had turned to go, stopped. "Check on the signs. Make sure they're ready to be loaded. We want all the bigwigs coming to the White House to know that we don't approve of that bigoted Russian schmuck."

"Right, Yorie. I'm on my way." Spinning around, Hackenschmidt slightly bumped into Bea, who was ushering Assad Izadi into the inner office.

"Excuse me, Bea," he said. The voice was contrite, but the eyes were full of mischief as he grabbed her by the bottom as if to steady her. Bea was annoyed, but reacted as though such minor assaults had occurred many times before.

"You're a dirty old man," she said to his retreating back. It was a flat statement of fact more than a protest. Izadi laughed openly.

Halevy managed to smile despite his general disapproval of horsing around and greeted the Iranian cordially. Izadi, who had come straight from the airport by taxi in a ride made endless by the rainstorm, dropped his two-suiter on the floor and flopped into the office's ancient armchair. Refusing Halevy's offer of coffee and a sandwich, he looked at the unframed pictures of Prime Minister Isadore Stein, Golda Meir, Yitzhak Rabin and Moshe Dayan that were tacked above the large map showing Israel in green and its bordering areas in white. He noted that parts of the Sinai, Syria, Jordan and Lebanon were crudely cross-hatched in green crayon to indicate areas still held by the Israeli army in defiance of more than a decade of pitiful United Nations efforts to restore them to their rightful owners.

Halevy's eyes followed Izadi's to the wall. "They're the reason why I spend most of my time in this dismal place. Dayan, the Old Lady and Rabin had the guts to put it all together, and Stein is making it stay together."

He looked back at Izadi, who was still inspecting the map. "I'm a Jew first and everything else second." The emotion in his voice reclaimed the full attention of the Iranian, who was surprised by the fever in Halevy's eyes. "That's the only way we Jews will avoid extinction. Never to relax, never to give those genocidal bastards a chance to destroy the homeland. When we say 'Israel Now and Forever,' we mean it."

Halevy leaned forward rigidly as if he would leap at his guest should there be the slightest sign of disagreement. Then suddenly the fierce expression dissolved and he relaxed back in his chair. "We'll make it all right, Assad. Jews are strong people, and, even though we're a small nation, we have powerful enclaves all over the world."

"With bright and dedicated people like you to support the Zionist cause, I have no doubt about it," Izadi said diplomatically.

"Yes, and it takes constant concentration to keep INAF on track," said Halevy, absorbing the flattery easily. "Except for a half-dozen old hands, most of our workers are young people. They come to us for a variety of reasons—to be part of a cause, to please their parents or their rabbi, to be with each other, to escape work or out of sheer boredom. Most are not deep thinkers, and sometimes it's difficult to keep the mob spirit in check. But they respect me, and I'm able to control them. We've been lucky enough to avoid convictions even though we've staged hundreds of demonstrations. Incidentally, we have a meeting here in a little while to plan a demonstration against the state dinner for Dradavov in Washington tomorrow."

He accepted a cigarette from the Iranian, then said, "Imagine a White House dinner for that communist murderer. Sometimes I wonder whether total nonviolence can accomplish our mission. We need coverage by the news media, and they are getting bored with ordinary demonstrations." He paused to listen as the sound of footsteps on the stairs and in the outer room announced that INAF members were beginning to arrive for the meeting.

Izadi was alert to the turn Halevy's ruminations were taking. "That's interesting, Yoram," he said. "I've noticed that it takes spectacular violence to make the international news. The media people have become fascinated by death and destruction."

Halevy nodded in agreement. "Yes, twenty years ago a few marchers would get you at least two minutes on the networks. Now it takes a riot or a shooting to get the cameras to the scene. That's why I say nonviolence may be on the way out."

"You're not thinking of starting a riot in Washington, are you?" said Izadi half-jokingly.

"No use, Assad. Not enough people churned up and not enough time. Besides, the security for the Russian will be strong—and I mean strong!"

He got up and switched off the air conditioner, which gave a tired shudder as it stopped. "But, Assad, my friend, we'll get some attention. Today there was a leak from our State Department that Dradavov has coldly rejected the suggestion that he liberalize his emigration policy for Soviet Jews. That issue's been around for a long time, but it's a chronic burr under the saddle to the American Jewish power structure—and they've got real clout with the big media. We'll have some catchy signs raising hell about persecuting Russian Jews, and the nets will dutifully film them."

The Iranian rose to his feet uncertainly. "Is it time for the meeting?"

"Not yet. I want to hear the news you've brought. But I didn't want you to have to yell over that groaning beast of an air conditioner along with all that noise outside. Come back here by the window and speak softly. It pays to be careful."

The two men walked to the far end of the room, and Halevy said, "Now, go ahead."

Well, here goes, thought Izadi to himself, hoping that he had made the right decision when he changed strategy without consulting either Reza or Anwar.

Thirteen hours before, the Alitalia 747 he was on had climbed out of Rome, where Izadi had stopped-over one night in order to make the trip from Tehran easier, and headed for New York. Something was annoying him, a formless worry that the plan to goad INAF into immediate violence was too quickly contrived and therefore probably contained imperfections. It was, after all, his plan, so he above all should be comfortable with it. Unfortunately, he wasn't. He sighed and squirmed slightly in the narrow middle seat. His armrest on both sides had been totally preempted by his neighbors—a large florid man whose muscles threatened to burst the seams of his jacket and a fragile, elderly lady who reeked of lavender. The bulk of the man caused Izadi to lean unconsciously toward the old lady, who cast disapproving side glances but did not budge her firmly anchored forearm from the armrest. Thus, depressed by mild claustrophobia, the Iranian's thoughts turned pessimistic. He knew so little about Halevy and INAF—he would be crazy to lead off with a proposal for violence. No, far better to go at it from the political side first. With Vice President Canfield already carrying the Israeli banner, and, according to the *Herald Tribune* on his lap, reaping benefits from it, perhaps the pro-Israel lobby in the United States could bring about enough diplomatic overstep to destroy the détente. Halevy, the man he was going to see, would support presidential-aspirant Canfield through thick and thin, and it was a safe bet that Isaac Miller, whom the *Herald Tribune* was already calling the brilliant architect of the Canfield campaign, was going out of his way to be very friendly with the INAF leader.

Unable to stand being cramped any longer, Izadi forced his elbow into a small opening behind the big man's forearm and was rewarded by a grunt and a grudging semiwithdrawal from the armrest. He was simultaneously relieved on the other side. The seat belt sign went off and the little old lady moved at flank speed toward the toilet. Taking a luxuriously deep breath, he began to structure a solution. His concentration sharpened, so he hardly noticed the return of the old lady, and the hostess who inquired about his drink order distracted him for only a moment.

A conservative plan was the answer. Radical action could always be employed later. For now it would be enough to encourage Canfield to carry the ball aggressively. How best to encourage him? Izadi chuckled to himself. Obviously, an ambitious politician needed minimum encouragement to jump into the spotlight. But it was important to keep him from becoming a bore or becoming ridiculous—like the American militant who said, during the time they were burning cities, "Let's burn down the Hoover Dam." Here the safety regulator was Isaac Miller. If he could control Miller, he could control Canfield. He picked up the *Herald Tribune* again and looked at the pictures over the double-column article entitled "Canfield Moves Out." There they were, the urbane, faintly smiling Vice President and his darkly handsome bachelor advisor, Prof. Zack Miller. The article described Miller with such superlatives as "brilliant iconoclast," "charismatic" and "highly sensitive," attributing the heavy praise to unnamed "associates" and "respected academic sources" in case Miller stubbed his toe in the future.

"Interested in American politics?" It was the man with the bulging biceps.

Izadi looked up to see his eyes on the newspaper.

"Sorry," the man continued, "but I couldn't help noticing your concentration on the Canfield story. These seats are so close together that it's impossible to avoid looking at your paper."

Izadi smiled pleasantly. "No apology needed. Yes, I guess everybody is interested in American politics. Always the unexpected can happen. And there's plenty of well-publicized nastiness."

"Yes, we cut each other up a lot; and the press loves blood—anybody's blood so long as it's not theirs."

"You sound close to it. Are you?"

"In a small way. I'm a city councilman from Albany, New York. I've been inspecting a new water-treatment plant in Rome."

The PPL leader saw a chance to increase his practical knowledge of the American political scene. "What do you think of your Vice President?"

The big man exhaled loudly. "I'm of his party, so I guess I can be objective. Personally, I don't think he's doing President Hurley any good trying to take the party back to the old days of speaking only for minorities. We grew strong on the working man—lost him for a while to the other party, but they screwed up and now we have him back. We fool around too much with those intellectuals and minorities; we're going to lose the working man again."

"But according to this article, Canfield's very popular."

"Yeah, he's popular, and if the liberals who publish that paper have anything to do with it, he'll become more popular." The big man shrugged. "They may ax him if he doesn't follow them on some issues, though. They're powerful enemies, but they aren't worth a damn as friends."

Izadi nodded understandingly. "You sound as though you have firsthand knowledge."

"Hell, yes! They bite me every chance they get. Like this inspection trip. They call it a junket, a waste of taxpayers' money. Maybe it is, but so are the federal Cabinet officers' trips around the world. And I'm alone, traveling economy class, while they have a whole damn airplane of their own. And it's loaded with staff." The man was glaring at Izadi in indignation.

"What do you think of the Arab-Israeli dispute?"

The city councilman shifted so that his left buttock took over the support function. The seat could not accommodate both sides of his massive posterior at the same time. "That's a tough one," he said evasively. "But I have to admire the Israelis. They're terrific people. Look at the guts it took to carve that country out of nothing. On the other hand, I like the Arab people I've met. Are you from that part of the world?"

Izadi was amused by the hedge. "Sort of," he said. "I'm from Iran."

The councilman nodded sagely. "That's a moderate Arab country, and your king's pretty sharp."

"No, we're not Arab. We're Persian."

"Oh, I see," he said, not really seeing at all.

"What I meant," persisted Izadi, "is—do you think the United States should supply war materials to Israel?"

"Sure I do. Aren't the Soviets supplying the other side? Look how the communists took over in Southeast Asia when we ducked out on the South Vietnamese."

"You have a good point there," said Izadi. He felt that he had had enough, so he excused himself and went to the lavatory. He stayed quite a while, and when he returned, his politician seatmate was, as he had hoped, sound asleep.

He stepped gingerly over the lavender lady, who sniffed lightly to show her annoyance, and sat down quietly so as not to disturb the sleeper. He ran the problem through his mind again. What was the best way to influence Miller? The news report said that Canfield was expected to fly to Singapore soon and that Miller would accompany him. Bachelor in the exotic Far East. Being a bachelor himself, he wondered how far it would be for the professor from exotic to erotic. For him, it had been a baby step. There was something about Singapore that stirred the loins. Wait! How about Sirana! Suppose he could get them to meet in Singapore? His mind raced. He had it! It was a moderate step—perfect. It did not foreclose other, more extreme solutions should they be necessary later. Of course, it depended on Sirana's impact on Miller, but given the right introduction, and the help of Singapore, she could do it. She hadn't disappointed him yet.

Now, standing in the stuffy INAF office, Izadi was going to give his decision its initial test. In a quiet, emotionless voice, he began: "You are familiar with the Persian Protective League's method of assembling information, so I won't bore you with the details of how we got this. I will emphasize that it has been cross-checked and we are convinced that it is accurate."

"Your information has been reliable in the past," agreed Halevy. The oppressive heat had quickly overcome the coolness left by the inactive air conditioner, and he was eager to get out of the office.

"Yes, we have worked well together in our fight against communists," Izadi said, "and now I'm afraid I have frightening news. Because of your effectiveness, the Soviets have slated INAF for destruction.'' He paused, watching the fleeting look of concern on Halevy's face turn to anger.

"Those genocidal maniacs! Those atheist swine!" The words were hissed, not spoken, but the hatred in them was not any the less for lack of volume. "How are they going to go about it?"

Izadi continued in a matter-of-fact tone. "The word they used was 'exterminate.' The instructions are being relayed by courier to KGB agents in the United States. I'd suggest you notify the FBI—if you're clean."

"We're clean, but the FBI doesn't admire us," said Halevy. "Besides, I don't want them skulking around here. We will take countermeasures, such as complaining to the news media about telephone threats from communist sympathizers, and we will lay any problems they give us squarely in the laps of Soviets. But I don't think they'll carry out the threat. It would bring every Zionist in the United States down on the Soviet Union with both feet."

"You are the best judge of that, Yoram. I just felt obligated to relay the information."

"Well, I appreciate it very much, Assad; however, it may be an intentional leak calculated to frighten us into going underground. Whatever it is, INAF won't give in and the Dradavov demonstration goes as planned tomorrow." Halevy looked fiercely determined.

"Your courage is admirable, Yoram," Izadi was generally pleased by Halevy's reaction up to this point. It showed just the right mix of worry and courage. Not to be frightened would evidence a degree of stupidity that would doom in advance any action INAF might be called on to undertake. Panic would remove INAF completely from the equation. It was apparent that Halevy was pleased by the compliment. "Anything worth doing requires risks," he said and he pointed to the map. "Real courage is a daily occurrence there. The least we can do is occasionally show a little fortitude here."

As though a thought had just come to him, Izadi snapped his fingers and said, "From the same sources, we obtained a name—an American who figures somewhere in the picture. We cannot tell whether he is a Russian agent dangerous to you or whether he is a target for the KGB. He appears to be an academic type. Professor Isaac Miller."

"Good God! Zack Miller?" Halevy's amazement was clear on his face. "Why would they be interested in Zack Miller?"

"You know him, then?" asked Izadi.

"Very well, and I can assure you that he's not a Russian agent. He's a highly respected professor of political science at New York

112

University. But what is more startling is that Miller is very close to Vice President Porter Canfield.''

"Well, I'd have to conclude that he's a target, just as you are,'' said Izadi, keeping his voice matter-of-fact.

Halevy's face left no doubt as to his concern. "Zack is a good friend of INAF. Not an out-and-out Zionist, you understand, because that would destroy his ability to maneuver politically and would hurt Canfield, but really supportive in a quiet way. Why, he is the Vice President's primary political strategist. If it wasn't for Zack, Canfield wouldn't be a seriously regarded presidential candidate. Zack is the brains behind Canfield.''

His excitement mounting, Halevy had become louder. Izadi placed a finger to his lips, and Halevy continued in a more subdued voice. "Zack is in Arizona right now with the Vice President. He expects to travel with Canfield for several months to get the campaign off on a solid footing.'' The INAF leader paused as a disturbing thought struck him. "Assad,'' he said, grabbing him by the arm. "Zack is going to the Far East with the Vice President. He may be in great danger there. They could kill him, and the reason would be lost in a maze of international politics. No one would suspect the real reason because we are hated for welshing on our commitments in that part of the world. An American could be assassinated for reasons totally unrelated to Israel. We must warn Zack immediately!''

"Wait a minute—calm yourself, Yoram. If you're right, and I think you are, nothing will happen to Miller right away. Is it public knowledge that he's going to the Far East?''

"It's been covered in the major news media.''

"Then the communists will reason the same way you have. If they're going to hit him, they'll do it where they can best cover their tracks, and that's overseas, not in the United States. And there's a way I can help protect your friend. The PPL maintains agents in that part of the world. We will instantly advise Mr. Miller if we find he is in danger. You see, our source of information is a continuing one.''

"But how can you approach him? He won't recognize your agent, nor expect a contact.''

Izadi smiled confidently. "It is easily arranged, Yoram. You are close to Miller. Explain the situation to him and tell him our agent will contact him by phone at his first stop. . . . What is his first stop?''

"Singapore.''

"We'll contact him in Singapore if there is any danger.''

"How will he identify your operative?''

"By code signal. Let's see. Our operative will contact him by phone—only should it be necessary, of course—and say that Professor Miller taught his brother at the university. That will identify the person as our agent, and Miller can arrange to see him to be briefed. We will use the same procedure in the other countries Canfield visits."

Halevy thought for a moment. "Okay, I'll get word to Zack. And I'm sure he'll appreciate your help—just as I do." He shook Izadi's hand firmly. The Iranian said modestly, "You would do the same for us, I'm sure."

The exchange of information completed, Halevy now seemed to adopt the air of a battlefield commander—grave but sure of himself—and Izadi was more than pleased that the first phase of his plan had been most successfully carried out. At the INAF leader's suggestion, he decided to stay for the meeting, but said he did not wish to be introduced or otherwise identified. They went at once to the larger outer room, where about a hundred people had assembled. Seventy or so were seated on wooden folding chairs, and the remainder stood around the sides and back of the room. Aside from the removable chairs, a long table loaded with tracts, and the stenographer's desk and chair, the room was without furniture. Bond-drive posters and other Israeli propaganda were scotch-taped to the cracked plaster walls.

Most of the people in the room were under thirty. Even a memory expert would have been hard-pressed to identify any twenty of them after a single introduction, for they clung to the same, stale peer image. The faded, shabby blue jeans; the formless sandals, showcases for feet coated with city-street grime; the color-uncoordinated T-shirts, sometimes charitably concealed by ill-fitting sweaters; the long, straight, center-parted hair that the girls pushed away from their faces at least once every fifteen seconds; the disheveled, tangled locks of the young men, wet and odorous from sweat and rain—all attested to a huddling together in what they thought was intellectual unity. And so the interminable umbilical cord remained unsevered, and from it depended the undisciplined emotions of the majority, cruelly burdening the few bright minds in the group.

At the very front sat the hyperactives, the self-appointed leaders who had been frustrated in their aspirations once too often. Off to one side, separated from the younger group by several empty chairs, were a few older people—born counselors without the intelligence to counsel, longing for recognition but always rejected.

The real shock troops of INAF were not present. They would be on the buses in the morning, but they had little patience with strategy sessions. Whatever they needed to know would be passed on to them by Halevy on the trip.

After bringing the meeting to order, the INAF leader lowered his arms and said with a smile, "Welcome, ladies and gentlemen. I am pleased that so many of you came tonight, and I hope all of you will be riding with us to Washington tomorrow."

"You bet we will, Yorie. I'm looking forward to doing a lot of riding tomorrow, and not all on the bus." The speaker was a wispy, bearded blond boy with rampant acne. There were a few snickers and giggles, but Halevy ignored the interruption.

"We leave at noon from here," he said. "We have one hundred and eighty paid, and we'll need everything in by the time we leave here tonight. The fare is fifteen bucks and that includes a box lunch from the deli. No dinner. We'll stop on the Jersey Pike coming back, but you'll have to buy your own then. We should be back here by two A.M." He paused, then said, "How many more have their money ready? Raise your hands."

About twenty hands went up. Halevy turned to Hackenschmidt, who was standing alongside him. "Just about what we figured, Hack. Let the bus company know."

Hackenschmidt left the room to phone, and Halevy resumed. "Now listen carefully. This is not some stoned-out rock concert; this is a serious demonstration. I want you people to bear that in mind. You are not going down there to play. This is for Israel. This is let the American people know we resent Hurley's entertaining that communist overlord who is repressing Russian Jews!"

There was a cheer and a good amount of applause. Then a serious-faced girl stood up and asked in a flat, dispassionate voice whether they should respect the police barricades if they couldn't get close enough to the White House to be seen by Dradavov and his party. Halevy said they should be nonviolent, but that didn't mean they couldn't fill a vacuum if they found one. The pimply-faced boy, who had apparently enjoyed his brief time in the spotlight, had a question.

"Yes, what is it?" said Halevy.

"How 'bout if we zing old Dradie's limo with a couple of rocks? That'll wake up those bastards and the cameras will love it."

"No. No rocks under any circumstances." Halevy turned to answer another question, but the boy was not satisfied.

"Look, Yorie, INAF is getting to be a sissy outfit. Nobody's going to pay any attention to us if we just stand there and let the pigs shove us around with their nightsticks."

The room became totally quiet. The audience waited to see how their leader would handle this challenge. Halevy said nothing. He just stood there looking at the boy. His lips were pressed tightly together, causing his mouth to become a thin, hard line, but his posture was relaxed and easy.

"What are we, a bunch of faggots?" Continuing to press his luck, the boy mimicked a falsetto: "No. No rocks. Or the big, bad police may spank you."

Yoram Halevy put his hands on his hips. "Are you through now?"

"No. I'm not through. We'll never be anything if we don't show some balls. Like Chicago. Like May Day. Like 'Bring Home the Navy Day.' Let's jam a sign up old Dradavov's exhaust pipe!" he said, waxing enthusiastic before his awed listeners.

"Sit down, Tommy. You're way off base," Halevy said, his voice quiet, but a trace metallic.

"No! I won't sit down! Let's get this out in the open. You want us to act like pansies. If the hassle is as important as you say, let's raise a little hell that they'll remember."

There were some mutters of agreement among the group. Out of the corner of his eyes, Halevy saw Assad Izadi watching him with a quizzical expression on his face.

He walked to the side of the room, picked up a small paperweight and tossed it to the boy. "Okay, Tommy. Let's see what you're made of. If you're so good at rock throwing, I want you to throw this through the two hundred fifty-sixth precinct window. I promise you the cops won't be a bit angrier at that than they will be if you bombard Dradavov's car. Now, go ahead. You don't like the pigs anyhow. Be a man, not a pansy."

The boy looked dazedly at the granite weight in his hand. He grew pale, and his mouth opened and closed twice without a sound.

"N-no, it's not the same," he said finally. "They'll lock me up, and my dad will beat hell out of me."

"They'd lock you up in Washington, and he'd still beat hell out of you—particularly if he has to take a day off from work to go all the way down there."

A few people began to taunt, and the boy's face turned red. Deeply embarrassed, he sat down to a chorus of catcalls.

Halevy took the weight from him and walked back to the front of the room. "That's enough," he said sternly to the crowd. "What happened to Tommy just now could have happened to a lot of you. Let's forget it. Tom is a good member. He just made a mistake, that's all. He's got guts enough, but he's also got brains, and his brains won't let him make a damn fool of himself when he understands the situation fully."

His face softened. "Tom," he said, "I want you to take responsibility for the signs tomorrow. See Mr. Hackenschmidt before you leave, okay?"

The boy smiled, grateful for the reprieve. "Yes, Yorie. I'll be glad to do that. Sorry I got carried away."

"No hard feelings, Tommy. We've all done it more than once."

There were several more desultory questions, all patiently answered by the INAF leader. It was obvious that the diffident questioners wanted to identify with Halevy, to gain attention more than information. There were no further challenges that night. Tommy's destruction had been too complete.

Halevy concluded the meeting with a fifteen-minute summary of the important aspects of the demonstration plan and gave the INAF members their final instructions. He invited them to partake of coffee and sandwiches in the back and brushed aside the forerunner of a new group of interrogators, referring them all to Hackenschmidt.

Before anything else could detain him, he beckoned to Izadi to follow him back to the inner office. Passing Bea Bernstein, he said, "No interruptions, Bea, until I tell you—that includes the phone."

"Yes, sir. You were sensational tonight, Yorie," she began obsequiously, the rest of her compliment truncated by Halevy's slamming of the door to his office.

Halevy switched on the air conditioner inside and sighed in audible relief. They both sat down.

Izadi made sure that the universal social lubricant, praise, was not neglected. "You handled the boy very well, Yoram," he said, his voice conveying more respect than the modest compliment would indicate. "Instead of leaving an enemy looking for revenge, you left a disciple seeking new ways to serve you. It was very well done, and your stature with the others grew, also."

Halevy leaned back, allowing himself the luxury of a replay. "You see the central point, Assad. Only an experienced leader would see it. A leader must think, not react emotionally. Above all, a leader must not crush those he leads. Tommy will be more loyal and more energetic because of his mistake. He will work to be praised before the group. I will see that he gets that praise."

"Very wise. I'm glad that we are working together. The PPL needs strong, intelligent allies; and we can help you in many ways."

"You've already helped with the dope on Zack Miller. I'll follow

117

up and see that he knows about the problem.''

Izadi hesitated for a moment, then decided to leave at least the nucleus of the original idea. "One more thing. We are checking out some incomplete information on American media people who have supported Israel up to now. The rumor is some may be selling out to the Arabs for oil money.''

"Good Lord," ejaculated Halevy, "that's unbelievably terrible.''

"Don't get excited, Yoram. It's not definite even though such reports have appeared in the international press.''

"What treachery—the contemptible vermin—''

"If it checks out," continued Izadi, "I'll write you with the usual precautions from Tehran, identifying the bad eggs.''

"Please do. We'd want to know the details.'' Halevy was visibly upset.

"Good. Then I'll get back to the city. My plane leaves in the morning. I have to stop in Frankfurt on the way back to check with one of my people who just returned from East Germany about Russian intentions in the Middle East.''

After refusing an offer of a ride to Manhattan, Izadi got to his feet and shook hands warmly with his host. "Good luck in Washington, Yoram, and watch yourself. The communists are angry about the internal problems you are giving them over the emigration policy. What I told you should not be taken lightly.''

"Let's keep in touch, Assad. Don't trust ordinary mail or phone with anything sensitive. The feds are getting nosier every day.''

"I thought things had improved. We heard that your government had lost its appetite for snooping.''

Halevy snorted his cynicism. "They did—briefly—but Hurley is a traditional conservative, and he likes the federal men to keep a close watch on people dissatisfied with his idea of democracy, especially when they demonstrate their disapproval.''

"Don't worry, Yoram. I'll use the utmost precautions. It's slower, but it's safer.'' Izadi picked up the battered two-suiter by the desk. "Best of luck. Don't forget to inform Professor Miller.'' He closed the door quietly behind him. Moving with easy, graceful strides that concealed his fatigue, he waved goodbye to a bemused Bea Bernstein, bounced down the single flight of stairs to the street and waited to hail the first passing cab. A flash from the deli's neon sign gave him a brief glimpse of Yoram Halevy's grave face looking out the window at him. Izadi was satisfied—satisfied that he had read Halevy correctly and that his new plan had every chance of being an outstanding success.

4

AFTERNOON CABINET meetings were anathema to Porter Canfield. His inability to concentrate was caused partly by his weakness for heavy lunches at Sans Souci, but mainly by the tedious, structured nature of the agenda. As he sat listening to the same ceremonious presentations he had heard a few hours before at the briefing for congressional leaders, he wondered what it had been like for Charles Dawes at Coolidge's Cabinet meetings. They must have had frank discussions back in those days. Now nothing controversial could be mentioned without it winding up in the morning news. Since the media march through Watergate, the executive branch had become a veritable sieve.

An economic advisor had the floor and was hanging on tenaciously. He was covertly known to the White House staff as "the Fly" because of his sudden insectlike head movements and his habit of rubbing his hands together rapidly.

"Here are some interesting second-quarter statistics, Mr. President," said the advisor ponderously to his semicomatose listeners. "We see that braking the economy by a restrictive fiscal and monetary policy causes an almost immediate fall-off in primary employment, but effects no quick reduction of inflation."

Canfield yawned in his ears and throat without opening his mouth. His eyes wandered to the wide French doors opening onto the porch. It was curious, the Vice President mused, that his chair commanded a breathtaking view of the Rose Garden, while all the President had to look at were curtained inner doors and a few somber portraits of admired predecessors. Canfield smiled to himself. This had to be an intentional abandonment of regal prerogative by Hurley—probably due to a fear of disturbing tradition. No President, as far as he knew, had ever been bashful about indulgence in the pleasures of the office—spiritual or material. More important, no President's staff would ever be careless enough not to call to his attention any advantage he overlooked.

The Vice President had to hide a smile as his attention was drawn to President Hurley's chief of staff, perched attentively behind his principal like an alert bird ready to take wing at the slightest movement. Canfield had his troubles with the President's top staff, just as had every Vice President in recent times.

"Now, Mr. President," continued the economic advisor, "I will take only about fifteen minutes more to cover this last group of data."

An audible groan escaped the secretary of labor. The secretary of defense looked quickly at his watch. Several other Cabinet members shifted nervously in their big leather chairs, and there was an impatient rustling of papers among the staff near the walls of the room.

President Walter Hurley sat up quickly and took a firm hold of the agenda in front of him. "I'm afraid we'll have to defer that until another time, Wally," he said, smiling gently to diminish the apparent discomfort of the economist. "We've still got to hear from Charlie on the budget, and, as you know, there is a state dinner tonight for our Soviet visitor."

"If I may have just five more minutes, Mr. President?" Wally's head bounced like a novice equestrian at the trot as he looked hopefully at Hurley.

"Sorry, Wally, we'll give you a rain check."

"But, Mr. President—"

"Mr. Grimm, please sit down." The President's usual pleasantness faded, and his voice revealed his irritation. He swung to the director of the Office of Management and Budget. "Make it short, Charlie," he said, gesturing the OMB man to the lectern at the end of the room.

"Yes, Mr. President," said Charles Voren, and he quickly, but without a trace of panic, laid out a few papers.

Behind Canfield and to his left the senior staffer from the Department of Housing and Urban Development nudged his counterpart from Commerce. "Check the Fly and the secretary of labor," he said in a barely audible undertone. "Old Maritime Marty is getting a kick out of watching the ivory tower put-down by the old man, and he's letting Wally know it."

Martin Muldrow, three years ago an international vice president and the chief legal officer of the Maritime Union, was enjoying the advisor's obvious suffering. Canfield remembered heated exchanges between them about union power. Now Muldrow was fixing Wally with a merciless, obsidian stare. Squirm, you little bastard, his expression seemed to say. Maybe that'll teach you not to lecture me about inflationary union pay raises.

Grimm sat down, rigid with embarrassment. Almost immediately he felt a gentle touch on his arm and turned to find Dr. Meredith Lord seeking his attention. The secretary of HEW was worth turning to look at. Softly arranged brown hair with just a hint of blonde highlights framed a lovely, expressive face. Her eyes were fawn-colored and wideset. Right now those warm brown eyes imparted concern and friendship.

"Don't take that personally, Wally," she said softly. "The President has great respect for you and relies heavily on your knowledge of the economy. He's just really tired, and he's thinking more of tomorrow's sessions with Dradavov than of this meeting."

"Thank you, Madam Secretary." Wally Grimm's eyes filmed with gratitude.

"Meredith, Wally. I keep telling you that. We're on the same team. Let's not be too formal."

This quiet exchange flustered the bashful statistician and he looked away quickly.

Charlie Voren had completed the budget process summary and was settling into his standard peroration. "The members of the Cabinet should be aware," he said ponderously, "that spending must be reduced in the fourth quarter if we are to remain within our projected deficit. That means *austerity.*" He banged his hand solidly against the lectern and glared at the secretary of HEW, who smiled disarmingly at him.

"And I would like to remind our two biggest spenders, HEW and HUD, that there are enough uncontrollables in their budgets without looking for new ways to dispose of the tax dollar."

The budget director angrily moved to one side to pick up a memorandum, almost knocking a coffeepot out of the hands of the navy steward who was making his third trip around the table. Reading from the memo, he puncuatted his explosive sentences with short jabs of his left forefinger.

"The secretary of Health, Education, and Welfare," he said, fully aware that an "undisclosed source" would repeat his words to the *Washington Globe,* "is recruiting influential members of the Senate Labor and Public Welfare Committee. The purpose is to initiate an amendment to the President's health bill. That amendment will authorize additional services at government expense by Total Health Care. I estimate that it will triple needed appropriations in that area."

Charlie Voren shook his head. "How are we going to trim the budget enough to keep within the overall congressional ceiling if our own people are encouraging new spending?"

"Now wait a minute, Charlie," Meredith Lord said very firmly. "The President should know that I tried for a week to brief him on that change, but I couldn't get past the chief of staff. I was told that so long as I did not alter the gross HEW budget figure, I could make internal reductions and increases. That was in the memo you—"

"Oh, for heaven's sake, Meredith, you know that memo referred to existing controllables and not to new legislation," said Voren. "Mr. President, we've been all through that a dozen times."

Meredith, who was seated on the same side of the conference table as Walter Hurley, three places to his right, leaned forward so that she could look directly at him. "But Mr. President," she said intensely, "those services are necessary if the THC concept is to work. I know Mr. Voren has difficult responsibilities, but this administration was elected to do something more than watch dollars. Six months ago we announced with fanfare a great new health breakthrough for the average citizen. Now we are virtually insuring public disillusionment by inadequately funding it. That's why I cut my budget in some of the community action programs and asked for this amendment in substitution."

Fatigue showed on Walter Hurley's face. Canfield felt a momentary twinge of sympathy. The presidency was a never-ending chain of judgments to be made between conflicting—and equally defensible—points of view. Hurley was openly proud of having appointed the first woman to head HEW since it had become the sprawling giant it now was, but this good-looking lady was some kind of firebrand. There was a stubbornness and independence within her that made it clear that she would not be a blind loyalist. It had taken only about ten weeks to prove that. The President probably wished that Jim Trahover, who until a year ago had headed the can of worms known as HEW, had not let the welfare lobby chase him into early retirement.

Hurley rubbed the side of his face ruefully. Old Walter's caught between a rock and a hard place, thought Canfield. Charlie Voren had a job to do or the Congress would be all over them like a swarm of mosquitoes. Yet Meredith had a point, too.

It was getting late. The President took the easy way out. "Hold it,

Meredith—Charlie. I can't take the time now to get to the bottom of the problem,'' he said gently, ''so I'm going to ask the Vice President to spend some time with both of you and try to work it out.''

Canfield looked up from his doodling in surprise. This was a new wrinkle.

The President continued, turning on the famous Hurley charm, ''Porter, I place in your hands the most beautiful and, I might add, one of the most intelligent members of our team. And I also leave to your tender ministrations the most loyal, patient and long-suffering budget director any President ever abused. Now, with your tact, skill and experience, you should be able to resolve the dispute.'' He stood up and looked at his watch. Chairs scraped the deep carpet as everyone rose respectfully with the thin, grayhaired chief executive.

It was now five-thirty and the President would be receiving Dradavov and his party at eight. He walked quickly toward the Oval Office, and a general exodus began. Canfield saw Meredith edging her way around small groups of people who had stopped to talk, and moved to intercept her at the door.

''Well, Mr. Vice President,'' she said teasingly as they walked together into the hall, ''what did you do to deserve such punishment? Delivered into the clutches of a middle-aged woman with a mission. My daddy used to opine that for sheer determination a middle-aged woman with a mission is far worse than a vacuum cleaner salesman.''

''You've made it clear that you have a mission, at least to Charlie,'' agreed Canfield, ''but I will not agree that thirty-four is middle-aged.'' He smiled wryly. ''That doesn't help us forty-eight-year-olds feel young.''

''Don't expect senior-citizen sympathy from me, Mr. Vice President,'' Meredith teased. ''You're hardly ready for a gerontologist, and I've been through enough campaign crowds with you to see that your impact on the ladies isn't purely intellectual.''

Canfield affected a stern look. ''I suppose you think that blarney will sway this impartial referee and help your case, Madam Secretary.'' His face relaxed into a smile. ''Well, it probably would except that my fear of Charlie Voren will keep me on the straight and narrow. He's been making noises about trimming the vice-presidential budget.''

Two young staffers, with the serious and urgent manner that is the hallmark of youth in the West Wing, approached, heading toward the press secretary's office. Meredith moved a step closer to Canfield to let them through the congested area, and the Vice President caught a trace of subtle floral perfume that pleasantly stirred his senses. Why, he wondered, did Amy wear that weird stuff that left the lingering impression of wet dog—at fifty dollars an ounce. He didn't know whether the price or the advertising annoyed him more. What was that obnoxious ad line—"Suggesting your secret earthiness and independence." Well, in another hour his independent, but far from earthy wife would arrive from Philadelphia, and the house on N Street would be full of it. And then he would have to hear ad nauseam about Women's League, the Theater Bunch, the Ladies' Bridge Club and whatever new group she might have joined in the three weeks since he had been in Philadelphia. He felt trapped.

Out of the corner of his eye, he noticed Josh Devers standing off to the side regarding him with a faintly amused expression. He wondered whether the political counselor could hear his conversation with Meredith.

One thing was certain. Devers' high-handedness in phoning instructions for him in Phoenix proved he was no friend. Moreover, he did not want the President's most intimate confidant reporting any lightweight vice-presidential conversation. Better to leave the banter for a more suitable moment.

"Meredith, we should get together as soon as possible," he said. "I'm leaving in about a week for the Far East, and I know the President would like your problem settled before I go."

He glanced openly at Devers, who now appeared to be waiting to speak to him. "Perhaps we could get together tomorrow afternoon. In any event, I'll see you at the Dradavov dinner tonight, and we'll set a definite time."

Shifting his stance in that practiced way that politicians use so skillfully to disengage from a conversation, he signaled Devers that he would join him in a moment.

"Fine, Mr. Vice President. I'll see you this evening." As Meredith moved gracefully toward the reception room, he could not resist a last look at her attractive, lithe figure. "Lord," he thought, "what sensational legs she has."

"They are nice, aren't they?" said a dry voice at his elbow. "They even look good to a sixty-seven-year-old arthritic."

Porter Canfield spun quickly toward Devers, embarrassed at having his thoughts read despite the friendly, conspiratorial tone of the remark. "I wasn't thinking about her body," he said, "but rather how to change her mind about the importance of following the spirit as well as the letter of presidential policy."

Devers had not given any indication that he was annoyed at Canfield's disregard of the message he had relayed through Zack Miller. Nor did he contest the Vice President's dissembling regarding Meredith. Four years as the party's national chairman and two more in the West Wing of the White House as President Hurley's political advisor had taught him not to press into sensitive areas at the wrong time or unnecessarily. It was tough enough when it was important. But, he reflected, he had got a good look at Canfield's face in that unguarded moment. The Vice President was clearly susceptible to sensual attraction. It showed a potential weakness. He would store this impression away in his massive memory file. Information and insights were the stock-in-trade of a political advisor.

"I'm glad you mentioned presidential policy, Newt, because it gives me the opportunity to come right to the point. I need an appointment with you tomorrow to pass on some sensitive information from the boss. What time can I see you?"

Canfield flinched slightly at the use of the nickname that he accepted graciously only from family and old friends. He didn't much care for Josh Devers. What gave this little dried-up busybody the right to patronize him? All Devers did was snoop around for Hurley. He'd really messed up Stanley Bedson by reporting verbatim to the President a rather pithy comment the senator made in a party caucus about the President's indecisiveness on Middle East policy. He could still see Bedson's face that day in the Oval Office when the President had asked acrimoniously whether Bedson thought it proper to suggest to senators that the President of the United States didn't know whether to perform a base body function or lose his eyesight.

But notwithstanding his desire to notify Devers that he didn't want to see him ever, much less tomorrow, Canfield was a realist; so he arranged an eleven o'clock appointment with the counselor and departed, followed by two of his Secret Service agents.

The Vice President took his usual route from the Cabinet Room to his suite in the Executive Office Building—past the Oval Office, the Roosevelt Room, a right turn at Devers's corner office (which once belonged to Sherman Adams), past the elevator and down the steps at a lope. Picking up another agent at the door, he hurried across Executive Avenue and up the drive to the ground-floor entrance of the Executive Office Building.

Steve Galdari met him just inside the swinging doors. "Sir, I'm going to get the cars moving," he said. "We don't have much time until the dinner."

"Right, Steve. What time am I due there?" he asked, backing toward the elevator.

"You should be at the Red Room no later than seven forty-five. It's almost six. With traffic the way it is this time of evening, that doesn't give you too much leeway."

The elevator doors opened. Canfield waited impatiently while a science advisor and a couple of stenographers from the budget office got off. Why did they gape at him like tourists? They must have seen him fifty times in the past four years.

Bill Shelby was standing under the official seal at the doorway of Canfield's suite.

"Anything hot, Bill?"

"Just unusual press activity," answered Shelby. "Since your speeches out West and the Phoenix Airport statement, the media have been driving your press secretary crazy. He's been pressing me for an appointment to talk with you about it."

"Well, hold him off for a while. Tell him to say the statements speak for themselves."

"Okay, Mr. Vice President, but I really think you should give him ten minutes sometime tomorrow."

"Very well, tell Pete I'll see him in the morning," he said absently.

Walking to his inner office, he nodded to the receptionist, who pushed the intercom and said, "He's back, Kathy."

The Vice President shuffled through the phone slips on his desk, discarding all but one that said to call Mrs. Canfield at Greystone. It was marked 5:30 P.M. What the hell was Amy doing in Philadelphia at that hour? She was supposed to be on the way to their place in Georgetown by four-thirty.

He was worried that Amy apparently hadn't yet left for Washington. She knew this dinner for the Russian chairman was important, and he knew how long it took her to dress for a White House dinner.

There was a knock at the door and Kathryn Dryden came in.

Canfield looked up, vaguely irritated at the interruption, but his stare quickly softened into a friendly smile. He liked this serious twenty-eight-year-old girl. With him only a year, she had proved herself to be cool, efficient and more than a match for his other senior staff at the tricky business of office politics. He had decided to look outside to replace Mrs. Grogan when she left to accompany her State Department husband to Brazil, and he hadn't been sorry. Kathryn Dryden had come with excellent references from the executive offices of a very high-pressure business, where mistakes were expensive and not tolerated. She was single, able to travel and willing to work long hours.

"Sorry I won't have time to sign this mail tonight," he said. "Cabinet meeting really dragged. Don't even tell me about anything that's not really urgent."

He picked up the phone and eased himself into the high-backed black leather chair. "Get my wife, please," he instructed the receptionist.

Kathy had taken the mail folder from the In bin and was going through the letters. Out of the twenty-five she extracted two and placed them in front of the Vice President. "These should go tonight, sir," she said firmly. "The speaker is pressing for this authorization for the Capitol architect, and the secretary of state needs a little time to get the briefing materials you are requesting before next week's departure."

"Nag, nag, nag," he teased, quickly signing the two letters. "Now, anything else that will rock the world if left undone?"

"Well, Peter Rosen's called me eight times today. He wants—"

"I know about that," Canfield interrupted quickly. "Bill's already warned me. But let's hold Pete and his crushing problems until tomorrow, shall we?"

"Of course, sir. I wasn't going to suggest you see him now."

The intercom rang, and he scooped up the phone. "Okay, thanks," he said, then pushed the flashing button. "Amy? What's happened? Why are you still there?" He leaned forward and drummed his fingers on the desk. Kathy quietly slipped out of the office as Canfield fell silent.

"Damn it, Amy, you know how important it is for you to be with me at state dinners, especially where major powers are involved. The President's going to be burned up about the last-minute seating change. Where the Russians are concerned, he wants everything to run smoothly."

Canfield closed his eyes for a moment in frustration. He listened to the inevitable recitation of excuses. Except for the first year, when he was a junior congressman and they had been still full of the excitement of public life, his wife had shown no interest in the capital. She preferred the familiar ground of Main Line Philadelphia—parties in Bryn Mawr, bridge games at the country club—to the complicated turmoil of national politics. As a matter of fact, Amy wasn't very good at being nice to people she didn't like, at least not on any sustained basis, and she was downright unforgiving about what she perceived as social flaws in her peers.

After a long moment Canfield said bitterly, "Forget it, Amy. It's too late to do anything about it now. If a luncheon at the Waldorf for Burmese refugees is more important than my career, there's really no use discussing the matter further.''

He listened for another long moment, and an incredulous look came over his face. ''Will-I-have-a-chance-to-ask-Mrs.-Hurley-about-coming-to-your-dinner-at-the-country-club?'' he repeated, spacing out the words as though each one was a rare curiosity. ''Sure, Amy. I'll brace the old girl in the receiving line.'' Then his patience dissolved completely. ''Amy, get this. I'm trying very hard to properly discharge the responsibilities of the nation's second highest office. Not often, but sometimes, those responsibilities include obligations on your part—like being at the White House tonight rather than resting up for a silly damn charity luncheon in New York. There is no time to discuss it now, but this can't go on.'' He pushed the buzzer for his secretary while listening to his wife's disingenuous reply. ''Okay, Amy. I'll call you in a day or so.''

God, he thought resignedly, what a totally self-centered woman. She seemed oblivious to the clumsy situation her default had placed him in. How could she be so meticulously courteous in Philadelphia and so rude in Washington? He was struck by the recurrence of a disturbing thought that had been annoying him lately. Maybe it wasn't thoughtlessness. Maybe she just didn't give a damn. She was spending less and less time in Washington, and that meant they were infrequently together. This did not bother him emotionally, but it was beginning to cause questions from the women of the press. He anticipated that they would become more and more persistent as he let his political intentions become better known. Something had to be done about it.

He got to his feet as his secretary reentered in response to his call. Masking his annoyance with his wife as best he could, he said, ''Kathy, Mrs. Canfield is unable to get down for the dinner tonight. She's not feeling well. Will you call Virginia Wells at the Social Office and let her know? A reseating is necessary.'' He moved quickly to the door. ''And suggest to Virginia that Secretary Lord fill in at the head table for Mrs. Canfield. I think the spot is between the Soviet foreign minister and their ambassador. Let me know if there's any problem.''

The heavy limousine moved slowly out of the Executive Office Building driveway past the guard booth and turned north on 17th Street. Close behind, like a puppy on the heels of a child, came the follow-up station wagon with Secret Service agents alertly watching in all directions. At the corner of Pennsylvania Avenue the cars paused briefly for the light and Steve Galdari completed his routine report to headquarters that the Vice President had left the EOB for his residence. He hung the mike on the dashboard and peered out the thick glass window toward Blair House.

"Looks like our Russian friends are going to be greeted by some demonstrators," Galdari said. "They're already gathering across from Blair House and in the park. Lots of signs, but I can't make out what's on them."

The Vice President shifted his attention from the newspaper he was reading to the street outside. It was a typical summer evening in Washington—warm and annoyingly muggy. The passersby looked uncomfortable and almost uniformly unhappy. "I'm not surprised, Steve," he said gloomily. "The Soviet policy in the Middle East is not pleasing to a lot of our people, especially those who are worried about the security of Israel. Some of our best minds resent Dradavov's visit at a time when the Iraqis got those new jets and the Russian navy is increasingly active in the Indian Ocean. They feel a peace visit is a charade."

"Well," Galdari replied guardedly, "I don't know much about international politics, Mr. Vice President, but I sure hope that we don't have any serious incidents during this demonstration. Some of these people going toward the park appear to be in an ugly mood."

By now the light had turned green, and the limousine poked its black nose into Pennsylvania Avenue and headed smoothly toward Georgetown.

"All deliberate speed, Jerry," said Galdari to the driver alongside him. "We don't have much time."

In a surprisingly short time, considering the difficult evening traffic, Galdari had the key in the lock and was pushing open the door to the house on N Street. Canfield entered and felt the pleasant rush of cool, dry air. He was glad he had turned down the residence at the Naval Observatory. Some in Congress had raised cain, but there wasn't anything in the Constitution that required him to live on government property. One good thing Amy had done was find this house, and she had fixed it up and furnished it beautifully. Old, solid and functional, with high ceilings and thick walls, it was a quiet retreat for a man who cherished the few hours he had to himself. He had complained about the cost at first, but the house was worth it and more.

The agents went to their command post in the basement, and Canfield walked back to the butler's pantry, where Sigmund Rawlins was polishing silver.

"Evening, Rawlins," Canfield said. "I have to hurry, so I'll change right away. Would you mix a V.O. and water and bring it up?"

The butler rose quickly and went to the sink to wash his hands. "Certainly, Mr. Vice President. I hope you had a good day," he said in a clipped, deferential way. "I'll bring the whiskey directly. Your evening clothes are laid out in your dressing room. I assumed you would want the most conservative ones for the Russians," he went on. "And Miss Dryden called to say that the assignment you left her had been completed as you wished."

"Thank you, Rawlins. Just leave the drink in the dressing room. I'll be in the shower."

He started for the stairs, then hesitated a moment to call back, "I guess you know Mrs. Canfield won't be coming. Let Betsy go home. I won't be needing her tonight." He was referring to the woman who doubled as maid and cook for them in Washington. When the Canfields refused the official residence, they lost the servants that went with it.

"I took the liberty of letting her go when I found out that Mrs. Canfield wouldn't be coming," the butler said, coming to the doorway in time to see his employer's feet disappearing up the stairs.

Canfield had taken a fast shower, run an electric shaver over his face, brushed his teeth and was in the process of slipping his studs in the tuxedo shirt when the intercom rang.

"Yes?" he questioned tersely, a bit unhappy at the interruption.

"It's Secretary Lord, sir," said Galdari. "Do you want me to tell her you'll call back?"

"No, I'll take it," said Canfield, stabbing the proper button. "Hello, Meredith," he said, all traces of irritation having magically disappeared from his voice. "What can I do for you?"

The voice in his ear was dulcet, exciting. "You've already done it, Mr. Vice President," Meredith said. "Virginia Wells just got me out of the tub to tell me I'm to be at the head table. I wanted to thank you for letting me act as your hostess tonight. I'm terribly sorry Mrs. Canfield can't come, but I welcome the chance to be the Vice President's lady for the evening." She laughed softly and, perhaps, provocatively.

He couldn't help visualizing her nude or nearly nude at the phone. "It's a pleasure. I appreciate your accepting the chore, and I'm positive that the foreign minister and the ambassador will enjoy having such a beautiful companion." It suddenly hit him that this could be construed as an indirect slap at his wife, so he added,

"How fortunate those Russians are. Deprived of the mature grace of Amy Canfield, they luck out with the alluring and exotic Meredith Lord." He took a sip of his drink, and the whiskey was warm and satisfying in his stomach.

Meredith laughed again. "Thank you, gracious sir. See you there. . . . Oh, one thing, Mr. Vice President. Could you possibly drop me at Foxhall after the entertainment? My driver has a miserable cold and I'd like to let him go as soon as he takes me to the White House."

"Of course, I'll be glad to take you home." Still entranced by his fantasy of a Meredith freshly out of the tub, Canfield allowed himself a few rather racy thoughts, then quickly suppressed them. "Thank you for calling, Meredith. See you soon." He hung up, pleased and hopeful.

As the cars approached the White House, the Vice President was mildly surprised to see that the demonstrators were out in larger numbers than usual. Nothing like the Vietnam war moratoriums or the recent antipollution marches, of course, but more than he expected. The dissenters had gathered in Lafayette Park. They spilled out onto the north side of Pennsylvania Avenue across from the Executive Mansion. Police barricades kept them from the Blair House area and the sidewalk in front of the White House. Canfield estimated that there were over five hundred people milling around. About thirty were carrying stenciled placards that appeared to have been mass produced. Some of them bore the legend ISRAEL NOW AND FOREVER. Some simply had the acronym INAF. One sign that Canfield caught a quick glimpse of displayed a crude sketch of a warship with a large red star on it and the words GET OUT OF SUEZ.

"That's Yoram Halevy's bunch from New York," he said to Galdari. "They won't cause any serious trouble. Zack Miller showed me a telegram they sent after my Phoenix speech. Very supportive. Zack knows Halevy and says he's quite responsible." In the front seat Galdari started to say something, then changed his mind.

The vice-presidential limousine and the follow-up station wagon slowed, nearing the northwest gate of the Mansion. Across the street the demonstrators were shouting and waving their signs. Four Secret Service men piled hurriedly from the wagon and took posts at the fenders of the Cadillac, running alongside as it pulled into the White House grounds. Once inside, they remounted, and the entourage rode up the stately drive. On each side of the pavement was a platoon of dress-suited marines, who brought their rifles smartly to present arms when the vehicles passed. Near the Portico, a detachment of resplendent buglers waited to sound the arrival of the guest of honor.

"Good evening, Mr. Vice President," Canfield's junior military aide said, opening the car door. "The President will be ready for you in a few minutes. In the meantime, I'll take you to the Red Room."

"Thank you, Major," said Canfield. Then, noticing the smiling White House butler who had come halfway down the white stone steps to greet him, he said, "Evening, Franklin. How're things with you?"

"Just fine, Mr. Vice President. Mrs. Canfield is not with you?" he inquired solicitously.

"Not feeling up to par, Franklin, but nothing serious." Canfield walked up the steps, nodding to press photographers and reporters who were clustered to the side, awaiting Chairman Dradavov.

"Mr. Vice President," called a reporter loudly, "what did you think of the INAF demonstration outside?"

Canfield turned his head toward the voice, but did not slow his pace. "They seemed orderly," he said quickly. "I believe in the First Amendment." With that, he hurried inside and into the Reception Hall.

The marine orchestra stopped playing chamber music for a moment to stand respectfully as the Vice President followed his aide into the Connecting Hall. There was a buzz of conversation to his left. Guests were arriving in substantial numbers, coming from the Diplomatic Reception Room downstairs. Canfield heard the rustle of expensive formal gowns. Beautifully dressed ladies and their escorts came up the marble stairs to the East Room, where cocktails were being served.

Canfield was aware of the eyes upon him. That sudden revealing lull, followed by a slight change in the pitch of the background sounds, told him as clearly as his eyes would have that he was being observed and commented on. He drew himself a little more erect, and his pulse quickened just a fraction. It was good, he thought, to be somebody, and particularly good to be somebody in this house, where so many somebodies had walked.

He had been in the Red Room with Secretary of State Woodhall and his wife but a few minutes when they were told that the President and Mrs. Hurley would receive them in the Yellow Oval Room upstairs. Perhaps it was just as well, thought Canfield.

132

Gordon Woodhall was beginning to probe into the rationale behind his West Coast speeches. One of the principal advocates of détente with the Soviets, Woodhall left little doubt that he saw the Vice President's forays into international diplomacy as amateurish at best and motivated more by personal ambition than statesmanship. Canfield generally didn't care. He considered Gordon Woodhall a political eunuch, a large fish in the pond at Foggy Bottom, but without clout elsewhere. Nevertheless, on this particular question, it wasn't wise to give the secretary of state any ammunition. The President was sensitive enough about the Middle East thing as it was. In the small elevator, Mrs. Woodhall gushed about some Washington social affair, trying to impress Canfield with her society connections. He nodded and smiled, concealing his impatience with difficulty. This frowzy little woman used her husband's office to force herself on the more established families. Amy always said that she had no more breeding than a ribbon clerk at Woody's. Canfield secretly was proud that he had "good blood," but it was poor politics to call attention to it. Damn it all, that was Amy's main problem. How was he to get the votes of the young, the black and the poor if she kept going to all those fancy, and highly restricted Philadelphia parties. The camouflage of the charity tag was not as effective as it used to be. And it wouldn't wash when the Pulitzer-hungry youngsters of the Washington press corps started their intensive sniffing out of new angles on presidential candidates.

At the doorway to the Yellow Oval Room the President greeted them courteously. Some members of the Russian delegation were already in the room, sipping sherry or vodka and toying with the caviar.

The President looked a little more tense than Canfield expected. Hurley was at his best in this kind of entertaining. He always had the proper blend of relaxed graciousness and dignified propriety. Tonight, somehow, he appeared distracted, mildly anxious.

The head-table guests were nearly through with their drinks, and the guest of honor still had not arrived. This was most unusual. Military aides were fidgeting in the hall, and Hurley kept looking up expectantly from his conversation with the Soviet foreign minister.

Canfield was curious. State dinners always ran on a rigid schedule. Where was Dradavov? He moved closer to the President and the foreign minister, hoping to be invited into the conversation. Hurley had noticed him and was about to say something to him, when an aide came up.

"Mr. President, the chairman has left Blair House. He will be at the North Portico in three minutes."

"Fine. Please excuse me, Mr. Minister. Here is the Vice President. I'm sure he would enjoy having a few words with you." The President departed to meet the arriving chairman at his car.

It was hard for Canfield to believe that the heavyset, disheveled man before him represented the most powerful military establishment in the world. This was the tough negotiator who had carved out the big bargains at SALT IV and V in Geneva—the agreements that left the United States at the fork in the road that led to eventual mediocrity.

Foreign Minister Buveney eyed the American Vice President cautiously and said ingratiatingly, "Your excellency, we do not get a chance to talk together. It is unfortunate, no? I fear you have been given some misimpressions of my country."

"It is indeed unfortunate, excellency, that the President has involved me deeply with other matters—principally domestic ones," Canfield said. "But I am sure you know," he continued with a smile, "that I am always a very interested observer of what goes on between our great nations."

"Yes, Mr. Vice President, we are aware of your interest, and we would hope to have a chance—perhaps through our ambassador here—to see that you have the very best information." Buveney looked full in Canfield's eyes in the way that had intimidated many an adversary. "Your recent speech in the West made us very sorry that we were negligent in not being sure you knew about certain important matters."

Canfield did not drop his gaze. "I am always interested in having the best possible information, Mr. Minister," he said gravely. "I will look forward to the opportunity to talk further. However, I must state in all candor that our interests probably will not always coincide."

There was a sudden hush in the room. Chairman Dradavov and Ambassador Rykovskiy and their wives entered with the President. Introductions were rapidly accomplished and the Soviet chairman accepted a glass of sherry. The men in the group gathered about the chairman while Mrs. Hurley took the wives in tow.

"Chairman Dradavov was delayed by a call from his representatives in Geneva," said Hurley with a slight smile. He raised his glass to Dradavov. "I hope that the conversation was encouraging, Mr. Chairman," he continued. "We all have great hopes for SALT Six."

Everyone waited deferentially for Dradavov to speak. This polished, assured, handsome man was the ultimate synthesis of the new Soviet image. The news media commented on his resemblance to Woodrow Wilson, and indeed there was some similarity. Fault-lessly dressed, impeccably mannered, fluent in six languages, Alexi Dradavov was never ill at ease. Put him on a film set with Walter Hurley and Hurley would be cast as the supporting actor. Dradavov had magnetism and presence. He represented a rejection both of the buffoonery of some former Soviet leaders and the diffidence of others. Here was a national figure of dimensions not encountered before in Russia—including Stalin. Stalin was feared and respected; Dradavov was loved and respected.

Canfield sensed the power and the confidence of the man. He hated him for always winning, even though appearing to lose at times. But most of all he resented the way he reduced other men just by being in their presence.

The Soviet chairman touched his lips gently with his napkin. "My conversation with Geneva would encourage anyone whose wish is for world peace, Mr. President," he said with a patronizing smile, "and I assume that includes all responsible individuals in both our countries."

There it was, thought Canfield. The arrogant barb, wrapped in velvet, Alexi Dradavov's trademark. *"Responsible* individuals." The clever insinuation that *he* was responsible even if others were not. The Vice President inwardly fumed. Hurley probably hadn't gotten it. It went right over his head.

Before he could hear the President's response the military aide drew him aside. "The President would like you to go down now, sir, and he requests that you be announced with Secretary of State and Mrs. Woodhall."

Canfield and the Woodhalls walked slowly down the Grand Staircase and into the East Room, where they were announced to the other guests. While the receiving line was being formed, the Vice President looked for Meredith Lord.

There were many beautiful women in the East Room, and they had spared neither effort nor expense to look their very best. Yet Meredith Lord attracted a lion's share of admiring glances from both sexes. She had selected her gown with imagination, shunning the overused cool blue and green pastels. Filmy chiffon of rich chocolate brown touched sparingly with pinpoints of gold in the bodice set off entrancingly her *café au lait* suntan and picked up the golden overtones of her hair and eyes. It was hard to keep in mind that here was the Cabinet secretary of the largest department of the federal government. To the men she was a graceful swirl of femi-ninity; to the women, a beautifully turned out competitor. To Porter Canfield, who had just caught sight of her across the room, she was a forbidden chocolate candy—one he was finding more and more difficult to resist.

Now the trumpeters and flags had preceded the principal actors to the appointed places in the receiving line. There was warm applause from the guests and the handshaking began. The Vice President was first through the line so that he could be in position to meet the Russian visitors in the Red Room. He and the Cabinet officers would entertain them there while the two leaders were completing the reception line and the guests already greeted were being shown to their seats in the State Dining Room.

When Meredith came into the Red Room, Canfield took her aside for a moment. "You look smashing, Madam Secretary," he said. Then he dropped his voice to a conspiratorial level: "You could probably get whatever you want from Charlie Voren tonight."

Meredith gave him an arch look. "Charlie is no longer in charge of my problem," she said mischievously. "How would I do with a Vice President?"

"Very well indeed," replied Canfield fervently, before moving off to find his dinner partner, the Soviet foreign minister's wife.

As the dinner entered the salad course, Canfield sipped his third glass of Château Margaux appreciatively. One good thing about a President's second term, he reflected, was that California wines were not served *all* the time. They were good, but not yet in a class with the best French reds.

The courses came and went. It hadn't been a big evening for table conversation. The foreign minister's wife became uncommunicative after the early amenities. She was probably unsure of her English and afraid of being misunderstood. For the fifth time he turned toward Mrs. Dradavov, but, as before, Hurley was deeply engaged in conversation with her instead of her husband. Canfield told himself that if he were President, he would never let a visiting head of state awe him to the extent that he would deliberately avoid informal table conversation. He suspected that Hurley feared unstructured encounters with the Soviet chairman.

Suddenly there was a swell of music from the hall and the Army Strolling Strings entered and distributed themselves around the room. The Vice President was not a connoisseur of music, nor did he particularly like violins, but the Strings were always a welcome diversion. He enjoyed watching the other guests, some buzzy with wine, hum along with the sentimental songs. Of course, there were always a number who continued talking over the music, exhibiting unbelievable rudeness. Manners were often lacking in the White House. He smiled. That was a direct quote from Amy.

136

Desserts were soon being finished and the champagne was poured. The little microphones were placed in front of Hurley and Dradovov. It was time for the toasts. Canfield could visualize the press outside the dining room with ears cocked and pens ready.

President Hurley stood up. Someone rapped a glass, and the room quickly half-quieted. A pause, then a more insistent rap on the glass made the loquacious remainder reluctantly turn their attention to the head table.

Speaking without notes, Walter Hurley offered the standard welcoming remarks. Then he apologized for the demonstration outside and moved to the usual compliments. The line between deference and obsequiousness is blurred in the habits of international diplomacy, but Canfield felt that others would agree with him that the President went beyond graciousness. At one point he said, "Great credit is owed our predecessors in these high offices, Mr. Chairman, for initiating the personal contacts that brought our nations to accords in principle a decade or more ago. But I must state here that the recent agreements on hard specifics are due in no small measure to the intellect, leadership and courage of one man— Alexi Dradavov—who through singular eloquence and forensic ability has convinced American leaders of the validity of many Soviet positions."

Good God, thought Canfield, he's ready to give the world away. Doesn't the fool know when a show of strength is necessary? The Russians are not only carnivorous, but they hunt for the fun of conquering the weak as well as to keep their bellies full.

When Hurley sat down to enthusiastic applause, Mrs. Dradavov for the first time turned to Canfield. "You have a great President," she said haltingly. "He understands other people and has a broad outlook."

Canfield smiled tightly. "He *is* the President," he said cryptically.

Now it was Dradavov's turn. He stood, then waited, relaxed and impassive, in the quiet room. The quiet became quieter. Even the muted background noises ceased, and an electric excitement seemed to grasp Canfield in spite of his hostility.

"There is Abraham Lincoln," opened the chairman, dramatically pointing at the famous solitary portrait on the wall opposite him. Again he paused a long moment, looking intently at the guests immediately in front of him.

"Lincoln was a great man because he did not think his country was more important than the tranquillity of its citizens," he went on in complete disregard of both logic and history. After another long moment he continued, "Lincoln was not just an American. He was a citizen of the world. What a pity that his global understanding was wasted in a time when it was hardly needed."

Walter Hurley shifted uncomfortably as a tipsy guest applauded to fill the void of another pregnant pause. Others bovinely followed suit until the senseless accolade became an active embarrassment to Canfield. Dradavov raised his hand imperiously.

"We must all try to be like Lincoln," he said, giving his audience a bright smile. "We must resist the chauvinists among us who peddle blind patriotism and distrust of our fellow citizens of the world."

Applause again, more general than before. The chairman sipped his water, still taking his time.

"In the past twelve years, Secretariat-level representatives of the Soviet Union and the United States have met fourteen times. I have met with President Hurley three times before this occasion. The meetings have helped, but they have been too cautious and guarded. Perhaps the next time we meet we will take the view of world citizens and not the selfish views of nationalists. Who knows, Mr. President, down the road may lie a future when the only lines on the map are topographical—when political unanimity guarantees peace and prosperity to every human being. Of course, for now, we must represent our countries. That is a political reality."

Not a single movement or cough disturbed the silence.

"Yes, representing our countries is necessary under the present conditions, but conscience mandates that we do so in a way that best serves the world citizenry. Only then," Dradavov concluded dramatically, "will we preserve the ideals and hopes of humankind."

This from a totalitarian leader?

There was a burst of applause like an explosion. People were on their feet, nodding and talking to one another. In an unprecedented breach of protocol, the toast was forgotten. People stood and continued applauding. Finally, Hurley rose, signaling the end of the dinner. Outside, the press broke for the phones.

Canfield felt a queasiness inside. He was suddenly very much afraid. He could see the headlines: "Dradavov Appeals for a United World." "People First, Flag Second—Dradavov." Why, that glib-talking snake-oil salesman had them in the palm of his hand. What drivel! World citizenship to Dradavov meant that we'd all live under the hammer and sickle. Canfield looked at Hurley, who was nodding and smiling as he led the guest of honor to the Blue Room for coffee and liqueurs. Could he really be so naive as to believe that propaganda? The Vice President hoped not, but he was worried about the softening process going on.

It was a long evening. The women reporters who customarily covered White House social events literally besieged Dradavov in the Blue Room, and the Soviet chairman showed no desire to escape. To the contrary, he did not avail himself of any of the devices provided by Hurley for his disengagement from the press and accepted a second brandy. This, of course, delayed the entertainment which followed and was the primary reason Porter Canfield and Meredith Lord turned into the driveway of her Foxhall apartment at 1:10 A.M.

"Well, let's drop the subject of the clever chairman of the Russians and talk about your troubles with the budget man for a minute," suggested Canfield.

"I'm glad you brought that up," said Meredith. "I know it's late, but could you stop just a minute for a nightcap? There's a memo I'd like to give you to read before you see Charlie Voren. It will help you ask a few questions that probably wouldn't occur to you because you haven't been heavily into THC."

"I'd be glad to have it and whatever other guidance you can give me. And after that marathon, I could use a drink." Canfield lowered the partition to speak to the Secret Service agent next to the driver. "Lee, I'm going to stop a moment to pick up some material at Secretary Lord's apartment."

"Okay, Mr. Vice President. A couple of us will come up and wait by the elevators for you." Lee Daniels, the assistant special agent in charge of the vice-presidential protective detail, was already marked by his superiors for a bright future. The successful product of the period of intensive black recruitment in the Seventies, he was respected and well liked by the other agents. Next to Hurley's top man and Steve Galdari, nearly everyone in Treasury regarded him as the best man in protection.

"All right, Lee. But keep as few as possible in the building. Men loitering in a hallway might frighten a tenant coming in at this hour."

"Just two, sir. But we will need that," Lee said, determined to carry out his mandate.

Inside the apartment, the Vice President waited for Meredith to return from the kitchen with the drinks.

Because Meredith did her official entertaining at the luxurious HEW complex, he'd never seen her home before. It was a comfortable apartment, informal and relaxing, done in oranges and yellows, with rough textures and rya rugs. Not overly feminine—but his idea of what Meredith would do. He doubted that she'd used a decorator.

"Here you are, Mr. Vice President." Meredith handed him his V.O. and water with a dazzling smile—or was he just dazzled more easily lately?

He was glad to see that she hadn't "slipped into something more comfortable." He was excited about being in this intimate setting with a beautiful and desirable woman, but curiously uneasy at the same time. When she let him out, he didn't want the agents to get any ideas.

"I'm sorry about the agents outside, but Daniels has to look for the worst. He probably visualizes a mugger clobbering me in the elevator and the Director chewing him out for leaving me alone."

"Oh, I understand," she said quickly. "Please sit down." She motioned him to an easy chair while she sat on the sofa opposite.

"Those men do a good job," continued Canfield. "They're very professional and try not to get in the way, but if the contest is between privacy and safety, safety wins every time."

Meredith looked at him impishly. "Do you suppose they are wise in trusting me?" With a teasing smile, she added, "After all, *Twiceweek* says your charm and looks will get you more votes from women than any other prospective candidate for President."

"But you forget the scathing letters that the women's rights leaders wrote in response to that article," said Canfield with mock solemnity. " 'Demeaning women's ability to make intelligent judgments on the basis of a candidate's qualifications for office,' I believe they said."

Meredith broke into a full-throated laugh. "Forget the libbers," she advised. "I'll take care of that segment. You just concentrate on the rest of womankind, eighteen to eighty-eight. Besides, a lot of militant women aren't beyond being attracted to men. They just don't want their minds trampled in the process."

"I think they're right about a lot of things," said Canfield. "Equal pay and equal opportunity make good sense. Now let's hear about THC."

Meredith went to a desk and returned with some typewritten papers. "If you'll come sit here beside me a minute, we can go over this together," she said in a businesslike voice, patting the sofa.

He eased himself down on the slubbed center cushion, half-finished drink in hand. "Now don't give me the standard health-care pitch, Dr. Lord. God knows how many meetings I've sat through getting the ABC's of how much better and cheaper it is to keep people well than to wait until they're ill to treat them."

140

"All right, I'll assume you know the basics, but I sure hope you understand them better than the President does." Meredith shook her head in exasperation, remembering an uncomfortable head-to-head with Hurley. "He is always thinking two meetings ahead, so he never really follows your arguments. If Charlie Voren says something is too expensive, forget it. The only way I kept this question alive long enough to get it assigned to you was by recruiting powerful congressional leaders of both parties to pressure the President."

Canfield watched her closely. It was obvious that she was serious about the dispute and also upset about the possibility of losing the battle to Charlie. He put his hand on her arm reassuringly, and was surprised at the tingle that coursed through him.

"Don't give up the fight, Meredith. I promise to give it careful attention, and you can be sure Charlie won't stampede me."

She turned directly toward him, tucking her legs under her in that little-girl way some women never abandon. Reaching out to take his hand, she said gravely, "Back in nineteen seventy-nine, after I helped you with the nomination, you told me I had an I.O.U. and to call if I needed you. Well, I never thought I would have to, but this is it. I want that extra funding for Total Health Care. It's life or death within the department for me. My credibility will be gone if Charlie wins. No one will believe I really tried."

"Meredith, you can be certain I'll do what I can." The Vice President smiled. "Now that you're cashing your chips with me, it really doesn't matter what's in the memo. I'll help."

Meredith's face broke into a smile of relief. "Thank you, Mr. Vice President, but please take the memo and study it. You must be well prepared to handle Voren."

"In situations like this when there's just the two of us, couldn't we forget the formal title and just make it Newt—the way it was that last night at Minneapolis?"

He squeezed her hand gently and took the papers from her. "Remember how you and I and Zack and Myrna sat in that little Italian restaurant and savored the victory until three A.M.—drinking Valpolicella until we were groggy?"

"Of course I remember."

"Then, just as I was about to take you back to the hotel, along came my new protectors, the intrepid Secret Service, and took over the custody of my body. That's one intrusion I've always resented."

The girl looked deep in his eyes and said, "In a way it was a relief for us both. Caught in the euphoria of the moment, we might have forgotten very important things—things like you're a married man.''

She stood up suddenly and pulled him to his feet. ''It's one-forty, sir, and time for you to join your trusty companions at the elevator,'' she said lightly. ''Thank you for bringing me home and even more for helping me.''

For several seconds they faced each other silently—and he wondered whether to embrace her. Then the moment passed, leaving only an awkward confrontation.

Canfield reached out whimsically and chucked her lightly under the chin. ''Good night, Meredith. Sleep well,'' he said.

5

THERE IS no greater insurance of privacy than the coupling of wealth with the ownership of a powerful news organ. The money insures remoteness and insulation. The control of snoops guarantees that they will not snoop on you. Mark O'Mara, publisher of the *Washington Globe,* met both criteria. It was a good thing that he did because he considered his personal privacy only slightly less sacred than the First Amendment. Moreover he had a notoriously low boiling point. Had he been subjected to the treatment routinely dished out by his hungry young muckrakers, the result would have been apoplexy or mayhem, or both.

Killarney, the magnificent sixty-acre O'Mara estate high above the Potomac, was only fifty minutes from the *Globe* offices in downtown Washington. Access was from MacArthur Boulevard on the Maryland side. Most of the fifteen acres of lawn were at the rear of the palatial twenty-room colonial mansion. There was a high stone wall along MacArthur Boulevard with a massive iron gate, electronically operated, opening to a long, treelined private drive. Running all the way back to the Potomac on each side boundary was a ten-foot-high chain-link fence with barbed wire along the top. The fences were screened from view by dense woods. After several recent burglaries in the area, O'Mara had purchased two Doberman pinschers. The dogs were specially trained and roamed the property after dark.

The O'Maras had acquired the renovated 1802 mansion from the estate of a Washington stockbroker only ten years before. Mark's chain of newspapers had flourished. The *Globe*, the jewel that he had always wanted, gave him power and gave Didi, a force in St. Louis society, the social "in" to the homes of Washington's political and diplomatic giants. They were overjoyed when a quiet stock corner was successful and the O'Mara organization took control. Didi found the house, and they moved immediately. Those years were happy ones. Mark moved the pawns, and the effervescent, gracious Didi was recognized as the premier hostess on the Washington scene.

Mark O'Mara's party affiliation was immaterial, for he had long ago been gelded by self-interest. He was simply a liberal. He had made his money in the newspaper business by favoring the "outs" against the "ins." Change and reform sold papers, and if the change was not good, then there was always another change. He was for "the people," that unspecified mass of humanity that always wanted what Mark O'Mara wanted. The bright politicians understood. The stupid ones had ideas of their own. O'Mara really enjoyed exposing their stupidity. And what if their images resisted casting them as Neanderthal? He could always brand them evil and corrupt. Sooner or later, he would emasculate them. "Operation Torch" rarely failed. That was a half-joking code name that he and his big-media associates used to describe the powerful focus of network television, news magazines, wire services and the New York-Washington newspaper axis. With the collective and continuing impact that they had every day on sixty million Americans, no politician could survive their wrath. The plain truth was that they had a much greater effect on foreign and domestic policy than any member of Congress.

One day during the week before Vice President Canfield's projected trip to the Far East, the squire of Killarney was relaxing with friends in the pastoral setting of his estate.

The early summer evening brought the magic of soft reds to the setting sun, transforming the western sky into an incredibly beautiful multilayering of blue, green and pink pastels. The single stately oak that had been allowed to remain close to the fieldstone patio cast a faint shadow across the four people in the comfortable wicker chairs. Below them the Potomac, jeweled here and there by the tangential light, wound its lazy way toward Washington.

Fresh from the six o'clock news, TBS anchorman Bradley Barton looked confident and relaxed in a tan cashmere jacket. He turned away from the hypnotic lulling of the river, gently shook the ice cubes in his drink and smiled at the editor of *Twiceweek* magazine.

Karen Rankin was quite attractive and unusually youthful for her forty-one years. Tennis kept her boyish figure trim, and the oversized eyeglasses gave her almost-pretty face an alert-schoolteacher look. She was sipping an obscure Spanish sherry she had found in Barcelona. She refused to drink anything else and insisted on having her chauffeur deliver a bottle in advance to any social function she attended. This was considered odd by her associates, particularly since the wine tasted like weak paregoric, but it was tolerated as just another eccentricity on the part of a woman who definitely relished being different.

"Did you catch our interview with Roland Gray tonight? Doug Drake caught him coming from a secret lunch with the speaker in one of those very private rooms in the Capitol." Barton's tone implied that discovering the Senate majority leader and the speaker of the House at such a luncheon was like finding Oral Roberts in a porno shop.

Karen Rankin put her glass down on the white metal table and looked disapprovingly at the television anchorman. "You know, Bradley, that I never watch your mobile crews. Your young people are so embarrassing. They're either vapid or boorish. In either case, they're performing more than seeking information. It's all I can stomach to read the transcripts the next day."

Barton was unaffected by the opprobrium, having heard it all many times before.

"Well, I know Didi and Mark heard it, and regardless of your opinion of Doug Drake, he did a hell of a good job on Gray—teased him about whether he was looking for the speaker to help him put the brakes on the Vice President. Then Doug baited him about the recent surge in Canfield's popularity and all the good press comment the Israel position is getting the Vice President.

"Believe me, he got old Roland hot under the collar. Then he asked whether Gray wasn't contributing to party disunity by snubbing Canfield at Phoenix. The senator said that the greatest threat to party unity was self-serving ambition and that his intention was to remain loyal to the President. Doug then asked him whether he meant that Canfield was self-serving and disloyal. Gray turned livid—said the question was not in good taste, and walked off in a huff. It was beautiful, just beautiful."

Karen Rankin laughed. She turned toward the O'Maras, who had been silently taking in her reactions, and said, "It sounds to me like Douglas Drake got a mite boorish, the way Brad tells it. What did you think, Didi?"

O'Mara frowned his disapproval at her for directing the question to his wife. For one thing, he was the expert, but that wasn't all. Ms. Rankin was too damn interested in Didi. "I know Didi feels the same as I do about that, Karen," he quickly interjected without waiting for Didi to respond. "Doug Drake's still inexperienced, but he's not a clod, nor is he vapid. Of course, he's not a master like Brad, but who is? Tonight he did a professional job on Senator Gray."

"Okay, Mark. I'll take your word for it. But the real tough digging to expose political phonies is done by the print people, not television."

Karen edged a look at Barton, who was still basking in the sun of the O'Mara compliment. Secretly she considered him a conceited ass and an aging stud who kept trying, according to rumor, but publicly they had to get along—consolidation of power for the common good.

Bradley Barton said good-naturedly, "You print people are great. Basically, we pilfer your ideas, but you need us, too. It's damn persuasive when the public actually *sees* the reaction of a person rather than just reading a description of it." He saluted her gravely. "Bouquets to the tough but lovely editor of *Twiceweek*; and many thanks to our host and hostess for arranging this opportunity to examine the Porter Canfields closely."

"I'm glad you recognize our worth, Brad," said Karen. "So many of your associates don't."

Barton did not continue the argument.

The shadows were deepening when the young black man came around the side of the house and approached O'Mara.

"Pardon me, Mr. O'Mara, but the Vice President and Mrs. Canfield are only three minutes away. I thought you might like to greet them at the car." Without waiting for a reply, Lee Daniels trotted back toward the front of the house. After a moment O'Mara followed him.

"It's getting dark. We may as well all go inside," said Didi. Walking through the house to the huge living room, she told Karen Rankin that it was wonderful to see qualified Negroes in the Secret Service. And they were so—so much more polite than some of the white policemen who ordered you around.

The heavy Cadillac swung slowly around the circle and stopped at the steps. Mark O'Mara escorted the Canfields into the reception hall.

"What a beautiful home," said Amy Canfield, looking into the magnificent paneled library. "And what an unusual desk! It's so big, and you have to step down to sit at it."

"I spend a lot of time in the library," replied O'Mara, pleased at the compliment. "It's my refuge from Didi when I need to be alone to think. But come and meet our dinner guests. I'll show you the house later if you're interested."

He led them to the living room, where Didi was waiting at the doorway.

Porter Canfield paid little attention to his surroundings or to the routine amenities of his host. He was going over in his mind the subjects he wished to touch on during the coming conversation and the likely impact of his views on those present. O'Mara, Barton and Rankin were not only powerful influences within their own large organizations but were acknowledged leaders in the entire big-media community. The verdict they reached about Porter Canfield would be multiplied in its effect and projected across the nation by thousands of feature articles, radio news items, talk shows and television analyses. Details were not important. What they sought was visceral, not intellectual. The image was everything. The key words that turned them on—compassionate, humanitarian, youth, minority, education, health, poor, freedom, opportunity, counter-culture, quality of life, overreact, dialogue, third world and mean-ingful, that most meaningless of the code words—must be used in abundance. On the other hand, it could be dangerous to use words like military, police, law and order, competitive, radical, earn, business, profit, balance, military-industrial complex, strength, suburban and middle class unless they were carefully qualified.

Of course, he was there to accent the positive, to place the emphasis on what these influential opinion-makers wanted to hear. He wanted to make them feel he was in fundamental agreement with their ideas, but to do so in a way that did not seem obsequious. He had found that a good technique was to state a noncontroversial point in a firm, challenging way, as though he expected disagree-ment but was too honest to care. His objective was to charm the pants off all of them. The general procedure was simple—make them feel he considered them the most intelligent, witty, important and attractive people in Washington. It wouldn't be hard. They already felt that way about themselves.

Canfield watched the constant movement of Amy's head as she took in everything in the beautifully done high-beamed room. Her love of things rather than people was bothering him more and more.

Again he thought of Meredith Lord, who had been on his mind all day. She was so much less materialistic. The meeting that morning at his office had confirmed his earlier impressions. She was interested and wanted him to go further. And it was very physical. The moment they had stood together looking at the map left no doubt of that. It happened so quickly: a touch of shoulders and she was in his arms. Their kiss left him literally aching. Meredith had handled the potentially awkward aftermath so well.

"It had to happen, Newt, and I'm glad," she said. Then looking into his eyes, she added, "Let's not worry about anything—just let go the reins and relax."

He had not admitted that the intensity of his feeling frightened him. "Letting go the reins may be dangerous advice, Meredith. I have a feeling that this horse wants to run," he replied lightly. Well, it was true, all right. The horse was already at a gallop. He could feel the hoofbeats in his chest just thinking about it.

Barton rose slowly to his feet with a nonchalance that announced to the world that he was far too sophisticated to be impressed by any living individual. "Good evening, Mr. Vice President," he said in the sincere-sounding voice that enraptured thirty millions viewers each night.

With a catlike smile at Amy, Karen Rankin said, "And what a pleasure to see Mrs. Canfield with you." The remark clearly implied that Amy's presence at such gatherings was unusual.

Amy eyed the seated woman, who gave no sign of rising. "Please don't get up, Miss Rankin," she said, throwing out her hand as though attempting to restrain a courtesy in progress. She smiled warmly at Barton. "The Vice President and I are delighted that Mr. and Mrs. O'Mara gave us this wonderful opportunity to learn more about our news-media celebrities, sir," she said.

Barton laughed. She's really quite attractive, he thought. He said, "Messengers are not very interesting, Mrs. Canfield, especially when the world is waiting for the message. What we want to hear are words of wisdom from the Vice President so we can help relay them to the American people. They are, I assure you, most interested in Porter Canfield."

Canfield glanced quizzically at Mark O'Mara, then back at Barton. "I thought this was to be a backgrounder and off the record."

"That's exactly right, Mr. Vice President. Brad didn't mean that you'd be quoted. Whatever information we use will appear attributed to 'close friends,' 'associates' or the like. I assure you that you will not be embarrassed. We want you to be as frank as possible."

Barton nodded his agreement, and Karen Rankin, still steaming over Amy Canfield's sarcasm, said with a trace of acid in her voice, "We're pros, Mr. Vice President. We understand that the President would not appreciate candor from you. And, regardless of what some people think, we have better manners than to embarrass a

148

guest in the home of our colleague.'' She did not look at Amy.

"That's entirely satisfactory, of course, but please don't get the impression that I don't speak candidly with the President. However, I see no reason to arm our opponents. They would misconstrue my remarks to create a fight between us.''

Didi O'Mara led them to a grouping of comfortable armchairs, and the butler took their drink orders. Amy kept looking around the room. "You're done a wonderful job of furnishing and decorating this house, Mrs. O'Mara,'' she said. "That painting is marvelous. Is it a Monet?''

"I wish it were,'' laughed Didi. "Monets are hard to find. That is a Childe Hassam. He is my favorite American impressionist.''

"Hassams are also hard to find. And art dealers extract the last pound of flesh for them,'' said Amy, enjoying the chance to move into areas where Karen Rankin had no superior knowledge. "Father had two Hassams in our home in Philadelphia. Unfortunately for us children, he has made an *intervivos* gift of them to the museum. He knows very well that three children would not agree on a division at his death, so he saved us that anguish.''

Didi grinned mischievously. "We had a similar problem in our family,'' she began. Mark O'Mara held up a hand in good-humored protest.

"Ladies, please! This gathering is social, but it has a more mundane purpose than a discussion of great artists.'' He favored the Vice President with a conspiratorial smile. "Our guest of honor is actively engaged in a baser art, and we want to learn the fascinating details of what he is plotting for the future— Please excuse me, Mr. Vice President, but news people are always honest.''

Canfield betrayed none of the irritation that he felt. "No apology necessary, Mr. O'Mara,'' he said jovially. "Politics *is* a baser art than painting. But every business, every profession, has its practitioners of politics. Politics is not confined to government. I would daresay that even the *Globe,* TBS and *Twiceweek* nurture political types occasionally.''

"Well, we've never had a Watergate,'' ventured Karen Rankin snidely.

"Not even a Bay of Pigs,'' laughed Bradley Barton. "So our politics must be of a gentle sort.''

Canfield faked another grin. How about an invasion of Haiti, he thought. Luck was all that saved a real mess there. He said nothing, however, and shifted in his chair. Best to let them think he was burdened with guilt over the real or imagined sins of every officeholder since George Washington. They really made it tough to be friendly. Hell, he agreed with them on foreign policy and the objectives of helping the young, the black and the poor. Why did they always have to cram their angelic attitude down your throat? They were hypocrites of an advanced breed, but hypocrites he needed to get to the presidency.

After an awkward pause, Didi proved she was the only one present with the compassion and sensitivity the others espoused. "I intend to be silent so the experts assembled can educate me," she announced, "but I do wish they'd get started."

There was a brief stir. Magically the small gathering was transformed into a session of "Meet the Nation."

"Mr. Vice President, why do you believe Israel should be given IRBM's? Isn't that a dangerous provocation of the Soviet Union?"

"Ms. Rankin, I've given long and serious study to the question. History has shown that Israeli leadership is responsible, compassionate and conservative. Defense-minded you might say. Now, my opponents don't agree with that conclusion. They point to the territories Israel has occupied since the nineteen-sixty-seven war. They call that aggression and there I disagree with them. The attacks were responsive, mainly. In the few cases where Israel seized the initiative, Lebanon, for example, the actions were pre-emptive in nature. Israel continues to hold those territories along the borders because of the threat of invasion. It's a matter of using geography to protect yourself."

Karen Rankin, who agreed entirely, pressed for total commitment. "But why IRBM's? The Israelis are doing very well with the weapons we've already made available to them."

"Because all the information I have been able to gather indicates that the Soviets are supplying the militant Arab nations with offensive weapons of a highly sophisticated nature."

"What kind of weapons—"

"I'm not at liberty to divulge the exact details, but I can say that they are weapons of frightening capability. Moreover, the information is persuasive to me because the Israelis themselves are convinced, and you know they have one of the finest intelligence organizations in the world."

Karen Rankin settled back in her chair like a lawyer who has successfully gotten the necessary information from her client on direct examination.

"What kind of reaction have you had from the American people about your outright advocacy of greater military assistance for Israel?" asked Bradley Barton.

"An excellent reaction. My mail on the subject is running seventy-four percent favorable." The Vice President added earnestly, "But more important than that, my posture has given reassurance and hope to hundreds of humanitarian Jewish organizations which felt that our country was reluctant to state the full implications of its foreign policy on this question—very responsible organizations of impeccable credentials."

"How about those Zionist organizations that have not always acted with restraint—those which have openly advocated a more militant policy for Israel. Have you heard from them?" Barton asked dramatically.

The Vice President summoned up his most statesmanlike expression. "I know the groups to which you probably refer, Mr. Barton," he said slowly. "Yes, I have heard from some of them, and they have discussed the matter with me in a most forthright and constructive fashion. I take the position that these people would be less volatile, and certainly a great deal less dangerous to the public peace, if we would talk more with them—if we would open a dialogue with them concerning their apprehensions and aspirations. I have tried to do just this. Particularly with a group known as 'Israel Now and Forever,' which functions under the leadership of a man named Yoram Halevy in New York."

"I've heard of them," said O'Mara. "They are quite militant, and they have been involved in numerous demonstrations. I think they were active in the crowd that protested the Dradavov appearance at the White House."

"I've checked them out carefully," said the Vice President, "and I don't find any evidence that they have ever acted in a violent manner. They do represent elements of the so-called counterculture, but that is not in itself objectionable given today's standards. Now, understand that I don't subscribe to everything they advocate or do. However, I think they have a right under the First Amendment—which we all cherish—to have their say and to dramatize their protest."

Canfield could barely resist striking a somewhat theatrical pose as he delivered these words of reassurance to the guardians of the Constitution.

"Hear, hear," said Bradley Barton. "It's good to know that we have a strong voice in such a high position who understands the critical need for freedom of speech. It seems that every week some disgruntled politician tries to blame the media for disclosing information about his activities which the public has the right to know."

Mark O'Mara leaned forward, looking around at his associates.

This signified that he was about to ask a very profound question, and they had best listen carefully.

"How are you getting along with President Hurley these days, Mr. Vice President? I don't imagine that he is particularly happy about your recent speeches, which go beyond what he is willing to say about Middle Eastern policy."

There was general nervous laughter, as though someone had exposed a dirty cartoon. It quickly subsided once the Vice President began to speak.

"The President has not talked with me about it, not personally. However, I would be less than frank if I tried to leave the impression that I have not been made aware of his feelings."

Karen Rankin and Mark O'Mara exchanged nods, as though in confirmation of a previously reached conclusion. Canfield continued. "It has been my position, and I have stated that position clearly to the traveling press, that my advocacy of IRBM's for Israel is merely a logical construction of what is inherent in existing presidential policy. Apparently, President Hurley does not wish to define his policy quite that precisely."

A chorus of exclamatory sounds from his listeners caused Canfield to tilt his chin back courageously before continuing. "To me, the situation is serious enough to require that I take the risk of displeasing some to make the American people aware of my concerns. A small nation, a bastion of freedom, is in grave danger should the United States be irresolute in defending her."

"Nicely said, Mr. Vice President. Does that mean that the President in effect sent you a message to please be quiet about the issue?" Karen Rankin directed a cold little smile at Amy, as if to indicate that she would not stand for any equivocation.

"I'm going to answer your question, Ms. Rankin," said the Vice President, "but I want to remind you that there are ground rules to this interview and that I am giving you this answer in total reliance on your assurances that I will not be directly quoted." He looked from face to face, waiting in each instance until he had received assent. "All right, then. You are correct in that conclusion."

He smiled faintly and gave a little sigh. "I guess I should have known better than to hope that your question would refer only to direct presidential contact. When one is dealing with sharp, experienced people like yourselves, one really can't get away with anything. On the road with the average reporter, perhaps, but certainly not with executives in the news business."

"How did he get the word to you?" asked Mark O'Mara.

"In a way that did not exactly massage my ego. He sent Joshua

Devers to my office this morning to convey his personal apprehensions about my statements and in substance to suggest that I return to more vice-presidential pursuits. The vice-presidency has never involved the exercise of power, you understand, but I told Mr. Devers my obligations to the American people would not permit me to remain silent on such a crucial issue. I explained to him that I wanted to be loyal to President Hurley in every way possible, but that ignoring severe danger to my country was not one of the ways."

Karen Rankin looked incredulous. "Severe danger, Mr. Vice President? Isn't that laying it on a little thick? Even if Israel were exterminated, I would not characterize the resulting situation as one involving immediate *severe* danger to the United States."

Canfield smiled patiently. "The question is when does severe danger exist? I did not say immediate, but I will accept the hypothesis that severity involves immediacy. In any event, the technology of today allows for very little reaction time. I would have to say that the loss of Israel on top of our recent weaknesses in that area could easily constitute an immediate and severe danger to the United States."

"You mean that the Russians might attack us if they were successful in destroying Israel?" asked Bradley Barton.

"No, that's not the way that I envisage the problem arising. I believe it would be more likely that American opinion would force the United States into an active confrontation should Israel be attacked. Furthermore, I believe it entirely plausible that Israel would be attacked should we be timid about acting in her defense."

"Good God," said Mark O'Mara. "You've given us some frightening ideas to chew on."

Karen Rankin waited impatiently for the passing of the few moments of respectful silence due O'Mara's somber pronouncement before she said, "Matters of foreign policy are a mystery to most *Twiceweek* readers. They enjoy following the personalities, but the issues are generally too complex and too far removed. Could we, gentlemen, turn Mr. Canfield's attention to more immediate matters?"

Hearing no dissent she went on. "Mr. Vice President, when will you announce your candidacy for President of the United States?"

Canfield chuckled disarmingly. "I am examining the possibility of running, Ms. Rankin, but am nowhere near a conclusion yet." He became serious. "I will be frank with you. Many of my friends and many leaders in my party want me to run. But broad-based support outside the party is an absolute necessity. I'm not sure yet whether that support exists. I must be sure that it does before I enter any contest with others in my party for the nomination.'' He looked down at his shoes, then said modestly, ''It's such a big job. Perhaps too big for any mortal.''

To Karen Rankin, this disingenuous response was an appropriate part of a familiar catechism. She would have been surprised at any other answer. Nevertheless, she continued the game. ''Too big for President Hurley?'' she asked, raising her eyebrows in mock surprise.

''Perhaps too big for Washington, and for Jefferson, and for Lincoln, and F.D.R., too,'' Canfield said. ''Please don't let it appear that I think President Hurley unable to do the job,'' he added quickly. ''After all, I am part of his administration.''

''But be frank, Mr. Vice President,'' the tenacious woman said, ignoring obvious indications that the others wanted to participate in the interrogation. ''Your views would require you to pursue a different course—a fundamentally different course, not just in foreign policy—if you were President. Isn't that so?''

''Of course the President and I have differences of opinion, Ms. Rankin. That's historically normal. It would serve no useful purpose to enlarge on those differences at this time.''

Karen continued probing. ''But Senator Gray does not seem to have differences with the President, does he?''

Bradley Barton, who was lighting his pipe, exclaimed between puffs, ''It's certainly not our purpose to cause any problems between you and the President, sir. I fully understand why you can't give us a laundry list of differences. What Karen was getting to, I believe, was something much more general—the broad philosophical distinctions between your thinking and President Hurley's.'' He took his pipe away from his face to focus a friendly, empathetic look at Canfield. ''Presidents, especially strong Presidents, are not predictable on every issue, but we need to understand what kind of men they are—their general beliefs and goals. For example, are you, Mr. Vice President, a Madison or a Franklin Roosevelt? They were both great Presidents. In the eyes of historians, Madison was perhaps the greater, but in the eyes of the people Roosevelt had no peer. Their differences result from, I believe, a basic difference in philosophy. Madison acted for the future, and Roosevelt for the present. How will you act, sir?''

Canfield touched his upper lip with his tongue. History was not his forte, and he had no desire to exhume old Presidents for detailed discussion. However, a comparison with Roosevelt, could be useful. He was about to begin a carefully phrased reply when Amy startled him by suddenly entering the conversation.

"James Madison was a great President, but Franklin Roosevelt was an opportunist—a genius at political huckstering with a large ego and no talent for government. He lucked his way through a depression and a war." Amy had been a history major. Moreover, her father had hated F.D.R. with the cold passion of an established financier. "Madison was brilliant," she said aggressively. "He didn't try to buy popularity with the federal dollar. He invested those dollars in the future of America. Look at—"

"I don't agree with that, Amy," cut in Porter Canfield with a cold smile. He composed himself with difficulty, and his face softened. "I'm proud that you have strong opinions, dear, but I suggest that I answer these questions." He laughed indulgently. "That is, unless you are thinking about following Ms. Rankin's advice that more women should seek high public office."

"Don't get Karen started on that," Mark O'Mara teased, but there was an undercurrent of malice in his voice. "I think she's for unisex, so long as it's all women."

"Please, Mark. This is a serious discussion." Didi O'Mara sounded a little jumpy to her husband. Could there be something to his vague worry that his wife was getting too friendly with this woman?

"I think Mr. Barton's question was a good one," Canfield said, grateful that the interplay had given him additional time to prepare an answer. "The American people need a Roosevelt more than a Madison right now. Events happen so quickly. The speed generated by our technology will not permit us to neglect the present for the future. We must meet today's problems today. Tomorrow may be too late. Our civilization can be extinguished by the pressure of a finger on a button." He raised his voice slightly to override an interruption by O'Mara.

"If I may just finish this thought, please. My party could use a Roosevelt. Bold, new actions are needed to help the poor and the minority groups. We provide token assistance and great promises, but they need money, not speeches. New legislation to give the poor a fair break in health care is one must, for example. Just the other day, Secretary Lord sought my assistance for Total Health Care. We must put our shoulders to the wheel—reduce waste in high places—so the people will know their needs are getting attention."

"Where would you get the money for these worthy but very expensive ideas, Mr. Vice President?" said Karen Rankin. "You're talking about billions. There are only two ways you could get billions, either by drastically cutting the defense budget or by heavy additional taxation. The way you're talking about Israel's

155

defense, it doesn't sound like you want to cut military spending. Does that indicate new taxes on the rich?''

Canfield smelled a trap. They needed to be assured that all their social objectives could be achieved but not at a heavy price to their businesses or themselves. It wouldn't be easy—it wouldn't make sense—but they would believe because they wanted to believe.

"There is an answer, and the penalties are not unduly onerous for any of our citizens,'' he said. "First, we must cut down waste in the government, reduce the size of the bureaucracy. Second, we must tax high-profit businesses, the ones that enjoy special exemptions or subsidies gained through years of skillful lobbying, such as the oil industry and the commodity exporters, and the military-industrialists. Third, we must cut down the advantages of big labor. Many of the benefits they negotiate wind up in the hands of a few labor politicians instead of the workers'. Finally, we can substantially reduce the defense budget without affecting our national security or our ability to safeguard freedom in the world. We can do it by selective emphasis in certain areas. We can close unneeded installations and consolidate our defenses at a much reduced cost. And we won't lose any appreciable strength by pulling into a smaller perimeter.''

This recitation was received with nods of agreement. Canfield was delighted. They *did* want to believe that it could be done—that all their do-gooder impulses could be satisfied without any cost to themselves. Well, if he got there, he would tax them, just as Roosevelt had taxed them. They had apparently forgotten the New Deal.

Luckily for the Vice President, any further examination of his banalities was averted by the entrance of the butler, who informed Didi O'Mara that dinner was ready to be served. As the small group made its way into the candlelit dining room, Canfield found a private moment to whisper to Amy, "Don't be disagreeable. We're here to make friends, not to prove points.'' She gave him her stubborn-little-girl look.

Canfield was seated to his hostess's right, and next to Karen Rankin. Across the table, Amy was between Mark O'Mara and Bradley Barton. Didi directed the dinner conversation into less formal channels, and throughout the dinner they bounced lightly through an assortment of small talk.

They were lingering over champagne and dessert and enjoying the sense of well-being engendered by an excellent meal and comfortable surroundings, when the sudden frantic barking of the dogs broke the tranquillity. Mark O'Mara paused with his wine glass halfway to his lips. "I've never heard the dogs carry on like that," he said. He slipped out of his chair. "Be right back. I'll just get Silas to take a look." A few minutes later he returned. "Silas has gone to check," he said.

"Do you let the dogs run at night? If you do, I'm not going outside without you," laughed Canfield. "They certainly sound formidable."

"Don't worry, Mr. Vice President," said Didi. "They are penned now. Silas won't release them until our guests are safely on their way home. Yes, we do let them run. We're pretty isolated out here, and they give us a great sense of security at night."

"If you think you need security here, you should live near Capitol Hill," Karen Rankin said. "I have a friend who has been burglarized five times in the past year. She was just lucky that she wasn't home on any of those occasions."

"I just have a terrible fear of being raped by a black man," said Amy Canfield, producing with the remark an instantaneous and embarrassing silence. Bradley Barton looked at his plate.

"Does that mean you would not object to a white rapist, Mrs. Canfield?" Karen Rankin asked sarcastically.

"Of course not," replied Amy, beginning to steam a little. "Everyone has a fear fantasy, and that just happens to be mine."

Bradley Barton looked troubled. "We've been fighting those illusions about the black community for years," he said. "It does no good to perpetuate them, even in fantasy."

"Well, I didn't expect everyone to get so uptight about it," Amy said. "It was just a private observation."

Bradley Barton sadly shook his handsome head in dismay. "Unfortunately, black people live in a world of *unconscious* prejudice," he observed, still looking at his plate. "It's not the hostility of the ignorant that drives them to crime and violence so much as the *thoughtless* prejudice that we all display now and then."

Canfield slid quickly into the opening. "I couldn't agree more, Mr. Barton," he said earnestly. Looking at Mark O'Mara, he said, "I want to congratulate the *Globe* for its years of courageous editorializing on the subject." His glance swung to Rankin. "And *Twiceweek* for its quota hiring policy and its consistently staunch defense of underprivileged black people."

The Vice President's praise had hit its mark.

"We must carry on the responsibilities of a free press, whatever the dangers," said O'Mara pompously. Canfield noted how O'Mara overlooked the fact that 80 percent of his circulation was black and 60 percent of his advertisers catered to black interests—so

157

that it took no courage at all to stroke them.

Karen Rankin regarded Canfield with new respect. "I'm really glad you understand the problem, Mr. Vice President. So few do. So much more remains to be done to overcome the decades of exploitation and the environmental handicaps that have warped and retarded black development."

"Exactly right," said the Vice President. "Rehabilitation for those who were forced into crime through their environment. Quota admissions for those who find themselves unprepared for college because of the deficiencies of segregated schools and poor home conditions for studying. Day care for working mothers and increased aid for dependent children. More food stamps, and controls over the bureaucracy to prevent snooping and other computerized invasions of privacy. More encouragement for the black and Puerto Rican disadvantaged to run candidates for office, waiving the standard requirements."

They sat enraptured. Canfield would have continued had not Amy said in a small, emotionless voice, "What about effort and ability and achievement—are they to be obliterated by all these compensating devices to mask mediocrity?"

"Not to mask mediocrity, Amy," Canfield answered grimly. "To encourage talent and remove the suffocating hood of discrimination."

Bradley Barton examined Amy through a cloud of pipe smoke, as though discovering her for the first time. "Mrs. Canfield," he said sorrowfully, "you don't seem to understand."

Amy thought angrily, There it is, the liberal cant. The escape hatch for editorial writers over their heads in a subject they know nothing about, the visceral avoidance of intellectual debate. Clothes for the emperor. She was furious. If ever she needed a reason for avoiding Washington society, this was it. At least her friends in Philadelphia were honest in their wealth and selfishness. She was about to force the issue, when she caught her husband's eye. Never had she seen such a threatening expression on his face.

"I don't want to keep our distinguished guests out too late, and I know the Vice President would not curtail our questioning," Mark O'Mara said, changing the subject. "So, I will not impose further on his generosity in speaking so frankly to us. Mr. Vice President, we were delighted to have you. I think the evening was enlightening for us and highly successful for you. You may stay as long as you wish, but the questions are declared ended."

As they wandered back to the living room, Karen Rankin took Canfield's arm and led him aside. "You were terrific, Mr. Vice

President. I'm really impressed. More newspeople should get to know you better. I think you're the kind of candidate *Twiceweek* has been searching for.''

"Thank you, Ms. Rankin. I assure you I will remain active in the support of those issues I spoke about.''

"Please do, especially about the minorities—all minorities.''

Bradley Barton, sipping a large brandy, descended upon them. "Good night, my Vice President," he said jovially. "A bravura performance, sir, I must say.''

After a brief tour of the house, the O'Maras saw the Vice President and Mrs. Canfield to their limousine and waved as the big car, followed by the Secret Service station wagon, pulled away from the house.

Canfield hardly heard the excited barking of the Dobermans. He was too busy preparing the lecture he would deliver to Amy when they were in the privacy of their bedroom. Thank God, he mused, gratified at the general outcome of the evening, I pulled it out of the fire in spite of her.

6

THE HANDS of the great clock in the rear of the chamber jumped into upright alignment, and the bell rang loudly, announcing that the noon hour had arrived. Vice President Porter Canfield, accompanied by the chaplain, stepped smartly through the lobby door. They moved together to the edge of the dais, where the Vice President stopped while the man of God mounted three steps to the rostrum and stood facing the nearly empty chamber. Canfield rapped once with the ivory gavel. The galleries, well filled with students on vacation and other summer tourists, hushed.

"The Senate will be in order," said the Vice President. "The chaplain will offer the opening prayer."

The brief invocation completed, Canfield assumed the Chair and nodded greetings to the parliamentarian and clerks, who were seating themselves in the tiers immediately below him. At that point he became the presiding officer of what has been called the world's greatest deliberative body. While in the Chair, he would be "Mr. President," and the business of the Senate would swirl about him, mocking him in his constitutional impotence to participate in either discussions or determinations—except to break a rare tie vote. His rulings would be in accordance with the Senate's rules, which were the Senate's wishes, which were nearly always the majority leader's wishes—which were Roland Gray's wishes. Should he rebel by construing a rule against the will of the Senate, the rule could easily be suspended by "unanimous consent"—the magic incantation with which the chief wizard, Roland Gray, directed the proceedings to suit the Senate.

The peculiar clubbishness of the Senate did not extend to Vice Presidents, not even when they were originally of the Senate. Vice Presidents belonged at the other end of Pennsylvania Avenue; they were part of the executive branch, dedicated to the extension of presidential power and, hence, not to be accepted fully into the brotherhood. Was it any wonder that most Vice Presidents spent as little time as possible discharging their ceremonial duty? It was not enough to be treated with courtesy when one was left out of the game and even out of the locker-room strategy sessions.

Porter Canfield was attending this session for two reasons. First, he needed some time in the Chair to avoid a spate of stories criticizing him for shirking his only constitutional duty; and second, his friend, Stanley Bedson, the junior senator from California, had tipped him off that Roland Gray was going to make a short speech supporting President Hurley's foreign policy. Few senators would be in the chamber to hear it, but the press and spectators would. Josh Devers wanted it because the statement would be printed in the *Congressional Record* and widely reported. It would be recognized for what it was—a public put-down of Canfield's Israel initiative.

"Mr. President!"

Canfield took his good time adjusting his notes before looking out at the majority leader. "The senator from Arizona," he said finally.

"Mr. President, I ask unanimous consent that the reading of the journal of the proceedings of the previous day be dispensed with."

"Without objection, it is so ordered," intoned the Vice President.

"Mr. President, I ask unanimous consent that statements during the morning hour be limited to three minutes," continued Gray.

"Without objection, it is so ordered."

The senator from Arizona whispered briefly across the aisle to the minority leader, who nodded agreement and resumed his chair to toy with the papers on his desk.

"Mr. President, I ask unanimous consent that I be recognized for seven minutes before the commencement of morning business," said Roland Gray, looking around to identify the few senators who were in the chamber.

"The Chair hears no objection. The Chair recognizes the senior senator from Arizona for seven minutes."

A staff assistant placed a portable lectern on the majority leader's front-row desk and handed him the speech. Two very junior back-bench senators on the minority side left their desks and strutted importantly to their cloakroom, conscious of the notice their movement drew to them. A half-dozen senators of Gray's party settled

162

back in their chairs attentively. Stanley Bedson pulled a note pad toward him and idly began to draw cubes on it.

Off to the right of the majority leader, five desks removed, sat Senator Leonard Hodgson, unpopular dean of the minority and fiscal watchdog. Hodgson had snorted in audible annoyance at having to wait seven minutes before he could get the floor to deliver a superheated three-minute blast at the latest HEW extravagance. He was now rechecking some figures in his statement and totally ignoring the opposition leader. He was a thorn in the side of every senator who had ever pushed a pet spending project—meaning virtually all of them—and he was powerful with the people. Even though the terrible political storm of the early Seventies had left his party with only twenty-five senators, he was still a force to be reckoned with.

At last the majority leader was ready.

"Mr. President," repeated Senator Gray, clearing his throat. The galleries stirred restlessly.

God, thought Canfield, checking his watch, why doesn't he get on with it?

While Gray launched into his encomium to Hurley's foreign policy, the parliamentarian leaned around toward the Vice President. "Senator Hodgson asks that he be recognized next, since he has an important committee meeting in progress."

Canfield nodded noncommittally. The rules required him to acknowledge whomever was first on his feet calling for recognition, but that still left him some latitude. They had to get his attention, and he could not be criticized for human imperfections of hearing and vision. In this case, however, there was no reason not to accommodate the little badger from Wisconsin.

The majority leader was doing a great job for Devers. Standing tall and straight, he read the speech with dignity, leaving the script now and then to play to the galleries. He was warming to his task.

"A precarious balance in the world has been maintained only by the cooperation of the three superpowers—the United States, the Soviet Union and the People's Republic of China. It was due to the initiative of President Hurley and Chairman Dradavov that the United Nations Security Council was recognized as dysfunctional for top-level decisions and the Tripartite Committee established as an independent entity outside the United Nations."

Gray paused and brushed back that contumacious shock of white hair. "Closer cooperation among the superpowers has resulted in increased understanding among them of security needs within their own geographic areas so that they can undertake movements to stabilize and consolidate their interests without arousing the fear of nuclear conflict.'' Gray rearranged a page before continuing. ''The United States has benefited. Without the agreement, the wishes of the people of Cuba, Haiti, the Dominican Republic and the Bahamas to be aligned with us could not have been realized. The other signatories have benefited, too, as witness the decisions of North Korea and Rumania to become part of the Soviet Union and the annexation of Cambodia and Laos by the People's Republic of China. All in all, these accommodations and the intensification of the Strategic Arms Limitation Talks between the parties have lessened tensions in the world.''

There was noisy movement among the spectators as one student group was moved out to make way for another. Canfield rapped his gavel sharply and asked that the galleries be in order. That's a rather ridiculous statement by Gray, he thought. Those accommodations have raised tensions in every small nation in the world, whether aligned or nonaligned. Not even satellites are safe from aggression. Actually, they are less safe, because when Big Brother gobbles them up, who is there to object?

A page brought the majority leader a fresh glass of water. More movement in the chamber accompanied the entrance of senators. They talked in small groups and left bills or resolutions at the clerk's desk. Gray was nearing the end of his allotted time, and Canfield waited for the signal from the timing clerk that the seven minutes were up.

The majority leader continued. ''Mr. President, the long-smoldering Middle East would have reached the flash point years ago had it not been for the policy of tripartite discussion among the superpowers. Only constant pressure by the Soviet Union on militant Arab interests and by the United States on Israel maintains the uneasy peace. Hopefully, ongoing discussions between Mr. Dradavov and our President will devise a lasting solution and defuse this incendiary situation.''

''The senator's time has expired,'' said Canfield, not without satisfaction.

''I ask unanimous consent that I be given two more minutes.''

Leonard Hodgson glared, coughed but remained in his chair.

The Vice President sighed. ''Without objection it is so ordered,'' he said tiredly.

The background noises swelled slightly, and a backbencher, a sycophant of Roland Gray, rose and complained, ''Mr. President, may we please have order in the chamber. I want to hear the remarks of the distinguished majority leader.''

164

Canfield rapped three times but avoided dignifying the complaint with a verbal response. The junior could hear perfectly well; all he wanted was attention.

Looking directly up at the Vice President, Roland Gray folded his papers and said gravely, "The Senate has always recognized that the conduct of foreign policy rests with the President of the United States. It has intervened only when a situation has been desperate, and then only to protest senseless killing. Now, because of the advocacy in high places that we again rattle the sword, the Senate will be pressured to abandon its support of the President's policy in the Middle East." Gray shook a finger slowly at the galleries. "What a tragedy it would be if a few zealots were to stampede us into a confrontation with our Tripartite partners. What a travesty of our present mature, reasonable approach to the grave problems that face us."

The majority leader's voice had sunk to the depths of despair, and he bowed his head. Then, suddenly, lifting his chin and tossing back his silver mane, he roared: "The United States was done with covert warmongering after Vietnam, and the United—"

Canfield brought the gavel down sharply.

"The senator's time has expired," he said evenly.

"One more minute," said Gray. "I ask unan—"

"Without objection," subsided Canfield.

"As I was saying," thundered on the majority leader, "we learned the futility of policing the world after Vietnam. Let us not listen to the voices that advocate aggressive actions that may bring the world to a nuclear catastrophe."

"Will the senator yield?" The backbencher had decided to try his luck again.

Gray turned toward the voice. "Of course I will yield to the distinguished senator from Delaware," he said graciously.

"The senator from Delaware," acknowledged the Chair.

"I thank the distinguished majority leader," said the beaming junior senator. "And I want to say that I endorse wholeheartedly his sage remarks today. We would be well advised as a nation to—"

The gavel came down with more force than necessary. "The time of the senator from Arizona has expired," said the Vice President. Then, before any renewal could be requested or the junior could ask recognition in his own right, he said firmly, "The Chair recognizes the senator from Wisconsin."

The junior senator from Delaware slowly sank into his seat, mouth still open in astonishment. Roland Gray was not upset. He only had a few more remarks. Besides, he knew the *Congressional*

Record would carry the complete speech in the morning. He never made a point of throwing around his power without a purpose. That was why he was majority leader.

Traffic in the Senate was increasing. Several important committee chairmen began to arrive to touch base with their assistant leaders on the latest head counts. The assistant leaders, or whips, always had the best information on voting inclinations. It was their job to stay in close touch with the members of their party, and they spent a great deal of time on the floor.

Although there was now considerably more noise than when the junior senator from Delaware had made his request that the Chair maintain order, it was a safe bet that no one would demand quiet to hear Leonard Hodgson. The senator from Wisconsin was not noted for his epideictic orations, but that did not stop him from drawing his saber during virtually every morning session to attack the wastefulness of HEW, HUD or some other freespending agency. His vast empirical knowledge of the bureaucracy made it virtually impossible to slip anything past him, so he was despised by the middle-level architects of social planning. The rotund little Wisconsin badger had one redeeming characteristic, so far as his brothers in the Senate were concerned. He was always mercifully brief. On this day he had asked three minutes to begin his attack on Secretary Meredith Lord's health program. Secretly, he was being assisted by Budget Director Charles Voren, his hidden ally in many causes. Of different parties, they nevertheless shared a draconian attitude on spending.

Canfield watched Hodgson literally belly up to his desk, which was the only way he could get close enough to see his notes. As usual, he was a sunburst of color—sport jacket of red, brown and yellow plaid; brown and white check trousers; and a lavender tie. Clearly, his conservatism did not extend to dress. Addressing the Chair in a high-pitched monotone, he expressed the view that HEW was set on proving the accuracy of his prior prediction that it would bankrupt the republic.

"Mr. President, a bill is presently moving through the Committee on Labor and Public Welfare to make mandatory the federal financing of *free*"—he was evidently unable to bear the whole egregious idea for at this point his voice cracked—"medical care to absolutely healthy people." The badger flushed in outrage. "This ridiculous idea, called 'Total Health Care,' belongs to the young lady who heads HEW, and I am sad to report that several of my colleagues are supporting it." Hodgson glared around the chamber, encountering no contest. No one was listening, not even the presiding officer. Canfield, barely visible, was leaning down to the side to converse with Stanley Bedson, who had come to the dais.

The badger was undaunted. "Mr. President, I send to the desk an amendment to S-3411 to strike from that bill the provisions on Total Health Care, sections three through eleven, relating to free health care for all individuals with incomes under"—he sputtered in rage—"fifty thousand dollars regardless of present health status. I ask that the amendment be referred to the same committee to which S-3411 was referred."

There was a long silence. Hodgson was craning his neck, trying to catch Canfield's eye. Finally the parliamentarian got the attention of the Chair.

"Uh, yes," said Canfield, straightening up in his chair and refocusing on the ritual of presiding. "The amendment will be received and appropriately referred."

"Thank you, Mr. President," said the badger, not at all upset by the lack of attention. He had been in the Senate longer than most and was used to contending with bored presiding officers. Once he had seen a Vice President fall asleep so soundly during debate that a senator had had to shake him gently to arouse him. Hodgson checked his watch. "I have about twenty-five seconds remaining and will use that time to put a few frightening figures before the Senate."

A loud hiss, impossible to ignore, erupted from the side gallery directly behind the senator from Wisconsin. All around the chamber, heads turned and the background noise abruptly diminished. Some of the onlookers in the balconies gave vent to nervous titters.

A trace of a smile was visible on Canfield's face. He rapped gently and said in a mild voice, "The galleries will please be in order."

Roland Gray was on his feet in an instant, his eyes flashing angrily. "Will the Chair please instruct the spectators," he said coldly, "that they are here at the invitation of the Senate and that the rules of the Senate forbid demonstrations of approval and disapproval. And, I would add, Mr. President, that while involuntary emotional responses are understandable, studied discourtesies such as hissing have never been tolerated in the chamber."

A murmur of disapproval swept through the audience of mostly young people. Canfield smiled openly and said, "The Chair has already requested order from the galleries, and so far as I can see, the galleries are in order now. The senator from Wisconsin will not be penalized by the interruption. He may have twenty seconds to finish.''

Face livid, the majority leader stood for a moment more looking at Canfield incredulously. Never in his long years in the Senate had he been dismissed so cavalierly by the Chair. He sat down, shaking his head in disbelief.

Leonard Hodgson, unflapped by the procedural discord, continued calmly. ''If the Congress should forsake common sense and enact to law this grandiose scheme, my extrapolations indicate the cost of the program in nineteen eighty-five will be two and a half billion dollars; and in nineteen eighty-six, it will be three billion.'' Hodgson pulled at his nose and looked around the galleries, seeming to address his next remarks directly to them. ''Someone must pay for that, and you know who that someone is. That someone is the people. A tax increase will be required. We just can't afford this pyramiding of frivolous spending. Before long, taxes will put American business out of the world competition.''

Another loud hiss, vicious in its intensity, was followed by scattered, more timid hisses and boos. Since most of the disruption came from the same balcony, a young Capitol policeman in the vicinity moved partway down the steps in an effort to locate the offenders.

This time the gavel rap was sharper. ''The Chair can understand the strong feelings of disagreement, but cannot condone the outburst. The Chair warns that should there be further violations, the galleries will be cleared.''

Roland Gray found the warning insufficient. ''Mr. President, I suggest that the Chair direct the sergeant-at-arms to clear the galleries now.''

Canfield was in a dilemma. He wanted to play to the youth in the audience to show his understanding and empathy. Trifling as it was, this incident could be used to establish him as an idol of the young, ready to stand with them against establishment repression at his own personal sacrifice. Certainly, it would be reported in a way that would make him look good and Gray bad. Quickly he made a decision. ''The Chair sees no need to clear the galleries at this point. It would be unfair to punish all these young people—here to learn firsthand about the democratic process—because of the lapses of a few among them. Thank God they have enough interest in their country to want to improve it by participating in great decisions.''

Gray quickly cut into the smattering of applause. ''I ask unanimous consent that the Chair direct the sergeant-at-arms to clear the galleries.'' Cold rage was in the majority leader's voice, and his contemptuous expression left no doubt that he regarded Canfield's action as cheap politicking.

So it's going to be a power play, thought Canfield. He heard a strong disapproving hum from the balconies, and then a clear voice said, ''Objection!'' instantly checking the steamroller known as ''unanimous consent.''

''The Chair hears an objection,'' said Canfield, noting that Gray was contemplating the objecting Senator Bedson as though he were a recalcitrant schoolchild.

''Then I *move* that the galleries be cleared,'' said the majority leader.

''I support the distinguished majority leader's motion,'' said the sycophant from Delaware as soon as his frantic demand for recognition got him the floor.

''Mr. President, I request the yeas and nays,'' said Gray. This time the murmur was one of surprise, and it came from the Senate, not the galleries. Gray was clearly out to humble the upstart Vice President. He could have accomplished his purpose easily with a simple voice vote, but he wanted the whole Senate to know about this contest, even though some senators might be embarrassed by having their votes recorded.

''The yeas and nays have been requested. The clerk will call the roll,'' said Canfield, wondering whether he had not pushed the whole thing too far.

As the bell rang summoning the absent senators to the roll-call vote, several solons already in the chamber made a hasty exit. This was a no-win proposition. It would be dangerous to defy the majority leader, who had a memory like an elephant—and it would be very harmful to be seen by the media as being against young people. The couriers now disappearing into the halls were from the third of the Senate that came up for reelection next year, and they would immediately warn the remainder of that group to get lost.

Meanwhile, the clerk began his sonorous recital of the roll, getting very few responses.

''Mr. Adams''—no answer. ''Mr. Ardell''—no answer. ''Mr. Bracey''—a weak aye, accompanied by another hiss from above. Canfield rapped for order, and the call proceeded.

It was a very small vote, but one safely acquiescent to his excellency, the majority leader. The Vice President, saying that he had no recourse, announced that a quorum was present and directed that the galleries be cleared.

Under the direction of the sergeant-at-arms, uniformed Capitol policemen at each exit began to move the crowd out. Most went without protest, although hisses were now heard in abundance. The balcony where the trouble had begun was not emptying as fast as the others, and a group of a dozen college-age youngsters of both sexes were apparently getting ready to stage a sit-down in the front row. Seeing that they were not moving from their seats, an equally young policeman began to make his way through the crowd toward them.

Lobbed underhand from the front of the balcony with deadly accuracy, the tomato underwent a spectacular chromatic disintegration as it struck the back of Leonard Hodgson's head. The startled senator, who had tarried too long watching Gray's power play, grunted his surprise, then cried out hoarsely when his exploring hand encountered what he mistook for blood and tissue. His colleagues rushed to him in alarm, but the Wisconsin badger's fear turned to wrath when he learned that he had been garnished rather than wounded.

Overhead, confusion reigned in the gallery section from which the offending fruit had been propelled. The officer had reached the knot of front-row troublemakers; indeed, he had identified the culprit—a bearded youth in faded denims with a motorcycle-chain belt. He was now attempting to handcuff the struggling boy while a screaming girl pushed at him from behind. Suddenly, while those below watched in horror, it happened.

Either the boy pushed the policeman or he lost his footing and fell back into the hysterical girl behind him. Later, witnesses differed about the cause, but not the result. The stockily built officer fell against the girl, and the low rail of the gallery provided the fulcrum. She went over the rail with a single, piercing scream and thudded heavily against the carpeted floor fifteen feet below. She was knocked out, but regained consciousness soon after the first help reached her.

The Senate was quickly recessed, and several people on the floor went to the girl, who was obviously severely hurt. Her face was pale and clammy, and she kept moaning, "My legs, I can't feel my legs." Someone covered her with a coat and placed a sweater under her head. Roland Gray knelt beside her. The ambulance and a doctor were already on the way. There was nothing more to be done at the moment.

The Vice President's senior Senate aide drew him discreetly to the side and, making certain that his message was not overheard by the group around the fallen girl, said softly, "Mr. Vice President, Senator Bedson is waiting in your office. He says the press are clamoring to see you, and he would like to give you some information before you talk to them."

"Okay, Jim. You stay here to keep an eye on things," said Canfield. He immediately crossed the deserted Senate hall on his way to his ceremonial office, where the senator awaited him.

Stanley Bedson was uneasy about what he had done. It was not every day that a middle-level senator challenged his leader on a sensitive matter—uppity attitudes were discouraged in the Congress. Usually the brazen one found himself at the end of the line when the best committee assignments, the desirable office space and other goodies were dispensed. For that reason Bedson was nervously pacing the ceremonial office, looking at himself every now and then in the mirror that, according to legend, had caused an uproar between Dolley Madison and the federal customs agents. It was also said that the resulting investigation over who should pay the thirty dollars duty on the mirror that Mrs. Madison had bought in Paris cost the taxpayers nearly three thousand dollars.

Bedson was much more worried about his major gamble on Porter Canfield's future than he was about the young woman who was at that very moment being carried from the Senate chamber on a stretcher. If the Vice President became President, all sorts of interesting possibilities might present themselves from California. A weakened Roland Gray could lose the leadership of the Senate, for example, or the known illness of a Supreme Court justice might force his early retirement. Coming as Bedson did from a large western state, there was an excellent chance that he might even be the vice-presidential choice.

On the other hand, if Canfield lost out, Gray would make mincemeat of him. Well, he was out on the point, so thoroughly committed that there was no disadvantage to being aggressive. And fortunately things were looking pretty good. His soundings in the House as well as the Senate indicated that the good ink Canfield was getting was gaining new friends.

Secret Service Agent Lee Daniels opened the door, put his head in and said, "The Vice President."

A moment later Canfield hustled into his office and flung himself into the high-backed swivel chair behind the desk. "Whew, what a mess," he said worriedly. "Gray was an idiot to inflame those kids, Stan. The girl never would have been hurt if Mr. Big hadn't insisted on playing the heavy." He loosened his collar. "Something must be wrong with the damned air conditioning. Can you imagine what this place was like during the summer in the old days?"

Canfield looked up at the ceiling and thought of the famous story about Teddy Roosevelt. It seems that on a particularly oppressive summer day Roosevelt was vexed by the clinking of a White House chandelier in the breeze and reportedly said, "Take the damn thing down and send it to the Vice President's office. It won't bother them because they don't have anything to do anyhow." Eying the thing, Canfield said, "No wonder Teddy Roosevelt sent this chandelier to Vice President Fairbanks just to annoy him. They were both probably suffering from diaper rash up to the armpits."

Bedson smiled dutifully. "How is the girl?"

"Not too good, I'm afraid. Aside from that, what's up?"

"Well, first you've got to see the reporters. They want to assess blame. With a little encouragement from you, they'll find old Roland guilty of insensitivity and other related fascist crimes."

"Let's get Zack here. He's right next door," said Canfield, touching the intercom button and directing the receptionist to tell Professor Miller he was wanted forthwith. He looked intently at the impatiently pacing Bedson. "Take it easy, Stan. Rushing makes mistakes. While we're waiting for Zack, tell me how Meredith is doing with her program. I see that Leonard has declared war on THC."

"Yes, but lost the first battle to a tomato grenade." Bedson laughed, relaxing a little. "Did you see what happened to his favorite sports jacket, not to mention his dignity?"

"No. I can't look at Leonard without my sunglasses," said Canfield, motioning the entering Zack Miller to take a seat on the divan. "What about Meredith?"

Bedson pulled a few sheets of paper from his pocket. "It's a little early to predict. We're doing all we can, and the lady herself is working like a beaver."

"I hope for her sake that beavers work harder than Wisconsin badgers. She's got her heart set on that new program." Canfield leaned his head back and looked into space. "She's a fantastic woman. Selfless. Totally dedicated to the underprivileged."

"And attractive," said Miller, glancing at Bedson, who raised his eyebrows slightly. The Vice President's feelings about Meredith Lord were no secret to either of them.

Abruptly Miller, who had already been thoroughly briefed on the Senate incident, brought Canfield back to reality. "I guess you know that the nets want you on film. The wires are also pressing for some quotes, not to mention the news magazines and the dailies. When do you want to see them?" It was characteristic of Miller that he had already decided that Canfield was going to see them—all he wanted to know was when.

"I was just talking to Stan about that. How about just giving them a statement?"

"N.G.," Miller said immediately. "They'd kill you. You have to have a short news conference. I'll set them up in the reception area, and you can catch them on your way out. Half an hour from now, okay?"

The Vice President looked at Stanley Bedson, who nodded in agreement. "Okay, Zack, but what do I tell them?"

"Well, for Christ's sake, don't tell them about THC." Miller's irreverence was due to too much familiarity with the officer rather than discourtesy to the office. "You know what they want to hear. They want you to nail Gray's ass to the wall. From the report I just got, the girl may never walk again. The press has to determine who is at fault. It has to have a villain—either Gray or you or the guy who made the rail too low or the cop. Now you know they're like a herd of cattle. Either Drake or Winehart or Atherton or another one of those clowns is going to decide irrevocably who's responsible. If his reasoning is plausible, the whole damn bunch of them will dance to the same tune."

Miller interrupted himself to pick up the buzzing phone. "Miller," he answered brusquely. "No, Mary. He's here, but he's not taking calls. No. Tell them to set up in the reception area and that we'll have something for them soon—okay?"

"They're homing in on you, Mr. V.P., and that's good. Gray has issued a statement of regret, but won't see them today. This is perfect! Philosophically, they don't admire Gray. Besides, he's the natural black hat in this scene. All you have to do is gently shove the manure into his corner. They'll do the rest."

Bedson broke in. "I agree, Newt. You can capitalize on this. It's a natural. Just be for young people, patience, participatory democracy and the little guy."

"Okay, Zack. Set it up. It's dangerous, but there's no other way." Canfield grimaced. "Oh for the good old days when nobody paid any attention to Vice Presidents."

Bedson laughed unsympathetically. "You're a hell of a lot better off than Henry Wilson, who came out of the Senate baths, got a chill and expired on this very divan."

"Let's get serious. It wouldn't hurt for me to have your best judgments on how we are progressing and how we are going to handle things here while I'm spreading good will for the Hurley administration in the Far East." There was just the slightest trace of a whine in Canfield's voice, a sign that the pressure was mounting. Miller and Bedson immediately became serious and soothingly deferential.

"I'm very optimistic about the Congress, Mr. Vice President," said Bedson encouragingly. "My explorations in the House show your stock way up among the Young Turks since the western trip. On top of that, Gray suffers the disadvantage of long tenure. He's been talked about for the presidency so many times that a lot of old hands are just tired of hearing about him—and maybe a little jealous that he's had the spotlight so long. I've been talking to a few key people—Bender, Jacobsen and Crowley you already know well, and they're for you one hundred percent. Anyhow, we have an intelligence system set up to watch the House, and we'll offer you to speak at luncheons and dinners in key districts before the actual campaign begins. Gray will be tied down in the Senate, and you'll be making friends all over."

Miller agreed enthusiastically, "Great setup, Stan. Newt'll be getting so much good press with the Israel position that he'll bury Gray before he can get on his mark."

"That's fine, but how about the Senate?" Canfield was guarded, fighting down the euphoria. It wouldn't be smart to let them know how pleased he was with the readings so far.

"The Senate will be tougher, of course," replied Bedson. "After all, that's Roland's power base, and he's been leader for a long time. Out of seventy-one senators of our party, only twenty presently support your initiative on Israel, and forty-five are openly hostile because of your slight of Gray in Arizona. But that can be turned around. You must play high-risk politics—gamble on swaying public opinion through the news media. Of course, you'll never convert bootlickers, like the junior senator from Delaware, but once we get up a head of steam, a lot of them will turn around. They're only loyal to their ambition."

Canfield nodded thoughtfully, thinking to himself how true that was and how it applied to all of them—himself, Bedson and even Zack Miller, who would want something when the number hit, just like all the others.

Aloud, he said, "I agree. I've done a lot of thinking about this. In my opinion, the intellectuals and the media are looking for a candidate who is philosophically equipped to lead our party away from the dreary middle-of-the-road policies of Hurley and back to the visonary liberalism that the party stood for from the time of the Great Depression until nineteen seventy-six, when Walter Hurley rejected the liberals for the hurt and disillusioned silent majority. For seven years, Hurley has provided a stable and totally dull administration—no sudden moves, no scandals, no tricky P.R. ploys, no jet-set diplomacy—and the media are tired of tranquillity. They need the saints and devils, the people-lovers and people-haters, the honey and the venom which are the raw materials of titillating stories. If we can restore some passion to the public scene, we'll roll.''

"That's a brilliant analysis, Newt," said Bedson. "The way I figure it, the Congress is ten times as important in swaying a convention when the incumbent president is of the majority party and cannot succeed himself for another term." He continued earnestly, "A lame-duck president can't use the promise of patronage to get delegates the way he can when seeking reelection, so the only permanence the party sees is in longtime congressional leaders. Governors have some clout, but not as much."

"We've got a lot of work to do in the Senate," said Miller, "but there's time enough. You're going to start us off with today's press conference."

"How do we stand with the governors?" asked the Vice President.

Bedson smiled. "Except for the forty or so who think they should be nominated for the presidency by acclaim, you should be about even at the moment."

Canfield turned to Miller. "Zack, ask Bill Shelby to feel out Gus Perry about handling our effort with the governors. He just retired from the staff of the National Governors' Conference after twenty-five years, and he knows them all personally. It's worth putting him on the payroll."

Miller made a note on his pad. "Sounds like a good idea," he said.

The strategy session lasted for another hour, and it was after four when a staff member knocked hesitantly at the door of the ceremonial office to inform the Vice President that the members of the news media had been set up in the Senate Reception Room for some time and were becoming restive about their deadlines.

"What about the girl? How is she?" Miller asked, quickly concentrating on the immediate problem.

"I heard one of the reporters say she's going to be in a wheelchair the rest of her life, but I don't see how they could know that already," said the staffer.

Zack Miller laughed cynically. "Makes no difference about facts. It's how they handle the story that counts. And obviously it's going to get full tragedy treatment."

"Tell them I'll be there in three minutes," said Canfield. He seemed totally at ease, but a little detached, as though he were trying to resummon a memorized line.

Miller began to orchestrate. "Now, Newt, here's how I think you should play it," he said firmly. "It's either you or Gray, so don't hold back. Let them know you didn't want the galleries cleared. Suggest that it's always dangerous to move crowds suddenly. Lay it right in Roland's lap. Be indignant. Agonize over the poor girl who has so unnecessarily lost the normal life she expected to enjoy when she got up this morning."

Stanley Bedson shook his head emphatically. "Wrong, Zack. That may do wonders outside, but it will create great sympathy for Gray in the Congress. You can throw out our predictions of converting those key people if Newt plays this too tough. I think he should be compassionate, but too statesmanlike to take a cheap shot at Gray."

"Statesmen don't win many elections," said Miller caustically. "Newt's got to be forceful, dynamic, fearless."

Canfield held up his hand. "We can't tell until I hear the questions," he said quietly. "I'll just have to play it by ear."

Zack leaped excitedly to his feet, striding back and forth with that characteristic nervous energy of his. "Okay, Mr. Vice President. You're the candidate, but don't be too polite. If you handle this according to Senate club rules, you'll get a few kind words in the cloakroom and a lousy press. Stanley's brain has been affected by too many committee meetings."

Bedson laughed tolerantly. "You've been radicalized in that ivory tower, Zack. The Vice President of the United States doesn't have to scream and throw rocks to get attention. This isn't nineteen sixty-five Berkeley, you know."

Canfield ran a comb through his hair and straightened his tie. "That's enough, friends. Don't worry. I'll handle it my way— probably somewhere in between your ideas." He went to the door. "Okay, Lee. I'm all set. Let's go," he said almost jauntily. "Lead me to the man-eaters."

The Reception Room was packed with curious tourists, drawn by the profusion of newsmen and their equipment.

As soon as Canfield stepped past the doorway, he was blinded by a powerful hand-held light. A cameraman blocked his path, focusing on a close-up shot of his face and backing up grudgingly when the Secret Service forced him out of the way.

"C'mon, c'mon," said Lee Daniels. "Let the Vice President get in position for everybody. Don't hog it."

Canfield moved easily to the spot that had been marked with a small adhesive-tape X. The lights accented the clash of the busy multihued tile with the ornate gilded filigree-work on the walls. Amy maintained that Brumidi was drunk when he did this room and that the Senate should sell it to a bordello operator; Canfield thought it could better be used as a waiting room in a big-city railroad station.

After a brief scurry, the room quieted. Spectators pressed forward, craning their necks to see over the front rank.

"Ready for your questions, gentlemen," the Vice President said pleasantly. He waited patiently at the "Hold-it-a-minute!" cry of a frantic cameraman who had to make a last-minute lens adjustment.

Finally they were ready, and Douglas Drake, a temporary celebrity because of his recent successful baiting of Roland Gray, began. "Mr. Vice President," he said, the salutation rolling resonantly from his tongue with a slightly accusatory ring, "this afternoon a young honor student either fell or was pushed from the Senate gallery as the result of a policeman's attempt to forcibly evict someone near her. Preliminary information indicates that she is seriously injured—may never walk again. The policeman was carrying out your instructions to clear the galleries. Do you have any comment on that?"

Maintaining his pleasant expression, the Vice President looked mildly at Drake as though the latter had handed him a piece of cake rather than a veiled indictment. "Mr. Drake, I am deeply disturbed by that unfortunate accident," he said earnestly. "I have instructed the sergeant-at-arms to make a full investigation of the matter and to have a report in my hands at the earliest possible moment." He frowned and shook his head. "It is indeed tragic that this young woman's interest in learning more about our democratic system led to such a sad result. On behalf of the entire Senate, I offer sincere condolences to her, her family and friends. We all pray that she will recover without suffering any disability."

Canfield waited as though he were through with the question, but he knew full well that this would not satisfy the ambitious Mr. Drake. It was much better, however, that he be a reluctant witness against Gray. Drake was quick upon him.

"You were in the Chair, sir, and could see the gallery. Was it necessary that the police use force in carrying out your order to clear out the spectators?"

"I was not looking at the spot where the accident occurred, so I did not see what brought about the struggle. The sergeant-at-arms will interview all witnesses and develop the facts." Canfield was in full control of himself.

Drake persisted. "Why did you find it necessary to order the chamber cleared?"

Ah, here it was—the opportunity to transfer the hounds to Gray.

"When the Senate orders, the presiding officer must carry out those orders. In this particular case, the order was by recorded vote after a proper motion."

"Who made the motion?"

Canfield hesitated just long enough to indicate that he was reluctant to point the finger of blame, then said evenly, "The majority leader, as I recall."

Sid Winehart couldn't stand it another minute. "Mr. Vice President, isn't it true that you resisted a request from the majority leader, Senator Gray, that you order the galleries cleared and that Senator Gray, after failing to get the Senate's unanimous consent, then forced the issue to a roll-call vote—you do recall that, don't you, sir?" Winehart was obviously impatient with the evasion, which he couldn't understand. Was Canfield going to stand there and miss the chance to clobber his archrival?

"Yes, I believe you are correct, Mr. Winehart," said Canfield, keeping all emotion out of his voice.

"The majority leader was angry because of some hissing, but you did not consider the disturbance sufficient to throw the spectators out, is that right?"

"That is correct. I cautioned the few onlookers who were hissing, but I did not feel the disturbance sufficiently widespread to warrant everyone being excluded from the galleries."

Winehard moved in for the kill. "If Senator Gray had not forced the issue, the accident wouldn't have happened, would it, sir?" he declared triumphantly.

"That's like saying that the accident wouldn't have happened if the Senate hadn't met—or if the young lady had been seated in a back row," Canfield said patiently, adroitly avoiding dealing the low blow. "Your question is too speculative for a fair answer. I'm sure that Senator Gray is as distressed as I am by what happened to the young lady."

Another reporter broke in. "The Students for a Participatory Society have condemned the brutal and repressive actions of the Senate and demand that the Senate formally apologize to the youth of America," he said, reading from a handbill. "What do you say to that, sir?"

"I have great respect for the principles that motivated the SPS to issue that statement. These sincere young people are justifiably anxious to guard the freedom of our democratic society. Their concern over any authoritarian action is understandable." The Vice President paused briefly to look directly into the camera with his "I-understand-the-kids" expression. "However, in this case, I do believe the SPS has overreacted a bit. The Senate, of course, is genuinely sorry about what happened, but in the absence of substantiating facts, it is premature to refer to brutality or repressiveness."

"One of the witnesses said that the girl handed her boyfriend the tomato that he threw at Senator Hodgson's head," said a gravelly voice from the side, "and that she was ecstatic at the senator's discomfort. If that is true, wouldn't you say that the policeman's intervention was proper, sir?" Bruce Atherton, cocking his head to one side, noticed the weight shift that was the first sign of nervousness from Canfield.

"I think it's only fair to wait for the sergeant-at-arm's report before speculating further. And now, gentlemen, please excuse me. I would like to telephone the young lady's parents," the Vice President said before stepping away from the microphone.

"Please, sir, one more question on another subject," called Douglas Drake, hoping to bail out what had turned out to be a less than polished performance on his part. Canfield smiled graciously and stepped back to the mike. "Okay, but only one more. I really must go, gentlemen."

"Mr. Vice President, in the past few days there have been several stories based on statements from White House sources that President Hurley has notified you of his disapproval of your statements about Israel. One usually reliable source says that the President sent Mr. Joshua Devers, his counselor, to deliver the message to you personally. Is there any truth to those rumors?"

Canfield laughed, thinking how quickly Bradley Barton had violated his promise to use only indirect references to what he had told him at the O'Mara home.

"I never discuss communications between the President and myself," he said, thereby confirming the spanking and at the same time being a good sport about it.

"But will you hold to your position on IRBM's?" asked Drake frantically when Canfield again moved to leave.

"Thank you, gentlemen," said the Vice President, hurrying out the door behind Lee Daniels, but finding time to wave and smile at several groups of applauding spectators.

The limousine was idling at the usual stop at the north entrance. Several Secret Service men waiting at the door ran to the follow-up car as Daniels swung the heavy armored door open for Canfield. In no time they were headed down Pennsylvania Avenue.

"EOB, sir?"

The Vice President gave Daniels the routine nod and picked up the news clips that had been left on the seat by a Senate aide. On top there was an early wire-service story carrying Bruce Atherton's by-line that dealt with the accident; it had the single-column headline: ACCIDENT IN SENATE. Canfield skimmed it quickly.

> Early this afternoon a seventeen-year-old girl was admitted to Georgetown University Hospital after a fall from the spectators' gallery to the floor of the U.S. Senate. The extent of her injuries is unknown, but while waiting for the ambulance, she complained of numbness in her legs. The hospital described her condition as "satisfactory." The girl, identified by friends as Diane Guthrie, a high school student, was visiting the Capitol with a group of young people. The cause of the accident has not been determined, but it is known that there was a scuffle between a youth and a policeman near the point where Miss Guthrie went over the low rail.

Atherton went on to report the events leading up to the order to clear the galleries and Senator Hodgson's misfortune. Regarding the confrontation between Canfield and Gray, he simply stated: "In spite of the reluctance of the Vice President to give the order, Senator Gray prevailed in his insistence that the galleries be cleared."

Canfield smiled. Apparently Atherton was not too excited about his head-knocking with the majority leader. Nor did the reporter seem interested that the incident would infallibly fan a confrontation between youth and the repressive Establishment. But he would be forced to cover those points later when the SPS and the media crusaders pushed them into the spotlight.

The next clip was from the *Washington Globe* city edition and was more in the modern-media style. The heavy black four-column headline announced:

POLICE-YOUTH CLASH INJURES GIRL
PUSHED FROM SENATE BALCONY

During a scuffle between Capitol police and a group of young people who were resisting forcible eviction from the spectators' gallery of the United States Senate, a high school honor student was pushed over the low rail of the balcony and fell nearly 20 feet to the floor below. The girl, Miss Diane Guthrie of 26 Wellington Avenue, was rushed to Georgetown University Hospital. Immediately after the fall, she was semiconscious. Several times she moaned that she had no feeling in her legs. A medical student present said that the position of her body suggested a back injury and perhaps paralysis of the lower limbs. Witnesses near the altercation stated that the policeman fell back into Miss Guthrie while scuffling with a young man he had been trying to handcuff. They said the girl's knees struck the low rail, causing her to lose her balance and fall to the floor of the Senate. Several senators in the chamber left immediately without attempting to assist the injured girl. Mr. Adam King, who was involved in the scuffle with the policeman, said he was suddenly seized and pulled from his seat before he had a chance to comply with the order to leave the gallery. He accused the officer of "police brutality" and reckless disregard for Miss Guthrie's safety.

Reached at home, Mr. Malcolm Guthrie, father of Diane, spoke out bitterly at what he called "strong-arm methods of the police."

"They never use persuasion," he said. "It's always force —aggression protected by the badge. My poor child was trying to learn about the American system, about freedom. What did she get—a demonstration of the real America—the brutal, ignorant, violent America. Now she may never walk again. All her ideas of studying and working for the under-privileged may have been for nothing. Instead of helping others, she may end up a pitiful invalid needing help."

The reporter went on to allege that the trouble in the Senate chamber started when several spectators demonstrated their disapproval of Wisconsin Senator Hodgson's attack on health care for the poor. In his recitation of the events prior to the order to clear the galleries, the writer mentioned that a "prankster" had dropped a tomato on Senator Hodgson. The conclusion of the article brought a glow of satisfaction to Canfield.

Vice President Canfield, who had been in the Chair since the Senate opened, did his best to calm both the galleries and the irate Senate majority leader, Mr. Gray. The Vice President refused a request by Senator Gray that the sergeant-at-arms be directed to remove the spectators, and it was not until the majority leader forced a vote on the issue that the Vice President reluctantly gave the instructions to clear the galleries. Sources knowledgeable about the Senate said the majority leader's actions were unprecedented so far as they could recall. Many observers expressed the opinion that it was

Senator Gray's forcing of the issue that brought about the ugly attitude between police and the spectators. Gray refused to see newsmen after the incident but issued a short statement expressing regret over the tragic accident.

Canfield flipped through the remaining stories. None was about the accident. He knew, however, that the nets and the big morning dailies would cover the story, and the odds were that they would follow the sensational approach of the *Globe*. The result would be a minus for Roland Gray and a plus for Porter Canfield.

In less than five minutes the limousine deposited the Vice President at the Executive Office Building.

He stuck his head into his secretary's office and waited a moment until the IBM stopped chattering.

"I'm back, Kathy. Give me a minute to wash up, and I'll be ready for the rundown." He slipped out of his coat and threw it over his shoulder.

"Okay, I'll come in about five from now. There is a lot to tell you. You've been busy up there on the Hill from the sound of things."

"Tired. Been a pressure day, but good results. Fill you in later." Canfield let the door close and headed for his private bathroom.

He rolled up his sleeves and loosened his collar. Then, after washing his hands and face, he soaked a washcloth in cold water and held it for several moments over his eyes. Toweling dry, he looked at himself in the mirror. Look a little bushed, he thought. Well, get used to it. From now on, it's going to be wild—but interesting. As he tightened his tie, he heard Kathy enter the big office. He quickly ran a comb through his hair and walked out, putting on his coat. Moving to a big leather chair, he stretched out with a sigh.

"Now, Kathy, let's have it. What momentous things have transpired while I was up at the funny farm?"

"First, the girl's parents called you. They heard you say on television that you were going to call them, and they were wondering why they hadn't heard. They want you to stop at the hospital and see her tomorrow. Seems she's a fan of yours and nothing would help her more—"

"Oh, God. I forgot to call before I left up there." Canfield frowned, then made a quick decision. "Have Shelby schedule me to see her for a few minutes in the morning. Photo opportunity would be good. Then ask him to call the parents and inform them I had to go into a meeting and that's why I didn't call. But assure them that I will be at the hospital in the morning. Better tell Bill right away."

The girl made a few shorthand notes on her pad, picked up the phone and relayed the instructions.

"Now," said Canfield, "let's start with a list of those who must see me immediately, according to their judgment."

Kathy smiled. It was a standing joke between them that she always had a few requests for emergency meetings.

"Well, there's Peter Rosen, who incidentally is quite disturbed that you undertook a press conference without his counsel. He says it's urgent."

"I'll see him before I leave. What else?"

"Then there's Professor Miller, who's on his way here from the Senate. Wants you to wait for him. That about takes care of the panic category."

"Phone calls?"

"Quite a few. Josh Devers, Yoram Halevy from INAF, Secretary Lord, Bradley Barton— Oh, yes, and Mrs. Canfield called to ask if you could free up tomorrow evening. One of the Smithsonian trustees is being honored in Philadelphia at an informal dinner at the country club."

Perceiving his irritation, Kathy paused, then said softly, "I didn't mention that you're already committed to that health-care dinner for Secretary Lord."

He threw her a quick glance, probing for any signs that might indicate her awareness of his unusual interest in Meredith Lord. There were none.

"I can't cancel now. The health lobby is too important," he said, drumming his fingers on the desk. "I'll explain the problem to Mrs. Canfield when I get home."

"Oh, didn't Lee Daniels tell you when he came on duty? Mrs. Canfield has already left for Philadelphia to help Mrs. Varlis plan for the flower show. I'm sorry. I would have called you at the Senate, but I assumed Lee would let you know." The girl was visibly upset at the communications failure.

"That's all right. No harm done," said Canfield with a quick smile. "I'm used to Amy heading for Philadelphia at every possible opportunity. Anything else?"

"Just one more thing. Steve Galdari would like to have a few minutes alone with you just before you leave for the residence."

"All right, run him in when we're all through." Canfield was mildly surprised. Usually his security chief did all the necessary communicating when they were on the move. It was unusual for Galdari to request a private meeting.

The intercom buzzed and the receptionist announced Miller's

arrival. He was immediately admitted to the inner sanctum and collapsed in a chair in front of the huge desk.

"Great job, Mr. Veep. The Senate gumshoes tell me the majority leader is tearing his hair," he began.

Canfield stepped quickly in behind the last word. "Hold it, Zack," he said crisply. "I've got just a few more things with Kathy, and then we'll talk." He turned toward the secretary. "Mail?"

"Nothing so important that you can't sign it tomorrow."

"Okay. Send Rosen and Shelby in, and get Yoram Halevy and Josh Devers on the phone—no special order. And call Secretary Lord. Tell her I'm in a meeting and will call her in about an hour, okay?"

"Right, sir," said Kathy, detouring around Zack Miller's dangling hand. The professor had a reputation for "accidentally" brushing against the more attractive female members of the staff.

After the girl had left the office, the ebullient Miller again began to dwell on the rumor of Senator Gray's rage, but was once more requested to wait—this time for the arrival of the others. A few minutes later Bill Shelby and Peter Rosen entered and were waved to seats on the comfortable sofa. Canfield noticed that Rosen looked sulky.

"Now, Peter, Kathy said you wanted to see me urgently. I guess it's about what happened at the Senate this afternoon. Zack is here with more information on that, and Bill Shelby needs to be brought up to date on the whole situation. I suggest we hear from you first, and then from Zack. Everyone feel free to interrupt at any time to ask whatever questions—damn!"

Canfield picked up the offending phone and learned that his call to Mr. Halevy was ready. He motioned the others to remain and punched the connecting button.

"Hello, Yoram, how're you? How are things in the big city? . . . Fine, fine. I have a friend of yours sitting in my office . . . Zack Miller . . . Yes, he's fine . . . Now, what can I do for you?"

The Vice President listened intently for several minutes, occasionally uttering monosyllabic words of agreement or understanding. Then he said, "That's very nice of you, Yoram. Thank you very much. It's reassuring to know I have such strong support from INAF, and you can rely on my dedication to the principle that that wonderfully courageous little nation across the ocean must remain free. All America admires Israel. Please thank your members for their resolution approving my position. . . . Yes, certainly, I'll tell him. . . . What? . . . Yes, we leave for the Far East in a few days. . . . Sure, I'll ask him to call you tonight at your home. Fine. Goodbye, Yoram.''

Canfield lowered the phone gently into its cradle and smiled broadly at the three staff men. ''INAF passed a resolution last night commending my support for Israel's defense,'' he said, a note of exhilaration in his voice. ''They call my stand 'statesmanlike, courageous, far-reaching and in the Truman tradition.' They have distributed the resolution to all major media, as well as to the principal national Jewish press organs. That should give us quite a lift.''

''That's great,'' said Zack. ''Yoram's a good organizer, and he'll be a tremendous help with the liberal vote in the big cities.''

''He wants you to call him at home this evening about an important matter, Zack. I suggest you keep in close touch with him.''

''I'll be sure to call him. What you said reminds me that we've got a lot of work to do in the three days left before we leave for Singapore.''

''We're about ready. I don't see any problems. The briefing books will be delivered tomorrow, and the logistics are all straight,'' Shelby said in the relaxed, unhurried manner that served him so well in the frantic environment of the vice-presidential operation.

''Good,'' said Canfield, swinging his chair around to face Peter Rosen. ''Now, Peter. What's on your mind?''

The press secretary, looking uncomfortable, squirmed forward on the couch. ''Well, Mr. Vice President, all hell's been breaking loose around here, and I didn't know what was going on, so I guess I looked pretty ridiculous.'' With obvious embarrassment he cleared his throat.

Canfield continued to look at him impassively, all the while thinking to himself, It's always their own dignity and credibility that worries them. Sometimes I think it's how they look more than how I look that's important.

Rosen went on, ''The phones started ringing off the hook right after your news conference at the Senate. Jack Ryner of the *Globe,* who has already done a story, wants an interview. Sid Winehart is clamoring for fifteen minutes with you. He's holding his definitive story until he sees you. Bradley Barton would like you to do a one-on-one with him within the next two days, before you leave for the Far East.''

The press secretary had delivered this summary at a machine-gun tempo. Pausing to take a deep breath, he continued, ''The thing that bothers me, Mr. Vice President, is that I don't know what's going on. These guys keep asking me for clarifications and constructions of your intent. They want to know whether you are taking on Roland Gray frontally, and they have a million questions about how the White House is reacting to all this. It's important that you keep me in the picture because I have to handle these calls on a day-to-day basis."

"Why don't you just tell them that the Vice President's words speak for themselves and that you don't have anything else to say," said Shelby dryly. "I don't see any reason to have to construe everything the boss does. Besides, a good way to get into trouble is to talk too much to those beagles."

Zack cut in sharply. "Wait a minute, Bill. Peter's got a point. He has a tough job. There's no sense antagonizing the media. He can do a lot of good by keeping them happy and well fed with tidbits."

Rosen looked at Miller gratefully. One thing was certain—he'd never get any support from the chief of staff.

"I know those guys," said Shelby. "You offer them a tidbit and they take your arm off at the elbow."

"That's ridiculous, Bill," shouted Peter Rosen. "That's a lousy attitude and a stupid way—"

"Hold it, hold it," said Canfield, raising his voice above the clamor. "Everybody just relax for a minute."

After a moment he said, "Now let's get this in perspective. First of all, Peter has a point. It was unfortunate that I did not get word to him about the news conference, but these oversights happen. I'll try to avoid leaving him out on that limb in the future.

"Now, with regard to how much Pete should say, I have to agree with Bill. It's much better to err on the side of silence than to say something that can be construed incorrectly. That doesn't mean, however, that we should not throw out a few stimulators that have been carefully thought out in advance. With regard to Sid Winehart, he's playing our side of the street in this controversy. I don't see any advantage in letting him ask those leading questions that permit further simplifications on his part. I think our present posture is just about right on this thing and we should leave it alone. The same thing applies to the guy from the *Globe*. He's in our corner already, so what else can he do but help? I know he'd like me to go to the Senate and throw a few punches at Roland Gray, but there is an intelligent electorate that wouldn't approve of that, even if some of the press would relish the confrontation."

The Vice President leaned back in his chair, stretched, then continued. "So, Pete, the verdict is no interviews prior to our departure for Singapore—that includes Bradley Barton, but I'll call and finesse him personally—and no clarifications unless they have been cleared through Bill and Zack and me in advance. Meanwhile, we'll try to think of a few handouts to feed the animals. One thing—I want you to go with me to the hospital to see the young lady. Make certain that it's well covered by the media. I'll do the visit in the morning."

"That's great, Mr. Vice President. Then you can stop and take a few questions after you see the girl," Rosen suggested enthusiastically.

"No," said Canfield flatly. "There will be no questions and no statement. I will play this strictly low key. Act like I'm sort of embarrassed to be caught in a humane act. You will then explain to the media that I do not want to politically exploit the serious injuries that the young woman has sustained in the unfortunate accident."

Miller cut in quickly, "That makes a lot of sense to me, Mr. Veep."

Bill Shelby nodded his agreement, and the press secretary also nodded as though the idea has been his in the first place.

The intercom buzzed again. "Put him on," Canfield said. In an aside to the staff, he said, "It's Josh Devers calling from Camp David. They want to know whether I'm ready for the call. I wonder what the old man's doing up there. This morning's *Globe* said he's closeted with his foreign policy advisors."

"Maybe he's about ready to take your advice on IRBM's for Israel," Zack said with a laugh.

Canfield removed his hand from the phone mouthpiece. "Yes? This is he. Oh, hello, Josh. What's up?" There was a long pause and Canfield's face hardened. Finally, he said, "Yes, I understand perfectly, but I think it's a bad decision. It's a disappointment. I'm afraid the press will make something of it. . . . Yes, I know the President considered that. Thank you for calling."

After the Vice President had put down the phone, he relayed the information he had just received in a tight, strained voice. "Devers called on the President's instructions to tell me that Hurley would not see me off for the Far East. The President feels that the press would use the occasion to demand that he comment on my stance about Israel. Besides, there's something more important going on, something that the President doesn't want to cancel. I can't imagine what that would be."

Zack jumped up and slammed his fist into his hand. "It's a damned insult," he said angrily. "Hurley knows very well that the media will construe this as a slap in the face to you, Newt. Also they'll conjecture that it shows his support of Gray. They'll play up the fact that he saw Gray that same morning. They know the leaders are having breakfast with the President that day."

"That's not all, Zack," said Canfield, restraining his fury with difficulty. "Josh Devers had more to say. This is the best I can reconstruct it: 'The President urges you in the strongest language possible to discontinue your public utterances concerning his policy in the Middle East. The President does not intend to mention this matter to you again. Particularly during your Far East visit, it is imperative that you confine yourself to the approved positions as defined in the briefing books.' Then he said, 'I am requested to ask you, Is that perfectly clear, Mr. Vice President?'"

"What a nerve," said Zack hotly, beginning his usual pacing. "Why in hell can't the President call you over and tell you that to your face?"

"Easy, Zack. You know very well that's not the way he operates," Canfield said, regaining his composure. "We'll just play this game our way. The power flow is all in our direction, but we must not reach too early. It's not the proper time for open rebellion."

He stood up and looked at his watch. "Nearly seven. Unless you have something very important, let's hold it for morning. I still have a couple of things to do."

"Just one second," said Zack. "I wanted to give you that report from the Senate."

"Oh, yes. Go ahead."

"As I indicated, Gray was really burned up about your meeting with the press. He wasn't so much angry with what you said as he was about putting him in a bad light by submitting to an interview without consulting him."

"That's a damned shame," said Canfield.

"But from what we've been able to garner, opinion in the Congress is much in your favor. Even the old guard in the Senate feels that you handled yourself beautifully and avoided the pitfalls well. They considered your conduct gentlemanly."

"Good, good. That's a big switch from the stiff-collared reaction Vice Presidents usually get from the Senate," Canfield said with a smile. "Now, gentlemen, if you'll excuse me."

Shelby, Rosen and Miller left immediately, and Kathy Dryden returned in answer to his call.

"Send in Steve Galdari," said Canfield, "and see if you can't rustle me up a V.O. and water, Kathy."

Waiting in the empty room, the Vice President permitted himself the luxury of a few sharp expletives. "That son of a bitch. From now on I'm looking after Number One. The hell with this 'loyalty to the administration' business."

Kathy had just put the drink on his desk when Steve Galdari entered.

"Sorry to bother you about this, sir, but I think it may be important enough to justify taking a few moments of your time."

"Sit down, Steve."

Galdari took a seat and leaned forward. "Mr. Vice President, I know you've had some contact with an organization called 'Israel Now and Forever,' run by a man named Yoram Halevy in New York. I believe they are supporting your present stand on Israel very strongly."

"Yes, that's true."

Galdari pulled some notes from his pocket and continued. "Yesterday, I was contacted by our liaison FBI operative. The organization INAF is under their surveillance and also under a concurrent investigation by the Internal Revenue Service. Although they are not under suspicion for any violent activities or unlawful conduct beyond the usual gray demonstration areas, there is grave concern about their funding. It seems that they accumulate and expend amounts of money that their known activities don't account for. Moreover, they are unable to properly explain the source of all those funds. Background checks on Halevy himself show he emigrated from Israel in nineteen seventy-seven and has been a full-time lobbyist for Israeli causes since that time. He became a United States citizen only last year. I thought I'd better let you know about this since you have been quoted as supportive of INAF and have publicly tangled with Senator Gray over INAF demonstrations. I would advise great caution in dealing with this particular group until we can get further information from the FBI and IRS investigations."

Canfield sat very still, thinking for a moment. "Steve, I appreciate your bringing this information to my attention. I am familiar with INAF and I know Yoram Halevy personally. As a matter of fact, I just talked with him on the phone this evening. I'll certainly be very guarded in my relations with this particular group, but of course I have to take advantage of the strategic political position it occupies at the moment."

He paused and rubbed his face reflectively. "Do you know who initiated these government investigations? And how long they've been in progress?"

"No, sir. But I don't think they've been under way too long, because we would have heard about this sooner."

"Would you try to find out who started the investigations? That is, if it can be done discreetly, without embarrassing the Service in any way."

"I'll do what I can," said Galdari, "but I don't want to push it too far. It's so easy for your office to be tagged with exerting undue influence."

"That's true, so be very careful."

After thanking Galdari, Canfield stood up and drained his glass. "Now, if the cars are ready, let's go home. This has been a real brute of a day."

CANFIELD PICKED up the briefing book and opened it to the tab marked "Summary." A quick skimming of the three single-spaced pages convinced him that State had done it again. The material was clean and succinct, uncluttered by the wordy editorializing so prevalent in current news reporting. He wondered about all the bad-mouthing that past and present elected officials had given the career foreign-service officers. Personally, he found them competent and professional.

He closed the dark-green three-ring binder, running his fingers idly across the smooth surface. It reminded him of those undemanding years at the elementary school on Wentworth Avenue in North Philadelphia. He remembered brush-penning covers of similar notebooks with initials, symbols and other esoteric trivia then popular among his peers. He and many of his schoolmates had shared a common problem—how to get out from under the suffocating blanket of great wealth. During early adolescence was the only time in his life, he reflected, that he found the accumulations of Great-grandfather Porter Starrat Canfield a disadvantage. Since he could remember, his privacy had been more or less continuously assaulted by a series of nurses, sitters, tutors, music teachers, butlers, cooks, maids and gardeners. Whether he or she intended to or not, each exerted a measure of restraint.

How he had envied his less affluent friends their freedom—bike rides in the country, skinny-dipping at Abrecht's quarry and just hanging out at Dundy's Soda Fountain—and how much more such bragged-about forbidden activities as walking the highest rafters of houses under construction, sneaking cigarettes and beer and hiding in the weeds to watch sexy movies at the outdoor theater.

Canfield looked at the words "Singapore—Top Secret" neatly printed on the smooth vinyl cover. There was a certain satisfaction in being at the top, even though it necessitated losing some of the freedom and privacy he had won later than most. He thought of the contrast between that final year at Wentworth and the wonderful less-controlled ones that followed at Hadston Prep. Living away from home for the first time was like being let out of a cage. During his third year he had learned that the glossy magazine fold-outs, stimulating as they were, were nothing compared to the real thing.

At a country club dance he discovered Wanda, a seventeen-year-old sophisticate, and she practically became an appendage to the red Ford convertible he had acquired on his sixteenth birthday. Wanda was light-years ahead of him in experience, but claimed to be tired of "older men," which was how she described the college boys she dated before Porter caught her fancy. She swam rings around him, dived from heights he would not attempt, embarrassed him at tennis, but salvaged his self-respect by preferring him to the hordes of attractive young jocks who clustered around her.

Golden hair and skin; slim body, incongruously voluptuous; violet eyes that made any encounter with a male dramatically personal; and a feline way of moving—that was Wanda. Unhurriedly, step by step, she brought him through the familiar kissing and touching rituals to that unforgettable August night on Wyndham Hill. He could still remember the night noises and the smell of honeysuckle, and the indelible sight of a very eager Wanda, skirt rucked high on tan thighs and breasts brushing his face as she moved into the automobile position.

His inexperienced, blundering early crescendo mortified him and might have left him with much to overcome in the future, but her matter-of-fact patience and experience reerected the fallen structure. In time, he drove her home proudly, colors flying. Whatever had happened to Wanda? Somehow, after his freshman year at Princeton, he lost track of her.

Canfield sighed restlessly and opened the notebook. There had been several others, before and after Amy, but no one who got under his skin—not until Meredith Lord. He leaned back and closed his eyes, preparing to drift down that increasingly used memory track labeled "Meredith." Only a few moments passed, however, before Steve Galdari's voice shattered his daydream.

"Sir, we're only fifteen minutes out. Will you be getting off at

Hickam to see General Waring? He and the governor will be waiting planeside for you.''

The Vice President opened his eyes without reaction. Such intrusions were commonplace. He expected them.

''Bill, I told you no greeting party—that we would just refuel and get on to Guam.''

Bill Shelby, standing beside Galdari, shook his head tiredly. ''I relayed that to both the governor's people and the general's aide. You should have heard the 'pony parade' they wanted to put you through originally.''

''Damn. Well, okay. I'll go down to them for a minute or two. But no moving to the lounge and positively no press accessibility. The governor would like to involve me in a local problem that has to be a loser no matter what I say.''

He turned back toward the window. The plane banked sharply, signifying the beginning of the approach pattern, but Oahu was not yet visisble.

''How about the people at the fence?'' asked Galdari.

''Have them park the plane so that we exit at the side away from them,'' replied Canfield without looking around. He made it clear that he wanted no further discussion, and the men moved away.

Air Force Two leveled out again. Porter Canfield replaced the green notebook alongside the Singapore schedule book on the table. As soon as they were airborne for Guam, he would get back to the briefing material. He'd better. The prime minister was going to be tough to handle.

In the rear of the plane, press secretary Peter Rosen was explaining to the traveling press that the Vice President of the United States did not intend to be interrogated during the fueling stop in Hawaii. This unwelcome news was being received with petulant stares and some overt expressions of incredulity.

''You call this access, Peter? You call this an open flow of information to the American people?'' Sid Winehart asked, putting an accusation of betrayal in his tone and misquoting a section of one of President Hurley's most misquoted speeches.

The press secretary's face froze, but he restrained the impulse to inform Winehart that the lack of accuracy and objectivity in modern reporting did more to impede the flow of information than anything else.

''Peetuh,'' enunciated Douglas Drake in his best Hollywood accent, ''you are freezing us out at the apex of a newsworthy nonevent. The President of the United States snubbed his Vice President when he departed for what the State Department has described as 'an important diplomatic mission.' The American people are curious about this developing bad blood between their Number One and Number Two. We, the guardians of the First Amendment, must explain what is happening. Running away won't help the Vice President. He has to come to grips with the problem sooner or later. We'll be together for the entire trip. He might as well get it over with.''

Rosen stiffened. "That's crap, Doug. It's not the first time a Vice President went through Hawaii without a news conference, nor is it the first time a President didn't wave goodbye to his Number Two.''

"But there is bad blood—you don't deny it, do you?'' pressed the television man. "The President is naturally pissed off about the IRBM's for Israel—and he likes Roland Gray better than Porter Canfield, *n'est-ce pas?*''

Rosen wiped a trickle of sweat from his forehead. "I think you're assuming a hell of a lot, Doug,'' he said heavily. "There's absolutely no confirmation of those rumors about a rift between the veep and President Hurley. Besides, the President's already said he will stay out of the jockeying by presidential aspirants.''

"Oh, God, Peter. Hurley's already in the race up to his neck. You aren't talking to yokels from Corn City, you know.''

Rosen hung on doggedly, maneuvering for escape. "I don't agree with you, Doug. . . . Now, that's all there is to it. I'll do the best I can to get you something before we get to Guam, okay?''

The grumbling tapered off as most of them returned to their seats to buckle in for landing. A familiar gravelly voice stopped Rosen from making his retreat. "I have it from an impeccable source that the Israeli ambassador to Singapore will seek a private meeting with Vice President Canfield,'' said Bruce Atherton. "First, if that is true, will the Vice President see him? Second, will you inform the press if the Israeli ambassador asks for the meeting?''

"I can't give you any information on that because I know nothing about it,'' said Peter Rosen, a hint of uncertainty in his voice. "I'll ask your questions and advise you of the Vice President's answers later.''

As *Air Force Two* banked around a few scattered rain clouds to begin its final descent into Hickam Air Force Base, Canfield had his first glimpse of the late afternoon sun through the port window by his chair. From this angle the Pacific seemed a placid sheet of silver reflecting the sun's oblique rays. Moments later, they came overland prior to landing, and he noted the exquisite contrast of Oahu's verdure against the now-azure sea. No matter how many times he came to Hawaii, the beauty of the islands never failed to move him.

In no time there was the cushioned shock of rubber on concrete, attesting to the skill of the men in the cockpit. While they taxied into the parking position, Bill Shelby and the stewards moved quickly down the banks of windows pulling the louvers shut in the Executive Cabin, thus assuring the Vice President's privacy during the fueling stop.

Ridge Potter swung the big bird around and parked it so that anyone disembarking would not be seen from the airport buildings. He shut the engines down, and the traveling press made a break for the base telephones as soon as the ladder was lowered.

Porter Canfield stood up, stretched and put on the jacket that Joe Hentz was holding for him.

"Just a second, Mr. Vice President," said Steve Galdari. "Shelby and I will make sure everything's lined up and ready before you exit. Peter is going to bird-dog the traveling press to make sure everybody gets back on the plane on time. We have forty-five minutes on the ground here."

Canfield stood in the forward part of the plane talking with some of the off-duty crew members until Shelby and Galdari returned. "What have we got out there?" asked the Vice President, his voice showing the lack of enthusiasm he felt about seeing the governor and the commander of the base. Coming on the heels of a frantic week, the five-hour flight over the Pacific had already taken its toll of his reserves. He wasn't exactly looking forward to going straight through to Guam, but it was much better that he rest there so that he would have only the short hop to Singapore before undertaking the ceremonies and discussions that were scheduled for his arrival.

"It's just Governor Kanuka and General Waring, a couple of junior officers and one still photographer. I've explained that a few pictures are okay, but that you will not make any statements to the press here. I also told them that you're pretty tired and they shouldn't keep you out there too long." Shelby smiled faintly. "The governor is quite unhappy. He had in mind a little tube time with you. The general shows his disappointment less, although I happen to know that he was looking forward to your having a cup of tea with his wife and some of the ladies of the senior officers."

"C'est dommage," said Canfield in mock regret. "Let's go." He followed the two aides out of the airplane, pausing at the top of the steps to wave the traditional greeting to the small group below for the benefit of the photographer.

The ten minutes with the governor and the general were not the most pleasant ones of his career. Kanuka, who had hoped to involve him in a political fight over a needed sales tax increase, looked set upon and sorrowful. He had been weaseling about supporting the tax and was looking for the opportunity publicly to demand federal assistance as an antidote to the unpopular legislation. The general, on the other hand, was courteous and accepted with good grace Canfield's refusal to go to the lounge for tea and sandwiches. After somewhat cheering the governor with a promise of a fund-raising appearance prior to the national election, the Vice President seized the first opportunity to escape into the cabin.

Back in the big chair, Canfield slipped out of his shoes and gratefully sipped the steaming cup of coffee that Joe brought him. He was beginning to feel civilized again. He drained the cup to the last drop, shook off the suggestion of a refill, tilted back and closed his eyes. He had been dozing only a moment when he was brought back to full consciousness by angry voices in the cabin of the airplane. The traveling press had returned and apparently were engaged in a heated argument.

There were a couple of dull thuds. Canfield at first thought they had come to blows, but then he felt the increased pressure in his ears that told him the airplane was being sealed for takeoff. The engines were just beginning to whine when the rear door to the Executive Cabin burst open and Peter Rosen hurried in, closing the door quickly behind him. He was wild-eyed.

"Sir, we've got a hell of a problem. I hate to disturb you, but this is urgent."

Bill Shelby, who had stretched out on one of the bunks, threw off the blanket he had pulled over him. "Didn't I tell you not to bother the Vice President without checking with me first, Peter?" He got to his feet and came to the conference table.

"I'm sorry, Bill. I'm so damned worried I forgot. This is a real emergency."

Canfield swung his chair out and gestured to the others to sit at the conference table across the aisle. "I heard all the racket back there. What the hell is the matter? Did you run out of whiskey? Or did you have to herd them all back before they made contact with the States?"

"Please don't joke, Mr. Vice President. You have been put in a position that's just murder."

"Well, for Christ's sake, what is it?" growled Bill Shelby. "Spit it out!"

"Easy, Bill," said Canfield quietly, thinking that Rosen interacted with Shelby like a tornado on a frame house.

Peter Rosen drew a deep breath. "Three hours ago, President Hurley held a news conference. That was eight P.M. Eastern Time. The media were given only two hours' notice. The President announced that new accords have been reached with the Soviet Union—and with the People's Republic of China—and that the first Tripartite SALT agreement would be executed in Geneva in forty-eight hours." The press secretary paused, carefully watching the Vice President's reaction to the news. It was obvious that the amazement on Canfield's face was genuine, that he was thunderstruck by the announcement.

Rosen continued, "The press in the back of our airplane is furious. They believe that you found out about this in advance of our landing and that's why you refused to have a press conference here. They caught hell when they called home—because they couldn't report your reactions."

Canfield sat perfectly still, the dazed look on his face testifying better than words to his complete surprise. A moment later, as though coming out of a dream, he shook his head and asked weakly, "Where's Zack?"

"He's in the back working on final arrival-statement changes with Parker, the State Department guy," said Shelby. "Do you want him?"

"Yes. Get him up here right away." Canfield's voice strengthened, and the color returned to his face. The adrenaline was beginning to flow. "And get Kathy," he added. "We need to focus everyone on this problem."

At the front of the rear section, Miller had been poring over briefing books with the career man from State assigned for the trip, when the turmoil interrupted them. Kathy Dryden was sitting across from them, waiting patiently for the dictation to resume. The 727 was halfway down the runway, ready to lift off for Guam, when Shelby, Miller and Kathy hurried in, closed the door on the pursuing Sid Winehart and buckled up for takeoff.

"I heard," said Zack before the Vice President could repeat Peter Rosen's message. "No one could be within two miles of Sid Winehart and not hear."

Canfield looked at Kathy, who nodded to indicate that she was also aware of the startling development, and then he leaned forward with both palms on the table.

"This duplicity on the part of the President places us in a difficult and potentially dangerous position," he said grimly. "Fortunately, we have time to prepare." His face twitched in a rictus that passed for a smile. "Those troublemakers in the back are our prisoners for eight hours. They are incommunicado so far as the rest of the world goes. Now, let's begin by getting what input Peter has."

"Excuse me, Mr. Vice President." Ridge Potter handed Canfield seven closely printed pages. "This was just received from the White House."

Canfield skimmed the top sheet. "Devers thought we might like to see what the President said at his news conference today," he said cynically. "Well, we'll hear from Peter first. The important thing is what our flying inquisitors have on their minds. Go ahead, Pete."

Rosen was at one and the same time frightened about facing the traveling press and puffed about being on center stage.

"They went to the phones at Hickam and I stood around talking to the duty officer and waiting for them to finish. Well, it didn't take but a few minutes to find out something was wrong. They were cursing and screaming back and forth on the phones and to each other. Then, one by one, as they hung up, they came rushing over to me. I thought they were going to attack me physically. They wouldn't give me a chance to say a word—just kept cussing me and calling me—and you, too, sir—every name in the book. They are convinced you had prior notice of this information when you refused to face the press in Hawaii."

"Wait a minute. Do they think that the President filled me in on the situation before his news conference? That doesn't make sense. They know he was angry at me and didn't even see me off," interjected Canfield angrily.

"No, sir. That wouldn't fit their scenario. They thrive on divisions between you and the President. What they are claiming is that after the President's news conference, but before you told them no press in Hawaii, you heard. They think you deliberately froze them out of a big story at its hottest so the thing could cool down before you commented."

"And you'll never convince them otherwise, because they have been raised to believe that all politicians are tricky, lying, deceptive bastards—pardon me, Kathy—so we might as well forget the disclaimers," Bill Shelby remarked with strong feeling.

Canfield groaned. "We'll have to make the effort anyhow, Bill, although I'm afraid you're right. What parts of the news conference attracted their attention most?"

"Apparently the President was overjoyed about the agreement, which involves the dismantling of one hundred offensive missiles each by the United States and the Soviet Union, and an agreement by the Chinese not to exceed the currently agreed levels of the other two powers. Naturally, the press made a few smart remarks about the PRC needing forty more years to get to those levels.''

"What pertained specifically to the boss?" Like most dedicated staff people, Shelby saw everything in relation to his principal.

Rosen thought a moment. "Well, the whole statement was essentially an ad for détente, reducing defense budgets and the elimination of force as a solution to international problems. Naturally, this idea of not needing weapons brought to the media minds that President Hurley's Vice President is stumping for more weapons for Israel. There were several questions about that which led to the ancient game of creating trouble between the President and Vice President.''

Canfield riffled through the sheets Potter had brought him. "Let's see if we can find that part," he said. "I suppose those questions will be near the front of the Q and A. . . . Yes, here they are. The very first question, of course." He read, " 'Mr. President, your policy of détente with the communist powers and gradual mutual disarmament seems to some to be impractical at a time when Russia, China and the United States are arming smaller nations that threaten each other around the world. Would it not be better to cooperate in eliminating the most serious flash points, such as the Middle East, before weakening the superpowers?' Here's the answer— 'We are negotiating only on the limitation of strategic nuclear weapons. That's a long way from disarmament. Of course, we will continue to exert our influence to reduce tensions around the world, but that doesn't mean we should abandon our efforts to defuse the danger of total destruction that is represented by nuclear warfare.' Question: 'But, sir, your own Vice President, Mr. Canfield, has on several occasions advocated that Israel be given nuclear weapons to protect her against what she sees as a nuclear threat from some of her Arab neighbors. Do you find the Vice President in opposition to your policy?*' "

Canfield raised his eyes to look dramatically from one person to the other in the small group. Zack Miller was uncharacteristically quiet, and Canfield wondered what he had on his mind. He had been listless and torpid much of the time since they left Washington. Shelby was composed but looked like he was ready to do battle. Rosen darted little side glances around him, not yet sure of how to react. Kathy Dryden looked straight at him, radiating loyalty and support. Canfield resumed reading. "Answer: 'The Vice President has a right to his own opinions, but I must candidly answer that on this issue his opinions do not represent the policy of this administration.' Question: 'Vice President Canfield has been sent by you to the Far East on a diplomatic mission. Are you not concerned that United States policy on this issue will be muddied and misunderstood because of his statements?' Answer''—Canfield read slowly for emphasis—'' 'I have instructed the Vice President to promulgate the foreign policy of the United States to the leaders of the countries he is visiting, and not his personal opinions.' ''

Bill Shelby sighed audibly. Canfield read silently for three more minutes, then tossed the papers on the table. ''There's more—a lot more. Does the President think my hawkishness disqualifies me for the presidency? —ducked. Does he prefer Roland Gray, who will carry on his foreign policy? —ducked. Will he recall me if I speak out during the trip? Ducked —he will not speculate.'' Canfield glowered at Rosen. ''What do those vultures in the back want?'' he asked rhetorically. He then answered his own question, ''They want to see a Vice President eat crow, cringe and cower.''

He suddenly banged his fist down on the table, making the cigarette butts in Rosen's ashtray jump. ''Well, we've got to figure out how to stick to our guns, yet not push Hurley to the point that he calls me back. Let's have some ideas.''

They spent the better part of the next two hours discussing various options. Hentz brought coffee and little sandwiches, which they demolished in a wave of nervous hunger. The ashtrays were emptied and reemptied. Finally, Canfield signaled the end of the discussion.

''We've talked it to death,'' he said quietly. ''There's no good way out. But the best thing for me to do is say I'm here to communicate United States policy to the leaders of the countries we visit, whether it happens to be my judgment or not. In selected situations, I will make it clear to the press that my personal opinions are unchanged, but will always state the administration policy at the same time. That's the best that can be done with a tough situation. What do you think, Zack?''

Miller looked uncertain. ''I don't know, sir. I guess that's the best you can do.'' The insouciance and the certainty that generally accompanied his recommendations were strangely missing.

''Better get some rest,'' said Canfield, peering at him intently. ''You look really bushed. Jump in the bunk for a couple hours. I'm going to need you functioning on all cylinders very shortly.''

He overrode Miller's protestations that the arrival statement was not complete, pointing out that the State Department man was fully competent to handle that. Without further argument, Miller climbed listlessly into one of the bunks and drew the curtain.

''He doesn't look like he's feeling very well,'' ventured Bill

Shelby, sounding more critical than sympathetic.

"Well, he's not used to chasing the sun halfway around the world. A little sleep will straighten him out. He has immense reserves of energy." Canfield felt uncomfortable, as though he were a sergeant and a member of his platoon had not been able to keep up at calisthenics. He was well aware that the regular staff secretly resented his grafting of Miller onto what they considered a smooth operation.

"What do you want me to tell the press people when I go back, sir?" Rosen asked anxiously. "They won't sit still for 'no comment' at this point."

The Vice President frowned a moment, and then his face relaxed as he came to a decision. "Tell them that I will come back to see them in about three hours and will answer all their questions on the record. That will give them a chance to have their stories ready for filing by the time we land at Guam."

The expression of relief on the press secretary's face was almost comical. He made a quick movement toward the door.

"Hold it a minute, Peter," said Canfield sharply. "I'm not finished. I want you to get this exactly right. Think first. It makes for fewer mistakes."

Rosen turned back to listen, chagrin showing on his face. Canfield continued in a softer tone. "Have copies of that stuff that Washington sent us made for the press, but make sure you delete any of Devers's side comments that might be damaging. Also give the press copies of the Singapore arrival statement, but embargo use until tomorrow noon. We want to soothe them, to cooperate in every possible way. It won't hurt to show that we trust them not to break anything before release date. Actually, it doesn't make any difference about the arrival statement. There's no great harm done if somebody breaks it before the release time."

Canfield thought for a moment longer, then said, "Think, now, Peter. Is there anything else they said to you that might be important for me to know?"

Rosen concentrated, biting his upper lip. "Oh, yes, sir, just one other thing. Atherton said his sources heard about a meeting you and the Israeli ambassador to Singapore have scheduled. He wanted to know whether you would confirm or deny that such a meeting was set. Also, whether you would let him know later if such a meeting did take place, scheduled or not."

Canfield did a good job of concealing his surprise. Meredith had told him the night of the health care dinner that his stock was soaring in Israel and that the Israeli ambassador in Washington wished to pass along a message of a confidential nature. Washington was not considered safe for this purpose, so the Israeli ambassador to Singapore would contact him at the Malaysia Hotel. How had Atherton discovered this, and how much did he know about it? Well, one thing was certain. No one in Washington was closer to the Israeli ambassador than Meredith, and since the meeting came through her and not to him directly, he could safely deny that any arrangements had been made.

"Tell Atherton that I have no arrangements for a meeting with the Israeli ambassador to Singapore. Naturally, if a high official, such as an ambassador, asked to see me, I would try to find time to accommodate him. Whatever meetings of an official nature I have in Singapore will be communicated to the traveling press. How's that?"

"That's perfect, sir. Saying these things now will go a long way toward reducing the hostility in the back. All the reporters know that you're the preferred presidential candidate of the liberal media, so they'll try to get back on a good footing if you massage their egos."

This time Rosen waited to make sure that Canfield was through before making his exit. Shelby and Kathy Dryden went with him to assist in preparing the distributions.

The Vice President opened the briefing book in his lap, but his thoughts were far away. The book was simply a prop that said "Do Not Disturb." Joe Hentz, who always seemed to know the right time to be there, put a darkish V.O. and water in front of him and told him that dinner would be ready fifteen minutes after he said he wanted it.

Canfield took a long sip of his drink. It has authority. He could feel the little tendrils of warmth stretching out in his stomach. The tensions started to ebb and a feeling of peace came over him. It was difficult to believe they were 38,000 feet above the broad expanse of the Pacific. *Air Force Two* whispered effortlessly at cruising speed, ticking off the miles at a rate of over five hundred per hour. There was no turbulence. Canfield looked out the window. He was struck by the beauty of the early evening sky. They were losing their race against the sun—a ball of maroon which now lay against the sea, its refracting rays painting the evening sky in subtle color modulations.

A sense of loneliness stabbed at the Vice President, an indefinable longing that was somehow the effect of the natural beauty of the sky rather than the state of his mind. He wondered whether other people reacted this way to the grandeur of God's work. So far as he was concerned, this experience was a strong argument against atheism.

He watched idly, his mind concious of nothing except the ever-changing spectacle, until the curtain of darkness had come down on nature's stage. Reluctantly, he turned his attention back to more mundane considerations.

The briefing book was opened to the section entitled "Sensitive Issues." He began to read the two single-spaced pages dealing with the gradually accumulated and understandable irritations of the prime minister of Singapore with twenty years of American foreign policy. It was obvious that the prime minister, a very intelligent and experienced man, was no longer a believer. He had watched with amazement the impudent victories of the Indochinese communists over the mightiest power in the world. Ultimately he had reached a sad conclusion—Tarzan had become Mickey Mouse and Mickey Mouse Tarzan. America's internal masochism had dropped her into the minor leagues. Canfield's task was to make the prime minister believe that the might of the United States was still available to protect his tiny gem of a nation, should it be attacked. It wasn't going to be easy. Canfield himself found it difficult to believe.

The paper blurred. Although the image of the words was being transmitted faithfully to the optic nerve, the brain had turned to a more pressing problem. Porter Canfield was organizing his defense against the anticipated thrusts of the traveling press. He was thoroughly aware of the importance of his impending conversation, since this conference would set the tone of the next two weeks—perhaps even of the coming months. It was up to him to dissipate the ill will resulting from his decision not to hold a press conference in Hawaii. Satisfying them would not be too difficult, but satisfying them without driving the President to the point of recalling him to Washington would require a very delicate balance of independence and caution. He would have to eat some crow, but he would do it in a way that made him look statesmanlike—more interested in the welfare of the country than in his own political fortunes.

But how to handle this thing with the Israeli ambassador in Singapore? That was a very sensitive matter, especially since someone not interested in his welfare had enough of an open line to know about it and leak it to Atherton. It had to be someone in the Israeli embassy in Washington or a person high up on Meredith Lord's staff. Knowing Meredith's political savvy and customary caution, he was inclined to believe the former. Well, if the meeting took place, he would have to admit it, but he certainly wasn't required to divulge the substance of the conversation.

Meredith. There she was again, elbowing aside everything else in his mind. He thought of their last meeting, the night of the health care dinner at the Sheraton Carlton in Washington. He had been caught in the inevitable cocktail small talk with a parchment-faced, guilt-ridden millionaire do-gooder, when she left a group of admiring men and walked over to him. Linking her arm in his, she drew him aside. "Please excuse me, Mr. Friedman, but I must have a private word with my Vice President. He's our best supporter, you know."

She had looked beautiful. To save his life, he couldn't remember what she had worn except that it was body hugging and low cut. The cloth clung to and outlined her shapely legs with every sinuous stride. They had talked of Charlie Voren and the Congress, but his mind was more on her bare tanned shoulders and her superb body.

Why was it that he couldn't think of Meredith without triggering awareness of his physical hunger for her? There was so much more to their mutual attraction.

He remembered the long telephone conversation the night Amy went to Philadelphia without even bothering to tell him. What a contrast in the two women. Meredith was aware of everything he did, supportive and sympathetic in times of stress. Amy was oblivious of his professional life, never mentioning the hopes and fears, the victories and defeats. To Amy, his career was no more important than a game of tennis. They never discussed it unless it conflicted with her own interests. She wasn't even aware of the ongoing desperate contest with Hurley and Gray. He doubted that she had even heard about the accident in the Senate, unless one of her social confidants had mentioned it.

Canfield wondered if Amy realized how rapidly they were drifting apart. No wonder he was a voyeur with Meredith. Amy always had a headache, or a hairdo to protect, or was "just exhausted." Sex was too much of a struggle; besides, she wasn't that great in bed anyhow. She had a good-looking, well-kept body, but making love with her was like seducing Snow White. She seemed happier when it was over than when it was in progress—as if she'd just come from a tough afternoon at the dentist's.

There was Meredith again, pushing her way back into his consciousness. "Forget Amy," she seemed to say. "You haven't finished remembering our last evening." He remembered all too well.

There had been no need to rush home when the dinner and speeches were over, so they sat in the holding room for nearly two hours sipping brandy nightcaps and talking about everything imaginable. At first Bill Shelby and Zack Miller were there too, but each had sensed the indefinable current and that their presence was not required forever. They had excused themselves in due course, and he was left with an hour and a quarter of Meredith Lord alone. The conversation moved quickly from governmental generalities to outright flirtation, with hints and hidden meanings. Then, as she started to leave, he pulled her to him and kissed her, his head swirling—drunk with her perfume and wondering at the speed with which his body notified him that it was ready to get down to serious business. For a moment they strained against one another. Finally, she broke away with a sigh and looked at him, her eyes pools of molten gold-flecked copper.

"Newt," she said, "we have to do something about this."

He had been more than willing, but with a full complement of Secret Service men waiting to escort him home, the situation was impossible. He had promised to exert all his efforts to find some way that they could be alone. The problem became even more evident when their kiss was interrupted by a knock at the door. It was Steve Galdari inquiring whether the shift change, due in fifteen minutes, should be there or back at the residence. And so they had parted, and Canfield went home to toss in his bed and dream fitfully of future nights with Meredith Lord.

The Vice President was roused from his pleasant reverie by Joe Hentz, who inquired whether another drink was needed. Canfield declined and ordered dinner. In the twenty minutes before the meal was brought, he managed to absorb the National Security Council cover paper and to skim most of the detailed background material in the briefing book.

When Joe Hentz put down the tray containing the steak, hobo potatoes and salad, the Vice President closed the book and pressed the button that slid his chair closer to the table. He began to eat in a deliberate, mechanical fashion, his mind again on other things.

He was convinced that Israel was the key to his campaign. He had been the first to recognize the power of the Middle East issue and the hunger of the American Jewish establishment for a foreign policy more visibly supportive of the beleaguered little nation. For years American diplomacy in the Middle East had been an elaborate formal dance, in which there was a great deal of bending over backward to waltz with all the other girls, but it fooled no one. The whole world knew that the last dance was reserved for Israel, the fiancée. However, the unspoken commitment didn't seem to be enough to satisfy the pro-Israel lobby in the United States. The American Zionists wanted the American sword to rattle every time a potential attacker made the slightest threat toward their darling. They, who had been the strongest advocates of abandoning Southeast Asia to the communists, were perfectly willing to send war materials, advisors and even armed troops if Israel was attacked. Canfield felt worry for any Palestinian communist who made the mistake of starting a war of national liberation. Such radical action drew the sympathy of the American left only so long as the homeland of the Jews was not threatened. It was perfectly all right for the North Vietnamese but not for the Palestinian reds.

Actually, the Vice President believed in Israel. He had tremendous admiration for the resiliency and courage of the poor immigrants who had carved a national identity out of so many diverse heritages. They were ambitious, energetic and tough. He was entirely comfortable with his support for them and his opposition to the communist powers. He was frank enough to admit that the Soviet Union frightened him. Certain that Dradavov was negotiating Hurley right out of his shoes, he was equally certain that neither the Russians nor the Chinese communists could be depended upon to adhere to the policy of coexistence with the free world that they currently seemed to support. Canfield was not deceived. He believed that the teachings of the old Marxist scholars would not be abandoned—that the revered idea of not resting until the world was communist was still active in Moscow and Peking.

People like Yoram Halevy fascinated him. Here was a man who had given up any chance for a pleasant existence to live in near poverty in a grubby section of Brooklyn. Besides the satisfaction gained from leading his little band of zealots, what were his rewards? What kind of fervor was it that made the man fight day after day to make Americans aware of real or imagined threats against a small nation thousands of miles away?

Halevy was volatile and intense. He found it easy to hate those who supported a point of view which might be erosive to Israel's continued existence. What a powerful man. Canfield remembered their recent meeting in the Vice President's office. Standing behind a heavy leather upholstered chair, Halevy seized the top of the back in his two hands and with straight arms raised the chair effortlessly. Referring to an Arab adversary, he said, ''Were I in Damascus, I would take that loudmouth in my two hands, lift him like this and crush him until he begged for mercy.''

That meeting had lasted for an hour and a half. He had been a bit uncertain when Zack Miller suggested he have Halevy into the Executive Office Building. It was three days after Steve Galdari's warning that INAF was being investigated, and Canfield knew that all visitors in the Executive complex were logged in by the White House police. Actually, he had been ready to veto the meeting, but two things changed his mind. First, Meredith informed him that her Israeli contacts had selected Halevy as the vehicle to channel two million dollars into his campaign, and second, Galdari reported that very morning that it was the White House that ordered the investigation of INAF. To Canfield, that meant it was a political investigation rather than a routine professional suspicion of wrongdoing. Hurley and Gray didn't want him to be on good terms with Halevy and they were trying to scare him off.

So on the spur of the moment, he had asked Zack to bring in Yoram Halevy, and it had been very worthwhile. Halevy pledged the full political and financial assistance of INAF and even referred to ''other interested Jewish groups'' and mentioned ''several million dollars.'' Canfield knew he had no worries about the strict campaign financing laws in effect since the Seventies. He would simply finance a great amount of his own effort with the family wealth and leave it to the lawyers to figure how to get the Israeli contributions in later, possibly through maneuvering in multinational corporations the Canfields controlled. For someone as rich as he was, the strict law could be evaded easily by using the leverage of his personal fortune.

Halevy had seemed unworried about the investigations—he said INAF had no problem about its donors. After a half-hour, Zack had excused himself to attend a meeting with key House members. Canfield could have broken it off there, but he was tremendously impressed with the Zionist and captured by the force of his personality.

The meeting had continued for another hour. Halevy confided to him his conviction that certain media leaders highly influential in the pro-Israel lobby had sold out to Arab oil money and would soon be dedicating their powerful news organs to the cause of Israel's Islamic opponents. Halevy mentioned Mark O'Mara. He said he knew O'Mara was involved and also knew who the others were because he had received detailed intelligence reports from overseas. He said that in some way they must be restrained—if necessary prevented by whatever means might be required—from acting on their nefarious ideas. Shocked by the disclosure about O'Mara, Canfield had agreed. It would be a tragedy, he told the INAF leader, if the powerful segments of the media now committed to helping Israel maintain a precarious existence were to go over to the enemy camp. Canfield had ventured the opinion that the defection of even a few media giants might easily tip the balance of American opinion, and therefore INAF was right to do whatever had to be done to prevent them from turning on Israel. Halevy said that now that he knew he had Canfield's full support, he was going to exert every effort to prevent this from happening.

Canfield pushed the tray aside and picked at a few grapes. He slid the chair back in its runners and picked up the briefing again. Only about fifteen minutes remained before he would have to go face the press.

In the back of the airplane, Peter Rosen and Bill Shelby were doing their best to get the reporters in a good frame of mind and had done remarkably well under the circumstances. In two hours the members of the flying Fourth Estate had gone from rabid to angry to sore to routinely surly. They had been given several big concessions in areas where they had been stonewalled before. Yes, they could each have a personal interview with the Vice President sometime before returning to Washington. Yes, the cameramen could photograph Canfield at work in the Executive Cabin. Yes, there would be a news conference in Singapore and also in Kuala Lumpur. Yes, the press vehicle could be positioned directly behind the Secret Service follow-up car so they could get to the Vice President quickly if anything interesting happened en route. Shelby bit his tongue to keep from asking if "anything interesting" meant an assassination attempt. Moreover, they had been promised a wingding party at the Malaysia Hotel at which the Canfield elbow would be bent in jolly camaraderie with them, so that they could glean from the casual contact his social idiosyncracies, which in time would be promulgated to the world— Item: he always had a drink in his hand. Item: he looked awkward with his tie undone. Item: he paid a lot of attention to the waitresses. Item: he lisps a little after a few drinks. Item: he told an ethnic joke.

When Porter Canfield, shirt-sleeved and tieless and with drink in hand, entered the rear cabin, the mollified media men crowded around him, bumping and shoving in the constricted space.

After getting them to quiet down, Canfield said, "Gentlemen, I think we will be more comfortable in the Executive Cabin. Bill, please clear the conference area for the press, will you?"

He led them for the first time to the private area and personally directed the arrangements until all were settled and satisfied. Before submitting to their questions, he said slowly, "I know you were disappointed that I turned down your request for a press conference during the refueling stop in Hawaii."

This obvious conclusion brought an incredulous snort from someone out of Canfield's line of view. The Vice President threw a quick glance toward the noise.

"Wait a minute," he said quickly, fearing that an ugly mood would be reestablished. "I know most of you believe I avoided you so I could duck questions about the President's news conference." Canfield looked directly at Sid Winehart, who dropped his eyes after an uncomfortable moment. He then turned toward Bruce Atherton, whose watery blue orbs stared penetratingly at the Vice President, and continued slowly, "I swear to you that I knew nothing of the President's press conference until after we left Hawaii."

The only sounds in the cabin were those of the subdued hum of the engines and the rushing noise made by the 727 knifing through the thin air. Then there was a crackle—Atherton, eyes still locked with Canfield's, crushed the empty cigarette package in his hand. The slightest trace of a smile showed on his thin lips.

"For one, I believe you, sir," he said. "You're too smart a politician to think that holding off the inevitable would do anything else but make the situation worse."

Douglas Drake cleared his throat importantly. "It looked very suspicious to us, Mr. Vice President. After all, we had assumed that you would talk to us at Hickam. No one said otherwise until the last minute."

"The important thing right now," said Sid Winehart impatiently, "is whether you will go on record, fully and frankly, about the subject."

"That is why we're here," said Canfield soothingly. "I am ready right now to go on the record with no limitations on subject matter."

The TV cameraman moved closer with his hand-held unit, and the single master microphone was laid on the Vice President's table. They were ready.

Peter Rosen suggested the time be limited to a half-hour, but was overruled by Canfield, who stated his willingness to talk until all their questions were answered. Assured that everyone was ready, Canfield gave the go-ahead, thinking how much simpler the mechanics had become since bright lights and multiple microphones were no longer necessary.

They spared him no embarrassment.

"Mr. Vice President, when did you first learn of the Tripartite agreement on the limitation of strategic arms which was announced by President Hurley, the Soviet chairman and the Chinese prime minister today?"

"Less than three hours ago when the White House sent me a transcript of the President's news conference."

"Were you aware of negotiations in this area among the three superpowers?"

"I was not informed about any negotiations with the People's Republic of China concerning nuclear weapons or, as a matter of fact, on any other subject."

"You are telling us that you, the Vice President of the United States and the vice chairman of the National Security Council, were not advised of the negotiations?"

"That is correct."

"You canceled your press conference in Hawaii. Was that because you were embarrassed by the President's announcement?"

"A press conference was never scheduled for Hawaii. When I refused the request for a press conference that you gentlemen made, I was not aware of the Tripartite agreement nor was I aware that President Hurley had had a news conference."

"How do you feel about being kept in the dark about a vital matter of national security?"

"Until I talk to the President and find out the reason that he did not inform me, I would prefer not to answer that question."

"The President made clear his disenchantment with your independent and widely reported views on the Middle East. Do you think he kept you in the dark because he does not trust you to support administration policy?"

"You'll have to ask the President. I cannot look into his mind."

"Since you obviously aren't trusted, are you going to resign?"

"I intend to serve out my term in this high office to which the people have elected me."

"President Hurley made it clear today that your ideas of what should be done for Israel differ from his, and that he sets the foreign policy of the United States. Will you support the administration policy or continue to advocate your own?"

"In discharging my responsibilities as a high diplomatic representative of the United States, I will enunciate the administration policy. When I am not performing diplomatic duties, I will feel free to speak out in favor of altering that policy in some respects."

"You say you will enunciate administration policy. That doesn't seem very strong. The question is—will you support the President's policy?"

"My oath of office requires me to support and defend the Constitution of the United States against all enemies, foreign and domestic. I do not believe it requires me to support a policy that I believe is bad for my country."

"Then you will not support the foreign policy of the United States, a policy approved by a man who chose you to be his deputy, and assist him in discharging his responsibilities?"

Canfield's working jaw muscles revealed his anger, but he quickly suppressed it and replied with a smile, "The United States has only one foreign policy at any given moment. Right now that policy is the policy of President Hurley. My ideas are only ideas— not a policy. Therefore, by making clear the policy of the United States as it exists, I am, in a sense, supporting it."

"Will you tell the foreign leaders that you disagree with the policy on Israel?"

"Only if they ask me about my personal opinions, which is not likely. But if they should, I will make sure they understand that my opinions are not the policy of the United States in the case of Israel."

"What will you say to the foreign press on this issue?"

"If I am asked for my opinions about Israel, I will state them truthfully—but again, let me emphasize that I will point out that those opinions are not the foreign policy of the United States. Now, gentlemen"—Canfield again smiled tolerantly—"there are so many areas where my opinions are in total agreement with administration policy. Can't we talk a little about those?"

"There is no news in a Vice President's agreeing with a President," Sid Winehart said officiously. "But there is real news when a President publicly warns a Vice President that he is off the reservation."

There was a long moment of silence while the reporters waited to see how Canfield would respond to this provocation. Then another voice said evenly, "Well, I think the Vice President has been frank and honest with us. This can't be the press conference he would most like to remember."

Several others around the conference table agreed with Bruce Atherton. Douglas Drake chimed in supportively. "The Vice President has been put in an awkward position and has admitted it. What more is there to say?"

They seemed to realize that the contest was over and a clear victory recorded, but Sid Winehart was enjoying the slaughter too much to let go.

"Mr. Vice President, on another subject, sir." He glanced at his notebook, a tiny bit uncertain about whether to proceed. Then, throwing caution to the winds, he said, "Andy Jackson, the syndicated columnist, reported yesterday that after the health care dinner in Washington a few days ago you and Secretary Lord adjourned to a private suite for more than two hours and that there was no staff present. Is that report accurate, sir, and if it is, could you tell us what you and the secretary were discussing at that late hour?''

There were several nervous coughs and expressions of acute embarrassment on most faces. Bill Shelby was about to object to the question when Canfield waved him off.

''I'm glad we have another subject, Mr. Winehart, and, for a change, a pleasant one. Secretary Lord and I certainly did meet after that dinner, but not in a private suite. We met in a downstairs holding room. Through part of the meeting, which concerned the HEW budget and Total Health Care, two members of my staff were present. From time to time, members of my Secret Service detail were in and out of the room. The meeting was necessary because the President had asked me to moderate a dispute between HEW and the budget people and I had to finish before leaving on this trip. I did apologize to Secretary Lord for inconveniencing her that evening. Does that answer your question?''

''Yes sir, it does,'' Winehart said sheepishly. It was impossible for him to ignore the disapproval of his associates. A good political reporter did not descend to the level of a scandal columnist unless he had his subject nailed cold. It was a risky business to deal in such stuff, even with the most disliked politicians, and the Vice President was not one of the targets on the big media's ''most wanted'' list.

As the reporters prepared to leave, Canfield could feel the improvement in their attitude toward him. There were several expressions of appreciation, a few wisecracks of the trade and even smiles from those who hadn't yet learned that journalists are expected to take themselves very, very seriously. The tension in the atmosphere had evaporated. Now relaxed and happy, Peter Rosen followed them back to the other cabin, where the portable typewriters were pulled from the beat-up traveling cases, and they settled down to write the story.

It was a new ball game. The family fight was now in the open. A firm basis had been established for all kinds of interesting speculation, and they now had a license to spin their rumors from the finest gossamer. Anything ''informed sources'' said about the ill feeling between the President and the Vice President would now be immediately believable.

Zack Miller was sitting at the work table in the aft cabin with his second Scotch and soda of the evening when Bill Shelby flopped down beside him. Miller looked up in surprise. It wasn't normal for the chief of staff to come near him unless he had a specific message to convey. And he never sat down with him unless it was for a meeting he couldn't avoid. Yet here he was, apparently with nothing special on his mind, yawning cavernously and ordering a drink from a passing steward. Miller glanced at him, saying nothing.

"Been a long day," offered Shelby, suppressing another yawn.

"Ummmm," Miller said. He was still depressed and worried about the warning that Yoram Halevy had given him. It was disconcerting to discover that someone wanted to kill you. It didn't help that Miller was a man of precipitous ups and downs. The information had caught him at the beginning of a downslide and sent him all the way to the bottom.

"The boss did very well with the press, don't you think?" asked Shelby, taking a long pull at the ice-cold drink that had just been put before him.

"Under the circumstances, excellent," said Miller. He thought that either the whiskey was beginning to soothe him or that he was getting his second wind, because suddenly he began to feel better. "Of course, we'll look badly left out of things at first, but Hurley will emerge as the real villain in a few days." He was beginning to warm to the flattery of a social visit from the chief of staff.

"I agree with your diagnosis, Doctor. We can steer the traveling press in the right direction so long as you and Peter and I stay on the same track. For the boss's sake, we all have to chug along together . . . and that includes Galdari and Kathy. If those media guys see any dissension, they'll dingdong us to death."

Miller kept his mouth shut, waiting to make certain that Shelby had got it all off his mind. It was a flag of truce, and at the right time. If the bad feelings between him and the regular staff could be eliminated, it was all to the good, especially since he might need Galdari's help before this trip was over.

Shelby watched him for a moment. Then, mistaking his silence for indecision, said firmly, "Look, Dr. Miller, I know that we haven't hit it off too well. Maybe a lot of the fault is mine. Anyhow, I'm willing to start over on a new footing. And I think I can change the attitude of the rest of the staff. At least, I'm willing to try if you are. We owe it to the boss."

For a long moment Miller seemed to wrestle with himself while he let the drama build, then a grin came over his handsome face and he stuck out his hand. "I'm with you, Bill. This is combat and we're all wearing the same uniform."

Bill Shelby's saturnine face broke into a big smile. He shook the proffered hand. "Great, Zack. From now on, we all work together. Let me get Pete, Kathy and Steve up here right now so we can bring them up to date."

There were a few curious glances, but the reporters were far too busy to pay much attention to the five principal staff people who gathered at the table. They were able to talk in complete privacy. The State Department man had gone forward to catch a nap in one of the crew bunks, and the reporters were seated too far behind them to overhear the conversation. Shelby gave a brief report of his agreement with Zack and made a short but eloquent plea for unity. All were pleased, and they sat talking about how to handle anticipated problems for over an hour. Finally the lowering of the wheels indicated that *Air Force Two* was about to sit down at Guam.

8

GALDARI LEANED forward and watched the lights of the runway rush past. As they taxied toward the hangars, he saw the shadowy shapes of a few old B-52's. The Secret Service man's thoughts leaped back through the years to other arrivals with other protectees at Guam—back to the days of the Vietnam war when the B-52's were shuttling back and forth with maximum bomb loads, doing their damnedest to prevent a communist victory in Indochina. Well, it had been useless. The American resolve was shattered from within. The political geniuses, assisted by the news media, had emasculated the greatest power in the world. Out there where the powerful new B-1's should be standing in the tropical night, there were only a few obsolete twenty-five-year-old B-52's. And it would get worse, thought Galdari. Much worse. Aloud, he said to the others at the table, "The Vice President is right about one thing. Dradavov *is* negotiating us out of our shoes. There's nothing here to make us a Pacific power—nothing here but words."

They completed the long taxi and pulled to a stop near the administration building. Galdari could see, outside in the beam of the lights, the military reception committee waiting for the stairs to be wheeled into place. The ranking officer was an air force brigadier general, a far cry from the lieutenant generals who had the command at Anderson when Guam was a repository of American military might. Now it was just a way station, a stop-off point allowing traveling military and political personnel to break the long overseas route from Hawaii to the Far East. Oh, yes, and something to talk about when politicians insisted that the United States intended to maintain a presence in the Pacific.

The ceremonial greeting having taken place, the Vice President and his top aides were taken by car to the guest cottage on the golf course. The others were directed to the guest dorms, which were actually bachelor officers' quarters allocated for visitors. The press asked and was permitted to file their stories immediately. It was 10:00 P.M. on the island, which made it 7:00 A.M. in the nation's capital. A quick report could make the early network news that day.

The Vice President was in the middle of a partial unpacking when the base public relations officer brought him a neatly arranged air force binder containing the day's important news stories and other selected items of probable interest. Canfield went to the kitchen, got himself a cold beer and talked for a few minutes with Joe Hentz, who was laying in a few items for breakfast. Returning to the bedroom, he sat down on the bed, removed his shoes, propped up the pillows to lean against and began to read. The top story, of course, was the presidential announcement and news conference of the night before. It was from Mark O'Mara's *Washington Globe*. The first two paragraphs were a straight report of the Tripartite Disarmament Pact with Russia and China. The mischief began with the third paragraph:

> President Hurley took an unprecedented slap at the man he selected to be Vice President just three years ago. Asked to reconcile his policy of gradually eliminating all nuclear weapons with Vice President Canfield's urging of IRBM's for Israel, the President left no doubt of his displeasure with Canfield.

Then, after reporting Hurley's exact words, it went on:

> There is considerable doubt as to whether the President even bothered to inform the Vice President about the negotiations in progress or that the Pact was ready for signature. The Vice President left Washington en route to a diplomatic mission in the Far East some ten hours before the announcement. The President did not see him off as is customary. An informed White House source had reported earlier that there was an open rift between the two men as the result of Canfield's outspoken disagreement with the Hurley policy on Israel. It now becomes obvious that those reports were accurate.

Another paragraph read:

Newsmen aboard *Air Force Two* reported from Hickam Air Force Base in Hawaii that Vice President Canfield canceled the press conference that normally would be held there without giving any reason. Old hands speculated that the Vice President was not informed of the President's attack in time to prepare for the embarrassing questions that he would undoubtedly face.

Well, it was about what he had expected, thought Canfield, flipping to the next story—an editorial in the most important New York newspaper, written before the announcement of the Tripartite Pact. It was headed "The Vice President Grows" and was brief:

In recent weeks, Vice President Porter Canfield has shown a surprising sensitivity to the continuing serious threat faced by Israel. We are uncertain about the stimulus for the Vice President's concern, but we applaud his interest. While we do not subscribe to all the strong specifics Mr. Canfield advocates for Israel, we are convinced that President Hurley's policy of benign neglect could result in disaster for this small, courageous nation. If Prime Minister Stein's allegation that an Arab attack is imminent can be verified, the United States should move quickly to reestablish a balance of power in the Middle East. Providing Israel with the capacity for an effective response to aggression need not, we believe, upset the ongoing negotiations with the Soviet Union to limit strategic arms.

Canfield was pleasantly surprised. Getting an editorial like this in the most influential newspaper in the country would be very helpful to him in the liberal community. He wondered what the follow-up would be in light of the announcement of the Tripartite Pact. The newspaper was all out for détente and all out for Israel. It would be interesting to see how they reconciled the conflict of interest.

There were several other stories related to the pact, as well as some columns about his split with presidential policy. Every one of the writers seemed to be looking forward to a brutal contest between Gray and him for the party nomination. Mentioned more than once was the Senate accident and his "excellent handling" of the situation compared to Gray's "insensitivity." There was a picture of Diane Guthrie delightedly receiving his autographed photograph at her hospital bedside, and some nice comments from her parents and friends in an article underneath. Miss Guthrie's opinion of him was in heavy type under the picture: "He's fantastic— So gentle, understanding and kind. And is he handsome—WOW!''

Canfield finished reading the clips. He was generally satisfied with the reports. They were not as hard on him about Hawaii as he had expected, and there were quite a few bonuses, such as the picture, the New York editorial and the columns.

He went back to his unpacking, turning on the portable radio on the dresser. The armed forces channel was rebroadcasting the President's press conference. As he listened, the press conference ended and the network commentators took over to burn up the ten minutes remaining until the hour's end.

Anchorman: Well, ladies and gentlemen, we have just heard the President of the United States announce the initial Tripartite accord on the limitation of nuclear arms. For the first time the three superpowers have agreed that the world powder keg must be defused. This is an important moment in world history.

First aspirant to anchorman's job: Yes, Brad, an important achievement—but what is more important, if I may be so bold as to suggest a slight modification of your statement, is that the superpowers have agreed on *how* we must begin to defuse the powder keg, not just that it must be defused.

Anchorman: Uh, yes, well, that is certainly inherent in what I said.

Second aspirant to anchorman's job: Well, I agree with you, Brad, and you, too, Don, that this ridiculous arms race was leading us to the brink of disaster. But I would advocate great caution in accepting this pact as the solution to our problems. It is a very small beginning, at best, and—

First aspirant, breaking in rudely: That is self-evident, Clive, but there must be a beginning, and this one at least cuts down on existing strategic weapons. As I said, it does something specific!

Anchorman, pompously: I think we are neglecting the most interesting development of the evening—that we face the future with a divided executive team. The President wants nukes out; the Vice President wants them in—at least IRBM's for Israel. Do you have any thoughts on that, Don?

Warning: The Surgeon General Has Determined That Cigarette Smoking Is Dangerous to Your Health.
True lowers tar to only
5 MGS. TAR
And has a taste worth changing to.
TRUE
FILTER CIGARETTES
5 MGS. TAR, 0.5 MGS. NICOTINE
TRUE 5 MGS. TAR
Regular: 5 mgs. "tar", 0.4 mgs. nicotine, av. per cigarette, FTC Report Dec. 1976.
©Lorillard, U.S.A., 1976

Alive with pleasure!
Newport

©Lorillard, U.S.A., 1976

18 mg. "tar", 1.2 mg. nicotine
av. per cigarette, FTC Report Dec. 1976.

First aspirant, slightly irritated: That's a point I was just getting ready to mention, Brad. Never, as far as I can remember, have we had such overt disagreement between the two men at the top of our executive structure. That's not good for our image abroad. It confuses our foreign friends—

Second aspirant, breaking in snidely: They've been confused for a long time, Don—ever since President Hurley's predecessors botched up Vietnam. But I disagree with you when you say that a public dispute between the President and the Vice President is a bad thing. That's our system. We always wash our dirty linen in public. And our public officials always seem to have a lot to be washed.

Anchorman, paternally: Yes, and the media are the laundry persons. That's why they try to hide things from us. We must tell the people the truth, no matter who gets hurt. So who's wrong in this case, Don? The President or the Vice President?

First aspirant, very seriously: Both are wrong to a degree, Brad. Of course, the President is the boss. He makes the foreign policy. The Vice President should follow orders, not take the President on publicly. If he feels so strongly that he must challenge the President, then he should resign first. However, I cannot excuse the President for not trying harder to convert his Number Two to his viewpoint. I don't think he made any effort to talk out the problem, and he owes that much to Vice President Canfield.

Second aspirant, tiredly: I have to agree with you that the whole thing might better have been settled in private. We don't seem to be able to attract men to high office who have the humility and the restraint to do what's best for the country if that means personal sacrifice.

Anchorman: To wrap this up, we have an important agreement with the communist powers, one that may be the forerunner of meaningful steps toward peace in the world. To dull the luster of this good news, we have a division at the highest level of our government, one that might have been avoided by greater effort on the part of the President and the Vice President of the United States. We can only hope that they will settle their personal problems for the good of the country. This is Bradley Barton, saying good night for Don Lowe, Clive Shuberger and myself from the TBS studios in Washington.

Wearily, Canfield switched off the radio, shaking his head in silent disbelief at what he had just heard. The shallowness of the national media never ceased to amaze him. Surely these were intelligent men. Were they ordered to check their brains at the entrances to the network studios? Or were they simply the victims of the unrelenting need to fill time with words—no matter how vacuous? Yes, that must be it. As a politician, he could understand that compulsion. The sad thing was that they exerted an almost hypnotic influence on millions of Americans. Their empty-headed mouthings were accepted without question, without analysis—and in time the listener was infected by the illogic they imparted. But never lose sight of one fact: They were powerful, powerful enough to destroy any public man or woman.

The Vice President prepared for bed. He would have no trouble sleeping, because he had had only a brief nap on the plane and it was now nearly 8:00 A.M. by his body clock. Departure was set for 10:00 A.M. the next morning, and the six-hour flight would bring them into Singapore International Airport at about 1:30 in the afternoon, local time. From then on he would be very busy with ceremonies, meetings and study. He turned off the bed lamp and slipped between the sheets. In a few minutes he was fast asleep, oblivious to the loud humming of the air conditioner. Without it, the incredibly humid tropical night would have made sleeping indoors impossible.

Outside, the equatorial night noises pulsed inexorably—a reminder that the jungle's retreat was only temporary. Now and then a brief but intense rain shower hushed the whistling tree frogs and the cicadas' shrill vibrations. The intermittent moonlight caught small rodents and sent them scurrying to their holes to avoid mongooses and other carnivorous prowlers.

Inside the guest dorm, activity was diminishing and one room after another darkened. Kathy Dryden lay wide awake in her bed, tired to the point of being nervous, but sleep would not come. She heard the water running in the bathroom she shared with the two girls in the adjoining room. Suddenly, the pipes groaned loudly. In frustration, Kathy threw back the covers, got up and put on her robe and slippers. Quietly, she opened the door to the center hallway. No one was about, so she went down the hall, out the small side door, and sat down on the wooden steps. It was warm, but a pleasant gentle breeze had come up.

She had been there but a short time, wondering about the twist of fate that had brought her from the glass-and-steel big-city corporation office to this small green island halfway around the world, when the door behind her opened and Steve Galdari came out. He had on a pair of worn khaki pants and a gray Columbia University T-shirt.

"Hi! What're you doing out here all alone?" he asked in surprise. "Don't you know that this is snake and spider country?"

"Couldn't sleep. I thought I'd sit out here and listen to the night noises for a while. They're much better than a sleeping pill. Sit down with me, Steve," she said softly, glad to see him. "Listen to the night. It's so lush on this island. Even here in this compound you can feel the primitiveness—there's so much life out there! I love the fragrance, the sounds of the insects, the frogs . . ."

Galdari was touched by the naturalness and freshness of the girl. He sat down on the step, closer than necessary to her. The faint breeze offered them a heady blend of bougainvillea and frangipani scents.

"I was restless, too, so I thought I'd go over and check the Command Post," he said awkwardly. God, he thought, she's feeling the romance of the moment, and you're talking about the C.P. Galdari, you're not the man of the world you thought you were. He quickly added aloud, "It's beautiful. I've been nearly everywhere, but there's a mystery about the tropics. I guess nature's full power of creation is here."

"Yes, it is beautiful—beautiful but cruel. Nature is very cruel, Steve. Out there in the dark, hundreds of living creatures will be slaughtered before the sun rises again so that others will have food to live."

Galdari reached out and took her hand. "I didn't realize you were such a philosopher. But since we're on the subject, I don't think 'cruel' is the word you want. Nature is savage and harsh, but not cruel. Humans, on the other hand, are cruel. Animals kill for food or to defend their young—maybe even for revenge. But men knowingly destroy each other in dozens of subtle ways—out of pure malice, out of evil, out of boredom, or perversion. There is no beauty in man's destructiveness, no honesty in it, because it has no link with real necessity."

The light from the hallway set Kathy's blue eyes aglow. "Now who's the philosopher?" she asked. "Wouldn't the SPS be amazed to know that a practitioner of police brutality could be so sensitive!"

Then she became serious again. "That was beautiful—but frightening." A tremor ran through her, as though she had had a

221

sudden chill. Steve put his arm around her, and she leaned against him willingly, her soft blonde hair touching his jaw. For a while nothing was said. Suddenly she asked anxiously, "Are the boss, the President and Senator Gray capable of that kind of cruelty? Will they try to destroy each other?"

"The greatest activator of the latent destructiveness in us all is ambition, and public men are known to be ambitious. Yes, it's possible that they will try to destroy each other." He tightened the pressure of his arm around her as she gave another involuntary shudder.

"Steve, it's going to get very dirty, isn't it?"

"It always has in election years." His arm still around her, he raised her to her feet and said firmly, "C'mon. It won't be as bad as you think. Our man can take care of himself. You're exhausted and that makes everything look worse than it is. Try to get some sleep."

"Steve." Her voice caressed the name, sending a wave of emotion through him. He lifted her chin and kissed her gently. She moved her mouth tenderly against his, and, lips parted, tongues entered the play. His hand cupped her breast outside the soft robe and began to tease. With a sigh, she reluctantly drew back. "Regardless of our better relations with Zack, there are too many eyes about. It's been a wonderful night."

"Sleep well, Kathy."

"Good night, Steve."

The SAIC of the vice-presidential protective detail edged his powerful body through the open doorway to the cockpit and touched the shoulder of the crewman closest to him. Without turning away from the complex communications panel, the man lifted one earphone to listen.

"How far out are we, Charlie?" Galdari asked.

The radio operator glanced at his wristwatch. "Should be about thirty minutes to touchdown, Steve." The inquiry was ritual and he did not have to wait for the next question. "I guess you'll want the C.P. at the Marco Polo Hotel."

"Right as rain, Charlie. Will you try to raise them for me in about ten minutes? I'll be in the back." Galdari closed the cockpit door and made his way through the crew section of the aircraft to the staff working area in the rear cabin. He was passing through the Executive Cabin when the Vice President looked up from his study of the Singapore arrival ceremony and raised his eyebrows inquiringly.

222

"Pardon me, sir. I'm looking for Dr. Miller, Bill and Pete. I didn't mean to interrupt you."

"No problem. They're all in the back having a final discussion of arrival plans."

Miller, Shelby, Rosen and the State Department man were in fact looking at a map of the airport reception ceremony, and in spite of last night's good intentions, an argument had broken out. The chief of staff, who disagreed with Dr. Miller and the press secretary, kept shaking his head slowly from side to side.

"I'm not going to recommend to the Vice President that he go to the crowd after the ceremony unless Galdari says it's okay," he said hotly. "We're not in the United States, and security considerations here are entirely different. We need a professional's opinion based on the latest information that the personnel on the ground have been able to develop." Looking up and seeing Galdari, he looked relieved. "Steve— I was just getting ready to send for you. Do you have any information about the situation on the ground?"

"I should have within five minutes," replied Galdari, "but I heard what you said as I came in, and regardless of how good it looks, I don't think the Vice President should wade into any crowd. Fifteen percent of the population here is Moslem, and there are always agents here from the militant Arab organizations. I don't believe they'll be very friendly to the boss's recommendations of intermediate range missiles for Israel. Anyhow, I recommend we don't take the chance."

"Now, wait just a minute, Steve," said Zack Miller. "We're trying hard to fight our way out of a very bad impression we inadvertently made on the press coming through Hawaii. Luckily, we've been able to overcome some of that, but I think it's terribly important that the Vice President conduct himself in the most open, straightforward way possible at this time. If your people are aware of specific dangers, that's different, but I think it would be a very bad mistake to apply extra tight security unless there is a reason for it."

"Rely on my experience in public relations, Steve. It would be extremely bad to wipe out the excellent impression that the boss created last night," Rosen added excitedly, but keeping his voice low to avoid being overheard by the reporters in back. "The traveling media people are expecting to get some excellent color shots of the Vice President being received by the common people of Singapore. This is our very first stop, and it will set the tone of the entire trip. I beg you, please don't prohibit the Vice President from going into the crowd."

"You know I can't take matters into my own hands unless I am acting to avoid a clear and present danger to the principal," said Galdari. "However, I must recommend, for the reasons I have already given, that the Vice President not go into any crowds at this stop."

Dr. Miller looked Steve in the eye. "I will have to recommend otherwise," he said firmly. The era of good feeling apparently had not survived a single twenty-four-hour period.

After five more minutes of discussion, an air force crewman came in to summon Galdari to the cockpit for his radio call. In his absence, Zack Miller and Peter Rosen continued to work on Bill Shelby without success.

A short time later Galdari returned to report to the others. "I have not been able to get in direct touch with the agent on the scene—we're too far away yet. But I did talk to the C.P. at the hotel. They have no special information from local intelligence sources about any planned attack on the Vice President. Nevertheless, I still recommend that he not go into the crowd."

They continued to argue for another ten minutes without reaching accord, and finally Miller said, "Well, I guess the Man himself will have to make the decision. Let's go and put it to him."

The Vice President, who was still studying the ceremonial procedure and looking over his arrival statement, did not seem to welcome the interruption. After hearing the arguments on both sides, he decided, "I cannot regard the risk as sufficient to prevent my being courteous to the people who have assembled to welcome me. After the ceremony is completed, I will go to the crowd." Looking at Galdari, he added, "Now, Steve, I won't go *into* the crowd. I'll just go along the edge, shaking hands with those I can reach without going into any congested area. I'm sorry, but I just have to do that much."

Galdari was a professional and did not argue further. "Yes, sir. That is your decision to make. I just wanted to make sure that you understood the reasons for my recommendation."

While the others returned to the rear to prepare for landing, Galdari went at once to the cockpit. They were now only five minutes out of Singapore International. The radioman handed him a transmitter. "Jestes, this is *Air Force Two*," Galdari said, trying to make direct contact with the agent on the ground.

"*Air Force Two*—Jestes," came the reply. "I read you loud and clear."

Galdari pushed the transmitter button and began. "Jestes—*Air Force Two*. Do you have any changes?"

"Everything goes as scheduled. We have you in view."

"Jestes—*Air Force Two*. Be advised we're going to smile and shake hands with the fans after the show. Send some people to take a good look around."

There was a long pause, then the agent on the ground said, "You mean he's planning to go to the crowd?"

"Yes. Listen, Jestes. Get as many people as you can over there right away to take a look."

After another pause, the Alabamian drawled, "*Air Force Two*—Jestes. Other than the American ambassador, the Singapore foreign minister, a dozen representatives of the diplomatic corps and the honor guard, the only crowd in sight is about two hundred civilians fifty yards away on an outside balcony of the second floor of the airport. If the boss is going to shake hands with them, he'll need wings."

Galdari heaved a sigh of relief. "Jestes, this is *Air Force Two*. Disregard. See you on the ground. Over and out."

9

CANFIELD PAUSED before descending from the plane and gave a smiling salutation to the applauding dignitaries at the foot of the steps. After hours in the airplane's dry, air-conditioned climate, the humid air seemed much warmer than eighty-eight degrees. The strong breeze did not evaporate the film of perspiration on his face, but whipped his hair about, giving him an almost boyish look. He tried hard not to squint in the bright afternoon sunlight.

Ambassador Oldham greeted him with an aseptic smile. Then, after conferring a brief handshake of the type usually given those with contagious disease, he presented the foreign minister of Singapore, who welcomed the Vice President warmly.

The foreign minister was a little nervous that Prime Minister Ling had not come to the airport to greet the distinguished visitor. He immediately expressed the prime minister's regrets that an unexpected and urgent communication from the Thai government had required his immediate personal attention. As soon as Canfield had been introduced to the four other Cabinet officers present, Oldham drew him aside to tell him that he should avoid being too friendly with the foreign minister. The idea was to show coolness because of what was thought to be an intentional slight to the United States by Ling.

The foreign minister led Canfield to a shallow platform in front of the troops, who were smartly attired in white jackets with red sashes, navy blue trousers with red stripes and matching garrison caps.

After the anthems had been played and the honor guard reviewed from the tailgate of a small vehicle, the Vice President went quickly down the line of waiting ambassadors and chargés d'affaires. There was a smattering of applause when he waved to the curious crowd on the airport balcony and climbed into the waiting limousine next to his host. Oldham took the jump seat on the left in front of the minister, and they sped away behind an impressive motorcycle escort, flags flying. Steve Galdari was sandwiched in the cramped front seat between the Singapore driver and the burly security chief.

As the convoy rolled at a good pace along the splendidly maintained highways, the Vice President blocked the minister's attempts at conversation with dead-end responses that were not quite discourteous. He simply left the very clear impression that he did not chitchat with foreign ministers Ambassador Oldham filled in the blanks by opening a lively dialogue with the grateful Singaporean.

For once Canfield was content to turn his full attention to the countryside. In hundreds of rides from airports to cities, he had never failed to be depressed by the dreary suburban shopping centers and gasoline stations followed by big-city slums. This was his initial visit to Singapore, and he was impressed by the intelligent planning in evidence everywhere. This microcosmic nation—only 226 square miles—was a sparkling combination of tropical parks, modern buildings and clean wide roads. One could sense the pride that allowed over two million people to live in such a small area and yet avoid the usual squalor of impacted living.

They crossed the Kallang River and continued down Serangood Road through the Indian community and into Selegie Road. Now and then Canfield caught a brief glimpse of the harbor off to his left. A moment later they were on Orchard Road, another impressive thoroughfare. Canfield could restrain his enthusiasm no longer.

"Your city is so clean and functional. The streets are paved. The parks are well kept. How do you do it with so many people crowded together?" he asked the foreign minister.

"Your excellency, we are a people of diverse and ancient cultures. Besides, we inherited the British love of order from Sir Stamford Raffles, who came here in eighteen nineteen. But our heritage alone was not enough. For over twenty-five years we have had the good fortune to be led by a genius who understands that freedom under reasonable legal restraints is preferable to unlimited license—a disciplinarian who will not allow the aberrations of a few individuals to destroy the well-being of the group." The foreign minister smiled. "In your country, you equate discipline with repression. Here, we feel it is necessary to progress."

Canfield felt a patriotic tremor. "But," he said defensively, "we had to free ourselves from racism, sexism and what amounted to a caste system. That is why we consider our personal freedom so precious."

"Our population is seventy-five percent Chinese, fifteen percent Malay, with most of the remaining ten percent from the Indian subcontinent," said the minister mildly. "We have had our share of racial troubles and exploitation, also. As for our women, they have won their fight for equality, but not by the establishment of a unisex counterculture such as your more extreme feminist leaders advocate. If you look, you will see that they still emphasize the female characteristics that men find desirable." The minister's expression revealed his appreciation of such characteristics. "The important truth we have learned is that harmony and progress cannot come without strong leadership. In the United States, your influential people in the private sector do not want strong leadership because it weakens their freedom to do as they please. That is why you have more waste and inefficiency than we."

Fearing that he had gone too far, the minister said deferentially, "Please excuse me, Mr. Vice President, for being frank, but your nation is so great, so talented, that it saddens your Asian friends to see its inability to cure the cancer within it."

Canfield smiled a tight, hurt little smile. "It is easy to govern two million on a small island," he said. "I doubt that you can appreciate what it is to deal with nearly two hundred and seventy million spread over a great continent. Perhaps the greatest weakness of the United States is its preoccupation with the security problems of small nations trying to survive."

"And you have done great things for the world, scientifically and in a humanitarian way," said the minister apologetically. "Again, please forgive my candor. It was generated out of respect for what the United States has meant for the free world and perhaps out of fear that its Pacific involvement is diminishing."

Arrival at the hotel ended further discussion, and the minister took his leave.

The Secret Service agents moved the Vice President and the American ambassador efficiently but unobtrusively through the busy hotel lobby, which was dotted with small groups of tourists. The Americans waved, called to the Vice President and extended their hands in greeting. Canfield smiled and exchanged brief pleasantries with them, here and there touching a proffered hand in passing, but not appreciably slowing his pace. By the time he was ushered to the elevator and whisked to the penthouse floor of the hotel, many were not yet aware of his presence.

They entered the master suite as the White House communications team and the technical security detail men were just leaving. Canfield now could be assured that his quarters were free from bugs and that he was hooked into the finest communications system in the world.

Noting that Oldham had followed him into the room and seemed to have something on his mind, he gestured him to a chair. The ambassador cleared his throat and began somewhat awkwardly: "I know you are tired, Mr. Vice President, and also that you have only an hour and a half before your ceremonial call on the president of Singapore, but I do have a few urgent matters to brief you on. With your permission, I'll do this as quickly as possible."

"Plenty of time, Mr. Ambassador. But would you mind holding just a couple of minutes while I get Shelby and Miller? I'd like them to be briefed also."

It took only a few moments to summon the staff people. When everyone was comfortably seated, the ambassador began again. "Washington asked me to be sure that you understood the delicacy of our situation here. Prime Minister Ling is quite upset about not being given any advance notice of the new Tripartite agreement. His policy has been to play the Russians against the Chinese. He sees the expanding big power détente as an encouragement to the communist rebels in Malaysia. It's rather awkward to say, Mr. Vice President, but he finds your presence here after the fact as little comfort—particularly since the press is playing up the supposition that you were excluded from the decision making."

Under Canfield's cold stare the ambassador shifted nervously in his chair. "Washington asked me to pass the word to you to do everything possible to reassure the prime minister," he resumed, "and, in these confusing times, to restrict yourself to the exact and simple definition of our foreign policy."

Canfield glanced impatiently away from the ambassador, looking from Miller, to Shelby, to the ceiling of the room, making it clear to Oldham that he was not at all happy with the information he was receiving. A few moments of absolute silence followed the remarks, and then Ambassador Oldham rose to his feet. "Well, that's about it, Mr. Vice President. I'll be back here in an hour and ten minutes to accompany you to Istana for your call on President Ramaha." He started toward the door.

"One moment, please, Mr. Ambassador," said Canfield, his voice frigid and commanding. The ambassador turned.

"Yes, sir?" he asked apprehensively.

"You may report to the secretary of state that you delivered the message to me and that I understood it. Now, since you are going to be with me for the next two days, there are a few things you should know for your private enlightenment. First, I find the information about reassuring the prime minister redundant. It has already been fully covered in my briefing materials. Second, I find the secretary's admonitions impertinent and insulting. This, of course, is not your fault. However, for the benefit of continuing our good relations, I would suggest that you confine yourself to a listening role during my conversations with the prime minister tomorrow. I will not countenance any interruptions for clarification or any other reason, however diplomatically they may be offered. At the first sign of your intervention, I will request that you remove yourself from the meeting. I am making these things clear to you in advance so that you may avoid potential embarrassment. Do you have any questions, Mr. Ambassador?"

Oldham flushed a deep red. Never in his long service had he been subjected to such a peremptory command. He had been put in an impossible position. It was inherent in his instructions that should the Vice President trespass into forbidden areas, he would interject himself into the conversation for the purpose of clarification. Now here he was being warned in advance against carrying out his orders. It placed him squarely in the middle, and he would have to think about the best way to handle it. Indicating his understanding of Canfield's instructions, he left immediately.

"Well, pretty risky stuff!" said Zack Miller, laughing. "Hurley may call you home immediately if Oldham reports that you're about to do your own thing."

Canfield shook his head. "No, I don't think so. These instructions are supposed to be coming from the secretary of state, not from the President. Of course, we know they really come from Hurley, but since they are allegedly from Secretary Woodhall, we can't get in too much trouble. Besides, Hurley knows that I'm not going to risk doing anything silly enough to justify his summoning me home. It would be too embarrassing."

Canfield picked up a copy of the *Straits Times* from the table and whistled approvingly. "Look at this. We're all over the front page, and it looks like real good ink."

They clustered around and together began to read the spread-out newspaper. The Vice President's most flattering handout photo graced the center of the front page. Underneath were the words:

231

"Next U.S. President?" The boldface headline read: VICE PRESIDENT CANFIELD DUE IN SINGAPORE.

Practically the entire paper was devoted to the Vice President: a biography, opposite a page of early pictures; excerpts from recent speeches, with emphasis on IRBM's for Israel; reactions from other nations. Canfield began to read aloud, his excitement mounting:

> The speech in Oregon struck sparks around the world. With rare independence, Vice President Canfield advocated that the United States send Israel nuclear weapons for her defense. He showed himself to be a presidential contender in his own right by not waiting timidly for a go-ahead from President Hurley. However, in adopting a stance which conflicts with Hurley's, Canfield has incurred the wrath of the administration. He can look for no help from the President, who seems to favor either the Senate majority leader, Mr. Gray, or the speaker of the House, Mr. Edmonds. Informed sources in Washington report that many of the younger members of Congress are lining up behind the Vice President for what promises to be America's most exciting campaign in years. Canfield has shown himself a likely factor in future global politics.

Zack Miller fairly danced with enthusiasm. "That's just super, Newt! We're really beginning to move! Can't you just see old Gray gnashing his teeth? He isn't even off the mark yet."

Canfield smiled in a restrained way, but it was apparent that he, too, assigned great importance to the news coverage. "The unusual thing here, Zack," he called to Miller, who had dashed into the kitchen to get some cold San Miguel beer, "is that the entire world is talking about us! And not just casually. They're taking us seriously. Listen to these world reactions about the Oregon speech—high praise from Israel, India, Australia and the non-Moslem African countries; guarded approval from Italy, Holland, West Germany, the Scandinavian countries and Indonesia; mixed reactions from France, England, Japan, and South America." Without pausing, Canfield accepted the glass of beer which Miller offered him. "The only adverse reactions are from Russia and its satellites, the Arab nations and Malaysia—every single one predictable."

"Fantastic!" said Zack, pouring beer for Shelby and himself. "I propose a toast to the next President of the United States."

"In view of the fact that they don't vote in United States elec-

232

tions, that's a little premature," laughed Canfield, but it was obvious that he had stars in his eyes.

Sensing a need to revert to reality, Bill Shelby said quietly, "The news coverage is excellent, and I'm sure that it is equally good in the United States, especially the *Globe, Twiceweek* and networks. But, Mr. Vice President, that can all change overnight. Nothing is less persuasive than yesterday's news, and the media are very fickle. And let's not forget, we've got to get through the convention. That won't be easy."

"Of course, you're right, Bill. Zack is only joking around, and I am first of all a realist." However, the manic look in Canfield's eyes belied his calm words. "But this is an important start. It's unusual for a Vice President to attract this much international attention, and to totally take over a newspaper like the *Straits Times.*"

"Even got a favorable editorial—and the *Straits Times* depends on Malaysian circulation," broke in Zack, starting to wolf the cold cuts that were on the hospitality table.

Shelby nodded. "The editorial was fine, but we shouldn't read too much into it. The Malaysian government is hostile to the veep because his policy hurts Islamic nations. But right at the moment the owners of the *Straits Times* are having a donnybrook with the Malaysian prime minister over a hot local issue—farming subsidies. It's my guess that they have seized on the Vice President's visit as an opportunity to stick it to the prime minister from another direction."

"Bill, Bill, don't be so gloomy," said Zack around a mouthful of cheese. "We need to keep spirits high, and we are going to win. Things are coming on like gang busters!"

"I'd better get changed," said Canfield. He got up and headed for the bedroom. Then, suddenly, he stopped and turned back toward them, his expression earnest. "The opportunity here must not be wasted. Zack, I want you to skip the ceremonial meeting today and write me a few paragraphs on Israel that are hard-hitting and can be inserted easily into informal remarks or answers to questions at news conferences. Modify the wording so it will sound extemporaneous. I'll spread a little of that around on this trip. I can assure you that it will be covered at home with an enthusiasm it wouldn't get if I said it there."

"Okay, I'll get right on it."

While Canfield changed clothes, Shelby and Miller talked for another five minutes about the same subject. Afterward, Shelby was not optimistic about the success of his effort to instill caution in the fervid Miller. The only statement he had made that had momentarily subdued Zack was his observation that recklessness would leave President Hurley no alternative but to call the Vice President home.

Zack Miller let himself into his suite—a large tastefully furnished living room with a small powder room near the hall. Sliding doors led to a balcony overlooking the greenery of the Tanglin Road area. A table to one side of the living room was spread with a spotless white cloth. It contained a large basket of fruit, including some tropical varieties he had not seen before, and a bar stocked with alcoholic basics of the best quality. A large bath with a separate shower adjoined the cheerful bedroom. Not bad for a bachelor college professor, thought Zack. And it sure beats moving around with a scheduled tour.

Noting that his baggage had already been delivered, he threw the nearest piece on the bed, unstrapped it and flipped the locks. He was carrying several clean shirts to the chest of drawers when his eye caught a blinking red light under the bed—the hotel phone. The communications men had placed it on the floor when they connected the White House system. He picked it up and put it on the table next to the official phone. Puzzled that someone outside the vice-presidential party would be calling him in Singapore, he dialed the operator and was informed that a Sirana Amiri had left a message that he should return her call at a local number. Frowning, Zack hung up and stared at the name and number he had just jotted down. He had never heard of a Sirana Amiri. Who was she? Where had she gotten his name? He was on the verge of calling her when the probable answer struck him. She must be a journalist who had been following the news about the Vice President and had seen his name somewhere. He crumpled the paper and tossed it into the wastebasket. There was certainly no advantage in being interviewed by a foreign newswoman. Besides, he would be too busy preparing the material the veep had just requested.

Quickly completing his unpacking, he pulled a yellow pad from his briefcase and went back into the living room. After mixing himself a strong drink, he sat in the large easy chair, propped his feet up on the hassock and began to rough out some statements on Canfield's Israeli position.

He had been working steadily for over an hour, interrupted only by Bill Shelby's call to tell him that the Vice President had returned from Istana, when Peter Rosen knocked on his door to invite him to dinner that evening with some of the traveling press. It seemed that they wanted a little background information.

"Can't do that, Pete, and neither can you. The whole traveling party, except the press, is invited to an informal dinner at Ambassador Oldham's tonight."

Rosen left, muttering to himself about never being told anything, and Miller, realizing that it was late, went into the bathroom to shave and shower. He had just begun to lather up after getting thoroughly wet under the hot needlelike shower when the White House phone rang. Unhurriedly, he continued his ablutions. He would get the call when he was through. A few minutes later the phone began to ring again, this time incessantly. Swearing, Zack climbed from the shower, wrapped a towel around himself and went into the bedroom, where he scooped up the receiver. "Miller," he said neutrally, giving no indication of his irritation as the knot slipped and the towel fell to the floor.

"Zack, how are you doing with the statements?" It was typical of Canfield that he would request a result in such a short time.

"Just about finished, Newt. I'll be able to give them to you sometime in the morning, and I think they'll be just what you want."

"That's fine. I'm figuring on saying a few things to the press after my morning meeting with the prime minister, and I'd like to look those over before I go. Let's have breakfast in my suite at nine, okay?"

"That'll be fine, Mr. Vice President. But I'll see you at the ambassador's dinner tonight, won't I?"

"Oh, yes, but I doubt that we'll have much chance to discuss anything then. Besides, it won't be a very relaxed affair, considering what I said to Oldham. And I'm figuring on turning in early tonight. For some reason, I feel tired, and I've just come from a ceremonial meeting at Istana, where President Ramaha finished me off."

"Was it tiresome?"

"Deadly. Complete with aides in full uniform, dowagers and dyspeptics. Ramaha must have inherited them from the former British governor. The house and gardens are beautiful, and the President is not a bad sort, but he—" At this point Miller stopped listening because without warning the door to the bedroom had opened and in walked the maid. She did not hesitate on her way to the bathroom with clean towels, propelling herself forward with real purpose. Zack swung quickly around to a less embarrassing position, but she moved right with him, staring with frank interest at what he sought to conceal. One could have hung a large family's Monday wash on the line that stretched between the woman's eyes and Zack's geometric center. She paid absolutely no attention to his frantic gestures for her to depart and finally disappeared into the bathroom.

"Zack, do you hear me?"

"Yes, sir. Just one minute, please." Picking up the towel and holding it around him, Zack stormed into the bathroom and escorted the bewildered, protesting woman to the door, hooking the night latch behind her.

"Pardon me, Mr. Vice President, but someone was at the door," he said, picking up the phone again.

"I was saying that I'd better be sharp for the prime minister. He's going to be a regular bearcat to handle."

Miller laughed. "You can handle him, Newt. You're getting to be a real expert. Look what you did to Roland Gray and the ambassador."

"This one requires more diplomacy," said Canfield, nevertheless pleased.

After hanging up, Zack mopped up the wet spot on the carpet where he had been standing and returned to the shower. His head was full of lather when the phone again began to ring insistently. Swearing more profusely this time, he rushed to the bedroom to find that the hotel phone was the violator of his peace. Thoroughly angry, he snapped into the receiver, "Yes? What is it?"

"Hello. Is this Dr. Miller?" The voice was low, sensuous, and gave only a slight hint that English was not the speaker's first language.

"Yes, yes. Who is this?" The last thing he wanted was a long conversation with a reporter while he stood dripping all over the floor again.

"Hello, Dr. Miller. My name is Sirana Amiri. You taught my brother at the university. Forgive me for imposing, but I would like to see you just to say hello."

The sudden chill that swept through Miller had nothing to do with the effect of the air conditioning on his wet, naked body. These were the code words that Yoram Halevy had told him would identify the undercover agent who would contact him in Asia if he was in danger. Zack tried his best to keep his voice steady and relaxed. "Oh, yes, Miss Amiri. I remember your brother very well. He transferred to us from the university in Tehran, I believe. We had many long, interesting discussions together. Of course I would be pleased to meet you." The sultry voice excited him in spite of his fear.

"Wonderful," she said with a delightful laugh. "I'm sure your time is much more occupied than mine. When would it be convenient for you?"

"We are only going to be here for a couple of days and, beginning tomorrow, it's going to get terribly busy. I do have a dinner engagement tonight, but it shouldn't last too long. How about meeting me later this evening, say about ten-thirty?"

"I think I can do that. Where shall I come?"

Miller thought rapidly. It wouldn't be advisable to meet her at the Marco Polo. Agents made the penthouse floor impossible, and the traveling press was always about the public rooms. He didn't want to be questioned about her identity.

"Where are you staying?" he asked.

"I'm at Raffles Hotel."

"Could I meet you there?"

"That would be fine. I'll be finishing dinner at the Palm Court about ten. Why don't I wait for you there? I'll leave word with the headwaiter that I'm expecting you."

"Perhaps I had better describe myself." Miller's acute edge of fear was dissipating and being replaced by a sense of impending adventure.

"That won't be necessary, sir. I've seen your picture—the one you were kind enough to let my brother take—and I never forget a handsome man." Again, the delightful laugh honed his desire to see this girl.

For a few moments after saying goodbye, Miller stood thinking; then he slowly replaced the receiver and went back to completing his long-delayed shower. With the hot water cascading sensuously over his body, he found himself becoming mildly stimulated. He turned on the cold water for a few moments, then stepped out. Ridiculous, he thought, toweling down vigorously. She's probably got a mustache, weighs two hundred thirty pounds and has never heard of deodorant.

Porter Canfield took a few bites, then pushed the *tournedos* and glazed carrots to new positions on his plate, roughing them up a little in the process. It wasn't that the Oldhams didn't set a fine table. On the contrary, he had never had a bad meal at an embassy residence. Ambassadors lived graciously, yet were never criticized for lacking the common touch. But envy had nothing to do with

237

Canfield's lack of appetite. It was just that he felt no hunger—only a gnawing at the pit of his stomach that told him he wanted nothing more than to get out of this elaborate house and away from the damask, dinnerware and dullness of Mrs. Oldham.

His crashing body block of the ambassador that afternoon had destroyed any chance of developing a cordial relationship. Not that his excellency wasn't being polite—his manners were impeccable—but it was the kind of courtesy that Emperor Theodosius might have extended Attila the Hun: motivated by fear and quiescent contempt. He could handle that, however, much better than Mrs. Oldham's chatter. Mrs. Oldham was an intellectual *manqué* who had taken a master's in journalism at a prestigious eastern university. She rattled on about how her great-great-grandfather had helped endow the college of journalism, thereby explaining her matriculation and graduation.

A few bites into the fish course, Canfield collided with a good idea. Drawing Zack Miller, who was seated to the lady's left, into the conversation, he handed off daringly to the professor by submitting that Miller, although an academic type himself, would be immensely grateful for insights into the journalistic mind. The old biddy took the bait beautifully, and he was left to exchange a few desultory words with the deputy chief of mission, who loyally was being as frigid as his boss.

Miller, on the other hand, was suffering mightily. His mind was on other things, and his absentminded nodding in agreement with the lady's monologues got him into trouble when a negative reply was in order. She would then stop abruptly, startling him by touching his arm and saying, ''Surely you don't really think so, do you?'' and he would have to explain that he had misunderstood her point.

Blissful was Zack when the traditional separation of the sexes took place after dinner. Over brandy, coffee and a good cigar, he glared at Canfield, who raised his eyebrows piously and commented to the deputy chief of mission that academicians had so much in common.

Promptly at nine-thirty Canfield complained of fatigue and indicated that he must go to rest up for the next day's meeting with the prime minister. Hypocritically deploring the quickness with which time had sped, the ambassador saw them to their cars, and thirty minutes later Zack Miller was leaving his hotel room for the second time that evening. He wasn't certain whether this meeting would be more enjoyable, but it was a cinch to be more interesting.

Dodging around the newsstand, where Douglas Drake was putting the make on a very pretty Eurasian girl, Zack went quickly past the bar entrance—there were sure to be newsies there—and out into the street. The doorman signaled one of the immaculately clean taxicabs and was volubly grateful for his tip of a Singapore half dollar—about eighteen U.S. cents.

Swinging expertly into the heavy traffic, the driver turned at Orchard Road and headed toward the Esplanade. The warm sea-and-flower-scented breeze brought Miller vivid memories of summer vacations long ago at the Montauk Point home of a wealthy college friend. Those were days of adventure and discovery. Now suddenly he wondered whether in this exotic city he would escape the loneliness and boredom that had become so ingrained a part of his life.

The Raffles Hotel looked graceful and beautifully pristine in its night-muted whiteness. The light of a yellow half moon touched the lawn and shrubbery, casting long shadows across the drive. Zack was impressed by the way the place had been maintained. It was old, but gracious, yielding nothing in style to the modern glass and steel giants. He went up the steps and then entered the spacious lobby, where his attention was drawn to the famous Raffles Bar to his left. Reputed to be the longest bar in the world, it had been a favorite retreat of Somerset Maugham and, before him, Rudyard Kipling. Curiously overcoming caution (this was a likely watering spot for a Bruce Atherton), he looked in. Gathered at the venerable polished wooden bar with its rattan awnings and tan shades of varying sizes was a crowd of people of all types and races. Overhead, ancient ceiling fans rotated lazily over bamboo and glass tables and comfortable bamboo armchairs, swirling the already cooled air. It was, indeed, a relic from Singapore's British colonial past.

Zack looked at his watch. It was ten-twenty—a bit early—but she had said she would be having dinner. Again a mixed feeling of apprehension and anticipation flowed through him. Perhaps he was magnifying the whole thing, both the danger and the erotic prospects. Nevertheless his heart was beating considerably faster than usual as he went across the lobby and out into the Palm Court.

A breeze fragrant with the intermingled scents of orchids and other tropical flowers stirred the tall palms. The muted noises of dining in the outdoors created an impression of pleasant refinement. The tall Malaysian headwaiter addressed him in perfect English, understood immediately and led him to a secluded corner table.

Approaching the girl, Zack's hopes soared. Even in the subtle lantern light, she was unmistakably beautiful. She appeared to be in her mid-twenties, with large brown eyes and finely sculpted features that indicated she was Middle Eastern. Her full lips were sensual without being puffy, and the delicate bone structure of her face would keep her young-looking for decades. She smiled, revealing the contrast of even white teeth against smooth olive skin.

"I'm Zack Miller," he said. "May I sit down?"

She extended a graceful hand to him. "Please do, Dr. Miller."

The waiter pulled out the chair, and he sat down, his eyes unavoidably drawn for a split second to the attractive swell above her low-cut gown. Sirana's eyes told him that she considered the optical detour a compliment. "Thank you for coming, sir. It is an honor to meet you. My brother had many kind things to say about you."

"He was one of my brightest students," said Zack, going along with the fable for the benefit of the waiter, who was waiting for his order. "Would you care for something to drink?" he added, noting that her coffee cup was nearly empty.

She looked pensive for a moment, then her eyes sparkled. "We were to have dessert together, but in honor of meeting my brother's favorite teacher, I think I'll have some champagne instead. Will you join me?"

"That's an excellent idea." Zack ordered Dom Pérignon, and the waiter nodded appreciatively, suggesting that 1977 was an excellent year.

Their conversation was confined to the type of small talk that newly-mets resort to until the champagne was poured and the waiter discreetly disappeared. Miller found it difficult to keep from staring at her. He was honest enough to admit to himself that he had been affected similarly on other occasions by other women. Besides, it had been a long time since he had been so close to an attractive woman. Meeting Newt's requirements usually left little time for play.

Sirana's glance around the room was casual, almost idle, but she missed nothing. Satisfied that no one was within earshot, she lifted her glass. "To your health, Dr. Miller. If I really had a brother, I'm sure he would have enjoyed studying under you."

He leaned a bit closer, touching her glass with his. "To you, with appreciation that such an attractive lady has an interest in my survival." Then the realization of the purpose of the meeting struck him, and he experienced a pang of anxiety. "I assume that you have some information for me? Naturally I'm interested."

The girl waited for a moment until a group of departing diners had passed. "First, I should identify myself exactly so that you will be certain that I come from people you know.'' She took a package of cigarettes from her purse, tapped one out and accepted a light. Blowing a thin trail of smoke toward the ceiling, she continued. ''I am Iranian, but I spend quite a bit of time in the Far East. I work for a secret anticommunist organization in Tehran, one that cooperates, where it is of mutual advantage, with other undercover organizations around the world. My organization also communicates, on a regular basis, with an overt American group called INAF. I have been told that you are familiar with that group.''

She watched his face carefully. What a handsome man, she thought. I won't have to fake my interest as I did with that Russian in Tehran. When he showed no desire to comment, she went on. ''In the course of our operation in Tehran, we intercepted some information in the hands of a visiting Soviet official that conclusively indicated INAF is a target of Soviet secret agents in America. Among a list of targeted individuals, your name was found.'' Sirana paused gravely to see the effect of her statement. Miller showed no reaction aside from a slight hunching of his shoulders.

''Yes, Mr. Halevy of INAF passed that information on to me,'' he said quietly.

''Then I assume Mr. Halevy also told you that we would be contacting you here only in the event that we became aware of a serious threat to your life,'' she said, her dark eyes professionally scanning his face for betrayal of the slightest reaction.

''I was informed of that,'' he said dryly, ''so I find myself more than a little curious about what you are going to tell me.'' He wondered how it would be to make love to her and was amazed that he could be thinking of such a thing at a time like this.

The waiter refilled the wine glasses, and Sirana made casual tourist conversation until he had departed again. Then she said, ''First, let me relieve your mind by telling you that you are in no danger in Singapore. However, we have information from a highly reliable source that Soviet and Arab communist agents are planning to assassinate you in Kuala Lumpur.''

This time there was a reaction—an involuntary, audible intake of breath.

''That is rather bad news.''

''You must not go to Kuala Lumpur,'' Sirana said earnestly, her face showing great concern. ''Conditions there fit right in with their plans. Already there is much violence, social unrest and animosity toward the United States due to intense communist undercover activity. If they were to kill you under such circumstances, the

241

supposition would be that it was a Malaysian protest against the Vice President's visit.''

Miller signalled the waiter to fill their glasses again. Those unpleasant crawling sensations in his stomach told him that he was really very scared. Sirana's revelation shocked him. That people whom he didn't even know not only wanted him dead, but had fixed the time and place of his demise, set his adrenal glands working overtime. He could feel a tightness around his eyes and he had paled noticeably. He needed a few moments to get hold of himself. As he watched the waiter pour the wine, he knew that the girl was looking at him, conscious of his discomfort. Trying to rally and feeling the need to say something even though the waiter was still there, he ventured, ''I think that we can handle any situation they throw at us. Our people are not without experience in this area.'' He drank off half his wine in one gulp and put the glass down quickly so that she would not see his hand shaking. Neither of them made any further comment until the waiter had replaced the nearly empty champagne bottle in the ice and departed.

Sirana said slowly, ''You are a courageous man, Dr. Miller, but you are too intelligent to allow your courage to become foolhardiness. I know your Secret Service is expert at protection. But their obligation is to Mr. Canfield and not to you.''

''But if I tell the Vice President, he will assign agents to me.''

''Then you would have to disclose the entire business to them, including my identity. Please, Dr. Miller, that would cause great complications for my organization. Besides, your press would make a big story of the whole thing, and it would completely overshadow the Vice President's efforts at diplomacy because it would embarrass the Malaysians.''

Zack pursed his lips in thought. A look of near panic on her face, the girl touched his hand impulsively. ''Dr. Miller, you do not know these people as I know them! They are desperate. They will take any risks to achieve their ends. Human life is cheap. They are a type of zealot that you have never before encountered.''

''I will have to tell the Vice President—'' began Zack.

''You must not tell the Vice President!'' she interrupted in dismay. ''You cannot predict his reaction. He may tell others and bring about the dangers we have just discussed. Whether he does or not, you will destroy his concentration and his chance to carry off his visit successfully. No, it is better that you make some excuse, find some urgent matter at home that requires your immediate return.''

The more Zack studied the situation, the less he liked it. If what

Sirana said was true, he was in grave danger. No matter how hard they might try to protect him, he was still vulnerable. And what she said made sense. Wrong handling of the situation could abort the mission and set back the Canfield campaign for no good reason. Yes, the intelligent course was for him to avoid Kuala Lumpur. He would figure out a reason. He squeezed Sirana's hand.

"I'm really not much of a gentleman," he said, smiling. "You've probably saved my life, and I haven't even thanked you." He grew pensive again. "It's going to be very difficult to explain why I can't complete this trip. Yet there is no pressing reason for me to go to Kuala. I've already completed the statements the Vice President wanted. Anyhow, I will be able to complete this part of the journey, and that's where he needs me most. Malaysia will be essentially a repeat of the same issues."

She made no effort to withdraw her hand. "Oh, Dr. Miller, I'm so relieved. I know it's difficult for you to understand how dangerous going to Kuala Lumpur would be, and I'm honored that you trust my judgment. Because of this assignment, I had to learn quite a bit about you, and I admire the stands you've taken, particularly your forthright statements against the Soviet Union's repression of dissent, and denial of the right of Soviet Jews to relocate wherever they wish."

Zack thanked her, wondering how she could accept an authoritarian, even though benign, government in her own country if she had such strong convictions about the right to demonstrate and dissent. There seemed little doubt that she was interested in helping him—or else she was a consummate actress. He had no way of knowing that her genuine relief came from being able to carry out her assignment —which was to influence him—rather than because of concern for his safety. Had he rejected her plea to abandon the trip to Kuala Lumpur, her mission would have ended in outright failure.

The champagne was doing its work; the nervous sensation in Miller's stomach had been replaced by a warm, comfortable glow.

"You make me feel very important. I doubt that many college professors in America have been noticed by pretty girls in Iran. But I wish you would call me Zack—that's short for Isaac, which I never liked—and I'm going to call you Sirana, if you'll allow me. It's awkward to be formal when you're discussing matters of life and death." When she nodded her assent, he gave a little laugh. "I don't suppose the women's revolution has penetrated Iran to the point where you would like to be called Ms.?"

She laughed gaily, her face lighting up in response to his lighter mood. "All female undercover agents are liberated, even the ones

243

who do their work in harems.'' She squeezed his fingers, sending a rush of desire through him. The wine was evidently making her feel warm and affectionate, and Zack decided it was time to begin moving in. Without consulting her, he ordered more champagne and began a subtle interrogation. He learned innocuous facts about her youth, unimportant details about her life in Tehran, how she became fluent in English and how she felt about higher education in the United States.

Although they spoke for a long time, he found out nothing about Assad Ali Izadi, and she was far too discreet to reveal anything about operations. It was important that she maintain the strict reserve of a professional agent.

Skillfully he asked, and deftly she evaded, until finally he said, ''I guess I'll give up trying to learn any more about your organization. But that just gives me greater confidence in your judgment, because it proves that you are a true professional. Now, let's talk about us—from tonight on—and forget the past. I have a feeling that that will keep me interested for a long time.''

He smiled his boldest and most charming smile, allowing his eyes to drop to her décolletage. Raising their joined hands, she lifted his chin. ''I'm up here,'' she said, ''at least the part of me that makes the decisions. And now, Dr. Miller—''

''Zack.''

''Zack. Now, Zack, I must leave you. I've had two very late nights developing and confirming the information about Kuala Lumpur and I must get some sleep. It's a pity, because I really am enjoying myself. Thank you for the champagne.'' She withdrew her hand and reached for her purse.

''Wait, Sirana! You can't just run off like this. Where are you staying? Where can I reach you?''

''I'm staying right here at Raffles, but I don't trust the phone system. If you need to talk to me, leave word with the concierge, and I will phone you back.''

''I'll see you to the door,'' he offered quickly.

She shook her head no. ''That wouldn't be wise, not tonight,'' she said, thus letting him know that his request to come in for a while would be denied and that she wished to spare him her refusal. ''You stay here for a bit, and I'll go on up. I think it's best that we leave separately. There are eyes about.''

''Wait, please!'' he said, frantic at the prospect of losing her for good. ''You know Singapore, and I'm sure you know where we could go to make an evening of it tomorrow. Would you join me for dinner and perhaps a show afterward tomorrow night?''

She hesitated as though considering the proposal, then gave him a warm smile. "I shouldn't, but I will." Then taking a slip of paper from her purse, she asked for his pen and wrote something on it, folded it and handed it to him. "Meet me there at eight-thirty tomorrow evening. Ask for Mr. Wong. The place is small, and each table is its own private dining room. Good night, Zack." She was gone almost before he got to his feet.

He sank back slowly in his chair, watching her lovely receding form.

The long dress revealed little; but the general dimensions and dynamics were encouraging.

10

THIRTY-TWO INFLUENTIAL men and women, eight to a side, sat around the outer perimeter of the adjoining luncheon tables, which were arranged in a hollow square in the State Dining Room. Besides twenty-four of the party's most powerful congressional leaders, there were the secretary of state; Counselor Joshua Devers; the party's national chairman; the director of OMB; the secretary of HEW; the President's chief of staff; the press secretary; and the President himself.

Coffee cups clinked and matches flared as smokers lit the excellent Coronas being passed by the White House waiters. President Hurley terminated a whispered conversation with the Senate majority leader and rose to his feet. Patches of conversation died down.

"Mr. Speaker, Mr. Majority Leader, and distinguished guests," he began. Gordon Woodhall, seated directly across from Hurley, bit his upper lip nervously. Unlike his predecessor he was a timid man and did not enjoy the prospect of having the stage.

"I apologize for disrupting the middle of your day on such short notice, but I thought that the leaders of our great party should have certain information that I gave the speaker and the majority and minority leaders of the Congress this morning." He smiled slightly. "Now, I'm sure most of you have already heard the rumblings—there are no secrets in bipartisan meetings or in any other White House meetings, for that matter—but I wanted you to get the accurate picture." There were a few chuckles, but Hurley went on without pausing, "Our top House and Senate committee chairmen are here, of course, as well as a few Cabinet and staff people who have political as well as governmental impact. Just about everyone in the room is a politician—except Secretary Woodhall. He is not permitted to be a politician, and I doubt that he could be one if he were permitted.''

There was a roar of laughter, some of it vicious. The party had not been pleased with the Woodhall appointment because Gordon had never worked in the political vineyards.

''One gentleman present is proud of his political credentials. He has the difficult responsibility of keeping our great party united. That's never easy, but when a transition in the presidency is required by the Twenty-second Amendment, it becomes a hellish task.'' Turning toward the national chairman, Hurley grinned and said graciously, ''Alfred Mann can do it if anyone can.'' A burst of applause caused the popular chairman to rise briefly to his feet and wave. ''Al is going to need every bit of assistance you can give him,'' said the President. ''The nature of our current problems makes it impossible for me to be of much help, except to see that Al gets the best information possible.''

What is he getting at, Meredith Lord wondered. Is he going to take Newt on in open battle before the whole party?

The President straightened his shoulders and adjusted his glasses. ''Yesterday, the Soviet ambassador called on the secretary of state to deliver a message from the Soviet foreign minister. I'll ask Gordon to take it from here.''

Woodhall rose, visibly edgy. Looking down at his notes for a moment, he slowly raised his head and began in a high, tight voice, ''Thank you, Mr. President. Gentlemen''—it would not be forgiven that, in his nervousness, he forgot to acknowledge the women—''the Soviet ambassador, Mr. Rykovskiy, was waiting for me when I arrived at my office yesterday at eight-thirty A.M. Although he had no appointment, I received him immediately because of our cordial relations.''

A pompous ass, the secretary, thought Meredith.

''The ambassador appeared uncomfortable. He handed me a note from his foreign minister, Mr. Buveney, and requested me to read it immediately.'' Woodhall cleared his throat several times. ''I'll not give you the exact words, but the note indicated that his government was seriously disturbed about a growing movement in some American governmental and academic circles to advocate the supplying of nuclear weapons to Israel. The Soviet government called this movement, quote, 'inappropriate and in conflict with the principles expressed by the intermediaries in the recent SALT negotiations,' unquote, and, quote, 'destructive of the advances made toward world peace in the recent successfully concluded Tripartite agreement,' unquote. The note closed by calling for, quote, 'strong presidential censure and control of those who seek to destroy the burgeoning understanding among the great powers,' unquote, and finally expressed grave concern that peace in the Middle East could not be maintained unless such, quote, 'irresponsible tirades were openly rejected by those in authority,' unquote. I told the ambassador that I would inform the President of the contents of the note immediately—it was addressed to me, not him—and would have no immediate reply. That's about it, Mr. President,'' said Woodhall with obvious relief.

"Secretary Woodhall and I discussed the matter thoroughly,'' Hurley said calmly. "Today the secretary responded with a note saying that the foreign policy of the United States had undergone no change with respect to the question raised, that we did not intend to supply nuclear weapons to Israel and that our system did not permit presidential censure and control. We did assure the Russians that we wanted peace as much as they and would continue to work for understanding and accords of the type we had just successfully completed.''

The President paused, took off his glasses and rubbed his eyes. He solemnly continued. "I am passing this on to you because pressure is mounting for us to alter our policy of restraint. Senator Gray and Speaker Edmonds tell me that there is much activity in Congress, and we can all see that a big media campaign is beginning. Some in our own party are proponents.

"Politics is politics,'' said Walter Hurley slowly, his words very distinct in the unusually silent room, "and this is a dynamite issue for people seeking attention. However, the CIA can find no evidence of any attack being prepared against Israel. Sometimes, the good of the country and world peace require politicians to forsake dynamite issues. Think it over,'' said the President of the United States; and he left the hushed room without the customary stops to chat with various guests.

There was an electric feeling in the air as the big room slowly emptied. Everyone realized that it would soon be time to choose between Hurley's man, probably Roland Gray, and Vice President Porter N. Canfield. Meredith Lord had already made her decision, and she had much to do.

At the very moment that President Hurley was leaving the luncheon meeting at the White House, the leader of the Persian Protective League slid into a rear booth in a sleazy bar on Mowlavi Street in Tehran. Reza bumped against Anwar to make space for Assad Izadi. Boldar and Little Man looked up quizzically; 10:30 P.M. was a little early to find Assad stirring.

"She's made the connection, and everything is going well," the leader said exultantly. "He'll be eating out of her hand in no time, and then we'll get some real action out of the candidate."

"That's very good," said Reza. "We'll need her to whip things up a little. Number One is really beginning to apply the brakes to Number Two. He shook him up pretty badly with what he said at the Tripartite Pact announcement."

Izadi smiled. "I just talked to her on the phone. She says he was thoroughly frightened about K.L., and he thinks she saved his life. Besides, he's panting for her."

"Miller's getting quite a bonus for heating up Canfield," Boldar said, leering. "I wouldn't mind a little of that action my—"

"Shut up, Boldar!" said Izadi savagely. "And stop mentioning names. You are stupid." However, the security slip bothered him less than the reminder of how Sirana was to carry out her assignment.

The big man bristled, but said nothing as Reza dug him sharply in the ribs.

Assad was too pleased at the progress of his plot to remain angry. "I'm going to call Yoram later to bring him up to date. He will think the plot is real and that we've saved his friend, the professor. We're lucky he's not the brightest guy around. He'll be plenty mad at the Russians and Arabs, but that'll be tame compared to his feelings about his Jewish friends in the American media who he thinks are selling out to the Arabs."

Izadi smiled craftily. "You should have heard him when I told him we had information on TBS, *Twiceweek* and the *Globe*. He couldn't believe it at first, but I referred him to the published rumor on TBS in the *Herald Tribune,* which naturally hadn't gotten much play there, and he really hit the ceiling. Said that kind of treachery could destroy Israel faster than Arab guns."

"What happens now? What do we do?" Boldar wanted to know.

"Just let the kettle boil, Boldar. I have a feeling we'll get action pretty quick. Our friends up north soon will be too busy to carry out their grand plan for taking over Afghanistan and Iran. They'll have their hands full holding détente together." He punched Anwar joyfully on the arm. "You gave me the whole idea that day at the house, Anwar. Now, let's have a drink to celebrate."

• • •

Nearly seven thousand miles away a big black Cadillac limousine followed by a Secret Service vehicle turned into a drive and pulled up before a stately fieldstone home in North Philadelphia. The tall blond uniformed chauffeur quickly got out and held the door for Amy Canfield. "Will you need the car more today, Mrs. Canfield?" he asked in a strong German accent.

"No, Gunther. It's past two-thirty, and I'm expecting a few friends for dinner. I won't need you until tomorrow morning." She walked quickly up the steps, and past the door, which had been opened by her maid.

"Hello, Elizabeth. Any calls?"

"No, ma'am, Mrs. C. But here's your mail."

"Thank you, Elizabeth. I'm going right up. The luncheon was tiring. I think I'll take a nap before I get ready for dinner." She started up the beautiful wide staircase, then turned. "Where's Jerome?" she asked. "I hope everything is ready for tonight."

"Everything's ready, Mrs. C. Jerome went to do some last-minute shopping."

"All right, Elizabeth. Call me at six, will you?"

"Yes, Mrs. C. I'll be sure you're up."

In her private bedroom suite Amy undressed, put on a robe and sank down in her favorite chair by the window overlooking the garden. She put on her reading glasses and began to go through her mail. There were two invitations to charity functions, an appeal for a contribution and a letter from a college friend in Virginia. Amy's brows arched in surprise. Mary Durban hadn't written her for years. There had been a great rivalry between them at Radcliffe, and Mary was piqued when Porter Canfield's star rose more rapidly than Robert Durban's. When Amy pulled out the letter and unfolded it, two newspaper clippings fell out on the floor. Disregarding them, she began to read the letter. Skimming the usual amenities, she came quickly to the reason she was hearing from Mary Durban.

"I do hope you and Newt are getting along well," Mary wrote. "Washington is so full of distractions for powerful men. While I have little confidence in the accuracy of the press, I thought you should know what some scandal columnists are saying. Remembering how you never had time for reading newspapers, I figured you might have missed these items. If they're wrong, as I suspect they are, you may want to sue the publications."

Amy was furious. "That gossiping cat!" she thought, picking up the clippings from the floor. As she read them, her face became suffused with color. One article was the Andy Jackerson item about which Sid Winehart had questioned Canfield on the plane. The other was from *Charade* magazine, a weekly publication distributed with several hundred Sunday newspapers. The *Charade* item, purportedly in answer to a reader's question, was written in a blend of righteous indignation and vicarious drooling.

Q. There have been reports that all is not well with the marriage of Vice President Porter Canfield. Is it true that he is involved with another well-known Washington celebrity?

A. It is no secret that Amy Canfield abhors the Washington scene, preferring the comfortable familiarity of old Main Line Philadelphia friends. This leaves the Vice President dependent on other companionship much of the time. Recent reports link him with the beautiful secretary of Health, Education, and Welfare, Dr. Meredith Lord. There is no verification that the attachment is a romantic one at this point, and that is unlikely to be verified in view of the Vice President's ambition to reside in the White House.

Amy flung letter and clippings down. How could she face her friends? Never had a breath of scandal ever touched anyone close to her before. She was devastated. Those miserable gossips! Her marriage was a lot more solid than most in their set. She and Newt had their separate interests, but they were comfortable together. Oh, they argued sometimes, but what married couple didn't? Suddenly she smiled. It was ridiculous to be upset over such drivel. The thing to do was to make a joke of it. That's what she'd do—treat it as a big joke, laugh about it to her friends. Feeling much better, she cleansed her face and stretched out on the bed. But sleep wouldn't come, and there was a gnawing uncertainty in her mind. Although Amy had not been in love with Porter Canfield for a long time, she was a proud woman and she would not suffer humiliation.

11

NOT YET fully awake, Miller frowned at the unfamiliar shadowy shapes around him, experiencing that moment of disorientation common to infrequent travelers. He lifted himself on one elbow and squinted into the gray near-darkness of early dawn. Awareness of his whereabouts, pleasant memories of the night before and mild physical discomfort came simultaneously. He smiled. A champagne headache was not a great price to pay for the privilege of knowing Sirana Amiri. And by tomorrow he hoped to know her ever so much better.

He looked at his watch. He had twenty minutes before he was due in the vice-presidential suite for breakfast. Leaping out of bed, he bolted a couple of aspirins, brushed his teeth and showered. By the time he was half through shaving, he was feeling fine. He had decided he wouldn't tell the veep that he couldn't accompany him to Kuala Lumpur until an hour before departure time tomorrow. That way, he would have his night with Sirana, and Canfield would be forced to fly out ahead of him. The excuse would be a fictitious phone call informing him of the sudden demise of a relative dear to him. Newt wouldn't have enough time to ask too many questions, and he would have to release him.

Finishing his shave and dressing quickly, Zack headed for Canfield's suite with the prepared statements. They would go over them at breakfast, before the Israeli ambassador was due. Miller had a good idea of what the ambassador wanted. Because of Atherton's tip, seeing him was a little awkward, but refusing would have been worse. The important thing was to be sure that he didn't say anything directly to the Vice President that would cause a problem later. Miller would take him aside to hear about the real purpose of his visit.

Thank heaven Meredith Lord had those close connections with the Israeli embassy in Washington. Otherwise, Canfield would certainly be embarrassed today. Meredith had early on recognized the Jewish community's activism regarding social programs and had taken advantage of it. She had been to Israel a dozen times, several of those times before her appointment to the Cabinet post. The Israelis loved her. She had sat at the head table at more Israeli bond drive dinners than any Cabinet officer before her and had appointed more Jews to high posts than all the preceding secretaries combined. It was she who had engineered the coming meeting in place of one the embassy asked for in Washington and she was the one who had learned the purpose of the meeting.

Bill Shelby and Kathy Dryden were already eating with the Vice President in the cheerful sunlit alcove. Canfield waved off Miller's apology for being slightly late and told him to sit down and eat. During the breakfast the Vice President read Miller's drafts, made a few amendments and dictated several inserts to Kathy. After a last cup of coffee, he handed the drafts to her and said, "These are marked to show where the inserts I have just dictated should go, Kathy. They are not for distribution, so I won't need a draft. Just type them in final and have them ready for me before nine-thirty. I want to get them anchored in my mind before I go to my ten-thirty appointment with the prime minister."

Watching the swing of Kathy's graceful body as she left the room reminded Zack of pleasant things to come that evening. It was nice to have frustration replaced by anticipation.

Shortly thereafter the C.P. notified Shelby that the Israeli ambassador had arrived and was waiting to see the Vice President. Miller quickly took control of the situation. "I suggest we bring Ambassador Morgenstern in for about ten minutes. He wants to express his government's appreciation for your strong support and tell you, in a roundabout way, that they favor your candidacy for the presidency. If he begins to be embarrassingly specific, I'll step in and shut him off. After ten minutes I'll take him to my suite, where specificity will be welcomed, even encouraged, if money is concerned."

"Be very careful, Zack," said Canfield. "Remember that Atherton will be probing for weak spots."

"The contributions law is murder since the nineteen seventy-two campaign reforms," added Shelby. "We're going to need money, but it's not worth taking chances."

Canfield nodded. "Whatever we spend visibly must be impeccable as to source. However, 'walking-around money' will be a problem to raise. That's a possible area where they can help. Certainly, no corporate or personal American sources will take the risk anymore. But be very careful, Zack, about the mechanics. Now, you might as well bring him in."

Galdari ushered the smiling diplomat into the suite. Morgenstern, a short, trim-looking man with alert blue eyes set in a round, smooth face, was completely bald except for a fringe of blond hair around his neck and ears. His handshake was firm as he clicked his heels and bowed to the Vice President. It occurred to Canfield how incongruous it was that so many Israelis he had met demonstrated the German military characteristics.

"Such an important man as your excellency is very generous to give me an audience when his schedule in Singapore is so crowded," said Morgenstern, taking the proffered seat.

"Not at all, Mr. Ambassador. I'm delighted to see you, although I wish my time were not so limited so that we could have a long talk," replied Canfield in conventional language that could be accurately translated as: "You're right. I'm busy. Let's get on with it."

Noting the ambassador's uncertainty, Canfield added, "It's all right to say whatever you want. I have total confidence in Dr. Miller and Mr. Shelby. However, you should be aware that elements of the American press have found out about your call on me, and they are curious about its purpose. It may be well that we bear in mind that both of us may be questioned about our conversation."

The ambassador seemed surprised. "How did the press know?" He thought a moment, and since no one volunteered to speculate, went on: "I will say nothing to them unless you want me to, sir."

The Vice President laughed. "Well, let's talk first; then decide that. It will be best if we can tell them something, of course, especially since they expect to get nothing."

"My purpose, Mr. Vice President, is to convey to you the gratitude of the government and people of Israel for your courageous public expressions of concern over the security of our country. No other major figure in the world has so forthrightly spoken out against the forces of aggression that are being prepared against us. The American people, for a long time our staunchest protectors, needed to be informed of these dangers. In the opinion of my government, they would not have been informed were it not for your excellency."

Canfield took a deep breath and smiled, a mannerism that

255

annoyed Shelby because he appeared to be preening himself. "Thank you, Mr. Ambassador. As you know, I greatly admire your people. I will continue to speak out when they are threatened. Please convey my appreciation to Prime Minister Stein for this expression of confidence."

"We hope for the day that you will be the President of the United States," said Morgenstern fervently, "and while our offices prevent our taking sides publicly, individually we will do all we can to convince our American friends to support your candidacy."

"But I am not yet a candidate. I must make certain that the American people want me to enter the race," said Canfield, trolling for more compliments.

"There is no doubt of that, Mr. Vice President! You are too modest! Everyone is talking about what a great President you would make."

"You are correct, Mr. Ambassador," interjected Zack Miller to save Canfield from an inane response.

"I know I am correct, Dr. Miller. Now, let me talk for a moment about how we can assist your campaign. First, about mon—"

"Forgive me for interrupting, Mr. Ambassador, but the Vice President is late for another meeting," Zack broke in firmly. He stood up, and Canfield and Shelby immediately took the cue and did the same. "Why don't you and I continue this discussion in my suite, your excellency," Zack said, moving the ambassador, who had also risen, toward the door.

The chief of protocol of Singapore pointed out of the window of the cruising limousine. "I brought you around Empress Place so you could see the statue of Sir Stamford Raffles." He indicated the impressive figure with the folded arms. Zack Miller and Bill Shelby twisted around on the jump seats to get a better look, and Canfield took the opportunity to show that he had done his homework.

"A lot of Westerners believe that Raffles actually discovered Singapore," he said to his staff members. "Actually, as the ambassador knows, the discovery of Singapore occurred six hundred years prior to Raffles's eighteen-nineteen landing. An Indian prince named Palembang landed here, thought he saw a lion and named the island 'Singapura,' meaning 'Lion City.' The English sent Raffles along much later to find a base so that they could contain the Dutch, who already controlled the Straits of Malacca and the Sundra Straits."

The chief of protocol laughed. "I am impressed with your excellency's knowledge of our history. It is true that the British were not the first here, but Raffles played a very important role in our development. He negotiated treaties with the Temengong and Sultan Hussein, thus creating stability on the island for the first time. As was true in the Pacific islands that the United States has developed, the Western influence was a beneficial one for Singapore. That is why we respect the British and are appreciative of the knowledge they brought us.''

The limousine drew away and turned toward City Hall, where Canfield would shortly meet the prime minister. "I'm glad that this afternoon will provide an opportunity for me to make a brief tour of the island," he said. "You are very kind, Mr. Ambassador, to take me around, and I look forward to seeing your famous Jurong Industrial Park, your harbor and the magnificent preserves and gardens for which you are so justly famous. I hope we also get the chance to ride through Serangoon and Chinatown and along the Singapore River so that I can sense the separate ethnic influences that make Singapore a model of human cooperation and understanding. If I could take a little of that back home with me, it would help my country a great deal.''

The ambassador was greatly pleased and assured Canfield that he was delighted to be tour guide for the afternoon. A few moments later, flags flying, the limousine drew up to City Hall, and the party entered accompanied by the usual herd of frantically scurrying and jostling newsmen.

Prime Minister Ling greeted them with the courteous reserve typical of the Chinese and then led them to his conference room, where the foreign minister, Ambassador Oldham and the State Department men waited. The room was immaculate and simple to the point of being austere. They sat in uncushioned, wooden-armed chairs around a modest eight-place conference table. The hardwood floors were bare except for a few Chinese throw rugs, and the pale yellow walls seemed almost institutional. Only a few pictures were on the walls and these were of various governmental projects— some completed and some in progress. It reminded Canfield of the kind of room that might be occupied by the director of public works of a big American city.

While a servant was pouring tea, Canfield took a good look at Ling. It was difficult to believe that this quiet, composed man had been the primary political force in Singapore for nearly thirty years. The broad, flat planes of his face were unmistakably Chinese, but the large expressive eyes were more Caucasian than Oriental. His supple, vigorous body, youthful unlined face and a shock of black hair made him appear much younger than sixty. But his appearance gave no hint of the singular qualities that made Ling so univerally respected.

After tea and small talk, the State Department man and his Singaporean counterpart opened their notebooks and prepared to record the discussions.

"Mr. Vice President," Ling began, "you come to us at a time when the intentions of your great nation are not entirely clear." Characteristically, the prime minister wasted no time getting to the important point.

"Over the past ten years, American Presidents and their envoys have told us over and over that the United States will continue its traditional policy of deterring aggression against the smaller nations. You say you will continue to protect your treaty partners. You say you will come to the aid of any small nation in the case of nuclear attack. And you say that you will help with money and materiel for those nations that are being undermined by a much more subtle kind of attack, known as a 'war of national liberation.'

"Notwithstanding those assurances, we have seen the much-maligned domino theory become a reality." The prime minister smiled, but there was little humor in the eyes that were fixed on Canfield. "Because we are the smallest nation of all, we have had to reassess and revise our position. In the past, our preferences for the West showed through our neutrality. We can no longer afford the luxury of even such covert unofficial alignment. Our eyes and our brains tell us that the United States is no longer an important military factor in the Pacific. Oh, your fleet moves about to maintain what you refer to as 'a presence,' but the cold fact of military readiness no longer exists.

"On the other hand, the communist powers have extended their capabilities. They have always had the advantage of proximity to home base. Now they have added military superiority, so they must be regarded as dominant should any military confrontation occur." The prime minister paused to give the note-takers a chance to catch up.

"The Japanese are beginning to rearm, but it will take years before they become any kind of balancing factor. Moreover, for historical reasons—" He laughed dryly. "Don't take this down," he cautioned the recorders. "—for historical reasons we find it difficult to consider them a protective force. But, to get to the point of my recitation, we hope that your visit will throw some light on the intentions of the United States in the area."

Canfield nodded agreeably and smiled as though he had all the answers well in hand. The briefing book had not exaggerated. The prime minister was going to be a pretty tough cookie to handle. However, he had to make the effort.

"Before I begin to respond to your observations, Mr. Prime Minister, let me first express my appreciation and that of my party for the cordial reception we have been given here in Singapore. For a long time I have wanted to visit your country, which many consider to be the finest example of economic and land-use planning in the world. Now that I am here, I see the justification for the accolade, and later today, when the chief of protocol takes me on a complete tour, I am certain that I will be even more impressed."

The prime minister, who had been through such pleasantries a hundred times over, smilingly acknowledged the tribute but made no comment.

Canfield continued, "As the person who has successfully guided the destinies of Singapore for such a long time you are wise to be cautious and pragmatic in your relations with the outside world. Your brand of activist, enterprise-oriented socialism is very closely attuned to the evolution of public conscience in the United States. And because our mutual aspirations for our people give us so much in common, our government takes a very active interest in encouraging what is going on here. That is the reason for my visit. President Hurley is well aware of apprehensions about America's ability to continue her nuclear umbrella over Southeast Asia. So I was sent here specifically to inform your excellency that American military cutbacks do not mean an end to America's capability to carry out commitments. Our military technology has become so advanced that it is possible today to provide the same safeguards without the cumbersome, highly visible and abrasive presence that was required twenty years ago!" The Vice President leaned forward in his seat as if to convince the prime minister by the very force of his delivery. "In other words, Mr. Prime Minister, our major Pacific base in Hawaii alone is now capable of providing the same strike force flexibility that formerly required additional large bases at Guam, Okinawa and other Far Eastern locations. The President has directed me to convey to you his pledge that the United States will not sit idly by should the direct actions of any other big power threaten the security of neutral nations in this part of the world."

The prime minister's large eyes continued to bore into Canfield, and several seconds of silence ensued. Finally, Ling gave a little sigh and said quietly, "You may mean well. There is no question in my mind that you mean well. But the American leaders who have preceded you also meant well, and look what we have come to.

Indochina is totally communist, and Thailand had been 'annexed' by the Chinese, supposedly at the request of the majority but actually through subtle duress. Active fighting rages in northern Malaysia, and the pattern of so-called wars of national liberation, a transparent fiction devised by Peking and Moscow, continues. Meanwhile, the United States accelerates the charade known as détente. While your intermediaries sit in Geneva drinking vodka and eating Peking duck with the communist diplomats, the secret political cadres of both Russia and China continue to exacerbate unrest in the area.'' The prime minister shifted his weight in the chair and shook his head from side to side sadly. ''I cannot tell you how many times I have sat here or in Washington and listened to assurances that the power and the resolve of the United States remain undiminished. Unfortunately, the facts say otherwise. The South Vietnamese, the Cambodians, the Laotians, the Thais, the South Koreans all learned that the hard way. We cannot resist the heavy winds that bear us away from the West. It is not a question of preference; it is a question of self-preservation. That is why we now repair Soviet naval vessels and why our finest technicians are on missions to assist the Chinese. That is why we are considering preferential trade arrangements with the communist nations. We recognize that the power has shifted to them. The United States has become impotent because it is no longer controlled by its government, but by its propagandists.''

The characterization of the United States as ''impotent'' angered Canfield. Who was this administrator of a country less than half the size of Rhode Island and containing only one-hundredth the population of the United States to denigrate the greatest democracy in the world? The Vice President's manner gave a hint of his indignation as he replied, ''The American people have a revulsion for senseless killing. They will endure a great deal to avoid it. But do not mistake their patience for impotence. The Germans and the Japanese made that error in World War Two, and some of them lived to rue it.''

The prime minister did not react in any way to Canfield's bristling. ''I'm afraid the communists understand you better than your World War Two adversaries. They are far too wise to give you such a clear-cut provocation. Their technique is to attack your credibility. First, they get your attention with an outrageous act of aggression by one of their small surrogates, such as North Korea or North Vietnam. Then, when you are forced to respond, they run to the rest of the world and complain that the Big Bully is at it again. Then the liberal propagandists of the Third World, aided and abetted by your masochistic news media, use the United Nations to chastise your government for warmongering and imperialism. Then the hacks of both your political parties rush to show compassion by emasculating your military effort. The end sees you withdraw in disgrace, apologizing for all the crimes others committed and laid at your doorstep. That is why I say you are impotent. If you were not impotent, North Vietnam would today be the only communist nation in Indochina."

"The major part of the problem was that a corrupt South Vietnamese government robbed the South Vietnamese people of their will to fight," said Canfield defensively.

"I cannot accept that thesis, Mr. Vice President," Ling said mildly. "Corruption was rampant in your country during both world wars and it did not rob you of your will to fight. Besides, nothing corrupts more, to paraphrase Lord Acton, than absolute power—and absolute power is the type exercised by the communists. There is no doubt that the secrecy with which totalitarian societies are run makes them more corrupt than free societies; the people see the results of the corruption even if the details are suppressed—yet their will to fight is not impaired.

"The South Vietnamese lost the will to fight only after their faith in their leadership was systematically destroyed. Not destroyed by the enemy, you understand, but destroyed by adversary journalists with American and European press passes who, caught up in the hysteria of the antiwar movement, parroted the communist line to the world and infected first the American troops, then the South Vietnamese troops, with lies that made right seem wrong and wrong seem right."

Canfield was shocked. "The news media were only the messengers who told the unpleasant truth!" he argued. "About My Lai, about the Cambodian invasion, about the horrible bombing of Hanoi and Haiphong. They also revealed the brutality of the tiger cages, criminal pilfering of troop rations for the black market and other abuses by the South Vietnamese government."

"The mass slaughters by the North Vietnamese dwarfed My Lai," Ling said patiently. "The North Vietnamese, not the Americans, were the uninvited invaders of Cambodia; the bombing was accurately restricted to war targets—nothing to compare with the ravages of Hue and other cities in the South—although some of your leftists made it sound like genocide. As to the tiger cages, talk to your prisoners of war about how they were treated. War is inherently cruel. Abuses of leadership? Who can say? There were no investigative reporters in North Vietnam then. Now there are none in all of Indochina, or Russia or China for that matter."

Canfield was annoyed. He glanced at Zack Miller, who was biting his lips to keep from entering the argument, then said loftily, "If we waited for perfection in others before improving ourselves, we would still be barbarians. Decency and justice win out in the end. The United States is stronger and more stable today than ever before because we admitted our faults and moved to correct them."

Ling perceived that his guest was not educable. Never one to beat a dead horse, he steered the conversation to less sensitive areas. Another half-hour elapsed. The ambassadors were looking for the proper moment to disengage their principals when Canfield suddenly asked if he could have a moment in private with the prime minister. Ling graciously acquiesced, and after the others had withdrawn to the anteroom—with Oldham obviously upset at the development—the Vice President reopened the conversation.

"Mr. Prime Minister, I want to speak to you man to man, frankly and confidentially."

"Sir, I am at your service," replied Ling, wondering what was on Canfield's mind. He had already formed an opinion of his perceptiveness and it wasn't flattering.

"What I want to say—and I speak as an individual and not as Vice President of the United States—is that I agree with you about the menace of communism," said Canfield cozily.

"I don't recall describing communism as a 'menace,'" said Ling carefully. "There are evils in every system." He smiled enigmatically. "The communists are no more ambitious than the capitalists, as witness the recent superpower accords. Greed is not the peculiar preserve of any political philosophy; it is a general infirmity of human nature. What I see as a real menace is big-power accord. Little nations have a way of disappearing when there is no balance of conflicting interests among the armipotent powers."

"Exactly!" said Canfield triumphantly. "I don't believe in President Hurley's policy of détente at any cost. I believe that the United States should look to its own interests and those interests are in conflict with communism, which is dedicated to the domination of all other systems. I want to see the United States remain strong and willing to take steps to prevent the forcing of communism on those who don't want it." He cleared his throat modestly. "Because I will be a candidate for the presidency next year, I wanted you to know my views. If I am elected, Singapore will have a firm friend to rely on."

The prime minister called on every bit of his self-control to mask the contempt he felt for this overly ambitious politician who had aborted his diplomatic assignment for self-aggrandizement. "How

262

do you propose to confront the problem?'' he asked with deceptive softness.

Canfield leaned back expansively. "First, I advocate facing them down on the issue of Israel," he said. "Israel must be given defensive nuclear capability or she will be destroyed by the Arab clients of the Soviet Union."

Ling was a man of strong feelings who could not stand sanctimonious stupidity. His control broke. Rigid with indignation, he said savagely, "Where were you with the big weapons when Indochina was being destroyed? I recall speeches by Representative Canfield and later by Senator Canfield demanding that the bombing be stopped, that Thieu resign, that funds for the war be cut off. I remember that you spoke out for your deserters and draft dodgers in Canada, that you encouraged those who flaunted the Viet Cong flag in the streets of Washington."

Paralyzed with surprise at Ling's outburst, Canfield sat motionless, watching the prime minister as a bird watches a stalking cat.

Ling deliberately got to his feet and said icily, "Man to man, Mr. Vice President, I abhor your politics. You believe in what serves you best at the moment. I am glad you did not say these things to me when others were present. For the good of our respective nations, what we have discussed privately should remain with us alone. But I want you to know that the respect I display during the remainder of your visit is respect for your office and not for you personally. Now, sir, if you will excuse me, I suggest we rejoin the others."

Canfield choked with rage. "Your ideas, sir are as parochial and impoverished as the nation you govern. And let me inform you that in all my years in public office, never have I been received so discourteously."

There was a look of total detachment on Prime Minister Ling's face. He swung open the door and stood back so that Canfield could precede him into the reception room. It was obvious to Zack Miller that the private meeting had not gone too well. Canfield walked with unnatural stiffness, his head carried a trifle higher than usual. Two bright spots of color on his cheeks contrasted with the general pallor of his face. The small muscles of his jaw hinges were rhythmically tensing and relaxing. and knowing those reliable signs of severe stress, Zack wondered what had happened to so upset Canfield.

The goodbyes were painstakingly correct. Ambassador Oldham shot the prime minister a curious glance when he saw that Ling was not going to accompany Canfield to his car. This was an unusually abrupt leave-taking for such a distinguished and high-ranking guest, but Oldham thought it was simply an extension of the strategy that began with the prime minister's absence at the airport.

At the driveway they were met by the traveling-media contingent and about a dozen members of the Singapore press. Canfield stopped to make a brief statement.

"The prime minister and I had a very useful and constructive meeting," he said. "I conveyed to him President Hurley's assurances that the United States would continue to maintain a presence in Southeast Asia and would assist with defense materiel any small nonaligned nation that might be attacked by a more powerful neighbor.

"Moreover, I stated that the United States would respect and honor its treaty obligations in the Pacific and would encourage regional cooperation by local groupings such as the Association of Southeast Asian Nations, whether for purposes of trade or defense.

"Our relations with the government of Singapore are very good. At the present time, there are no difficult issues that need to be resolved between us. The prime minister was interested in our future intentions in Southeast Asia, and I assured him that we are contemplating no changes in American policy.

"Now, gentlemen, if you have any questions, I'll try to answer them."

Douglas Drake edged forward with his microphone. "Mr. Vice President, is the prime minister concerned about the escalation of the fighting along the Thai-Malaysian border?"

"As you know, these disturbances have been going on for some time. However, as you say, they have escalated in recent months. The prime minister mentioned them in a general sense, but said nothing that would make me believe he lacked confidence in the ability of Malaysia to contain the incursions."

"Sir, we had a report this morning that Russian-built aircraft manned by North Vietnamese pilots are being used in air strikes along that border. In line with your recommendations regarding Israel, would you ask the President to send ground-to-air missiles to Malaysia?" asked Sid Winehart.

"We do not know whether or not the report is correct. Moreover, the Malaysian government has not asked for such assistance, to my knowledge."

"But as a matter of principle, if they did ask, would you recommend we help them?" pressed Winehart.

"I doubt that reopening American involvement in this part of the world would be acceptable to the American people unless there were greater provocation than you mention," said Canfield. He was visibly uneasy about the answer, perceiving that he was being led into dangerous territory.

The raspy voice of Bruce Atherton came out of the background. "Then you would not recommend for Malaysia what you have recommended for Israel—not even conventional weapons of a lesser degree, is that right, sir?"

"Based on what we know at the moment, I would have to say that I would be very careful about involving the United States at this stage of the matter. The American people have indicated very forcefully that they do not wish to involve themselves in land wars in Asia."

"But Israel is different, is that it?" continued Atherton.

Canfield reviewed in his mind the notes that Zack Miller had given him that morning. "Yes. We have a very special relationship with Israel and have been involved with Israel's defense on a more or less continuing basis since the nation was formed. We have never had that kind of relationship with Malaysia."

"Do you think we should have that kind of relationship with Israel—one that involves us in dangerous confrontations?" asked Atherton.

"We have to face the fact that a stand against aggression must be made somewhere. We cannot always withdraw."

"Were we wrong to withdraw in Vietnam?"

"That was a totally different situation. Events proved that the Vietnamese people wanted communism."

"Do you think the Thais and Malaysians want communism?"

"I am not sure what they want, but I know the Israelis don't want it."

"But according to my understanding of American foreign policy, if Malaysia is under all-out attack by a more powerful neighbor, the United States would send defense materiel and equipment to assist her. Is that not the policy?"

"Yes, but Malaysia is not under all-out enemy attack at the moment. The war, if you can call it that, is civil in nature. Besides, to my knowledge, Malaysia has not requested such assistance."

"Sir, would your reluctance to assist Malaysia be at all connected with the fact that Malaysia has an Islamic rather than a Judaic culture and that Jews are politically strong in America?" The questioner was a Malay reporter from the Singapore *News,* and a hush fell over the assembled press people as they realized the implications of the question.

"Absolutely not!" snapped Canfield. "And I must say that I find your question offensive."

Miller steered him away from his interrogators, recognizing that his frame of mind made him vulnerable to goading. There could be very dangerous results and little to be gained by continuing the interview.

The chief of protocol bid them goodbye at the limousine, promising to pick Canfield up for the tour in one hour. As they climbed into the back seat, Ambassador Oldham said, "I wish that wasn't the only question that had been asked by a Singapore newsman. I'm afraid that we're not going to be treated too kindly by the local press, even though I agree with you that the question was impertinent."

"They'll just have to make what they will of it," said Canfield irritably. "I did give them a rundown on the meeting and that should make enough for a story."

Oldham did not respond. Aside from being thoroughly angry at being excluded from the latter part of the meeting with the prime minister, the more he saw of the Vice President, the less he liked him.

They rode back to the hotel in silence. On the way up to the suite Miller whispered to Canfield, "What went wrong back there that upset you so much, Newt?"

Canfield, stony-faced, swung angrily out of the elevator, and Miller hurried along beside him. "Nothing really important, Zack. I just found Ling a little too big-headed for a serious, down-to-earth discussion," he said testily.

Miller could sense that this was not the time to probe. Probably the Vice President had made a minor gaffe and was too embarrassed to talk about it. In time he would give him a laundered version of what happened. He always did.

"I wish we didn't have to take this damned guided tour with the chief of protocol," Canfield said. "Then there's the prime minister's dinner this evening. That'll be deadly."

Zack saw his opportunity to free up the evening for Sirana. "Oh, am I invited to go on the tour?" he said, surprise in his voice. "That's great! It should be interesting. But, Newt, I'd like to beg off as far as the dinner is concerned. An old friend from the university who lives here now has invited me out for the entire evening. I'd really like to accept if it's all right with you."

"No reason you shouldn't enjoy yourself. It's enough that I have to suffer the smug opinions of Ling all evening. Besides, Shelby will be there with enough staff to fill in."

Zack was a little surprised at the vehemence with which the bitter remark about the prime minister was delivered. "Incidentally, what time are we leaving in the morning?" he asked.

Canfield smiled tolerantly. "Not until noon, Zack. You can sleep late after your big night on the town. Call me when you get up. I'll be working on the briefings for Kuala Lumpur."

Perfect, thought Miller. I'll tell him about Uncle Henry shortly before departure.

It was nearly 7:00 P.M. when the chief of protocol finally brought them back to the Marco Polo. They had visited the Jurong Industrial Park, taken a boat ride around the harbor, driven to the Kranji War Memorial so that Canfield could lay a wreath, seen the Botanic Gardens, the crocodile farm, the Mandai orchids and walked through a block of the Thieves' Market on Sengei Road. Canfield's sulkiness had disappeared during a luncheon of delicious Chinese tidbits, and he had seemed truly to enjoy the afternoon, even showing flashes of courtesy to Ambassador Oldham. Miller was delighted because now no Canfield bad mood would interfere with his evening with Sirana Amiri.

The taxi deposited him in front of a restaurant on South Bridge Road in Singapore's Chinatown just before nine. Hastily zigzagging his way through the crowd of shoppers and strollers, he entered and found himself in a cool, softly lit room. The floor was covered with a neutral-shade all-weather carpet, and the rough paneled walls reached up to an acoustic-tiled ceiling. Bright seascapes decorated the walls. An L-shaped bar to the right was filled with well-dressed, mostly young people—an easy, relaxed blending of Chinese, Indian, Malay and Caucasian races. Beyond the latticed boundaries of the bar, diners sat at dark wooden booths and small tables, each table pinpointed by a colorful Chinese lantern. A subdued buzz of multilingual conversation permeated the place.

Miller walked past the bar and approached the attentive *maitre d'hôtel,* who bowed courteously. "I am looking for Mr. Wong. Is he here?"

"I am Wong. You are Dr. Miller?" Hardly pausing to receive the the acknowledgment, he summoned a slender Chinese who led Zack to the rear of the restaurant and up a small curving stairway to the floor above.

Here the decor was more luxurious. A pale blue Chinese carpet covered most of the floor. In the center of the room was an enormous Ming-style rosewood chest, with a beautiful yellow jade Merlion on top. Around the perimeter of the room were a dozen curtained areas which Miller assumed to be the private dining alcoves that Sirana had mentioned. Smaller pieces of Ming rosewood were scattered around, each topped by Chinese porcelain, ivory or jade.

The man led him to one of the private areas and pulled back the curtain to admit him to an alcove of about six by four feet. Except for the soft glow of a lantern on the spotless white tablecloth and the light from an illuminated picture along the outer wall, the alcove was unlit. Zack's heart sank because it was also empty. The Chinese man held his chair. "Please sit down," he said. "The lady will be here very soon. If you will tell me what you would like to drink, I will have the waiter bring it."

Zack sighed with relief. For a moment he'd been afraid she wasn't going to show. When his drink came, he settled back to enjoy the restful surroundings. Only the Chinese could have made so much of so small an area. The pale blue of the rug, which he recognized from his travel literature as a Tai Ping reproduction, had been picked up by the plain carpet outside. Small teakwood end tables, each with a delicately carved Balinese figurine holding an ashtray, were placed alongside the comfortable armchair he now occupied and the empty one across the table.

Zack was relaxed and very satisfied except for a remote twinge of concern about his impending lie to Canfield. However, a few sips of his drink brought that beast totally to heel, and he turned his mind to fantasies about Sirana.

While he was so occupied, there was a discreet knock on the partition outside, and the same slight Chinese man held back the curtain to admit the subject of his reverie.

He found it difficult to believe that his memory had been so inadequate. She looked incredibly lovely, but in a totally different way.

Sirana had gotten ready carefully to show her versatility. The long pageboy of the night before she had pinned into a white-ribboned upsweep, thus accenting the clean, flawless line of her jaw and making her look younger than twenty-six. The slight touch of lip and eye makeup was just enough to bring out the natural beauty of her features.

Small earrings of gold filigree complemented a narrow gold-chain necklace. She wore white calf medium-heel pumps, and her sleeveless dress, just barely above knee length, was of clinging white silk jersey with a green, blue and white belt of the same material.

All of the details were lost on Zack, but the overall effect was what she desired. He was convinced that she was the most attractive woman he had ever seen.

"Do you like it, Zack?"

"I like it more all the time," he said, blowing out the match with which he was lighting her cigarette and without taking his eyes off her.

"I meant Mr. Wong's place, Professor." She laughed, pleased at his frank appreciation.

"Oh, Mr. Wong's place is charming, but it fades to insignificance in your presence," he said theatrically, but somehow failing to conceal his underlying seriousness.

"You are clearly a Casanova, a man to be watched carefully by innocent and impressionable ladies. But on a serious subject, have you been able to avoid the dangerous trip? What was his reaction?"

"I have arranged to skip Malaysia. Sudden illness of a close relative requires me to return home. I haven't told him yet."

"But what if he won't release you?" she asked, her dark eyes becoming grave.

Zack smiled reassuringly. "Don't worry, he will. I didn't want to give him too much time to decide, so I'll tell him tomorrow morning about an hour before departure time. Even more important, if I had told him already I'd be on a plane for New York right now instead of here in exotic Singapore with the most beautiful girl I've ever met. That didn't seem like good planning to me."

She smiled pensively. "I do have to be careful about you, Zack. I've always been able to keep myself detached from individuals I meet in the course of my work. I'm enjoying this assignment too much."

He was about to reach across the table for her hand when the waiter knocked lightly on the partition. They took the menus and the conversation turned to Chinese food and other light subjects.

Zack accepted Sirana's suggestion that she order family style for both of them, and he was not disappointed. Beginning with a delicious shark's fin soup, they were served a sumptuous dinner of Shanghai-style food. There were paper-thin fried puffs of squid and shrimp, a succulent local fish baked and served whole, steamed and fried rice, a tangy lobster dish, steak with fresh pea pods, and roast duckling. Each course seemed more tasty than the last. They took their time, consuming a bottle of excellent white wine and many cups of Chinese tea.

Because of the lightness of the food and the leisurely pace, Zack did not feel sated. Their talk was rambling, full of the nuances and subtle glances that seed a budding love affair. Zack was thoroughly smitten. Sirana was doing her job well and enjoying it.

The waiter had disappeared.

When the last of the tea had been drunk, Sirana suggested a stroll through Chinatown. Zack came around the table to hold her chair.

Her perfume was an exciting, elusive impression, gone in a minute. As she moved toward the curtain, he saw that Sirana had the kind of body that drew glances the way a magnet attracts iron filings. The white pumps and short dress set off her tanned legs to perfection. He wanted to touch her, to restrain her from ending their privacy, but something told him that this wasn't the time and he pulled the curtain aside and followed her down the steps, noting with pride the many heads that turned to look at her.

The streets were teeming with window-shoppers, although most of the stores had closed. Zack and Sirana strolled through Temple, Smith and Banda streets, looking at the attractively displayed handicrafts, carpets, antiques and jewelry. When they were tired of walking, he stopped a cab, and they cruised about town while she pointed out things of interest.

"Look, Zack. They're just closing up a *pasar malam*. It's a sort of roving night-bazaar. They have a different location for each night of the week." Her face was alive with enthusiasm—so different, he thought, from the ennui of the New York girls he dated. "Oh, I wish I had time to really show you Singapore," She looked at him obliquely. "Perhaps you'd rather see a theater show. There's a Las Vegas-type thing at the Tropicana. It's near the Marco Polo Hotel."

He glanced at her curiously. Was this reference to his hotel a signal? Probably not. In any event, he didn't want to get tied up in a big nightclub.

"Let's skip the show," he said. "I'd rather see Singapore with you. You're much prettier than those hothouse flowers they parade around at such places."

Her bright smile showed that the answer pleased her. "Thank you, sir. I'm glad you'd rather move around. Those places give me claustrophobia."

They continued to ride around, to the delight of their driver. They rode along the canal on Bukit Timah Road, inspected the beautiful MacRitchie Reservoir and drove through the wharf areas to Mount Faber, where they parked for a while to watch the lights of the city below. Zack, wishing the driver were a million miles away, moved closer to look out the same window as Sirana and held her hand.

It was past two when they returned downtown. After a brief stop at the Singapore River promontory to look at the statue of Merlion —that fictitious beast, half lion and half fish—they dismissed the driver at Queen Elizabeth Walk.

She took his arm, and they strolled along the pleasant promenade, past the now dark satay stalls. There was a cool sea breeze and harbor lights in the distance. The decrescent moon near the horizon provided only enough light to make them vaguely aware of other couples. Suddenly she stopped and turned toward the sea.

"Isn't it beautiful, Zack? Sometimes I feel more Asian than Iranian. I really love Singapore."

He put his hands on her shoulders. "It has to be a dream, Sirana. International intrigues set in the exotic Far East, a romantic evening with a beautiful girl sent to warn of danger—"

"More like a popular novel," she said dreamily, her head resting against his cheek. "The hero is on an important mission for his country. He is warned by the girl. They are attracted to one another, but duty calls him home, and they never see each other again."

"Not quite. In a novel the hero would continue on into the danger and conquer it, rather than run away."

She looked up at him and put her fingers across his lips. "Only a stupid hero would do that. I wouldn't want to be involved with a stupid hero," she said, smiling.

His arms went around her slim waist, and he felt the soft pressure of her breasts when she leaned against him. "Only a stupid hero would go away and never see the girl again," he said slowly. They lost themselves in one another's eyes for a long moment, then she lifted her lips in an unmistakable invitation. He kissed her gently, and her arms reached around his neck. She pressed the full length of her body against him. Suddenly free of the uncharacteristic school-boylike timidity he had felt with her, Zack now began to respond with passion. He opened his lips and the kiss became an expression of fundamental need. Finally, she broke away.

"Raffles is only a short walk. Let's go to my room," she said matter-of-factly.

He remembered her caution the previous evening. "Is it safe for you there? I mean, weren't you concerned about someone seeing us?"

"It's all right. I checked him out, and that was a false alarm." She took his hand. "Now come on, Professor, before I begin to feel like a seductress and change my mind."

Sunlight crept around the edges of the heavy night curtain, routing the timid grays of dawn. Sirana awakened and frowned at the sudden stab of pain the brightness caused. Her eyes focused on the curly black hairs on the powerful forearm draped across her

271

waist, and she instantly remembered the most exciting, sexually satisfying two hours of her life.

She twisted around to look at her lover, who responded to her movement with a cross between a snort and a grunt, then sighed heavily and cupped her breast. A delicious feeling of belonging swept over Sirana. He had taken her so gently. Used to Assad's urgent rapacity, she had been unprepared for the tenderness of this man, which extended beyond lovemaking. He treated her as a treasure he was not sure he deserved, showing an innocent wonderment at her interest in him. She found it difficult to reconcile his obvious experience with his shyness. There was no way for her to know that this modesty was for her alone. With her, he was the antithesis of the blunt-talking, aggressive Zack who had chased the broads of Washington and Manhattan.

"Zack." She shook him gently. "Zack, darling, it's six-thirty. You'd better be getting back to the Marco Polo."

"Hi, lovely," he said, pulling her against him and kissing her lips and eyes. "I don't want to be anywhere except right here in bed with you. I may never get up."

His hands were busy, as though reading her body Braille, and she felt the sudden rush of reawakened desire. This time, the current flowed faster and before the clock hand had moved twenty minutes, she was carried in crashing waves over the falls and deposited in the tranquil pool of slaked desire.

They talked endearingly until Zack grew nervous about the time and got up to dress quickly. "Call my room at twelve-thirty. He leaves for Malaysia just before noon," he said.

"Yes, I will." The girl giggled. "You look like Bluebeard."

"It's my badge of virility." He grinned at her as she yawned languorously. "And, sleepyhead, don't make any plane reservations until you talk to me." He came to the bed and kissed her lightly.

She sat up and put her arms around his neck. Another quick kiss and he was gone. She fell asleep almost immediately.

Shortly before seven-thirty, Zack stopped at the desk of the Marco Polo to pick up his messages, choosing to ignore the clerk's disapproving glance at his unkempt appearance but glad there were so few people in the lobby. He read the messages as he walked toward the elevators. Alone, inside the ascending cage, he was perplexed. Why had Senator Bedson called him from Washington three times since ten o'clock the night before? But more important, why hadn't he used the White House line that went through the Command Post? It was much quicker, and the Secret Service would have run him down if necessary. He doubted that they could have found him, and it certainly would have screwed up a great night if they had. He looked at the slips more closely. The most recent was stamped six-forty, less than an hour ago. On each was written, "Please have the hotel return call regardless of time." Then he understood. Stanley didn't want him to use the White House line. There must be something sensitive to report—something that shouldn't get back to the President.

Zack got off at the penthouse floor and headed toward the C.P., still reading. The other messages were unimportant—a Singapore journalist, Peter Rosen and a Chinese name that meant nothing to him. He walked past two agents on post in the hall and into the C.P., where Billy Jestes was in charge.

"Mornin', Dr. Miller. You're up early." Jestes peered at him closely. "Or should I say, out late." He winked.

Miller was in no mood for joking. Anyway, Jestes was too ribald for his taste. It was none of the agent's business where he had been.

"I've been out awhile. Anyone looking for me or any phone calls?" he asked, trying to keep his manner pleasant.

"Nothing here that I see." Jestes wafted a dense cloud of cigar smoke toward him, then grinned. "This is quite a town, isn't it, Professor? Any man who leaves here hurtin', it's his own fault."

"I wouldn't know," said Miller coolly, quickly turning away. He nodded at the serious young agent at the end of the hall, let himself into his suite and undressed immediately. Picking up the shirt he had just removed and was about to throw into the laundry bag, his heart sank. There was an obvious smudge of lipstick on the collar. Why hadn't Sirana told him? Oh, well, the hell with Jestes and the clerk. They didn't mean anything to him.

Miller placed the call to Bedson and was pleased to learn that the delay would be only ten minutes. The phone rang in five, catching him in the bathroom. It seemed he was destined to undergo these small tortures.

"Hello—hello." The phone was dead.

He hung up, cursing. Before he had taken two steps, the phone rang again with imperial insistence.

"Your call to Senator Bedson," said the operator.

"Hello, Stanley. Sorry I'm so late getting back to you, but I've been out to a friend's home for the night. What's up?"

The voice on the other end was guarded. "Are you on the white?"

"No, I understood your messages. Go ahead."

"The top guy has been very active here and the progress we'd made is disappearing. There's a lot of wooing going on in the media and on the Hill, do you understand?''

"Yes, yes, I understand."

"Well, tell the Man he's got to hit harder. You know how these people are. They want action, and they want a winner."

Miller frowned. "He can only go so far while he's on this job," he said patiently. "It wouldn't do for him to get jerked home."

Bedson hesitated a moment. "I know that, but this push against us is being done very professionally. They're revving up every isolationist and antiwar activist they can find. You know the theme: The President has kept us out of war and cooled the long confrontation, so don't let an ambitious candidate destroy that."

"Okay, Stan. I'll tell him. Now listen. I'll be home in a couple of days or so—one of my uncles died—and I'll talk to you more about it then, okay?''

"Oh, sorry to hear about that."

"And look, Stan, call Yorie. Tell him our guy wants him to push harder. Let's get our troops moving and get the initiative back again!''

"Right, Zack. Be sure to tell the Man to say something newsworthy. See you when you get back. Goodbye."

Miller hung up and sneezed explosively. If I get a cold, he thought, I'll sue all the telephone companies in the world.

At ten he called the Vice President and asked to see him right away on an urgent matter. He was told to come in at once.

Porter Canfield was still in bathrobe and pajamas when Zack sat down in the living room. Piled on the floor around the Vice President were several briefing and research books. Newspapers and magazines were lying on the sofa and end tables. Dirty coffee cups seemed to be everywhere. It looked like the Vice President had been working for some time. Reading glasses perched midway down his narrow nose, he was perusing his Kuala Lumpur schedule.

"Quite a mess, eh, Zack? I've been preparing for the talks in Malaysia and also for a press conference there." He smiled warmly. "Did you have a good evening with your old faculty friend?''

"Excellent, Newt. Thank you for releasing me. I didn't get in until very late." Miller let his face fall. "And then I got some very bad news this morning," he said dolefully.

"What's the trouble?"

"Death in the family. You've heard me talk about my Uncle Henry from Detroit?" Canfield hadn't, but he nodded just the same. "Well," continued Zack, "he and Aunt Elsie practically raised me until I was twelve. Uncle Henry had a sudden stroke yesterday and died three hours later. I hate to ask you, but there's nobody to help Aunt Elsie with things. He told her nothing of his financial affairs. They have no children. I should catch a plane back immediately. Luckily, his lawyer, Morty Sugarman, is vacationing in Hawaii. I can stop there on the way home and talk to him about matters concerning the estate."

"Zack, I'm sorry. Of course you have to go. I understand perfectly." Canfield was sincerely compassionate, and Miller felt a twinge of guilt. "Now, there's no reason to be concerned about me," continued Canfield. "Everything is in order, and I'm well prepared for the Malaysians. Shelby and Kathy can handle it without any problem."

A wonderful feeling of relief flowed through Zack. The danger of Kuala Lumpur was avoided, and avoided without unpleasantness. Best of all, he was free for several days to continue his affair with Sirana.

During the next half-hour's conference Zack discussed Stanley Bedson's telephone call. The Vice President was a little disappointed, but soon recovered his good humor.

"There's a long way to go, Zack. We can turn that back around when I get home. I know the Congress. If they get enough mail and media pressure, Hurley won't be able to keep them in line. It's always easier to sell change, particularly radical change, than the status quo."

Miller nodded. "I'll do what I can to energize INAF, and I'll talk to Meredith and Bedson, too," he said, watching Canfield's eyes light up at the mention of the secretary of Health, Education, and Welfare.

"Tell Meredith that I've lots of things to discuss with her," Canfield said eagerly. "If I have to stop somewhere on the way in, I may want her to fly out for an early conference."

Zack got up. "Take care of yourself, Mr. Vice President," he said, extending his hand. "Knock 'em dead in Kuala Lumpur."

"Goodbye, Zack. Sympathy to your Aunt Elsie. Let Shelby know if you need money or any help getting home. I'll see you back in the States."

Zack went immediately to his suite. He notified the Secret Service and Bill Shelby that he wouldn't be going on to Kuala Lumpur. At eleven, he walked out to the hall to bid the others goodbye and then flopped on his bed for an hour's sleep. The phone rang, and her voice sent a thrill through him.

"Hello, baby," he said. "How'd you like to go to Hawaii?"

12

SUNDAY NIGHT suppers at the O'Maras were late, light and without guests. From the very beginnings of success, Didi had been sensitive to the danger that affluence might destroy their closeness. So Sunday evening together was instituted as a fortress against the divisive separate interests that money and social involvement bred—although now it had become simply a tradition without meaning. Except for one of the men who remained to handle the door, telephone and any emergency that might arise, the servants had the evening off. Most went to visit relatives in Washington, but Bridget Hennegan, the cook, stayed in her attic room. Mr. O'Mara liked to startle some groups of the *Globe*'s employees with an early walk-through every Monday morning, so Bridget served breakfast at six-thirty in the study while he listened to the morning news.

On the Sunday following Canfield's departure for the Far East, Didi O'Mara sat wondering why Mark was so quiet. Usually, he took complete control of the Sunday night conversation, regaling her with political gossip and anecdotes about his media associates, but this night he seemed preoccupied. He ate mechanically, without even commenting once on the excellent Maryland crab, a favorite dish.

"What kind of response did you get on your front-page editorial calling for greater support for Israel?" Didi asked, trying again to start a conversation and hoping that pride of authorship would arouse his interest.

"Not as good as I expected," he said morosely. "Hurley has

been working hard on the congressional leaders. Old Devers practically lives on the Hill, promising them all sorts of boodle for their districts if they'll stay in line.''

"But your associates in the media—certainly Karen Rankin and Operation Torch—are supporting the effort. And Canfield—''

"Didi, I told you before to forget you ever heard of Operation Torch," he broke in irritably. "If it ever became known that media leaders were cooperating on important issues, there'd be hell to pay. No one would understand that we're doing it for the good of the country.'' He stabbed a tomato slice viciously. "Unfortunately, Operation Torch lacks balls. They're all waiting to assess Hurley's strength before they jump in," he added with a mirthless laugh.

"But Karen is chairperson this year. Certainly you'll agree that she has guts.''

O'Mara looked at her a longer-than-necessary moment. "Yes, she has guts. She may even have balls, and that brings me to another subject I've been wanting to talk to you about," he said acidulously, pushing his cup toward her for a refill.

Didi knew what was coming. "What is it, Mark?" she asked, trying to keep her voice calm and her hand steady as she poured the coffee.

He looked at her intently. "I've tried to hint to you in many ways that your friendship with Karen is beginning to cause comment in Washington," he said carefully. "You know as well as I do that she has a reputation for highly incandescent and transitory involvements with women. To be blunt, she's thought to be a lesbian and does nothing to change her image. She's never married, and she doesn't date *male* men. Oh, she'll show up with a man when it's required, but it's usually some decorator or artist who'd rather squeeze a bicep than a breast.'' His voice grew harsher. "Didi, I want you to taper off your twosomes with Karen. In a group, it's okay—there are plenty of business reasons why we should see her, and she moves in our social circles. But I want you to cut out the private luncheons, the shopping forays and, above all, I don't want her here for an afternoon swim or an overnight visit when I'm out of town.''

"Mark, you're a dirty-minded beast!" Didi's face had turned scarlet, and she half-rose from her chair.

"Sit down. I'm not through," he said, his voice dangerously ugly. "Don't think I'm blind, Didi. Look, we lost the physical magic years ago. I don't care what you do so long as you're discreet. But I won't be cuckolded by a hen." His voice rose to a near shout. "I don't want you to embarrass me again, do you hear?"

"You're embarrassing both of us in front of Bridget," she said savagely. "Your voice is carrying all over the house." She stood up suddenly. "I'm going to my room. I suggest you think over this unreasonable and insulting demand and we'll talk about it again in the morning." Near tears, she stormed out of the room.

O'Mara sat for a while watching his untouched coffee get cold. Then, with a tired sigh, he went into his study and closed the heavy door behind him. He switched on the dim candelabra wall lights and walked heavily, with shoulders uncharacteristically bent, to his desk. He felt hot, distracted and depressed. He turned on the bright desk lamp, stepped down into the unusual well in which the big desk was set and slumped in the high-backed leather chair. He had conceived the idea for the desk arrangement from a console organ, being impressed with how many places the organist could reach from one seat. In addition to being a conversation piece, it was his sanctuary when he needed to think.

Wearily, he pulled a manila folder toward him and dumped out the week's clippings and transcripts of the most influential media voices. He mopped his face with his handkerchief. Either he was coming down with something or the air conditioner wasn't working right. Perhaps he should get that physical he had been putting off for so long—it was not like him to feel so enervated. Forcing himself to concentrate, he began to read the first article—an analysis by a former foreign policy advisor who once had been highly respected but who lost his exalted status after trying to negotiate a durable accord between the Israelis and the Arabs. Now his principal occupation was writing and lecturing on the diabolical and unforeseeable forces that had robbed him of the place in history he so richly deserved.

O'Mara forced his eyes to focus on the print. He was midway through the second paragraph when the cold wire bit into the tender skin of his neck, instantly closing the windpipe and shutting off his unborn scream. Eyes bulging, tongue protruding, hands tearing uselessly at the garrote, he reared back and came halfway to his feet in a reflexive effort to escape. For a few seconds, attacker and victim strained motionlessly against each other, etched against the single powerful lamp's bright light; then O'Mara collapsed, unconscious, as his brain ceased to receive oxygen from the pinched carotid arteries and he began to die. The powerful assailant gave the wire a few extra twists so that the pressure would not ease. Then, releasing the ends, he seized the rapidly expiring publisher under the arms and lowered him quietly into the carpeted desk well. Moving efficiently and without panic, the man took a paper from his jacket pocket and slid it onto the desk, his black gloved hand moving like a giant spider in the harsh circle of light. Then, bending over the inert body, he turned his flashlight on O'Mara's face. The eyes were beginning to go glassy with death stare, and rivulets of blood had dribbled down the neck and stained the fresh white collar.

Now the man moved quickly back to the open window through which he had entered. Ducking below the sill so that he would not be visible to anyone watching from outside, he crawled back behind the closed draperies that had hidden him from O'Mara and gave a short, low whistle. Immediately on receiving a similar response from somewhere in the shrubbery outside, he stood up and climbed out with athletic grace, taking care not to shake loose the glass remaining at the edges of the cut pane. He dropped silently to the soft earth and joined his partner. The two men whispered briefly in their native language. Then, hugging the shrubbery line at the edge of the house, they crawled noiselessly to the corner nearest the large oak tree off the patio. There they waited several minutes, listening carefully for any signs of activity. Hearing nothing, they ran together at a crouch to the shelter of the low-limbed oak, their black clothing and fully masked faces reflecting none of the dim light from the cook's upper window. A minute later they entered the wooded area and moved at a run to the fence. Quickly mounting the strong galvanized mesh, they carefully climbed over the cut upper wires, avoiding the circuit bridge they had connected to prevent triggering the alarm. The withdrawal had taken only four minutes.

A mile farther into the woods they found their stolen panel truck. They changed clothes, then dug a hole and buried their sneakers, along with the masks and gloves. They packed the remainder of their clothing in small airlines bags, then, without lights, eased the truck out on the dirt trail, turned into the main road and drove to Dulles International Airport, where they parked the truck on an outer lot and walked toward the terminal.

They walked leisurely through the terminal building and exited at the taxi stand, where they took a cab to a motel on New York Avenue in Washington. There they separated. The assassin boarded another cab and headed for Baltimore-Washington International Airport.

The airline clerk was courteous and efficient to the pleasant passenger. "Yes, sir. Your flight to New York is on time. Gate Four A, Mr. Halevy."

Capt. Frank Galen, chief of the Montgomery County Homicide Squad, had a reputation in Maryland police circles for thoroughness. In a high-profile case, he liked to do his own interviews, which was why he had arrived at the O'Mara estate early on this Monday morning.

Galen wasted little time with the tearful widow. There was no possibility that a woman of average strength could have committed the crime, and no reason at this point to suspect that Didi O'Mara was an accomplice.

The captain went again to the study. The grotesquely staring corpse was being photographed by one member of his unit while others took measurements, chalked in the outline and dusted for fingerprints. The note was already on its way downtown to be processed by the experts. The crudely cut-out newspaper-headline letters had been scotch-taped to a piece of ordinary notebook paper. The message was clear:

O'MARA CHOKED TO DEATH ON HIS OWN LIES IN SUPPORT OF ZIONIST PERFIDY. OTHER JEW-LOVERS WILL FOLLOW HIM TO HELL.

It was signed:

DEFENDERS OF ARAB MILITANT NATIONALISM DAMN

Along with the note had gone the saliva-stained crumpled paper that had been forced into O'Mara's mouth. It was the front-page *Globe* editorial supporting Israel that had been run the week before under the publisher's name.

Downtown, nobody had heard of DAMN. They were checking it out with the FBI. Galen grunted in disgust. The media would have a picnic with the acronym, and a few nuts would be blown up into an army of terrorists in no time at all.

A detective came in and went to Galen. "Chief just radioed you this." He read from his note pad, "Press called by party who identified self as a member of DAMN and claimed credit for murder. Might as well reveal contents of note. Media know about it."

The captain groaned aloud. "Are those bloodhounds still waiting outside the gate?"

A sardonic smile crossed the face of the detective. "In company force, sir. They're all over the place, like a swarm of locusts. We caught two trying to get over the fence."

"Okay. Tell them I'll brief them in a few minutes. We might as well give them what we can."

He drove out to the gate and answered their morbid questions as completely as good criminal practice allowed. During the interview the ambulance bearing the cadaver came out, heading for the morgue, and the reporters broke for their cars like a pack of hyenas. Galen drove slowly back to the house and resumed his work.

The thing that puzzled Captain Galen was that no one had heard the dogs bark. How did the killer get near enough to kill them without their barking at him? But kill them he did. The stiff bodies of the two magnificent black Dobermans were now on the way to the animal clinic for autopsy. The dogs had looked very peaceful, with no evidence of strychnine rictus or distress prior to their deaths. There was no food on the ground—nothing to indicate they had been poisoned. Were they gassed or struck with darts? He doubted it. No one could have gotten close enough for that without being barked at. Yet the crude murder note indicated an outside job by terrorists. Possibly the murderer or an accomplice was someone the dogs knew? That was one reason Galen took his time questioning Silas Crade, the watchman-handyman who had been, but for Bridget Hennegan, the only servant on the premises the night before. Seated comfortably at the big kitchen table, with a cup of steaming black coffee at his elbow, the white-haired captain eyed Crade.

"You're the watchman at night, except for Wednesday—is that right?" Galen asked.

"That's right. Wensdy's my day off," said Silas, shifting his weight from one side to the other.

"Do you carry a weapon?"

"Yessir, mostly a twelve-gauge double barrel when I go out to check. Inside, I keep a thirty-eight special. Here's my permit for the handgun." He pulled a dirty old wallet out of his coveralls.

"Never mind that now." Galen stared hard at the watchman. "Didn't you go outside at all last night to check around?" he asked, surprised that inspection wasn't made routinely in an area where burglars were feared.

"No, sir," said Silas nervously. His coffee cup trembled slightly in his hand, but that didn't have to mean anything. Silas's face showed that he was not unfamiliar with the bottle. Yet there was no odor of alcohol on him. He looked imploringly at the captain, as though willing him to understand.

"You see, Cap'n, we always turned the dogs loose when it got dark. They was real good watchdogs, sir—they'd bark and carry on to beat hell if anyone came near the proppity. Wasn't no call for me to go out'n check unless they was barkin', and I didn' hear no barkin' last night."

"Where are the dogs kept during the day?"

"Kennel over'n t'other side of the house."

"You mean the side away from where the entry was made?"

"That's right, Cap'n. On t'other side." Delighted to have made a contribution, Silas smiled, showing a beautiful set of Poli-gripped uppers.

"When you let them out last night, what did they do?"

"You mean the dogs?"

Galen smiled kindly. "You didn't let anybody else out last night, did you? Yes, I mean the dogs."

"Well, they didn' do nothin' unusyal. Just lit out for the fence nearest them. See, Cap'n, they're critters of habit. They'd always go to that fence, run clear down to the water an' then work their way 'round the whole place. They'd keep that up all night an' if anything upset 'em, they'd bark up a storm."

"Did you ever have to go out at night and check to see what they were barking at?"

"Oh, yes, sir. T'wasn't unusyal. I went out about a week ago."

"What did you find?"

"They was over on that same side where the murderer got in—y'know, where I found 'em dead s'morn'n—rais'n hell 'bout somethin'. I figgered it was prob'ly 'n animal in the woods. Didn't see nothin' an' they finally quieted down." Silas was beginning to relax a little and enjoy the spotlight. "Did hear a car drive off somewhere in that direction though. Wasn't too close t' our pro-pitty," he added thoughtfully.

Captain Galen thought a moment. "When do you feed the dogs, Silas?"

"Feed 'em once a day, early in the mornin'. Mist' O'Mara, he allus said he wanted 'em t'be good'n hungry at night."

"One more question, Silas, and then you can go on about your duties. You don't seem much affected by the dogs being killed. Taking care of them every day, I'd think you would have grown attached to them."

Silas looked him straight in the eye and said firmly, "They was good watchdogs, but I din't really trust those black devils. Wouldn't go out with 'em at night without my gun. They gave me some funny looks sometimes. Only time they was friendly was when I fed 'em. I saw 'em kill some squirrels once, jus' out of meanness. I won't miss 'em."

"Will you miss Mr. O'Mara?" asked Galen softly.

A hint of wetness welled in the old man's eyes. "Yes, sir. Expect I will, Cap'n. Can I go now?"

"You can go now, Silas," said the captain, closing his notebook.

In an hour Frank Galen had completed his questioning and sat down in the study with his homicide team to receive a report of the information thus far developed.

Entry to the house was accomplished by cutting the glass and unlatching the side study window.

The O'Maras had no internal alarm system. They relied on the fence, the dogs and the watchman for protection.

Footprints in the soft shrubbery bed outside the window indicated that there were at least two persons involved and that they wore cheap sneakers of the type sold in most discount stores.

Galen theorized that one entered while the O'Maras were still at dinner and hid behind the curtains. It appeared that O'Mara went to his study to work and was garroted at his desk by the assailant, who crept up behind him.

There were no fingerprints on the desk except O'Mara's, and none on the windowsill or the fence.

The lab report on the dogs had come in. It indicated death was caused by a potent new derivative of a drug used by veterinarians for animal euthanasia. The Dobermans were poisoned after ingesting meat containing the barbiturate. From the concentrations found in their vital organs, the lab estimated that the dogs became unconscious about two hours after eating the poisoned meat and died an hour later without awakening. That accounted for their placid attitudes in death. It also explained why no meat scraps were found near them. They had had plenty of time to wander before the drug made them sleepy enough to lie down.

From the information already obtained, Galen theorized that the murderers threw the meat over the fence in a secluded area not visible from the house. This probably was done during the late afternoon, before the dogs were released to patrol the property. Then the murderers withdrew. After dark Crade released the hungry dogs, and they began to prowl the property. They found the meat, ate it and in time went to sleep. Their bodies were found a good hundred yards away from the spot the entry was made, which suggested that they were already unconscious when the intruders appeared to do their highly professional job of bridging the electric fence alarm.

A search of the woods produced nothing. There was a dirt road about a mile from the O'Mara property, but it was well used by lovers seeking privacy and dozens of tire marks were found. The police set about the laborious job of checking them out against those of recently recovered stolen vehicles.

Galen reported to the chief of police at headquarters late that evening. "It's a professional job, Chief. Looks like a real toughie. I'm not optimistic unless we get a break from the outside that gives us a lead on that bunch of nuts who call themselves DAMN."

The early afternoon thundershower had moved to the horizon for some final grumbling before yielding to the reemerging sun. Executive Avenue gleamed wetly under the feet of grim-faced workers hurrying from hive to hive.

Josh Devers watched from his window in the principal hive, the West Wing of the White House. He could see the steady pedestrian traffic to and from the Executive Office Building, as well as the vehicles pulling up to discharge passengers every few minutes. Both sides of Executive Avenue were filled with the diagonally parked cars of staffers high enough in the pecking order to hold the coveted special parking permits. Devers had no personal knowledge of what it was like to fight the parking problem in downtown Washington. As counselor to the President, he had enjoyed a chauffeur-driven limousine for nearly seven years.

The old man turned stiffly from the window and eased himself into a comfortable armchair. Propping his feet on a hassock, he contemplated the rather severe portrait of Harry Truman on the opposite wall. What would Harry have done with a Vice President who wouldn't listen to reason? Josh thought he knew; no Vice President could be a tougher case than Douglas MacArthur had been.

But the fact remained that in exactly fifteen minutes, Walter Hurley wanted his recommendation on what to do about Vice President Porter Canfield, who, despite seven thousand miles of insulation, was shorting the presidential machine. Devers stretched his stiff neck and grimaced as the familiar arthritic pain coursed down his back. He cursed therapeutically, partly at the pain and partly at the Vice President. Why couldn't Canfield play his politics conventionally—raise hell in safe domestic areas? Why couldn't he submerge personal ambition and be loyal for the good of the country? He grinned wryly at the Truman picture. If he were honest with himself, the way the man on the wall usually had been, he would admit that he had become a bit lazy in the easygoing Hurley years.

Walter Hurley came to the presidency in 1977, at a time when the country was emotionally exhausted from the paroxysms of the early Seventies. The Hurley team recognized that the American people were tired and discouraged. For ten years they had been deluged with criticism of their leaders, their system and their selfishness. The time had come to end this self-destructive campaign. Devers used sensible elements of the news media to shift the focus to pride in what America had accomplished. Playing heavily on the Bicentennial, they brought about a new era of good feeling.

After the election Josh became political counselor, with Cabinet rank. He was proud that he had had much to do with the success of the Hurley administration. He called himself the Vice President in Charge of Important People, and he was a master at ego massage, which is what politics is all about—provided, of course, one made the right decisions about which egos came first.

Josh knew the priorities: 1. the big media; 2. the academicians; 3. the politicians. Big business and big labor he put at the end of the list—the problems of vested interests could be identified and solved with simple financial equations. But the Big Three—the media, the intellectuals and the pols—ran on emotion. Handling them was an inexact science or, more properly, an art.

Devers lit his pipe, managing to spill tobacco and ashes on his jacket in the process. He blew smoke at President Truman. That damned Canfield had sensed the latent dissatisfaction of the Big Three. Six and a half years of healing was dull, dull, dull. The old villains had been vilified in every way imaginable and the heroes honored by their mutual-admiration societies. Now new protein was needed—red meat to send the blood racing through the veins—shock and danger to stimulate the adrenal glands and vitalize the heart. Well, the thing would be hard to brake now that Canfield had it rolling. All the signs pointed to a buildup. Congress was restless, the academicians were ominously quiet, and the big media were wondering whether P.N.C. could become another J.F.K.

The buzzer jarred Devers out of his reflections and sent him down the gold-carpeted hallway to the Oval Office. He spoke briefly to the Secret Service agent at the door, then walked right in without knocking.

Tall and erect in a neat gray herringbone suit, the President stood beside his desk reading a memorandum. He took off his glasses and came quickly across the room. There were marks of fatigue at the corners of his mouth, but he greeted the counselor warmly and gestured him to one of the two wing chairs before the fireplace.

"Make yourself comfortable in the most photographed chair in the White House, Josh," he said with a smile. "Just about every dignitary I receive sits there. We've got a lot to discuss, so we might as well relax. Care for coffee or tea?"

Eupepsia was not the lot of Josh Devers. He chose tea, which was easier on his stomach in the afternoon. After the navy steward had brought it and departed, Hurley moved with characteristic directness to the subject.

"Canfield's become quite a problem," he said.

"I've been reading and hearing about that," Devers's smile was without humor—a politician's habit. "Also, I've been hearing disturbing talk in the Congress about a joint resolution calling for IRBM's for Israel, and I don't like the looks on the faces of some of your Cabinet members."

"It's worse than you think. I may have to bring Canfield home," said Hurley calmly, carefully watching the counselor's reaction.

Devers raised his eyebrows, but said nothing. Dragging a Vice President home in the course of a foreign trip was radical surgery, not at all typical of Hurley. He wanted to hear more before he commented.

"You read what he said to the Singapore press about the difference between Israel and Malaysia. He ignored my warning delivered through State to stay off Israel."

"Yes, sir; and I also read that Prime Minister Ling said that he should keep in mind that he is the Vice President of the United States, not the Vice President of Israel. Ling rapped his knuckles pretty hard."

Hurley smiled wanly. "Not uncharacteristic of the prime minister. He abhors stupidity." The President's expression left no doubt that he, too, abhorred it. "But," he continued, "instead of shutting up, Canfield threw down the gauntlet in Kuala Lumpur. He told the press there that he disagreed with our policy of refusing Israel, the IRBM's they'd requested. Then, pressed about Malaysia's border problems, he again volunteered the opinion that America's experience in the Far East made it unlikely that we would involve ourselves there again unless there was extreme provocation."

"Yes, I read that, too. At least he recovered his senses in time to refuse to define 'extreme provocation.' "

Hurley's face hardened. "The Vice President deliberately disregarded instructions which have been passed to him several times. How could he misunderstand my news conference or Oldham's warning? He's causing one hell of a lot of trouble, and now this damned terrorist murder of O'Mara has provided an explosive ingredient." He sipped his tea glumly. "Canfield's being used as the centerpiece for a big media campaign against the Arabs that must also involve the Soviets. Look at today's television, wire service stories and big-city newspapers. They know what they're doing is dangerous, but they ignore danger if they can help Israel. They feel that the Vice President is getting stronger every day. I can sense a different attitude among the congressional leaders, too. They were fine right after the luncheon, but they're getting unresponsive and somewhat evasive again.''

"It's true we're losing strength there," the counselor agreed, "and in the sub-Cabinet also. The murder put big pressure on. Gray's another problem. He just doesn't come over as concerned and sincere. The media are killing him day after day.''

Hurley leaned back in his chair and thought a few moments. "Josh," he said slowly and emphatically, "I want you to listen carefully to what I'm going to say now. You've known right along that I don't believe Porter Canfield has the maturity for this job. And you also know I think Roland Gray has—and Marty Edmonds, too, but I prefer Roland's politics. Be that as it may''—here the President paused to look Devers straight in the eye—"there's much more at stake here than an election. This burning ambition of Canfield's, coupled with unexpected incidents of high emotional impact, conceivably can bring us to nuclear war.''

Devers leaned forward. "I understand and appreciate your grave concern, Mr. President,'' he said soothingly. "Do not forget, however, your brilliant successes at détente—the SALT agreements and the unprecedented new Tripartite Pact. Your relations with Dradavov are so excellent, I doubt that this crisis will destroy them.''

"I have to tell you something." The President's voice was unnaturally strained. "Dradavov called me today on the red phone. He was quite pleasant, but his words were ominous. He said that *my* Vice President was a threat to the peace that he and I had worked so hard to achieve. He said that the personal call was because of his high regard for me, but that strong anti-American influences in the Communist party were already threatening his leadership. It was his opinion that increasing United States involvement with Israel would bring about grave dangers of confrontation. He said I must take whatever steps I considered appropriate to ease the tensions.''

"Well, I daresay the Soviets are uncomfortable about it all,'' said Devers, trying not to reveal his concern.

"Josh, I've got to order Canfield back. It's the only way we can quiet him.''

"Mr. President, I strongly urge you to reconsider. If you call him back before he completes the schedule, the press will make it a major confrontation. They will line up behind him, and much of the establishment will defect to him. A lame-duck President has a tough time holding things in the best of times. If you call him back, he is forever alienated and will be a burr in your side from then on.''

''What alternative have I? He's flaunting his independence and making us look ridiculous. Worse, he's endangering the country.''

''I suggest that you yourself telephone him on the scrambler. Tell him you know he means well, but he's endangering the country with his intemperate remarks. Tell him you are relying on him as a member of the team to carry out administration policy. Hint that you may support him at the convention next year if he behaves himself. Say you want to have a long political discussion with him when he gets home.''

''His plane will land in Japan in three hours. The Japanese media are really tough,'' said Hurley.

''Get him on the scrambler while he's airborne,'' suggested Devers. ''It's worth a try. But in any event, don't bring him home. You'll create a monster that will destroy you if you do.''

Nine days after Mark O'Mara's sudden and violent death the police were no closer to solving the case than on the day the body was found. There had been few promising clues. Tire tracks on the road near the house matched the treads of a stolen panel truck found parked at Dulles Airport, but the vehicle had been wiped clean of fingerprints. Questioning of personnel in the terminal building led nowhere. Examinations of the airlines' manifests produced nothing. There were just no leads, mainly because all efforts to learn anything about the terrorist organization DAMN were fruitless. No one had ever heard of it. The FBI had entered the case on the assumption that the truck was the escape vehicle and that it was moved the night of the murder from Maryland to Virginia, but the federal police were having no better luck than Captain Galen and his Montgomery County cops.

Quite naturally the case caused a furor in the news media, for O'Mara had been a respected leader, one of the original ''welders'' who put together Operation Torch, that loose-knit but influential group of media people who secretly cooperated on the big issues so that America ''would not come apart at the seams.'' There were five full days of the most intensive media coverage: eulogies to O'Mara; the chasing down of investigative details; and much footage and words on and by Arab terrorists, and by the outraged and unintimidated giants of the Fourth Estate and the Congress.

President Hurley attended the mass for O'Mara and issued the sternest statement imaginable against ''these terrorist outlaws who weaken the laboriously woven fabric of peace,'' but that was hardly enough to satisfy the hard-liners. The moderate Arab nations denied any connection with or knowledge of DAMN, but that won them no respite from the fire-spitters in the press and government. There was a mounting swell of sympathy for Israel and much pressure for assuring her of American support.

The Soviet propaganda organs ignored the murder, but began issuing warnings against new Israeli aggression. They cautioned the United States that providing nuclear weapons of any sort to the Israelis would jeopardize the SALT and Tripartite agreements. The Chinese kept absolutely quiet, hoping to benefit from a confrontation between America and Russia.

Sensing a receptive audience, the Israelis floated tons of propaganda allegedly documenting plans of an Arab-Soviet attack on them. The plea for IRBM's was intensified, and the American press and public demanded that the Congress and the President of the United States deliver the weapons.

There was no question that the most vocal elements of the American public were demanding that IRBM's be delivered for Israeli defense. It made little difference to them that cooler heads were pointing out that the IRBM was primarily an offensive weapon.

For the first time in recent years Russian warships were patrolling near Israeli waters, and an Israeli report stated that Egyptian troopships had been sighted off the Island of Cyprus.

Now the reflective columns and intellectual articles were beginning to appear, pointing out the threat to international stability if America let itself be frightened into abandoning tiny, dependent Israel. The Zionist lobby and the anticommunists of the right wing, unlikely allies, thundered their outrage in concert, and the timid in the government needed no wet fingers to tell them which way the wind was blowing. Indeed, the deluge of one-sided telegrams and letters proved to the sensitive politicians in the nation's capital that it was no ordinary wind, but a veritable hurricane.

13

In FARSI, and then in English, the smooth male voice announced that they would touch down at Mehrabad Airport in one hour. Iran Air Flight 226, a Boeing 747 bound from London to Tehran, was on time and would land at 12:15 A.M..

The attractive dark-haired girl in the first-class section switched on her reading light to check her watch. She sighed and stretched out a shapely leg. Across the wide aisle, a young British businessman noted its contour with approval, but failed for the fifth time to make eye contact with the lady. Wearily, he turned back to his paperback novel.

Sirana Amiri was tired and irritable. The long flight from London had been preceded by an even longer one from Los Angeles and a two-hour layover at Heathrow Airport. She had had her fill of airplanes for a while. In less than one month, she had flown from Tehran to Singapore to Honolulu to Los Angeles to London to Tehran—completely around the world. Strangely, she felt no exhilaration at returning home; even the prospect of seeing Assad in an hour failed to excite her. It was fatigue, she reasoned. That and the ridiculously late hours at which eastbound flights arrive in Tehran. She would feel much better when Assad met her at the airport.

She pulled the blanket around her and turned off the light. Leaning back against the pillow, she closed her eyes and thought about the unbelievable month she had just lived through.

It had been considerate of Assad to give her the week at Raffles to rest before Zack Miller arrived. She had been fond of Singapore since the time her indulgent father allowed her a vacation in the Far

291

East, and she fully enjoyed refreshing her memories of that exciting and cosmopolitan city. All too soon her week had flown by and it was with some reluctance that she faced her meeting with Zack Miller. The idea of being a toy for a man she did not know and probably would not like was not appealing.

Then she had met him, and something happened. She wasn't sure just what, but the following days became a blur of pure pleasure— two of the most exotic places in the world, romance and the most exquisite physical sensations she had ever known had numbed her conscience. She hoped that she could conceal from Assad that she had given Zack Miller more than her body.

Sirana squirmed in the seat, confused and uncomfortable about her emotions. Surely the memory of Zack would dim now that she was away from those fairylands. But for now that night at Queen Elizabeth Walk, the distant harbor lights, the intensity of their first kiss were much on her mind. Would she ever forget their total possession of each other and the tenderness of their lovemaking? How surprised she had been when he took her to Hawaii, and how surprised she had been when Assad consented to let her go. Hawaii was fabulous. The hot sand on the beach at the Kahala Hilton—his strong body next to hers—the lilting Hawaiian music—the soft fragrant nights. They explored each other well, and she did her job as instructed. It really had not been too difficult to inflame his nascent hatred of the Russians. The repressive Soviet system was alien to his devotion to individual freedom. In bed she had talked of real and imagined atrocities committed by the communists, and she had felt his body stiffen with revulsion. Then he told her of the persecution of Israel, of Russian goading of the Arabs, of the interminable assaults on Jews over the ages; and he worked himself into a frenzy until she pulled his head to her breast and soothed him.

The decision. I must not even think about the decision, she told herself. But she did. She had to. It kept forcing itself into her mind. Zack wanted her to marry him. When she said that it was too fast, that they were cultures apart, he asked her to come and live with him in Washington for six months and then decide. At the Los Angeles airport, he said, "Please come to Washington, darling. I need you." And she promised to phone him her decision within a month. Because she visited with her sister in Los Angeles for ten days, she had less than three weeks in which to make up her mind.

But Assad was waiting, and when she was in his arms again this foolish interlude would dissolve into nothing more than a pleasant memory. In fifteen minutes her dilemma would be over. She closed her eyes, already imagining herself at Mehrabad Airport.

292

The airport had come a long way since part of the roof of the old building collapsed under the weight of a wet snow in the winter of 1975. The Shah ordered the modernization of both Iran Air and the airport so that Tehran now boasted the most up-to-date computerized facility in the world. Moreover, the customs machinery was streamlined, so that foreign travelers were usually on the street with their baggage within a half-hour of arrival.

At last the time had come. Once she was outside, following the porter with her luggage, Sirana looked anxiously about for Assad Izadi. He was nowhere to be seen. She waved away the aggressive cabdrivers who reached for her bags. She stopped the porter and searched for the familiar face in the hurrying crowd, but still no sign of Assad. The strong, hot night wind blew her hair in her face, and fatigue took hold of her again. Suddenly she saw a familiar burly form coming toward her.

"Welcome, Sirana," said Boldar, giving her a bear hug that turned into an inventory of her flanks. "Assad is sorry he could not come to meet you. Important business. Let's get out of this crowd. I'll tell you about it when we can talk."

The girl broke loose, repelled by the big man's wandering hands and the overpowering odor of garlic he exuded. "Business at one o'clock in the morning?" she asked bitterly. "What business that could not be handled by Reza or Anwar?"

Boldar shrugged. "It's another Russian who likes Shokoufeh Now, I think. He's been in town for several days. Assad couldn't get close to him, but Nina Divahdi has taken him over and is making some progress. Assad had to check with Nina tonight." Boldar picked up the bags, and Sirana, inwardly fuming, followed him to a waiting cab.

"Nina Divahdi," said Sirana angrily once they were inside the cab and had taken off, "isn't that the girl who dances at Shokoufeh?"

Before Boldar could answer, the cabdriver, forgetting about the decrepit truck he was tailgating, turned around and said, "You know it, lady." He rolled his eyes expressively and turned back just in time to fling the cab between the slowing truck and an oncoming car with lights off.

"Well, what—" Sirana suddenly stopped. "Please drive more carefully," she admonished the driver, who smiled, oblivious to such reminders.

Saying no more, she retreated into an ominous silence and, despite Boldar's efforts at casual conversation, remained silent until they reached her apartment. Boldar carried her bags inside the door of her apartment and withdrew to the hall.

"Good night, Sirana," he said tentatively, vaguely sensing her fury. "Assad will call you in the late morning."

"Wait." Her tone was nasty, and he unhappily turned back to her. "How does Assad know this woman? She is a trashy entertainer. She has never worked with us."

Boldar wiped his eyes uncomfortably. Little waves of garlic accompanied his reply. "While you were away, Assad met her. He liked her, checked her out and now she is doing the same thing you do." Without any regard for diplomacy, he added, "Assad says she has a natural talent for getting information from men."

"Does she know about the house on Mowlavi Street?"

Boldar did not recognize the significance of the question. "She's been there several times for instruction," he said innocently, quickly jerking back his head as she slammed the door hard in his face. Shrugging his shoulders and muttering to himself, he returned to the cab.

Sirana dejectedly picked up two of the suitcases and carried them into the bedroom. Her quick flash of anger had subsided, leaving only fatigue and an aching lump of loneliness in her throat. She walked slowly back into the living room. Under the cold glare of the single overhead light near the door, the apartment looked bleak— not at all like the cozy home she remembered. She turned on the air conditioner, thankful for the relief from the summer heat, and shot the heavy night-bolt on the door. Wearily, she lugged the remaining bags to the bedroom and began to undress. She felt numb—outside of herself—as though the lump in her throat were the leading edge of a great pain temporarily anesthetized.

She blocked out everything, concentrating on what she was doing—unpacking, preparing for bed. Finally, she got into bed and reached over to switch off the lamp. Her eyes fell on the small silver-framed picture on the night table—Assad and Sirana on a Caspian beach—and suddenly the numbness gave way to a rush of self-pity and hot tears. Throwing herself across the bed, she sobbed out her frustration and anguish until the tensions drained and sleep claimed her tired body.

The sun was beginning to touch the corner of her window when she awakened. For a moment she was confused to find herself lying sideways outside the covers. Then full awareness came, and with it the recollection of Assad's cruel neglect.

Oddly, she had no headache or severe depression from her crying. She felt amazingly good and even a little surprised that Assad's cavalier treatment had devastated her the night before.

After all, she knew how he rejected any possessive moves from her. But her philosophical rationalization of his infidelity left room for wounded pride, if not for grief. At least he could have given up his dancer for one night to meet her at the airport. She felt the beginning of anger. She had carried out the PPL mission successfully, and while she was working, Assad was playing with a Shahre Now trollop.

Sirana pouted for a moment; then, as the incongruity of her reaction struck her, laughed aloud. It really had not been work for her, either. Remembering Zack Miller and all those delicious nights exhilarated her. She had thought she had a very difficult decision to make—Assad or Zack. Now it became clear to her that the decision seemed difficult only because of guilt about hurting Assad.

She got up, closed the draperies to shut out the daylight come too soon, then crawled under the covers and thought it over. In five minutes she fell asleep again with a contented expression on her face.

Under the beating rays of the late morning sun, the house on Mowlavi Street was undergoing its daily transformation from oven to furnace. Thoroughly exhausted, Assad Izadi dragged the phone across the floor to the side of the bed in order to make the call he had been delaying since Boldar's visit routed Nina Divahdi from his side an hour ago.

He should have known better than to trust Boldar with the delicate job of meeting Sirana at the airport. Although it was good for Sirana to know that he was independent and not accountable to her, it was not wise to flaunt his dalliance with another woman—particularly not with a sex symbol like Nina. He smiled with smug self-satisfaction. Nina was a machine—a smooth-muscled, beautifully constructed machine. He had thought that Sirana's appetites were formidable, but they were hardly comparable to this dancer's never-quenched fires. And she was doing an excellent job of getting information from the Russian. He laughed. Thank God for the Russian. If the Russian were not helping to fill Nina's requirements, he doubted that he could be sitting upright on the bed. He lifted the phone off the cradle and dialed her number.

The point, however, was that Sirana had quickly trapped Boldar into an admission that Nina had been coming to the house on Mowlavi Street. And Sirana was angry. Boldar's dramatic description of how narrowly his nose escaped the slammed door left no question of that. The damage was done, and now it was up to him to quiet her down. She was far too valuable an operative to lose.

"Sirana." Into the expression of her name he tried to put delight, enthusiasm and unawareness that he had done anything to deserve her wrath. "How wonderful to have you back. I'm sorry that I couldn't meet you at the airport, but I sent Boldar to get you. I hope he took good care of you."

"Yes, Boldar brought me home." After a pregnant pause, she said, her voice level and controlled, "Assad, you haven't changed a bit. I go all the way around the world for you, and when I come home, you're sitting in Shokoufeh Now so occupied with a cheap dancer that you can't even get to the airport to meet me." Her voice rose. "Well, from now on, Mr. Izadi, just do your own dirty work. I'm sick and tired of being treated like a messenger girl. You've no appreciation for the sacrifices I make for you."

He interrupted quickly as she paused for breath, "Now Sirana, don't be upset. You've got it all wrong. The meeting with Nina was absolutely necessary, and it turned out to develop some very important information for us. I'll explain everything to you when I see you."

"You'll not see me again. You don't care about me." Her voice broke.

"Please, darling. I do care about you, and you're jumping to conclusions. Look. I'll be over there in ten minutes, and I promsie you I'll explain everything."

"I won't let you in." The words were final, but the tone was uncertain.

He put every possible bit of blandishment into his voice: "You can't do this, Sirana. I love you. I must see you to make you understand that what happened last night was not a matter of choice. Now, please, let me come over and see you."

There was a slight pause, and she said in a small voice, "Well, all right, but I don't think it's going to do any good. You've been terribly inconsiderate and didn't even bother to call me after I got home." She continued hesitatingly, "You can come if you promise me you'll leave when I ask you to."

Assad hid his exuberance and said with relief, "Thank you, darling. You won't regret it. I'll be there in ten minutes." He hung up and rolled out of bed, a complacent smile on his face.

First Izadi went to the bazaar, where a check with Ali produced no new information on the Russian currently under surveillance. This was discouraging, because Nina's efforts had been similarly fruitless so far. Izadi was worried that this Russian would turn out to be a wild goose chase. He had given Nina a list of specific questions to ask the Russian when she saw him that afternoon. If they failed to give a lead, he would be hard pressed to know how to tell Reza and Anwar that the investigation had failed, particularly after painting such a rosy picture of Nina's effectiveness.

Hurrying along the dark passageways of the leaky old building, his eye caught a flash of color. In a booth to his right, fresh flowers were exhibited, and their fragrance overcame the more unpleasant bazaar smells in that area. He stopped, bought a dozen yellow tulips for Sirana, went back to the street and hailed a cab.

When she opened the door and gave him a manikin smile, he knew he had his work cut out for him.

"I've brought you some flowers," he said, holding out the tulips with what was intended to be charming uncertainty.

She took the peace offering and thanked him, little crystals of ice adhering to her voice. "Come in and sit down, Assad. I'll be with you just as soon as I put these in some water." Avoiding any hesitation that might have led to an embrace, she went quickly to the kitchen. She filled a vase, arranged the tulips and carried them back to the living room. As she put them down on the coffee table, Assad came to her and put his arms around her.

"I'm very sorry about last night, but we have another Russian on the string, and he's producing some very helpful information. Nina Divahdi has been helping with him. Last night was critical, and I had to be certain that she knew the correct questions to ask. That's why I had to go to Shokoufeh Now just as the moment your plane was arriving. Then I got tied up until late, and I was afraid to call you, knowing how tired you must have been from the long trip."

When he reached for her, she made no effort to escape or to turn her face away when he kissed her. Her lips were cool, and her body was passively resistant. Almost immediately she broke away, saying, "I am no longer as angry as I was last night, but neither am I ready to forgive you. It seems to me that you could have sent Reza or Anwar to give the necessary instructions to your new agent." The last words were delivered with contempt.

"Nina is inexperienced, and instructing her was too sensitive to entrust to someone else," Assad said defensively.

She tossed her head in annoyance, showing for the first time a break in her glacial reserve. "Everything I've heard about Nina Divahdi makes me think that she is fully experienced."

Izadi sat down uncomfortably. Pursuing this line of discussion could only lead to trouble. After a few awkward moments, he said, "Please, Sirana, let's put all that behind us. You're back now, and things are exactly as they were." He lit a cigarette nervously. "I'm very anxious to hear about the learned Professor Miller.'' He smiled beguilingly. ''We are all delighted with your success and the way you have gained his confidence. I hope your assignment did not turn out to be too unpleasant.'' He looked sympathetic. ''It must be very boring to pretend intimacy with these foreigners.'' Without admitting it to himself, Izadi needed to be reassured that she considered him infinitely more attractive than Zack Miller.

''Actually, I found him quite refined and interesting,'' she said. ''He does have a great influence on Vice President Canfield, and he hates the brutality of communism. I was able to stimulate the response we wanted by telling him of outrages perpetrated by the Soviets.''

Izadi tried to conceal his twinge of disappointment, but she detected it as surely as a seismograph detects a faint earth tremor, although she did not betray what satisfaction she derived from hurting him. Women play these games so much better than men, she thought.

''Well, tell me more about Dr. Miller,'' said Izadi with feigned heartiness.

She related in detail Zack Miller's political and international observations, his opinions about Canfield and his general philosophy. Beyond a doubt, she had done a superlative job, and Izadi was well pleased, if also sad that her attitude toward him showed a newfound independence. Well, he would get her over her pique, and she would want him again. He would give her a glimpse into what made Izadi a force in international intelligence despite the paltry resources available to the Persian Protective League.

''You have done a very thorough and professional job, dear Sirana,'' he began, assuming a didactic manner. ''Now let me tell you—in the strictest confidence because only Reza and Anwar know this—about the big picture.''

Her natural curiosity triumphed over her desire for revenge, and she came and sat beside him on the couch. He turned toward her, his eyes burning with fervor. ''Before long, the Zionist sympathizers in the United States will have their ranks swelled by hundreds of thousands of Americans who normally pay little or no attention to international affairs. You may have read while you were away about the murder of Mark O'Mara, the influential Washington newspaper publisher—''

She nodded.

''O'Mara was killed, and an Arab extemist group called DAMN took credit for his murder, stating that he died because he supported Israel in its plea for nuclear weapons.''

298

Again the girl nodded, indicating her familiarity with the celebrated crime.

"This helped our cause immeasurably," continued Izadi. "We want the Soviets and the Americans to tangle so that the Russians will forget about their plan to take over Afghanistan and the Persian Gulf. Destroying détente will save Iran."

She watched his excitement mount, as it always did when he discussed the subject. When he finished, he would want sex; but today there would be none with her.

"And there will be other killings of opinion leaders in the American news media, Sirana. That will bring the superpowers to confrontation over Arab terrorism and the United States' actions in favor of Israel."

"Wait a minute, Assad. All this does help us, I'm sure, but how can you predict that DAMN will strike again and at the same target?"

He regarded her silently, as though her question had broken his train of thought. Then, aiming for the maximum effect, he said simply, "Because we control the assassins. They act at our direction."

"But how?" She truly was confused. "We don't work with Arab extremists. They are affiliated with the Russians. They are not our friends. Why would DAMN do what we want, and why would we want innocent people killed?"

He smiled smugly. "There is no DAMN," he said, enjoying the astonishment on her face. "Selected agents of Yoram Halevy's organization, INAF, killed O'Mara; and Halevy will soon see to the elimination of others in influential positions in the American media."

Her perplexed expression indicated that this shocking new information confused her even more. She remembered Zack Miller's high praise of Halevy's personal integrity and dedication to the Zionist cause.

"That doesn't make sense, Assad. Yoram Halevy's no murderer. We've worked with INAF several times, and violence is not their style. Besides, they would have no motive for attacking people supportive of their own cause. O'Mara was a strong supporter of Israel."

"On its face, it doesn't make sense," he admitted. "That's why it's so beautifully invulnerable." He lit her cigarette and then his own. "Suppose several big-shot owners of powerful American media were approached by wealthy Arab interests and offered ten times the value of their properties to allow the Arabs to dictate their editorial and news policies. Suppose they agreed, and Halevy found out about it. Suppose Halevy believed that the impact of this Arab propaganda from such an unexpected source could turn the United States away from Israel and leave it defenseless against Soviet-backed Arab attack.'' He watched her eyes grow round with wonder. ''Finally, suppose Halevy thought that killing the conspirators and leaving clues pointing to a fictitious Arab terrorist group called DAMN would not only save Israel from the media conspiracy but would release waves of American sympathy that would help get Israel nuclear weapons. Assume that Halevy believed all that, whether true or not. Now do you see the motive?''

Her dark complexion had blanched to a chalky gray. ''But murder,'' she whispered. ''Yoram Halevy is respected by Canfield and by Dr. Miller. He would not stoop to murder. He has a national voice. He could expose the media plot to the country and accomplish the same result.''

''The point is, Sirana, that he did kill,'' Izadi said patiently, ''and will kill again, because he thinks it necessary to save Israel. His advisor has told him that exposing the plot without tangible proof will result only in his being discredited and ridiculed as an unbalanced extremist.''

''Who is this advisor who knows so much?'' she asked belligerently.

''The same person who made up the lie about the media conspiracy in the first place. The same person who is willing to go to any lengths to provoke a confrontation over Israel between the Soviet Union and the United States.'' He let the anticipation build. ''A person whom Yoram Halevy knows well, has worked with successfully in the past and trusts completely. Me. Assad Izadi.''

The girl sat stock-still, seemingly stunned, but her mind was racing, trying to cope with the shock of discovering that this man she had once loved could be the author of such an inhuman and diabolical plot—could cause, with lies and deception, the deaths of innocent people. And Zack—poor Zack—when this came out, he would certainly be regarded as an unwitting accomplice. She must warn him. But now, she must not show her horror or revulsion. This man Assad was crazy. He might kill her if he knew what was in her mind. ''Assad, I'm staggered,'' she said truthfully.

He smiled, taking the remark as high praise.

''But Assad, suppose Halevy is caught and tells the American police of your part in this scheme. The FBI has a working agreement with the Savak. They will prosecute you.'' She let the tears come, but for other reasons, and leaned against his shoulder. He put his arm around her.

"Now, now, darling. No tears. Nothing like that will happen. We are going to take certain precautions."

She looked at him suspiciously. "What precautions?"

"Never mind. Don't bother your pretty head about it. Just relax, knowing that I have neglected nothing in my planning." He saw no reason for her to know that Yoram Halevy and the other INAF leaders would have to go, too, somewhere on down the line. These killings would be laid at the door of the Soviets, since Halevy said he had already complained about Russian threats.

Sirana seemed satisfied. "It's all very frightening, but if you say it's necessary, then I guess it is," she said in a tired voice.

"It is necessary, but it is not your concern," he said gently. "Now, let's forget it and turn our minds to more pleasant things." He pulled her to him and kissed her, his hands automatically beginning to explore her body. But there was not the usual spark. His loins seemed dead, probably not recovered from Nina's prolonged ministrations that morning. Sirana was responding, but slowly. God, if only he knew how to avoid this—he wasn't even sure he could perform!

Suddenly, she pulled away and sat up. "Assad, I'm not ready to leap right into bed with you after what you did last night," she said petulantly. "If you want to talk, that's all right, but no lovemaking, thank you."

He sighed and smiled woefully. "I don't deserve to be punished, but if you insist on it, then I'll have to accept it. What do you want to talk about?"

She laughed at his downcast expression, then asked seriously, "What do you want me to do now?"

"Rest for a week or so." He peered closely at her, then deciding that her mood was improved, ventured, "I know it's asking an awful lot of you, but would you be willing to rejoin Miller in Washington for about another month? We're nearing a critical point, and I would like to know what he's thinking—and, of course, to keep him at fever pitch against the Arabs and the Soviets."

She exploded with indignation. "Assad Izadi," she screamed, "you have colossal nerve. Here I've just returned after a month away, and you want to send me out again before I can catch my breath. I've said it before and will say it again. You are a heartless beast. Now get out of here!"

Muttering soothing words, he allowed himself to be forced out the door. This was familiar ground to him—part of the old pattern. Later she would call and all would be well again.

Behind the closed door, Sirana did not smile, because she was still thoroughly frightened. Yet she was grateful for the way things stood. Within a week she would be on her way to warn Zack. Later in the year, when she returned to Tehran with her new husband, Assad Izadi would be behind bars, where he belonged.

14

AFTER HIS two weeks' visit to Singapore, Malaysia, Japan and Korea, Vice President Canfield made the Fairmont in San Francisco, which ranks among the ten finest hotels in the world, his first stop on his return to the United States.

During the late afternoon of the day he was scheduled to give a speech, he spent the time lounging in his hotel living room. In robe and slippers, he reclined lazily in a comfortable armchair, half-watching a baseball game on television. The Vice President was happy with himself and the world. Sipping a fragrant and deliciously pulpy glass of fresh orange juice, he allowed his thoughts to wander again over the pleasant events of the past week.

The President was beginning to feel the developing vacuum, that was for sure. The power, so long part of Hurley's life that it was taken for granted, was seeping away, and there was nothing to take its place. Canfield savored again the call from the White House that he had received aboard *Air Force Two* just out of Tokyo. He had made Hurley come to him—and come to him with a request, not a demand or a peremptory order. It was beautiful.

"I appreciate your good intentions," the President had said, "but you are inadvertently causing serious diplomatic problems." He did not say a damn thing—just waited for that uncertain voice to get on with it. The President then said, "I would appreciate it, Newt, if you, as a vital member of the team, would not say anything more about weapons for Israel."

Canfield swirled his juice and smiled at the pitcher on the television screen, who was leaning forward in that awkward, ritualistic pose to get the sign. ''Mr. President, I will not open the subject in Japan or Korea,'' he promised, and Hurley expressed his relief. ''But, Mr. President,'' he added, ''I cannot retract my previous statements. They, sir, represent my honest convictions. If I am asked about Israel again, I will simply say that I have already addressed the subject and have nothing more to say at the present time. I believe that will comply with your wishes, sir.''

After a long pause, the tired voice said, ''That will do for the time being, but I want to have Woodhall brief you when you return. There are things that may change your mind.''

That had made Canfield recall his acute embarrassment at having no warning of the Tripartite Pact announcement. It was a little late to talk of briefings. Why hadn't Hurley let him know what was going on? Stifling his anger, he replied, ''All right, sir. It would be helpful to be kept informed of developing events.'' They talked only a few more moments before Hurley ended the conversation. It was a clear victory—a far cry from a chewing-out or an order to abort the mission and return home.

There was a rhubarb with the plate umpire, and Canfield darkened the screen with the remote control switch and gave his complete attention to remembering.

Shelby had been pleased and Rosen gleeful at the news of the White House call. The traveling media had asked every day whether the Vice President had talked to the President since they left Washington. On learning that he had not, they wrote that bad blood continued to exist between Number One and Number Two. Now that Hurley's call made it possible for Rosen to put a stop to that, the press asked the inevitable question—had he been muzzled? But Porter Canfield stood by his past statements on Israel. That had shown them he wasn't running for cover.

From that moment on, they had treated him with new respect. Everything was turned around. The hazing period was over, and the trip changed in their eyes from a useless junket to get Canfield out of the way to a brilliant diplomatic success. Zack Miller had called to congratulate him and say that Meredith wanted him to do a speech for the Western Welfare Union on his way back, and here he was. Giving up a two-day layover in Hawaii was a sacrifice, but the chance to spend some time with Meredith in San Francisco overcame any hesitation on his part. He looked at his watch. In just two hours, Meredith, Senator Bedson and a few staff people would be joining him for a cocktail before he went down to speak. After the dinner, he would invite them back for a nightcap. The possibilities were interesting.

Reminded of Zack Miller, Canfield picked up the phone and asked for him. Almost instantly the WHCA operator had him on the wire.

"Hi, Zack. Where are you?"

"Hello, Mr. Vice President. Good to hear you sounding so cheerful. I'm at my house in Washington. The whole Capitol Hill area is about to wash away in the rain. It's a regular flood."

Canfield laughed. "Too bad. It's beautiful here. Don't go out on a rainy night in that neighborhood. Not unless you want to get your head cracked."

"Don't worry. I bolt myself in at night. You could yell your head off here, and no one would come to investigate. What's new, Newt?"

"Everything's going well. How did you make out with Aunt Elsie? Did you get the estate straightened out?"

"It's all settled, and Elsie's doing pretty well. When are you coming back to Washington?"

"Be back tomorrow. Anything important happening there?"

"I'll be on the Hill a few days beginning tomorrow, so I can get you the latest evaluation. Oh, yes, and Halevy wants to come in to see you. Shall I hold him off until I can be there?"

"Hold him off a couple of weeks. I'm sure he just wants to establish access."

After putting down the receiver, the Vice President poured himself a little more orange juice and again looked approvingly at his picture on the front page of the *Examiner*. The story had been unbelievably good, as had the commentary. He glanced at the big mirror. "You, Porter Canfield, are going to be the next President of these United States," he exulted aloud.

He began to plan. Yoram Halevy wanted to see him as soon as he returned to Washington. Okay, INAF was on his side, and Zack had extracted a few pounds of flesh from the Israelis that Halevy would deliver in due time, but it wouldn't hurt to make him wait for a while. Then an unpleasant thought intruded. When he had called Amy, there was something in her voice that worried him—a new coldness, beyond the lack of interest he had come to expect. Perhaps he was imagining things because he had not talked to her for nearly two weeks, or perhaps he was experiencing guilt because of his increasing preoccupation with Meredith Lord. Whatever the reason, he thought her voice was different. The impersonal matter-of-factness was gone, and there were traces of little-girl hurt. Why did she ask who was with him? That was an atypical question for Amy. He shook his head. He was certainly imagining things. She

305

probably had a headache or had had an argument with one of her friends over a charity luncheon. In any event, he was not going to spook himself out of the chance to pursue his infatuation with Meredith. He had lots of time to worry about how to handle Amy if and when she became a problem.

He wandered into his bedroom. The time change had made him sleepy. Why not a short nap before dressing for the evening? After leaving a call with Trent Gilbert in the C.P., he stretched out and soon fell asleep.

Galdari eased himself out of Kathy Dryden's room and walked nonchalantly around the corner of the hall to the C.P. He was relaxed and happy. What had blossomed that night on the porch in Guam had been nurtured in Singapore, Malaysia, Tokyo and Korea. The SAIC was in love. He was whistling when he walked into the C.P.

"Hi, Trent, Jack. Anything happening?" He picked up the schedule and quickly checked the evening's movements.

"No problems, Steve. We go as scheduled." Gilbert handed him a slip of paper. "Atherton's been trying to get you. He's in six twenty-two."

"Atherton?" Galdari's voice showed his surprise. It wasn't often that the press had direct contact with the Secret Service. There was a natural difference of interest over access to the Vice President, and communication was generally through the press secretary. "Did Pete Rosen leave any explanation of why he wants me?"

"No. Want me to get Pete?" asked Gilbert, reaching for the telephone.

"No, it isn't necessary, Trent." Atherton knew the routine. If he had called directly, there must be a reason for it. Drunk or sober, he never bothered the SAIC with trivial matters.

Galdari went to his room and called the AP reporter. "Sure, Bruce," he said. "I'll be right down."

Atherton's room looked as though it had been hurriedly searched. A week's dirty laundry was piled on the floor under half-open dresser drawers. A crumpled cigarette package and a spilled ashtray littered the bedspread alongside the wrinkled pillow. Half a fifth of gin and a dirty glass decorated the nearby end table. A valise lay carelessly opened on the floor so that one would have to step over it to get to the bathroom.

"Sit down, Steve. Nice of you to come down." Atherton pulled a chair toward the agent and perched himself on the edge of the disheveled bed.

Galdari sat down and watched the reporter swirl the gin in his glass.

Atherton looked at him intently. "I'd offer you a drink, but I know better." He smiled, crinkling his red-lined face, but the bloodshot ice-blue eyes were serious. "You know me pretty well, Steve. I've been around the pols a long time. Maybe I'm cynical, but that's what I've learned. I do try to call 'em like I see 'em." The veteran paused to watch Galdari's reaction.

"Most of the time you're fair, Bruce. Just about all the time, you're fairer than the average," said Galdari, wondering what was on the man's mind.

Atherton took a swig of gin and grimaced. "I've got something to tell you that the Vice President should know." He pointed an ink-stained finger at the agent to emphasize the seriousness of his next words. "I want you to understand, Steve, that I don't particularly like Canfield." He put a twisted cigarette in his mouth and quickly removed it, spitting out a flake of tobacco. "There's something about him I don't quite trust, and I feel he's playing the Israel thing for all it's worth to him—not them. But that's just suspicion for now, and he's entitled to be treated fairly in any case." Atherton lit the cigarette and inhaled a long drag. He continued talking, but very little smoke came out. "Today, a friend of mine here in San Francisco told me something. This guy's got a pipeline out of Andy Jackerson's office. He says that Jackerson's laying for your guy. Josh Devers has fed him a load of juicy stuff about Canfield and Meredith Lord."

"Son of a bitch," said Galdari. It was a quiet statement of fact rather than an expletive.

"When I found out that Ms. Lord was going to be here tonight, I thought you should know that Jackerson's got the Fairmont covered like a tent. You know—he's twenty-bucked a lot of the help. I'd hate to see Canfield set up for a cheap shot. That's why I'm passing this on to you." The reporter drained his glass. "I don't trust Rosen, either," he said emphatically.

"Thanks, Bruce. We owe you one." Galdari got up to go.

"I'd rather Canfield didn't know where you got the information," said Atherton, following him to the door.

"There's no need to tell him how I heard it. But again, thanks. I wish there were more people in your business with your ethics."

"Take it easy," Atherton said, gently closing the door.

● ● ●

While he was getting ready for the evening, Galdari puzzled over Atherton's surprising disclosure and how best to make the Vice President aware that his personal life was under surveillance. The question was whether to go to Bill Shelby or directly to Canfield. He finally decided to bypass the chief of staff due to the very personal nature of the problem. He glanced at his Seiko—six-thirty. Canfield had invited Bedson, Lord and the staff for cocktails at seven. Perhaps he could slip in just before that. He dialed the Vice President's suite, and Canfield himself answered instantaneously. Galdari asked whether he could see him for five minutes alone before his guests arrived, and the Vice President told him to come right then.

Five minutes later, he was informing the Vice President about Jackerson's tip from the White House. "I promised not to disclose my source to you, sir. I know that sounds like our media friends," he added sheepishly, "but I can vouch for the reliability of the informant."

Canfield laughed. He was obviously in a good humor and didn't appear upset at the news. "I'm glad you told me, Steve. We'll have to be careful about a frame." He cleared his throat and continued in a somewhat stilted way, "Uh, the requirements of our offices will bring Secretary Lord and me into frequent close contact during the coming months. I suppose a filthy scavenger like Jackerson could make something of that if he were given the opportunity. Private meetings especially might be grist for the mill, so I guess it would be well to keep those as secret as possible."

"Yes, sir, I think you're absolutely right," said Galdari. He felt a little sorry for Canfield. The office was a glass cage.

"Well, I'm not going to stop functioning just because that dried-up fossil, Devers, is spreading vicious rumors." Canfield pursed his lips thoughtfully. "About tonight, Steve. I may confer with Secretary Lord right here after the dinner. Since some of the hotel help may be on Jackerson's payroll, can you see that none are on the floor?"

"I'll take care of that, Mr. Vice President; and if you'll call the C.P. when the secretary is ready to leave, I'll see that she gets back to her room without being observed."

The Vice President showed just a trace of embarrassment. "We won't be getting through with the dinner until after ten, Steve, so it will be kind of late. I don't want to make a big production of it."

"No need for anyone else to know. I'm in the C.P. from eleven to seven. If you'll ring me when Dr. Lord is ready to leave, I'll escort her back to her suite, and I'll make sure that no curious eyes are about.''

Canfield looked relieved. "That's fine. The whole thing's ridiculous, of course, but people like Jackerson can make a lot of trouble out of nothing.''

After Galdari's visit, Canfield felt a little uneasy about his half-formed plans to finish his conference with Meredith in the bedroom that very night—or to be more accurate, early the next morning. The whole idea of someone trying to prove he was doing something he hadn't been doing but wanted to do made him angry. But he would have to be careful. Devers would go to any lengths, apparently, to derail his presidential train. He shook his head in disbelief. Paying hotel employees for information practically assured that they would try very hard to come up with something—even out of the flimsiest circumstantial evidence. Yes, he would have to be very careful, or some maid would be finding makeup on the pillow or discovering a hairpin left by a previous occupant.

He was spared further fretting by the arrival of his guests—Senator Bedson, Secretary Lord, Shelby, Kathy Dryden and Peter Rosen. Meredith shocked him by being even more beautiful than he remembered, but his anxiety caused him to scrap a kiss on the cheek for a warm handshake.

Shelby and Rosen mixed the drinks while the other guests found chairs and settled down. Stanley Bedson was wound up. Wildly enthusiastic about the developing campaign and the progress he had noted in the Congress, he talked a blue streak and fired off numerous questions about Canfield's trip.

With less than ten minutes remaining before they would have to go downstairs to the WWU dinner, Canfield decided he would have to cap the Bedson gusher. "Hold it, hold it, Stan,'' he said, holding up his hands in mock surrender, "we'll have days to devote to the campaign when we get back to Washington. This is a moment to relax, so enjoy your drink. You haven't even taken time to touch it yet, you know.''

Bedson smiled good-naturedly and held up his full glass. "Okay, I get the message, Mr. Vice President. I'll never be an alcoholic so long as I'm a wordoholic.''

Meredith Lord instinctively moved to take the edge off Canfield's rather abrupt interruption. "You'll probably have to quiet me, too, sir. We're all tremendously up about what's been happening. But, bearing in mind your warning, I'll restrict my business to one question. Mrs. Archibald Brown, who is president of Western Welfare, was a bit upset about your not attending the reception tonight. I took the liberty of asking her and the three other top officers to come by my suite for a little while after the dinner." Meredith used her most persuasive smile. "Could you stop by for a few moments? It would do a world of good to keep things totally friendly."

Canfield reacted quickly. He didn't like the idea of getting stranded in Meredith's suite with people who wouldn't know when to leave. Then, also, how would he get her upstairs to his rooms at such a late hour? "I have an idea you may like even better, Meredith. How about having them here? Then Bill and Pete can move them out after a reasonable time. Pete can ask them to his room to discuss some ideas he has about the news release from the dinner." He glanced at Kathy Dryden, wondering what she would think about what he was going to say next. "And, Meredith"—he risked it anyhow; damn Andy Jackerson—"I would really appreciate it if you would stay on awhile after they leave to bring me up to date on Charlie Voren and the THC budget problem. I know he'll be on me with both feet the minute I get back."

"Of course. I'll be glad to," Meredith said.

He got up, looking around at the others. Was it an accident that no eyes met his eyes, or was he being hypersensitive in imagining the moment was awkward? "It's about time for you all to go down," he said. "I'll be coming along in just a few minutes."

The dinner was well attended. Thanks to a subsidy from the union's treasury and generosity on the part of the Fairmont, five hundred people heard a Vice President and ate breast of chicken for a modest $7.50. There were no big givers, no Herman Poparchs to annoy the guest of honor; and the two-tiered head table kept him well insulated from the guests. Unfortunately, there was nothing he could do to protect his ear from Mrs. Archibald Brown, who served him, unbidden, her baffling assortment of ideas on welfare reform. Mrs. Brown was certain the federal welfare budget should be increased threefold immediately and that all demeaning work requirements should be eliminated. Her most provocative idea was to have HEW operate, at government expense, certain "in-services," as she called them, for welfare mothers. She thought mothers of several children were far too busy to shop for the necessities of life. With its immense resources, HEW could have food delivered to the welfare household each week, thus sparing the busy mother the chore of shopping and giving her more time with her children to help them overcome the trauma of being poor. And,

Mrs. Brown added, eyes sparkling with zeal, nutritious meals would result. Wasn't it well known that malnutrition caused the welfare cycle? If such a distribution plan proved too costly, the deliveries could be cut down to once a month after providing families with freezers—a simple one-time expense for HEW.

Canfield told her that her ideas were remarkably innovative and asked her how many children she had. It turned out that she had ten—but not more than two by the same father. Oh yes, she was married, but had not heard from her husband for seventeen years. How were the children doing? Not too well, unfortunately. The oldest boy, eighteen, had died in a motorcycle accident last year. The sixteen-year-old girl had found a job, but then had runaway with a traveling salesman. The remaining eight were still with her. Only the nine-year-old girl was still in school. The older boys were here and there—you know how boys are. The twelve-year-old girl had to watch the little ones when she was away on union business. Her job took her away from home so often, you know. It hadn't been easy, according to Mrs. Brown, to raise all those children on the little bit that the welfare provided and still work herself up to this position of responsibility in the union.

Canfield assured her that she was another Eleanor Roosevelt and that he was fully sympathetic to the legitimate goals of that greatly misunderstood group, the welfare recipients.

It was ten-thirty when the parade of limelighters finally yielded the microphone to the Vice President. Fully conscious of the red eye of the TV camera upon him, he stuck to the mealy-mouthed script, intoning platitudes in the approved liberal canon.

A light-year later, it seemed to him, he was alone in his living room with Meredith Lord, and the clock read 12:30 A.M. He mixed himself a strong V.O. and water and poured her a brandy.

"Mrs. Brown is a lunatic," he said matter-of-factly, handing Meredith her brandy and sitting beside her on the sofa.

She chuckled. "No more than that fellow in Phoenix you told me about," she said, snuggling up close.

"You mean Herman Poparch?" Canfield put his arm around her. "No. Poparch isn't crazy. A little self-centered, maybe. On the other hand, Mrs. Brown is completely bananas."

"Have it your way, Newt. They both bore me. Let's talk about Charlie Voren."

"All three bore me." He found her lips warm and inviting. Finally, he pulled his head back a few inches and looked directly at her. "I missed you very much."

"And I missed you. I was worried about you. You're so controversial and there is so much political violence these days. Promise me you'll be careful in this campaign."

He gently held her face and kissed her again, this time without passion. "Dear Meredith," he said, his voice husky with emotion. "You *are* concerned." Then he said perplexedly, "Why did we waste those years after Minneapolis? I'd forgotten what it feels like to be worried about." With great tenderness, he drew her to him. "Of course I'll be careful, but that really doesn't mean anything. Neither does the best professional protection assure safety. If an assassin wants to get you, and he's willing to give up his life to do so, there's no way you can be protected. Risk is part of politics, Meredith." In the flow, he couldn't help hamming it up. "Risk is part of leadership. People at the top of the mountain against the skyline make good targets." Seeing the fear in her eyes, he held her tightly. "I know what's on your mind. You're thinking about the O'Mara murder—that the same people would like to see me dead."

"They would, you know. Arab extremists have good reason to hate you with all this publicity about your stand for arming Israel."

"If you'll think about it carefully, Meredith, you'll see that I'm of more value to them alive. I'm their greatest rallying force." He picked up the brandy glass and handed it to her. "Now, let's talk about something less scary but even more dangerous at the moment."

He told her about Galdari's warning—about Devers and Jackerson. "You can understand, Meredith, why this infuriates me," he said with a forced laugh as he went to the bar to freshen his drink. "It's a good reason for us to walk away from each other—like we did before—because love can be too damned much trouble."

"I didn't walk away, Newt." Her voice was flat, not accusatory.

"No, you didn't, to be fair. I walked away. I was infatuated with the vice-presidency, and you were a complication. I saw a sign on you that said, 'Warning. Loving may be injurious to your political health,' and I gave you up for ambition." He walked back slowly, gravely looking down at her. "I was wrong, Meredith, and I won't let Devers or Jackerson frighten me away from happiness now. That is, if you still feel as deeply as I think you do."

She laughed. "We're talking like two teen-agers having their first crush, Newt. We haven't even made love. Suppose we're awful in bed together?" She took an unladylike gulp of brandy.

Canfield jiggled the ice cubes in his drink and smiled at her frankness. "We won't be," he said positively. "I'll prove it to you." And without another word, he kissed her. Then he picked her up in his arms and carried her into the bedroom.

Much later, close to 4:00 A.M., Galdari picked up the C.P.

intercom and said, "Yes, sir. I'll be right there." In fifteen minutes he was back in the C.P., pouring himself a black coffee. Why was it, he mused, that two people who had just made love couldn't conceal it, no matter how hard they tried?

Back in Washington, Karen Rankin, attractive in a pearl-gray western-style slack suit, entered the Sans Souci, meeting place of Washington celebrities and their trackers. On the way to her table, she stopped briefly to greet the famous—a political satirist, the secretary of labor, two senators and a visiting milkmaid from Hollywood.

"You are twenty minutes late, bitch goddess," Bradley Barton whispered when she reached the corner table. His smile was broad for the benefit of the swivel-heads. "Don't you think anyone's time but yours is important?"

Karen smiled sweetly, her eyes wide with feigned surprise. "Why, Brad, you know how the phone can tie you up at the last minute. I was talking to Secretary Meredith Lord in California about our show," she dissembled. "I'm a little tired of doing all the work for the show, Bradley, so don't give me the 'outraged man' routine. What's the matter, am I cutting into your matinee time with one of your young groupies?"

Barton said nothing while the waiter put down a very dry martini for Barton and a glass of the Spanish sherry for Rankin. Barton sighed and touched his dyed brown hair to make sure the woven-in rug on his crown was in place. He should know better than to lose his temper; it didn't do any good. But she was so damned irritating. He came at her again, this time from ambush.

"How is Didi bearing up under the strain?"

"Didi's still hurting a lot. They were together a long time. What's bugging her is that they had some sort of tiff the night he was killed, and she walked out on him. She never saw him alive again. Poor Didi, she's full of guilt about that."

He knew he shouldn't say it but say it he did. "Well, you've done everything possible to, uh—distract her—staying with her every night. Maybe she'll get over it."

Karen's eyes showed the wound. "Look, you ancient lecher," she said with quiet savagery, "let's get off this subject. If it weren't for business, I'd never give you the time of day. Now, let's talk about the big picture. We're here because we're both welders of Operation Torch, and Mark's murder threatens the country. What do you have to report from the television and radio people you've talked to?"

Bradley Barton was an expert at maintaining outward composure. Covering the news was excellent training; there the most that one could do was lift an eyebrow now and then. But to be called an ancient lecher was sorely trying and to pass it off required his best effort. He glanced at the young actress two tables away, caught her eye and smiled. Lecher, yes—but not ancient. Vintage maybe, but certainly not ancient.

Directing a superior and tolerant look at Karen, he answered, "I've seen all the network people in our group—both television and radio. The opinion is unanimous. The situation comes under the general guidelines we set up for Torch. They agree with us that there is no single target to be scorched. Hurley, of course, but he alone is not enough. The congressional leaders and the Cabinet must also be pressured. Sending the missiles is only a beginning. Above all, Canfield must be encouraged. He is the most useful instrument for putting backbone in our foreign policy."

"What do they see as our purpose, our objective?"

"To confront Arab terrorism, first. If we let these bandits dictate our foreign policy, we will lose the entire world's respect. But more important, to let the Soviet Union know that we will not permit Israel to fall. No one I have talked to believes that supporting Israel to the hilt will destroy the SALT agreements or seriously damage détente."

"Of course not," said Rankin emphatically. "Facing them down in the Cuban missile crisis actually helped bring about détente. The Russians admire strength. They'll push you as far as they can when they detect weakness—" She stopped, suddenly aware that Andy Jackerson was standing beside her.

He had come to their table to inform them that his morning column would contain an interesting item about Meredith Lord rushing to San Francisco for the convention of the Western Welfare Union, an obscure organization with less than a thousand members. "Who was the principal speaker at the WWU?" the gossip columnist asked, savoring the rhetorical question, then telling them that it was no one but Vice President Porter Canfield. Jackerson leaned toward them conspiratorially. "And I'm working on other leads," he said. "This isn't the first time they've found excuses to be together."

Rankin and Barton pretended to be impressed. Like most media people, they secretly held Jackerson in contempt, but their private lives were not sufficiently innocent to withstand his muckraking. It was the better part of valor to be friendly to Andy Jackerson.

"What an abominable man," said Barton, after Jackerson had

314

left. "Imagine having to live with a job where you must make some poor devil unhappy every day."

Karen nodded vaguely but said nothing. Two years before, Jackerson had put a couple of his snoops on her, but fortunately her friends with certain big-city newspapers intervened and Jackerson abandoned the project. Wide syndication was his bread and butter.

"Perhaps we'd better let some of the people close to Jackerson try to turn him off that target," added Barton. "If Canfield's the vehicle for Torch, we don't want him slaughtered in the Bible Belt."

"Andy's stubborn. It could backfire if it's not done with finesse. Perhaps you'd better handle it personally," said Karen slyly, blowing smoke and watching the ice melt magically.

Barton put on his modest face. "I'll do what I can, Karen," he said.

By the time they finished eating the excellent lunch, the tension between them had completely eased. They agreed on the tactical approaches to the problem as well as broad strategy. Over a second cup of coffee, Karen had a new idea.

"Let's give some attention to the Zionist organizations," she said. "For too long we've soft-pedaled them, put them on the back burner publicity-wise. The result has been that groups like INAF, the infantrymen for Israel propaganda here, are regarded by the general public as being a little kooky. Yoram Halevy, who leads INAF, is very attractive to young people. I think I'll have *Twiceweek* do a spread on INAF next week."

"Good idea. Maybe I'll have Doug Drake interview him. If he's really good, I'll see if we can't get him on 'Meet the Nation' later."

Barton looked at his watch apologetically. "I have to run along. Nothing personal, however, Karen. This isn't my month for sex," he added jocularly.

She laughed. "No hard feelings, Brad," she said. "We both got our digs in and that's over. Now there's work to do."

15

THE EXTRAORDINARY amount of attention that the Vice President had attracted in the course of his Far Eastern trip yielded very concrete results. A new just-released poll showed a dramatic increase in his popularity. People were beginning to think seriously about Porter Canfield as a presidential candidate, with the result that Vincent Jendar could foresee a time when the members of the Hurley Cabinet would have to choose between the President and the Vice President.

Except for Ramon Fernandez, Martin Muldrow and Vince Jendar, the males in the Hurley Cabinet lacked drive. In fairness, one had to admit that the President's cautious approach to government did not encourage bold departures from well-worn bureaucratic grooves. Another deterrent to strength in the Cabinet was the immense power of the sub-Cabinet career people, derived from the early Seventies when they discovered their ultimate weapon, the amoral leak.

Although government departments had always had media informants, the amoral leak was something new. In this type of leak, the leaker took upon himself the divine task of assigning moral standards, in this way becoming amoral—not to be judged by external criteria of morality. The conventional leaker had been inhibited by reluctance to commit a traitorous act or to destroy a reputation with lies, but the amoral leaker, taking a leaf from revolutionaries, rewrote the commandments to suit his own needs. He characterized as immoral whatever he attacked—immoral war, immoral wealth, immoral discrimination, immoral waste of natural resources—and ignored the immorality of subverting the orderly processes of an elected government. He became a celebrated hero, a leader of the underground, and was worshiped by the media for the constant turmoil he provided. Naturally he eroded the authority above him, and his presence in increasing numbers was no small cause for timidity in high places.

The third reason the Cabinet lacked fire—and it hurt Josh Devers to admit it—was that most of its members were past their energetic years. They came from earned or inherited successes in various areas of the private sector, and they were basically status quo people—content to accept the honor, talk loftily and pursue their pleasant established lives.

Amon Meadows, the secretary of agriculture, had been a successful wheat farmer and was a longtime spokesman for farm interests. He and the secretary of the treasury, Craig Elbrook, a retired Texas financier, were the only original Hurley appointees—every other post had turned over at least once. They were still there because they satisfied their constituencies. They shunned change, walked away from controversy and double-talked with ease. Although they were not especially popular, they were not so unpopular as to have become Washington targets.

Edward West, the secretary of the interior, and Elias Pangborn, the secretary of commerce, would have hated each other except that it was too much trouble. West, a fragile septuagenarian, was propped up in office by the conservationist lobby, which utterly owned him. Pangborn was an irascible man who had terrorized the board room as chairman of one of the nation's largest corporations. He had been secretary of commerce only a year, and the gamblers gave him two more months at the most. Frustrated by the unintimidated civil servants under him and unable to solve the riddle of how to deal with them, he sat around and glowered.

John Abbott, disdained by the Joint Chiefs of Staff of the Armed Services, was an unusually vapid secretary of defense except where China was concerned. He came from a diplomatic assignment in the Far East and believed that the future well-being of the United States lay in advancing Sino-American cooperation. The new Tripartite agreement pleased him greatly because he had been afraid that the Russians would swallow the Chinese before they reached nuclear maturity.

Secretary of State Gordon Woodhall had attached himself gradually to the federal government through long service with esoteric foreign policy journals. He was an insider at State, but the career people considered him over his head in the secretary's job. He

318

usually did what Hurley wanted him to do, but his loyalty had undergone no severe strains.

Ninety percent of the Cabinet's vitality resided in the secretaries of HEW, HUD and Labor, and a young, dynamic attorney general. Fernandez of HUD was a second-generation American of Mexican descent. He was bright and aggressive, and the versatile executive team at HUD was one of the Hurley administration's strong assets.

Muldrow, the shrewd, blunt, legally trained man at Labor, had been an international vice president of the Maritime Union. He had a no-nonsense approach to government, but had been less than evenhanded in clashes between big business and big labor. He considered Pangborn a relic from the prehistoric ages.

The most surprisingly effective and powerful member of the Hurley Cabinet by far was Jendar, the thirty-seven-year-old attorney general. A frequent victim of migraine headaches, Jendar lost a full day's work nearly every week. Yet such was his dedication and brilliance that the justice department functioned admirably under his leadership. A trial lawyer by profession, Jendar had been disturbed for a long time about abuses in the criminal justice division. Politically ambitious prosecutors were perverting the immunity statutes and using the news media to undermine the traditional protections of the grand jury system. At the time that Jendar took office, the liberal community was clamoring for the abolition of grand juries. Using great skill and devastating logic, Jendar pioneered amendments to the immunity statutes and cleaned house in the U.S. attorney's offices. Twelve federal prosecutors were dismissed for abuses of their powers, and the seemingly interminable wave of political investigations finally came to a long-awaited end. It was expected that Jendar would return to Illinois to become a candidate for the Senate in 1984. Experienced political observers were sure that he had a promising future.

But as he stepped up to the eighteenth tee at Burning Tree Club, Jendar was thinking only of the five-dollar Nassau that he and Ramon Fernandez had going against John Abbott and Marty Muldrow.

Muldrow, whose team was closed out in the back nine and one down on the eighteenth, counseled his opponent, "Water out there, Vince. Better use an old one." He was a fierce competitor and not above gamesmanship. As Jendar waggled, he stopped him. "Wait a minute, we're three down on the back side. We press you, right, John?"

Abbott nodded assent, and Jendar smoothly stroked the ball 230 yards down the fairway. Fernandez followed with a slice into the right rough, and then Abbott addressed his ball.

"Hit it a good one, John," encouraged Marty. With a peculiar, hitched swing that looked impossible, Abbott hit the ball in the fairway just behind Jendar. Then the powerfully built Muldrow, trying for extra distance, pushed his drive into the right rough about thirty yards in front of Fernandez.

All second shots were good, but no one made the green, which was not unusual at the difficult eighteenth. Ramon, who was away, shanked his five iron into the right trap. Having previously hit fat from a bad lie in the rough, Muldrow was strong with his eight to the back fringe of the green, and then Abbott, stepped up and knocked his ball five feet from the cup.

"Ho, boy," chortled the secretary of labor. "Looks like old Vince is under real pressure. Better get it up close, Vince."

Jendar gripped his seven iron expertly. Once he had been pretty good, a ten handicap, but he played very seldom these days. The shot was a thirty-five-yard chip, and he had a lot of green to work with. A short, smooth punch and the ball struck the edge of the green and rolled toward the cup. Up the hill, losing speed, it broke sharply left and dropped in for a birdie.

"With your luck, Vince, you should run for President," said Muldrow disappointedly. "Neither Gray nor Edmonds nor Canfield would stand a chance."

"Don't fret, Marty. I'll buy you a drink while you and John pay us. Let's see, back side, eighteen, and press, minus front side— that's ten bucks each," said Vince laughing.

Sitting comfortably over drinks at the club bar and card room, with its caricatures of the famous on the walls, Vince waited until the end of the golf talk and then said, "You spoke of luck and Presidents out there, Marty. How do you see things developing?"

"Unless they take your seven iron away from you, you gotta win it easy," said Muldrow. "But, seriously, I feel a change is in the making. Four months ago I would have said it'll be who the old man picks, probably Gray. But today, Canfield looks lots stronger than he did. I'd say he's got a good chance."

"What do you think, John?" asked Jendar, turning to Abbott. "You're the most experienced in national elections."

"The Vice President has made progress," said Abbott thoughtfully, "but he is advocating a dangerous policy. In my opinion, the President will still be able to pick his successor, either Gray or Edmonds. However, any more violence that is politically motivated, like the O'Mara killing, could strengthen Canfield."

"Ramon?"

"These are funny times, Vince," said the HUD secretary. "We've had a long healing period, and the animals are hungry. Canfield is the hunter and their best prospect for putting meat on the table. The Israeli lobby is potent. I'd have to make the Vice President the favorite, based on the media swing to him lately."

The attorney general toyed with his Scotch. "I've been sampling Cabinet opinion on this," he said slowly, "and you'd be surprised how many take Porter Canfield very seriously—Pangborn, for example."

Muldrow snorted contemptuously, but said nothing.

"And Meadows at agriculture—you'd hardly think he would see it any way but Hurley's. Of course, Elbrook and West are about as unaware politically as any two high appointees I've ever seen. They have no opinion. Meredith Lord is solid Canfield, and Woodhall will go with the probable winner."

"Meredith Lord's an asset," said Fernandez.

"Meredith Lord's got assets," said Marty Muldrow with a frank leer. "I'll negotiate a long-term agreement with fringe benefits with her any time."

Vince laughed. "Marty, I'd advise you to stay out of Porter Newton's potato patch. You wouldn't want to wind up in Andy Jackerson's column cast as the victim of unrequited love, would you?"

"Deliver me from that jackal," said Muldrow. "I'd rather be a eunuch than take that chance." He looked at Vince penetratingly. "But how about you, Mr. Gallup. What's your feeling about the situation as it now stands?"

Abbott and Fernandez looked at Jendar with interest. It wasn't like him to go around polling Cabinet officers; there had to be something on his mind.

"Marty, I have a feeling that we in the Cabinet are going to be put in a position of having to choose up sides."

John Abbott disagreed. "Oh, I doubt that, Vince. I've been around the national scene for a long time—mostly in appointive positions—and I've never been pushed into a corner that easily by presidential aspirants. Besides, the Cabinet of a lame-duck President is the least vulnerable. We can always say we serve President Hurley and our offices. In that way, we'll be above the fray."

"I respect your opinion, John, and it would normally apply," said Jendar earnestly, "but here we have a Vice President bolting ship and drawing the President directly into battle. More is involved than Hurley saving face. Canfield has the Russians angry, and Hurley's entire foreign strategy is jeopardized." He munched a peanut thoughtfully. "My guess is that there will be a confrontation; that Canfield will not retreat; and that we will be asked to line up behind the President."

"I don't see how the confrontation would come about. Hurley is not the type to challenge the Vice President in a Cabinet meeting," said Fernandez.

"Hell, yes, Vince. The President has never said a really harsh word to anyone in a Cabinet meeting," added Muldrow, "and God knows I've provoked him a number of times."

Jendar shook his head, slightly impatient that they had not grasped the point. "I don't mean that it would happen in a Cabinet meeting," he said. "It's more likely that we will be asked to take sides in a less direct way—by the way we respond to press inquiries, for example, or by inserting signals in our speeches. Believe me, gentlemen, I'm giving it a lot of thought these days. Canfield is not to be taken lightly."

At that moment a retired senator came over to speak to them, and the conversation turned back to golf. Within ten minutes, four black limousines quietly left the famous club. They carried four very thoughtful Cabinet officers.

The passions aroused by the O'Mara murder and the concerted efforts by Operation Torch soon caused the Israel issue to become a boiling pot. In the week that followed the Vice President's return, the pot boiled over.

With singular speed and uncharacteristic efficiency, Congress rushed through a joint resolution urging President Hurley to send Israel the necessary weapons to protect her sovereignty, including but not limited to intermediate range ballistic missiles, so that the balance of power could be maintained in the Middle East.

Armed with the joint resolution, the media and the intellectual community stimulated a formidable series of provocative demonstrations and a flood of mail and phone calls to the White House. President Hurley was placed under more severe and unremitting pressure than any White House occupant since the Watergate days.

After three days of turmoil, the President capitulated, announcing that he was taking appropriate action to maintain the balance of power in the Middle East. He dispatched to Haifa, without announcement of further definition, two ships carrying technicians and launch-site hardware for IRBM's. Within three hours of sailing time, one of the networks which had special contacts among Pentagon malcontents broke the story that United States technicians,

322

hardware and intermediate-range warheads were on the way to Israel. The story made page one around the world. When the White House refused to comment, the media quickly assumed the rumor to be an established fact.

Throughout the successful campaign, Vice President Canfield maintained a statesmanlike restraint, refusing to be drawn into any overstatement of the situation. He simply repeated that his position was well known and of long standing. Because he refused to gloat or hog the credit, he converted scores of congressmen who had been opposed to him or undecided.

16

IT WAS not very often that a speaker of the House of Representatives walked over to the Senate wing of the Capitol to visit a Vice President in his small ceremonial office. As a matter of fact, it was usually the Vice President who sailed with full security escort into the speaker's impressive suite, there to be kept waiting by superannuated House functionaries for the moment or two thought necessary to prove that the congressional pecking order was not the same as the constitutional pecking order. It was a question of Capitol Hill power: The speaker had an abundance of it and the Vice President had none.

One could understand therefore the buzz of excitement that ran through the Senate chamber and cloakrooms on this warm, slow late-summer afternoon.

"The speaker's in the veep's office! Wonder what's up? Well, you can bet that it's something good for Canfield. Marty Edmonds doesn't call on people unless they're important to him or have a good chance of becoming important to him." This observation by a Hill-wise senator was the standard reaction to the unusual event.

Inside the ceremonial office, Porter Canfield regarded his visitor with a thoughtful smile. He had been listening without much comment for ten minutes while the young, dynamic speaker explained the reason for his call. Now it was his turn to respond, and he knew that what he said might very well determine the success or failure of his embryonic presidential bid. He searched the face of this thirty-nine-year-old master politician—one of the youngest speakers in recent history—for the slightest sign of duplicity. Edmonds, a compact, square-jawed man, met his gaze confidently. After a long moment, Canfield began to talk.

"First of all, Mr. Speaker, I want you to know how much I appreciate your coming to see me this afternoon and how much I admire your candor. Before you leave, though, I suggest that we agree on a short statement to be released to the press." He smiled engagingly. "Otherwise, they'll imagine and print some very peculiar things."

"I agree, Mr. Vice President."

Canfield's smile broadened. "And despite the seriousness of our talk, I think we'd be more comfortable without the formality. Let's make it Newt and Marty, shall we?"

"By all means, Newt." The gray eyes behind the horn rims twinkled. "At least, until after the election."

Canfield's expression showed that that version of the future pleased him. "Now, I want to answer you with equal frankness, Marty. Naturally, I am glad to know that you turned down Devers's suggestion that you take the stump here and there to support the Tripartite Pact and urge restraint regarding the Middle East. We both know what the media would have done with that. They would have played it as Edmonds to his own use and to the use of Hurley versus Canfield."

"Exactly how I figured it, Newt. And, incidentally, John wouldn't have stopped there had I agreed to take on the assignment. Next, he would have wanted me to deplore the warmongering of ambitious candidates willing to risk nuclear confrontation just to attract a few votes. I have the distinct impression that the President had tremendous respect for me and thought I was one of the few people around who are really qualified for the presidency."

"Old Joshua is clever, no question about that," said Canfield. "It must have been tempting hearing all those nice compliments along with a teaser about possible presidential support."

"Maybe for a sophomore congressman but not for old Marty. I know from experience that those hints don't mean anything. They are about as exclusive as a direct mail solicitation." Edmonds took off his glasses and polished them with his handkerchief. "But I'm interrupting you. You were about to answer my question."

Canfield had a moment of fleeting doubt. Was he being pumped and set up for a sandbagging? It was possible, but not probable. He decided to take the chance. "You are correct in your assumption that I intend to seek the presidency regardless of how actively Hurley opposes me. You are also correct in your conclusion that I am irreversibly committed to my stand on short-range nukes for Israel, whether Dradavov likes it or not.''

The speaker nodded gravely, and Canfield continued. ''You tell me you have no intention of running for the presidency for at least eight years—that would make you forty-six, still a very young candidate, so that makes sense to me. Now''—Canfield leaned forward in his chair, his manner tense—''you tell me you are seriously considering supporting my candidacy—covertly for the moment, but not so covertly that the influential House members won't know how you are leaning. But before you make this decision, you want me to assure you that there are no skeletons in my closet. Particularly, you want me to assure you that the vicious rumors now circulating that Andy Jackerson has caught me in a major scandal but will not break it until just before the convention are untrue—is that right?''

A less tested politician might have squirmed a little at Canfield's stark exposition, but Marty Edmonds was a pro all the way.

''That's about it. Before I put my chips on you, Newt, I want you to swear to me that Jackerson has nothing on you.'' The speaker's eyes narrowed. ''More than that, I want to hear that no matter how hard he digs, no matter who talks, he will still have nothing on you.''

Canfield did not blink. His face remained impassive. ''Unequivocally, I give you that assurance,'' he said firmly.

Edmonds softened. ''Thank you, Newt. It's embarrassing to be so blunt, but we both know this is a cold, hard business. If a man doesn't protect himself, he doesn't last long.'' He stood up and extended his hand. ''You're my candidate, Mr. V.P., and I think you'll see some early results of my support when the House members go home to campaign. I'm with you all the way, because I feel exactly as you do about protecting Israel. Our international image depends on our honoring our commitments there.''

The Vice President shook hands solemnly. ''Thank you, Marty. Now, before you go, let's decide on what to tell the reporters. I suggest we issue a joint statement of our concern over the increased use of terrorism as a political tool in the world and our determination that the Congress of the United States will not be intimidated by any international criminals.''

''That sounds great, Newt. If you'll have it drafted and send it over, I'll sign it, and we'll release it simultaneously.''

''Fine. I'll have it in your office tonight.'' Canfield walked to the door with Edmonds and stepped into the hallway so that the loungers in the Senate lobby could observe the speaker's cordial departure.

Scarcely able to contain his joy, Canfield immediately reached Zack Miller at Stanley Bedson's office in the New Senate Office Building and quickly filled him in on the encouraging development.

The advisor was gleeful. "What a fantastic break to nail down Edmonds this early! This will do more than ten weeks of wooing individual House members. Shall I come right over?"

"No need, Zack. Get hold of Peter and begin drafting the statement for joint signature. I have an appointment with Halevy now—just a walk-through—been putting him off for weeks. As soon as I stroke him a little, I'll come over there. . . . And Zack—don't tell Rosen any more than what's in the statement, understand?"

Hanging up the phone, Canfield smiled at the famous portrait of George Washington. Already he envisaged himself in the role of Commander-in-Chief.

Five minutes later the Secret Service agent on duty outside opened the door to admit Yoram Halevy, clad in faded jeans and Earth Shoes. He moved with an arrogance that fell just short of being a swagger, and the agent's woodenly expressionless face left little doubt that the INAF leader was not one of his favorite people.

"Come in, Yoram. I'm sorry it took so long to arrange this appointment. Nice of you to stop by." Canfield came from behind his desk to shake hands warmly. "I don't believe you've been in the ceremonial office," he continued. "Sit right here under George Washington's portrait. It was purchased in 1832 by order of the Senate from Rembrandt Peale, the artist who painted it. It is reputed to be one of our first President's best likenesses."

Although Halevy did not appear to be impressed, Canfield nevertheless bombarded him for ten minutes with the standard anecdotes about the memorabilia in the office. The Vice President was unusually talkative, flying high because of Martin Edmonds's surprising commitment, and he did not notice his visitor's indifference for some time. But suddenly Canfield sensed that he was becoming a bore, and that, moreover, he was prolonging a meeting he had intended to keep as brief as possible.

"I've been rattling on too long, Yoram," he said apologetically. "What's new? How are things going with INAF?"

Halevy at once became alert and interested. "Very well. For some time, I've been wanting to report to you that we have accomplished one of the objectives that you and I discussed in our last meeting."

"Wonderful! I'm extremely pleased with the support INAF is

giving me. It isn't often that a candidate gets such enthusiastic backing—especially from people who are willing to get out on the firing line and do the hard things that are required to win elections.'' Canfield smiled. ''Not to mention the valuable work you are doing to coordinate with our friends overseas.''

Halevy nodded impatiently. ''That's not what I meant.'' He looked intently at the Vice President. ''Is it secure here? Can we talk freely?''

''Quite secure. I have it swept every day. Lately, I've been worried about electronic surveillance. Too many things I've never released appear in the press.''

''While we're in this dangerous stage, we can't be too careful,'' Halevy said. He leaned forward. ''We've got two more in mind to accompany O'Mara.''

For a moment Canfield did not follow him. Then he felt a chill run from his shoulders up to his scalp, raising the small hairs on the nape of his neck. He must have misunderstood. ''What do you mean?'' he stammered, anxiety stripping his voice of its customary resonance.

Halevy looked at him incredulously, as though he had lost his senses. ''You and I discussed this,'' he said evenly. ''We decided that we had to use whatever means might be required to prevent those people from selling out. We got O'Mara. Now we're going to get the rest.''

A sick feeling spread through the Vice President. This couldn't be real. He took a deep breath. ''But O'Mara was killed by Arab terrorists—some organization called DAMN—''

For the first time since he had entered the room, Yoram Halevy smiled. ''That's right, and so will the others be the victims of DAMN.'' He winked at Canfield. ''It's a very useful cover. The police don't know where to start.''

Canfield sat stunned. This fanatic, sitting so calmly in the Capitol of the United States, was attempting to involve its second highest officer in a murder. Halevy was talking to him as though he were a conspirator in a political killing—as though he, Porter Newton Canfield, Vice President of the United States, had agreed that Mark O'Mara should be murdered. It was ridiculous, bizarre. He must put a stop to this foolishness immediately. Assuming a stern expression and fighting down panic, he said firmly, ''Mr. Halevy, I don't know exactly what you are trying to tell me, and I have a feeling that, for your benefit, I shouldn't know. Perhaps it would be best if we leave the matter as it is now. It is certainly none of my business how INAF functions internally. We have a common purpose—

helping to protect Israel from aggression. INAF has given me political support because of that purpose, and I have accepted it, knowing from my investigation that INAF has always operated lawfully.'' He rose to his feet, signifying the end of the meeting. "Thank you very much for coming by to see me—''

"Sit down, Mr. Vice President.'' The words cracked like a whip in the old room. Canfield hesitated, fear flickering in his eyes. The cold-eyed man in the rough clothes looked at him clinically and said, "You're in this up to your neck. Don't give me that thank-you-very-much-but-I-don't-know-what-you-are-talking-about crap. Mister, you agreed that O'Mara had to go—for the good of our common purpose.'' Halevy mimicked the Vice President's self-important manner: "So sit down and be sensible.'' Then he relented a little. "There is no trouble, and the matters we are talking about may just make you the next President of the United States.''

The Vice President decided that it was best to humor this madman while he sought a solution. There would be no turning back from a confrontation that might easily involve the agent outside the door. Forcing himself to smile, Canfield resumed his seat and began to improvise.

"Yoram, you're not thinking very clearly. Apparently, you have some information on the O'Mara case. If you insist on telling it to me, I will be obligated to inform the FBI—which may not be in either of our interests. As things stand now, no harm has been done.'' His voice became intimate, persuasive. "Why don't we drop that whole discussion right here and talk about the many constructive ways in which I can help the worthwhile cause of INAF?''

"It's too late for that, Porter.'' Halevy stared impudently, noting the Vice President's unsuccessful effort to conceal his irritation at the use of his first name. "Far too late,'' he repeated, stretching his long legs out and lacing his fingers behind his head. "Let me lay it out for you very simply. I got reliable information from the Middle East that O'Mara and several other media bigwigs were selling out quietly to the Arabs for a bundle. I came to see you downtown about the problem. We—and I mean *we*, Porter—agreed that such treachery would be a disaster for Israel. *We* agreed O'Mara had to be stopped. You said—'' Halevy looked at the ornate ceiling reflectively. "Let's see, your exact words were—'' he fished in his jacket and brought out a folded piece of paper and read from it—'' 'INAF is right in doing whatever needs to be done to prevent the most influential media from turning on Israel. They must be stopped.' '' He looked at the Vice President's ashen face. "I'm sure you remember saying that, Porter, but in case you don't, I have it all recorded—your voice.'' He produced a small cassette tape from a jacket pocket and tossed it to Canfield, who looked at it dazedly. ''That's just a copy of the real thing, Porter, so you can keep it. The original is in a safe place, just so you'll remember that it won't help a bit for the CIA to arrange an unfortunate accident for me.'' Halevy's contemptuous smile turned suddenly to a cruel slash. ''You said they must be stopped, Mr. Vice President. Well, I agreed with you. I stopped O'Mara.''

He stood up suddenly, and, leaning over the quaking Canfield so that their faces were only inches apart, delivered the *coup de grâce* in more of a hiss than a voice: ''I killed Mark O'Mara at your suggestion, Porter. I choked him to death, and you are as guilty of his murder as if your two hands twisted the wire that killed him. You are a coconspirator, and your absence from the scene of the crime does not lessen your accountability for first degree murder. You, as a lawyer, know that.''

With a faint cry of anguish, Canfield pushed the malevolent presence away and leaped to his feet. ''You are crazy! Murder never crossed my mind!'' he said wildly. ''I meant that whatever lawful means were necessary should be used. No one talked or thought of killing anyone. No one would believe that I meant to agree to a killing.''

''No one except the late Mr. O'Mara's friends in the news media, and several million political enemies you have enraged during your time in politics, and several thousand ciphers you believe to be friends but who will turn on you because they envy you your position and wealth,'' said Halevy, suddenly becoming calm. ''Think, man. You have a good brain. If you turn me in and I play this tape, you are through. No presidency. No more vice-presidency. Indictment. Wild rumors and speculation. Hatred. Disgrace. Humiliation. Defeat. And then long imprisonment.'' Halevy watched the crushing impact of these dire words on Canfield. ''Remember,'' continued the INAF leader in the same soft, confident voice, ''you are tied to INAF. We have issued public statements supporting you. We have raised money for you, some unlawfully. You have commended us publicly, and even defended us publicly against the attacks of others. If you turn us in, you will not be praised. They will say that the case was about to be broken and you tried to bail out at the expense of your friends.'' Halevy got up and took the Vice President's arm. ''Sit down, Porter,'' he said gently, ''and listen to me for a few more minutes.''

Canfield allowed himself to be led to a chair. He sat down heavily and stared vacantly at his tormentor. He just wanted to close his eyes and sleep, to shut out this horrible dream.

The big man's voice became even more soothing. "The way things stand now, everything is fine," he said. "No one knows. The operation was handled perfectly. It forced Hurley to send the missiles. It is having the desired effect on American opinion. Your campaign is moving splendidly, and you are picking up support every day."

Halevy offered Canfield a cigarette, but the Vice President declined it absently. Lighting his own, Halevy continued in the same hypnotic tone: "You are going to be President of the United States—one of the most respected Presidents in our history. It will be President Canfield whom scholars will credit with saving the United States from Russian domination. You will reverse this terrible tide that is running against freedom in the world, rescue the United States from the jaws of that shark, Dradavov. Because of you, Israel will survive the conspiracy against her and become an anchor of democracy in the Middle East. Your position in history will be unique, incomparable. You will take your place alongside Washington, Lincoln and Roosevelt."

Canfield shook his head. "I've got to think," he said. "I've got to think about this."

"Of course you must," said Halevy soothingly. "I'm going to go along now. Don't worry about anything. What's been done has been done well, and what is still to be done will be done with equal expertness."

He stopped and turned back. "You have the tape," he said offhandedly. "I suggest you destroy it after you have refreshed your memory. Wouldn't do to leave it lying around." Then he frowned. "And I wouldn't mention our conversation to anyone—not to anyone, understand? Nobody but you and me know. The original tape of our previous conversation will not come into anyone's possession unless I die under suspicious circumstances. It's just you and me. You can trust me because my life is at stake, just as yours is, but you can't trust anyone else—But no more about that. Just keep up the good work. I'll be checking with you from time to time, Porter."

Pure habit alone moved the stunned Vice President to the door with his departing visitor and through the farewell formalities. He stared distractedly at the retreating back of the man who had destroyed his peace of mind.

"Do you want the car now, sir?" The agent was looking at him uncertainly.

"In ten minutes, please. I'll be stopping for a while at Senator Bedson's office in the New Senate Office Building," said Canfield, pulling himself back to reality. He closed the opaque glass door gently and sat down at his desk numbly.

His eyes shifted morosely from one familiar object to another in the office, but he didn't experience the usual pride of being part of a great tradition. It had been so pleasurable to sit alone in this room so full of history and imagine future visitors referring in hushed tones to Porter Canfield, a Vice President of such brilliance that he eclipsed his President in the final years of the Hurley administration. And now all of that great promise was threatened by a radical Zionist who stopped at nothing, not even murder. The Vice President's hand trembled as he answered the buzz of the phone. No, he didn't want to talk to Dr. Miller. Just tell him he was on the way over there. Yes, he would take his wife's call.

"Hello, Amy," he said, without the usual brisk impatience. "No, nothing's wrong. Somewhat tired, I guess." After a short pause, he added, "I may be a little late for dinner. Have to go to a meeting." A hint of irritation forced aside the despair. "No, at Stanley Bedson's office. Whatever made you think it was at HEW? . . . Well, don't believe everything you read in the *Globe*. They never know what meetings are where. Okay, should be there by eight-thirty. Bye."

He shook his head in wonderment. Since when was Amy Canfield interested enough in government to read the daily agenda of supposed meetings in the media? Quickly, he reverted to the problem. Somehow the interruption had helped. The panic was subsiding, and clear thoughts were pushing aside the hopeless depression. Halevy had tricked him—that was undeniable—but there was no use crying over spilt milk. Besides, Halevy was right. Just the two of them knew, and there was no crisis at the moment. Things were going splendidly for the campaign, and O'Mara's death had strengthened his hand and weakened Hurley's. He began to feel alive again. What a plus Marty Edmonds would be. Politically, everything was coming up roses. It would have been perfect if Halevy had had the sense not to inform him of such details. People always thought of themselves. Actually, he wasn't involved, but no sense in irritating Halevy. The man was dangerous, capable of turning against him. Best to leave things as they were and tell no one. Political assassinations were not uncommon. One shouldn't consider them as shocking as an ordinary murder. The queasy feeling began to creep back into his stomach. He didn't really believe that.

Suddenly he stood up purposefully, took a deep breath and threw back his shoulders. He was just as much a soldier as an infantryman in battle. The mission came first. The country was being endangered by that sly Russian, Dradavov. He must never lose sight of the priorities. He would put this shock behind him and go forward. Leadership was a terrible burden, but those who were called to important tasks must bear up under the strain.

He went into the tiny washroom, converted from an ordinary coat closet by a predecessor who liked his plumbing proximate, and splashed cold water on his face. The mirror showed a tired man. The lines of middle age stood out more sharply under the unusual stress of the day, but the blue eyes were clear and the complexion had regained its healthy ruddiness. He would survive this crisis just as he had survived all the others.

He had no sooner stepped into the Senate lobby when the Capitol reporters came at him with questions about his meeting with Edmonds. Refusing their specific inquiries, he told them that a joint statement would be released by himself and the speaker within an hour.

During the short ride to Stanley Bedson's suite Yoram Halevy's awful disclosure seemed to recede further and further in the still-bright late-afternoon sunlight, and it was with a springy step and cheerful mien that he entered the office where Bedson, Zack Miller and Peter Rosen awaited him. The three automatically came to their feet in acknowledgment of high office. Canfield took the center chair and smilingly waved them back to their seats. After several years as Vice President, he had come to believe that such gestures implied something more personal than customary respect to the office he held.

"Mr. Vice President, we were afraid you had forgotten us," said Stanley Bedson. "The speaker's press secretary called Pete's office at the EOB and wanted to know when the speaker could expect the statement. He's going to leave in a half-hour from now and wants to sign it before he goes so that the press won't be all over him."

"We have it finished, sir, and I'll run it right over as soon as you sign—that is, of course, if you approve of what we drafted," said Peter Rosen eagerly. "It's fantastic P.R., Mr. Vice President," he added, "to have the speaker join in a statement of any kind that issues from your office, and particularly for him to be seen coming to you to discuss it."

"It won't hurt us." Canfield laughed lightly, thinking that Rosen would be dancing with joy if he knew how fantastic it really was. Rosen's demonstrativeness was sometimes unkindly characterized by Bill Shelby as "wriggling like a puppy." The trouble was that when Rosen wriggled, the press wormed the reason for it out of him within twenty-four hours.

Miller handed him a single-page release on the vice-presidential stationery, with a line for his signature and one for the speaker's below. "It's simple and to the point, sir. In a way, it's understated. The news is in the fact of the visit and the cooperation between you and Edmonds, not in the words."

Canfield read it through quickly and signed it without alteration. He then handed it to Rosen, who left immediately for the speaker's office.

"Let's have a drink, Stan. It's been a long day, and I'm a little bushed. If I know senators, that cabinet over there doesn't hold files."

"Coming right up, Mr. Vice President," said Bedson. He lifted and slid back the false drawer front of the walnut highboy to reveal a well-stocked bar and minifridge. Quickly mixing drinks for the three of them, he handed the strong V.O. and water to Canfield. "You've earned us the right to celebrate. We kept it from Rosen, of course, but I confess I almost wet myself when Zack got me to the side and let me in on Edmonds's capitulation. That makes our job in the House a cinch."

Canfield drank off a good bit of his whiskey without a pause. "You deserve a lot of credit for the skillful way you've handled things in Congress, Stan," he said, ever the political animal. The liquor, quickly absorbed by his empty stomach, began at once to deaden his suppressed anxiety. Halevy and his frightening revelation were no longer a cause for panic. Concern, yes, but careful monitoring and good judgment would keep things under control.

"How was your meeting with Yoram?" The question startled Canfield for a moment, as though it had been plucked from his own mind. He looked at Zack casually, alert for any signal of something hidden behind the perfectly normal question. There was no sign.

"Fine, fine. INAF is doing a good job with the middle-class Jewish community. Don't you think so, Zack?"

"Yes, I do. I'm glad you took my suggestion and challenged Gray's criticism of INAF. It made us a lot of friends we didn't have before."

"We took a calculated risk, and it's turned out well," said Canfield. He wondered what Miller would do if he were confronted with the fact that Halevy was a political assassin. One thing was certain. He couldn't afford to take the chance of finding out—not with that tape in existence. Unobtrusively, he dropped his hand to his coat pocket. The hard outline of the cassette gave him a momentary chill in spite of the alcohol.

Three drinks and an hour and a half later Canfield left his two advisors. Peter Rosen had called to announce the distribution of the statement and his opinion that it would be a lead story on the eleven o'clock news. The Vice President had one more stop to make, a drop-by at a cocktail party given by the Spanish-American Society at the Washington Hilton. He went through the vast room like a brush fire. Twenty minutes from the time the limousine pulled up at the hotel, he was locked in his bedroom, scissoring the tape to shreds and calling to Amy that he would be down to dinner in just a minute.

A week of relative calm followed, and the vice-presidential staff took advantage of the summer's end to prepare for the hectic pace anticipated after Labor Day. Bill Shelby dropped into Zack Miller's office one morning to chat about routine matters.

"You look exhausted, Zack. Why don't you take a couple of days off before you come down with a virus or something. After Labor Day, the boss will need you a lot more than now." A month before a remark like that from Bill Shelby would have been sardonic, but it was a testimonial to the smooth progress of the Canfield campaign that it was said and received sincerely. Success and a happy principal are the best lubricants for staff frictions.

Zack sat glumly behind his EOB desk, nursing a steaming cup of black coffee. He tried to acknowledge that he appreciated the solicitude of the chief of staff. "This is not one of my better days, Bill, but I'll snap out of it. Too many things cooking to flake off now."

"Well, at least look over your open matters and see if I can't reassign some of the work. We took on a new speechwriter yesterday, and he has a clear desk. Try to get rid of some of the detail." Shelby pushed back his chair and started toward the door.

"Thanks, Bill. I'll do that."

Shelby hesitated, hand on the doorknob. He had become accustomed to Miller's ups and downs, but had never seen him look so worried. "Can I help in any way, Zack? Is there something bothering you that you need to talk out?"

Miller made a determined effort to appear more cheerful. "Don't pay any attention to this gloom, Bill. Right now I happen to feel like the north end of a southbound skunk, but it will pass. And I will try to unload some detail, as you suggested."

"Good. If you need me, I'll be in my office until one."

The heavy door clicked shut behind the chief of staff, and Zack Miller slumped back into his chair, sinking even deeper into the dark despair that had overwhelmed him the night before. He had been plunged from ecstasy to misery with the speed of a toboggan on a steep hill.

Just three days ago, the call from Sirana that she was flying to him had put him in the clouds. Then came two days of delicious anticipation, of putting the house on C Street in order and preparing for her arrival. He had stood like a schoolboy outside Customs at Dulles Airport, waiting for her with a bouquet of red roses. It would have been easy to arrange to wait for her inside, but he wanted their reunion to be private, and nothing was more private than the middle of a crowd of people greeting their own loved ones.

She was one of the last travelers to check through, and he was looking at the clock for the umpteenth time when she finally appeared. For a second or so, he had not called to her, allowing himself the sensual pleasure of enjoying her beauty unobserved. Then she caught sight of him and ran into his arms. In her face he read the certainty of her love, and at that moment he became equally certain of his. He took her home and carried her across the threshold as though she were his bride. Her spontaneous delight with the old house pleased him greatly, and they frolicked like children while carrying in her luggage from the car.

Zack had rented the entire place at an unbelievably cheap price from a professor at American University who was leaving for a two-year sabbatical in Asia and wanted a reliable tenant to keep an eye on the property in his absence. C Street's residents were varied—some well off and some drifters—but the surrounding neighborhood was a high-crime district, and few people ventured from their tightly barricaded homes after dark. Vandalism was rampant, particularly in vacant properties or areas shared in common by several renters.

Situated on a long, narrow lot close to the adjacent dwellings, Zack's house had a small front yard and porch. On entering, one immediately faced the stairs to the second and third floors. The first floor, from front to rear, contained a fairly good-size living room, dining room and den. Next to the den and behind the staircase was an adequate kitchen. The upstairs floors had two bedrooms and one bath each—a great deal too much space for Zack, who only used the third floor for storage. Out the kitchen door was a fenced backyard and a one-car garage opening into an alley. The home, which was well furnished and carpeted, had a certain old-town charm that Zack liked.

He had helped her get settled in the front bedroom with him, laughing at her when she took one look at the tiny closet and promptly claimed the back bedroom as her province also. He pulled her roughly to him, exacting the promise that any other bed in the house was off limits. She broke loose, laughing hysterically, and he chased her around the room until he caught her and threw her on the bed. There their mock wrestling match had become urgent love-making, and they thundered through the act, unaware that the curtains were not completely closed.

Then, bathed and refreshed, they crept downstairs in robes and slippers to raid the refrigerator and drink steaming cups of tea. He noticed her exhilaration flagging and attributed it to fatigue, but later in bed she tossed fitfully until a few sobs broke through. It was then, when he had cradled her in his arms to comfort her, that she had blown his world apart.

He got up slowly and looked out the window at the porch with its broad rails encrusted with pigeon excrement. Beyond, the pedestrian traffic streamed relentlessly to and from the White House across the street. Suddenly he felt a sharp flash of pain across his temples, and his heart fibrillated wildly for a few seconds. Fighting dizziness, he sat down again and buried his face in his hands. The problem could not be avoided. There was no choice. He had to tell Newt the terrifying news that Sirana had brought him. Tears of regret stung his eyes. In his inexperience and stupidity he had demolished Canfield's chance to be President of the United States. He had been brought to Washington to help elect a President; instead, he had destroyed a Vice President.

Wearily, he rubbed the back of his hands across his eyes and reached for the phone. "Kathy, this is Zack Miller. Is he in yet?"

"Yes, sir. He's reading the National Security reports."

"Would you see if I can go right in?" Noting her hesitation, he quickly added, "It's urgent."

"Hold a minute, please. I'll check." She was back almost instantly. "He says to come right in, Dr. Miller."

Zack hung up, irrelevantly wondering if she had noticed the absence of his usual flippancies.

Shrugging on his coat, he walked stiffly across the hall, without hearing the greeting of the receptionist, and knocked on the door of the Vice President's office. He was calm, almost detached, and aware of the irreversibility of what he was going to do. Entering on

338

summons, he waited just inside the door. Canfield was bent over an open leather-bound folder marked TOP SECRET in large gold letters. He looked up over his glasses for a brief moment. "Morning, Zack. Get yourself a cup of coffee from the kitchen. Be with you in two shakes."

Zack went into the adjoining kitchen. Looking at the framed cartoons on the walls brought a tightness to his diaphragm; they would soon be but memories to the man in the other room. His hand shook slightly as he poured the coffee. Brushing back a new wave of emotion, he carried the cup into the office and sat down near the desk. The Vice President initialed the reports, replaced them in the folder and buzzed for Kathy.

"Got something important, huh?" Canfield gave his full attention to his advisor, who nodded in agreement. "Well, we might as well wait until Kathy takes this stuff." At that moment, the door opened and Kathy came in to pick up the secret material, which was always returned immediately to its source through cleared personnel.

"Cut off all interruptions, Kathy," said Canfield. When she had departed, he leaned back and peered quizzically at his visitor. "You look grim, Zack," he said, putting his glasses aside. "No more bad news of a family nature, I hope."

"I wish it were as simple as that." Miller nervously lit another cigarette. "What I have to tell you about is an absolute disaster—for you, for all of your people, for everything we've worked to achieve."

Canfield forced a laugh. "Those are dire words, Zack. Come now, it can't be that bad, can it?" God, he thought, more trouble on top of what I went through with Halevy last week?

Miller hung his head for an instant, then looked directly into Canfield's eyes. "It's worse. I've gotten you involved with a murderer."

There was an instant of surprise in which time seemed to be suspended for Porter Canfield. Then a karate chop of fear struck his solar plexus. "What are you talking about?" he asked faintly. Already he had hypothesized that Halevy had been apprehended and had revealed the tape.

"I don't blame you for being confused," said Miller dejectedly. "It's a crazy, unbelievable tragedy. Our friend, Yoram Halevy, has been conned into committing a murder." Miller lit a fresh cigarette off the old one and savagely ground out the butt.

"Take it easy, Zack," said Canfield impatiently, trying to prepare himself for the worst. "You're not making much sense.

"Suppose you start at the beginning and tell me the whole business."

"Sorry, Newt. This thing's got me half off my rocker." Miller straightened up, seeming to pull himself together. "Okay, here it is. Halevy was told that O'Mara and some other very influential news-media owners were selling out to the Arabs and would quietly become anti-Israeli propagandists. He saw this as the end of American support for Israel and ultimately the fall of Israel to Arab aggression. His informant suggested that INAF could stop the plot by killing the media conspirators—moreover, that Arab extremists could be blamed, pointing to the media people's support for Israel up to that time as the motive. Halevy was sold the bill of goods that this would help Israel get IRBM's and reinforce America's ties with Israel." Miller sucked at his cigarette and resumed, "In other words, turn the thing around from defeat to victory. Well, Yoram fell for it. He murdered O'Mara and succeeded in having a phony Arab group called DAMN blamed for it. Having been successful once, he's ready to try again." Zack shook his head in torment. "Oh, God, why did I let you get publicly identified with Halevy?" he moaned. "It's the end of your presidential hopes."

Canfield was stunned. What would Halevy do when he learned he had killed for nothing—and murdered a friend, at that.

"How do you know all this? It sounds like some wild Washington rumor to me," he said, fishing for more information.

"I wish to hell it were, Newt. Oh, how I wish it were. Look, you have to know everything, so listen carefully."

He then related in detail the history of his relationship with Sirana Amiri and her startling revelations.

By the end of his narrative, Zack was much calmer. Having made his confession, he felt purged and prepared to take the censure for ruining a political career. An advisor who gives poor advice cannot be tolerated any more than a doctor who prescribes medicine that harms the patient. He and Meredith Lord had pushed Halevy on Canfield, and now Halevy would be Canfield's nemesis. Guilt by association had punctured many a political balloon. Zack waited for the bitter words of blame, or worse—perhaps even a recrudescence of the old Canfield temper tantrum.

"How do you know you can trust this girl? She may have a grudge against the Persian, what's his name—Izadi? You said they were very close—she may want to hurt him. How do we know she isn't making the whole thing up?" Canfield displayed no emotion. His manner was almost pedantic, and his question reasonable to anyone unaware of his conversation with Halevy.

Zack was surprised. He had not expected an examination of his

340

witness's credibility. "I trust her completely," he said simply. "We're going to be married very soon. Besides, all this hurts me and you—and Halevy, especially—more than Izadi. Izadi never became involved in planning the crime. There is no way he could be extradited from Iran on the flimsy charge that he passed vicious and false rumors to Halevy—rumors that caused him to commit murder. And even if they went after Izadi, he'd just disappear into the Tehran underground. No, Newt, there's no reason for Sirana to make this up."

"Then why would she mention it to you at all? If it's true, it destroys Halevy. It ruins my chances for the presidency because my enemies will point to my close association with INAF and imply dark and dirty secret connections. That will be obviously agonizing for you. Why would the girl who loves you subject you to such torture?"

Zack looked very closely at Canfield, searching for some clue to explain this curious refusal to believe Sirana. He had blown up Canfield's world in his face. Instead of addressing the problem, Canfield was groping in the dark to prove that it didn't exist. Had the shock been so great, the pain so severe, that he refused to face reality? "Newt, old friend," he said gently, "Sirana feared that I might become an unwitting accomplice to a future killing by Halevy. She is worried primarily about me, but she is also a decent person who doesn't want to see innocent people killed. Halevy must be taken into custody to save lives. He could murder again at any moment."

The expression on Canfield's face was bland. Smoothly, he abandoned the issue of Sirana's credibility and pulled back to a new position.

"He won't kill again if you tell him he has been duped by Izadi and there has been no treachery by the media people," he said, keeping an iron grip on his composure. "Zack," he said beguilingly, "Yoram is your friend. He is a good man who has been exploited. With the most patriotic motives, he has done a wrong. You are in a position to save him from doing other wrongs. You owe him that. He would do the same for you."

Zack found it hard to believe his ears. Was the Vice President of the United States suggesting that a premeditated murder be ignored? Mark O'Mara was dead and buried. Sorry, old boy, it was all a mistake. Rotten luck for you, you know. "I owe Yoram nothing," Zack said, beginning to become agitated again. "He has killed in cold blood. Forget about the deception and the false motive. We are supposed to be civilized. Even if Halevy had been right about O'Mara, he cannot be excused for murder." He got up and began his usual pacing. "We must inform the FBI immediately."

Canfield's heart raced. Halevy's frightening threats—indictment, hatred, disgrace, imprisonment—sounded in his ears like the hollow reverberations of a jungle drum. He swallowed back the panic. "That will be the end for me as well as for Halevy," he said soberly. "A man can be very vindictive against those who cause him to lose his freedom forever. He may try to involve us in the plot. Certainly, he'll bring out his arrangement with you that resulted in the girl contacting you in Singapore. But whether or not he is successful in involving us legally, the media will have a field day with his accusations." Canfield let the bitterness show in his voice. "It's a hell of a thing when your whole life is ruined because you listened to your friends and let some kook get too close to you."

Miller stopped, as though impaled by a real rather than verbal spear. The hurt in his eyes proved that Canfield had not overestimated his sensitivity. His voice was broken with remorse. "God, Newt. I'd give anything if this hadn't happened. I take the responsibility of misjudging Halevy, but remember, others did, too— Meredith Lord, for one, and she is a political expert. If I could do something to make this nightmare go away, I would; but I can't." He slumped in the chair.

"Zack, be practical." The Vice President's tone was no longer accusatory. "Halevy won't go on with his plan once he learns that the media conspiracy is a fake, so there is no immediate crisis once he is notified that Izadi deceived him. That gives us time to think."

"O'Mara is dead, Newt. We are morally obligated to turn in his killer, now that we know who it is."

Canfield walked slowly up and down behind his desk, saying nothing for a few moments. Then, stopping suddenly, he wheeled to face Miller. "We haven't done anything illegal. What is a moral obligation, Zack? Are we not morally obligated to prevent Israel from being extinguished in the interest of the Russian predators? Are we not morally obligated to do what we can to prevent the eventual enslavement of the world by communist dictators? Is the moral obligation to report an individual murder, committed by mistake, greater than these moral obligations?"

"I believe it is at this moment," Miller said firmly. "No individual is safe if laws can be broken because of our rationalizations. Total anarchy would result."

Canfield shook his head in disagreement. "I'm not asking for an affirmative act—only silence," he said.

342

"That's another rationalization." Miller walked over and sympathetically put his arm around the Vice President's shoulders. "Losing the presidency for this time is not as bad as losing your self-respect, Newt," he said softly. "We'd never be able to live with ourselves if we didn't do the right thing."

"But it isn't just you and I, Zack. The whole administration will suffer. The party may be defeated next year because of the capital that can be made of this!"

"No use, Newt. You know it's no use. We must call in the FBI."

Canfield let his shoulders slump in total defeat. "At least let me warn the President of what's coming," he said. "Give me some time to figure out how to explain all this to him. I'm obligated that much to the administration and the party." He smiled ironically. "I haven't been the most loyal Vice President, you know."

"I don't think Hurley's entitled to any consideration," said Miller flatly. "However, that's your call. You think about it overnight, and we'll meet again in the morning. I'm afraid if we delay too long, we may have more blood on our hands."

"Tomorrow's Saturday. I have nothing scheduled except reading briefing materials. Suppose we meet here at nine. It will help both of us to sleep on it."

"Okay, that's a good idea," said Zack, happy that the decision had been made. "But remember, it's got to be done. All we're considering is how."

"Absolutely," said Canfield solemnly, "you've convinced me there's no other way."

Zack put his hand on the doorknob and looked at the man he had wounded so grievously. Canfield's face was pale, but composed. He was smiling wanly.

Never in his life had Zack Miller felt such pity. He stepped back toward Canfield and extended his hand. "Mr. Vice President, I'm very proud—" his voice broke uncontrollably "—to be your friend." In acute embarrassment, he turned and hurried from the office.

Alone now and very alarmed, the Vice President checked his schedule. What he needed desperately was time to think, to figure a way out of this impending disaster.

The schedule was not helpful. Executive schedulers, like nature, abhor a vacuum, and this Friday was typical. Beginning at ten, he had a half-hour magazine interview with *American News,* followed by a meeting with a congressman who was stopping by with an important constituent to have him stroked. Ten forty-five would bring the poster child for a well-known charity. At eleven, he would receive the prime minister of a minor African nation for coffee and an hour's discussion. At one, he was due at the Senate for morale purposes and in case he was needed to break a tie vote on a critical and highly controversial issue. Two o'clock would find him in the ceremonial office posing for campaign photographs with members of the House who were preparing their reelection campaigns. The fatiguing and excruciatingly boring session of smiling and posing would last until four-thirty, when he was due at the Department of Agriculture to present awards to the Four-H clubs. Five-thirty and six were scheduled for cocktail-reception drop-bys with the Young Federalists and at a dinner honoring a congressman who couldn't quite decide between him and Senator Gray. But there was one plus. The evening was free—or was it? No, damn it. He had promised Amy they would go up to Greystone for the weekend. It wasn't on the schedule because he had not told Kathy yet.

The tendons in the back of his neck felt like two steel bands. He cursed the schedule and its authors. Well, something had to give; he must have time to think. His practiced eye ran through the list of appointments again. Quickly, he made two decisions and picked up his phone. Peter Rosen answered immediately.

"Morning, Peter. Is the man from *American News* here yet?"

"Yes, sir. We're just leaving to come over to your office."

"Well, don't. An emergency has come up. I'll have to postpone the interview."

"But, Mr. Vice President"—Rosen's voice was a near whine—"Raymond Dow, the senior editor, is here. The article is all set for Thursday release, and the mag goes to bed tomorrow. They'll have to cancel the entire layout."

"I can't do it now, Pete. It's impossible. Wait a minute." Canfield looked at the schedule again. "Amuse him until noon. I'll see him then."

"But that's nearly two hours, sir."

"It is indeed," said Canfield tersely and hung up. There, that's a half-hour to think and get settled down, he thought.

Grabbing the phone again, he dialed his secretary. "Kathy, I've moved *American News* to noon. Get the last hour of the photo session at the Capitol canceled. And don't let anyone interrupt me until ten-thirty."

"Yes, sir." the secretary said, without surprise. She was used to sudden changes. In a few minutes she rang back and told him that the cancellation had been accomplished.

Canfield pushed his schedule aside. Now that the preliminary, mechanical things were done, worry flooded back over him. He had encountered enough troubles during his lifetime to know that seemingly insurmountable problems had a way of eventually being solved. It was difficult, however, to find any comfort in comparing this crisis to his past difficulties. Never before had he faced the possibility of ruin and imprisonment.

He sat for ten minutes in the deepest kind of funk, fear stripping his mind of productive thoughts. Then, with a great effort, he pulled himself together and began to isolate the critical aspects of his problems.

In the entire situation, which was fraught with danger, only Zack Miller was a time bomb, ticking away. The chance of Halevy being linked by the police investigation to the O'Mara murder lessened every day. The greatest risk of detection lay in poor execution of the future killings, and, now that Zack's new information had removed the motive for Halevy's punishment of the media people, that risk no longer existed. So, aside from Zack's sanctimonious attitude that he was morally obligated to identify Halevy as a murderer, the probability was that everything could continue to run smoothly. But if he failed to deter Zack from informing, that would be catastrophic—much worse than Zack himself realized. Zack did not know the extent of Canfield's involvement with Halevy. The worst that Zack saw was political loss.

Canfield wondered if his advisor's attitude would change if he knew about the ace that Halevy held. Suppose he told Zack the whole story and relied on friendship to dissuade him from talking. That could solve the immediate problem. "But wait," said a cunning corner of his mind, "what if you try and can't dissuade him? Then all is lost. You have foreclosed all possibility of other solutions."

The Vice President shuddered. Was he thinking, even subconsciously, of forcible prevention? Good God! Was he capable of considering that—the ultimate solution? Face it, he told himself; he was. That would make him no better than Yoram Halevy. Wrong. That would make him worse, because Halevy had not acted for himself, but for Israel.

He looked at his watch. Only five more minutes. He simply had to devise a strategy to keep Miller from going to the FBI. Obviously, he had only two alternatives: to convince Zack not to sound the alarm or to restrain him in some way. First, he would have another try at convincing him when he saw him the next morning. Then, if that failed, he would have to figure out how to restrain him, how to prevent him from carrying out his intentions.

For the second time in as many minutes, Canfield felt chilled.

"Restrain." "Prevent." Those were the words that Halevy had turned against him.

He made his decision. If he could not deter Zack from his foolish course of action, he would get word to Halevy that Miller must be somehow prevented—by abduction or some other means—from going to the FBI. Then it would be in Halevy's hands. If the INAF leader again read the signal wrong, Canfield could not be blamed. And even if he were blamed, you could only be hung once.

Now, how should he get word to Halevy? The phone was not safe; a personal message must be delivered. There was no way he could do that himself—not with the whole protective detail on his heels. Whom could he trust? No one. But no, wait. There was one person—the person he trusted above all. Meredith. His hopes soared when he remembered that she was going to New York this weekend to make some appearances promoting THC. That was perfect. She knew Halevy, and INAF was supporting THC. It would be a natural for her to see him and convey the message.

He quickly checked his calendar to verify that this was the weekend she was going. It was. There was almost no time. He would have to see her tonight, since she was leaving the next morning.

The intercom interrupted his thoughts. The congressman was waiting with his friend.

"Hold them a few minutes more, Kathy. I'll let you know when to send them in. And please get me Mrs. Canfield on the phone right away. She's in town."

Almost instantly, Kathy was back to him.

"Amy? I—"

"What good luck that you should call now, dear." Amy's voice was bright, and, as usual, she was totally immersed in her own interests. "The Claridges want us to come to their country place tomorrow evening and go to the polo match with them Sunday. I told them I thought that would be to your liking. Do you want me to pack your gray cashmere jacket?"

"I'm really sorry, Amy, but I'm going to have to cancel out. The President wants me to take a final shot at making peace between the budget director and the secretary of HEW tonight. I have to catch her before she goes out of town for the weekend. I'm having them both come to the house after dinner. Josh Devers is coming, too, to help mediate. But you go ahead, dear. Make my apologies to the Mastersons about tonight—and to the Claridges. This thing is probably going to keep me busy all weekend. I have meetings in the office Saturday morning from eight-thirty to noon."

346

"But, Newton, you promised me we would fly up for the week-end."

"I know I did, dear, but the job comes first. You know I can't refuse the President."

There was a self-pitying sigh, then a moment of silence. "Why are you having them to the house?" she asked. "Now I'll have to keep Rawlins, and I promised he could leave early. And Betsy was supposed to be off, but I'll ask her to stay to get your dinner." She sighed again. "I suppose I'd better cancel, too. Since you're not going, I'd have to be driven all the way to Philadelphia."

"Nonsense. There is no need for Betsy to stay. I won't starve. And I can get along without Rawlins for one night. There's no reason why your agents can't drive you to Greystone. You have plenty of time."

"Oh, it's just too complicated. I don't see how I can be ready in time to drive. I'll just call everyone and tell them we can't make it this time."

"Amy, there is no reason for you to stay in Washington," he insisted. "I'll be tied up in the meeting until late, and I'll be gone early in the morning. There will be nothing for you to do here."

"Newt, I get so exasperated with politics! Why can't we live like ordinary people?"

He laughed shortly. "Because neither of us would be satisfied to be ordinary. Now you go ahead and have a good time. If something breaks and I can join you tomorrow night, I will."

"I know what that means," she said sarcastically. "Well, I might as well go as sit around here looking at the walls. I'll be gone before you get home, so I'll see you Monday."

"Take care, dear. I'll phone you tomorrow," he said, listening for her disconnect and then switching to the intercom again.

"Have Bill Shelby set up a meeting at my house tonight at seven-thirty with Secretary Lord, Charlie Voren and Josh Devers. Tell their appointments secretaries that the meeting is urgent to get THC funding settled, and have them confirm as soon as possible, understand? . . . Good. Let me know when it's settled, and now you can send in the congressman and his friend."

Canfield was still thinking about his plans as he rose to welcome his visitors. He would keep Meredith after the others departed that evening, and he was certain that she would help him. During his free afternoon hour, he would figure out how to handle Zack in the morning, but he was less optimistic about him.

● ● ●

The town house on N Street was not one of Amy Canfield's favorite places. It was true that she had found it, exclaimed over its charm, bought it, redecorated it, exhibited it to her Philadelphia friends and enjoyed accepting their plaudits for her perspicacity. But soon the novelty wore off, leaving her with the realization that a house and the things in it were hardly the raw materials for happiness. Much more important were the things and people around the house, and there was nothing and nobody in Washington to interest her. Amy saw her unhappiness as imposed from outside. In her mind, it was her husband's selfish preoccupation with politics that forced this ridiculous and artificial life-style on them. She supposed that some men needed public office as a means of livelihood—particularly those who had not had the advantages of a Porter Newton Canfield—but she was genuinely perplexed that a man of wealth and impeccable social background should gravitate to politics when he could be conducting a comfortable law practice among his own kind.

There was a time when she had forgiven him his sudden absences and the embarrassment of having to show up without him at important social functions. Then the frequent overnight separations began. She cried, threatened, gave him the deep-freeze treatment—all to no avail. His promises and the poignant reconciliations had meant nothing. Gradually, they learned to cope with routines that shut them off from one another. She had retreated to the security of Greystone and her old crowd, and he had immersed himself completely in his work. Other places and other people filled up the voids. She didn't even know exactly when they lost each other.

Amy let go the curtain. The wrinkle where she had held the material was evidence of the intensity of her feelings. Why was she suddenly so concerned about her marriage? Why should their sterile arrangement of mutual convenience suddenly cause a rumbling in her like a latent Vesuvius? And what about this constriction in her stomach with the unpleasant radiating tickles? Could she be jealous?

Angrily, she pulled the curtain aside again. On this beautiful summer morning she would forget the unpleasant thoughts that had been nagging at her since she hung up the phone a few moments ago.

Her tiny garden in the postage-stamp front lawn below was a taunting reminder of Greystone's spacious, well-landscaped grounds. There were people strolling on N Street—a full-bearded young man wearing a Georgetown University T-shirt hanging out of dirty corduroy cut-offs and an unkempt girl in tight shorts. Their arms around each other, they stopped right in front of the house to kiss, oblivious to the people around them. Amy's eyes rounded as they ground their bodies together in open sensuality and the boy slipped his hand under the girl's thin blouse. After what seemed an interminable exhibition of mutual stimulation, the boy pulled his pliant companion to the ground. They laughed and rolled in the flowers, apparently bombed on liquor or drugs. Amy watched in immobilized horror the serious precoital preparations. Then, rage overcoming revulsion, she raised the window and screamed at them, "Get off my property, you—you animals—before I call the police." Pedestrians looked up at the window curiously, but the couple paid no heed until Amy had yelled several times. Finally, they got up and stood weaving, looking toward the disturbing voice.

"Whatssamatter, man? Don't you dig love?" The boy was trying through bleary eyes to locate Amy.

"She's up there, Kevin," said the girl, pointing. "C'mon, she's a frigid old rich-bitch, mad because she needs a little and can't get it. Let's get back. I've got a sociology class in a half-hour."

"Well, screw you, ma'am," said the boy, holding up a finger just as an agent came running to chase them away.

"Are you okay, Mrs. Canfield?" he called.

"I'm all right, Dexter. Don't bother with them." The last thing she wanted was to prolong the incident.

Amy was weak with impotent fury as she pulled down the window and locked it. This was what she hated about Washington. One of the finest residential neighborhoods was a promenade for arrogant, lascivious juveniles, supposedly intelligent enough to be attending a prestigious institution of higher learning. And that wasn't all. At various times she had seen common drunks, strutting homosexuals and beggars on N Street. Washington was decadent. Her eyes became wet with tears. Why couldn't they go back to North Philadelphia, among their own kind, for good? Damn Newt's career. How could he be so selfish? Couldn't he see what this was doing to her?

She collapsed wearily in a comfortable chair. When she furnished this small sitting room, she had expected it to become her refuge in Washington. To cut out street noise and assure privacy in the bedroom, she had moved partitions to make this small front room and place the master bedroom in the back. So many good ideas, but no happiness. She ran to the bedroom, locked herself in and let the tears flow. There was no doubt, absolutely none. Newton was having an affair with that aggressive woman in the Cabinet. She was undeniably attractive, and Amy had noticed that she turned on

349

all her candlepower when the Vice President was around. Every time Amy was not able to attend an official function, that woman somehow managed to fill in for her. And all these night meetings. Neither the budget nor HEW matters required night meetings before she was appointed.

Amy muffled her sobs in the pillow. There was also that hateful trash printed by Andy Jackerson that Mary Durban had been so eager for her to see. And they recently had been together in San Francisco; she knew that. After a half-hour of uncontrolled sobbing, she found her nerves quieting. Her head was pounding from crying, so she got up and took two aspirins. Sitting on the side of the bed, she thought about Newt's call and a cold fury came over her. There was no doubt that her philandering husband wanted her out of the house and the servants gone for a purpose. She wouldn't put it past him to sleep with that hussy right here in her bed. Her anger mounted. Oh, she would like to come and catch them, but there was no way. Her agents always called the C.P. when she was nearly home, and the C.P. always notified the Vice President that she would be arriving soon.

She jumped when the intercom rang. "Yes?"

"This is Lee, Mrs. C. The Vice President would like to have the whole house swept before his meeting tonight. The men from Technical Security Division are here now. They've finished downstairs. May they come up?"

"Certainly, Lee. I'll be out of the bedroom in a few minutes. Have them begin with the sitting room." That sly husband of hers wanted to be sure no one overheard any of his conversations.

Amy fixed her face, straightened the room and then waited downstairs while the TSD men made an electronic sweep of all the upstairs rooms. Strange. This was generally done about once a week, and to the best of her recollection it had been only three days since last time.

She was telling Betsy that there was no reason for her to change her plan to leave early when an idea struck her with the force of a hammer.

Two hours later, Amy Canfield, calm and composed, left by car for North Philadelphia with two of the three Secret Service agents regularly assigned to her.

Just before six Steve Galdari entered the basement C.P. and received a report of the day's activities from Lee Daniels. The disturbing incident on the front lawn was duly noted. A routine

350

follow-up would be made the next morning in the form of a visit to the dean of Georgetown University. There would be no accusations, just a general description of the pair and a report of the obscene remarks to the Vice President's wife—strictly for the information of the school authorities.

"Mrs. Canfield departed at four-ten P.M. by auto with agents Kevin O'Leary and Bill Rados," said Daniels. "They should be reporting arrival at Greystone in about an hour."

"Okay," said Galdari. "Did TSD make the sweep?"

"Just after two."

Galdari dialed the Vice President's bedroom and got no answer. He then dialed the living room. The phone rang several times before Canfield answered.

"Can't a fellow have time to build himself a drink?" The prospect of seeing Meredith had improved his spirits.

"Sorry, sir. You wanted confirmation on the TSD sweep. It was done early this afternoon. Negative."

"Fine, Steve. Thanks. I'm going to clean up. Will you admit my visitors to the living room when they arrive? I've put some whiskey, ice and mixers out, and a bottle of chilled Chablis for Secretary Lord." Although agents are not permitted to perform personal services for their principals, Canfield had found that when the occasion required it, they made fine substitute hosts because of their natural courtesy.

When the Vice President came downstairs, he found that Josh Devers had arrived early and was fidgeting in the living room. Devers was in black tie, a clear signal that he had other things to do that evening and did not wish to be detained too long.

"Good evening, Mr. Vice President. You're looking well," said Devers, turning from the painting he was examining to shake hands. His words were polite, but his manner always made Canfield feel that he was being patronized.

"Good evening, Counselor." Devers's hand was as soft and dry as facial tissue. "Sorry to bother you on such short notice. Especially when you have a black-tie affair to attend. But I'll get you out of here as soon as I can." He smiled amiably. You can bet your life on that, he thought to himself.

"Thank you. The President had to go to Camp David suddenly, and I was tapped to do his regrets at the Farm Bureau dinner. I don't have to be there until shortly before nine."

Canfield looked at the counselor shrewdly. With an airtight excuse like that, he didn't have to show up for the meeting. He must have something on his mind, some other reason for being here, he thought.

Devers did not leave him wondering long. "I came a little early in the hope that I might have a few minutes in private with you, Newt." There it was again—that annoying trespass.

"Of course, Counselor," Canfield said tepidly. He led the way to the upstairs sitting room, motioned Devers to a chair and seated himself on the chintz-covered love seat.

Even his enemies conceded that Josh Devers knew how to organize what he wanted to say and say it without beating around the bush. But what made him valuable enough to be a counselor to the President of the United States was his ability to combine directness with tact so that he was quickly understood without arousing hostility. Devers admitted to himself that Porter Canfield was a hard case to handle because there already was latent hostility there. Nevertheless, he was ready to give it his best effort.

"Mr. Vice President, the President asked me to alert you to the possibility that there will be an emergency meeting of the National Security Council on Monday," he said. "The President thought it might be useful if you were filled in ahead of time about the situation."

"That's very kind of the President, Counselor. Please proceed." What was the old man up to now? He knew the White House was investigating INAF.

"All right to smoke here?" Devers had fished out his pipe and a venerable tobacco pouch and glanced around the obviously feminine room.

"Of course." Amy would raise hell, but she wasn't around. He'd air the whole place out later. It wouldn't do to let Devers think him henpecked.

The counselor lit up, put the burnt match in his pocket without asking for an ashtray, and continued unhurriedly. "Woodhall and Kalter are with the boss at Camp David. There's a serious situation developing with the Russians about those ships headed for Israel. They're entering the Mediterranean tonight."

Canfield felt his neck relax. Apparently it wasn't about Halevy. Devers was referring to the two ships that had left the United States nine days before and were carrying "convincer" nuclear missiles, launch silo components and sixty American technicians to Haifa to begin construction of several IRBM sites. In spite of an effort at secrecy, the Pentagon had leaked; and the world press had trumpeted the disclosure that President Hurley had yielded to congres-

352

sional and public pressure and was sending intermediate range nuclear weapons to embattled Israel.

Devers breathed his pipe back to life. His eyes met and held the Vice President's. "You know how hard the boss fought against that joint resolution. Even after it passed overwhelmingly, he held out for a while, knowing it did not *compel* him to act." The old man sighed audibly. "But so much of the team was for it, and so much of the media raised hell, and so damned many letters flooded in that he compromised."

Canfield suppressed a cynical smile. Indeed, Hurley had been inundated with proof that the country did not agree with his timidity.

"No one knew he compromised, because he didn't correct the erroneous leak. He didn't even tell the NSC because that seems to leak like a sieve, too." Devers brushed an ash off the chair arm. "You see, Mr. Vice President, there aren't any convincer warheads on those ships. The boss pulled them off. He just sent the site components and the advisors."

Canfield was startled by this revelation. It was deceiving the American people not to correct the faulty news reports—but typical of Hurley's trickiness. "So the President didn't comply after all," he said, his voice carrying overtones of outrage.

"Damn good thing he didn't, sir." Devers's famous tact almost deserted him, but he quickly got control of the icemaker behind his eyes.

"Look, Mr. Vice President, I know you have deep and sincere convictions about this issue, and I admire your courage as well as your candor." The smile was placating. "But I think you'll agree, when you hear what the President has directed me to tell you, that he was right in holding back the warheads." He became very serious. "Two days ago, the Soviet ambassador called on Secretary Woodhall at Foggy Bottom. It was not a pleasant meeting. The ambassador said that the Soviet government considered the entry of American ships carrying nuclear war materials for Israel into the Mediterranean Sea a grave breach of the Tripartite Pact and the SALT agreements. He said that unless the ships were directed to abandon their mission, the Soviet Union would be forced to take such actions as it considered necessary to protect itself and other nations threatened by this warlike act."

Canfield vented his outrage. "Who does that son of a bitch Dradavov think he is?" he said indignantly. "I hope the President told him to mind his own business. What nerve from a country that is arming the Arabs to the teeth."

"On the contrary, sir. The President directed Woodhall to inform the Soviet ambassador that the news reports were in error—that there were no missiles on the ships, only site hardware and advisors, and that he felt sure that this information would allow the withdrawal of the complaint.''

The Vice President clenched his teeth savagely. ''Why,'' he fumed, ''do we have to knuckle under to those arrogant primitives?''

The old man smiled a sad smile. ''Because we want to avoid having the world blown apart, perhaps.''

''Well, in view of what you've told me, what's the crisis? Why the NSC standby?''

The counselor got to his feet stiffly and responded with the ageless tolerance that greater intellects summon to cope with lesser ones. ''Because, Mr. Vice President, there are indications that the mere absence of the missiles themselves may not be enough to satisfy the Russians. In order to demonstrate their strength, they may try to stop the ships anyway.'' He looked at his watch. ''Good Lord, it's nearly ten of eight. I apologize for keeping you from your meeting.''

Porter Canfield was seething inside, frustrated at his helplessness to do anything about his President's weakness. ''That's all right, Counselor. I'm sure they didn't mind waiting. I appreciate your briefing me.'' He started to precede Devers down the stairs, but hesitated on the top step. ''Counselor, I know how busy you are at this time. I don't think I should detain you on this budgetary matter. Suppose you go along to the dinner, and I will send you a summary of the meeting later in the week.''

After a few routine protestations, Devers made his escape with alacrity, pausing only for a word of greeting to the secretary of HEW and the budget director. Even in that instant, his eyes moved from Meredith to Canfield in a way that reminded the Vice President that here was the source of his trouble with Andy Jackerson.

Meredith Lord had a tall V.O. and water waiting for him when he returned from seeing Devers to the door. ''Charlie and I have talked over our dispute for fifteen minutes,'' she said with a bewitching smile. ''We are hopelessly deadlocked, and we thought you might need this.''

Canfield took the drink from her, feeling the familiar surge as their fingers touched. She was as radiant as ever, dressed in hip-hugging forest-green slacks and a pale-yellow chiffon blouse.

For the first time since the beginning of that long, unpleasant day, Canfield felt the pressure begin to ease. How lucky he was to have this exceptional woman, superior in mind and body, to ease his torment. He knew that she would share his terrible burden, willingly, and best of all, had the fiber and capacity to help him solve the problem.

"Let's sit down and see what can be done about this hopeless deadlock," he said. "Suppose you lead off, Charlie."

With the clipped, sure delivery of a man who measures life in mathematical absolutes, Voren laid out the HEW budget and its projections based on existing programs. The figures were astronomical, but they did not shock the Vice President for two reasons. First, he was used to big spending, and second, he was thinking mostly about what he was going to do with Meredith Lord as soon as he could decently send the budget man away.

Charlie moved into high gear when he reached his favorite subject, "imponderables." Imponderables referred to new ideas for spending the federal tax dollar—ideas so new that there was no experience on which to base extrapolation of the eventual costs. Federally built, operated and funded THC was this kind of new idea.

Two hours dragged by, and the conflict seemed no closer to being resolved than when they had started. Finally Canfield said, "Meredith has the votes on both sides of the aisle to force the bill out of committee and pass it in the House and in the Senate. If she goes ahead and does that with the bill in its present form, Charlie will urge the President to veto it; and I think he will take that advice. There don't seem to be enough votes to override, so that will end the bill—but it will also damage party unity. Now listen, you two. You're both sincere and conscientious, but we've been stalemated with this too long—there have to be reasonable compromises. Meredith, I want you to put a ten-year limit on disaster coverage. The private sector will just have to pick up the slack. Also, I want the number of institutions per half million of population reduced by twenty percent, and I want a tighter schedule of physician's allowances along with better auditing procedures. And I'd like to see mandatory individual contributions beginning at incomes of twenty thousand and increasing proportionately with each five thousand above that."

"But, Mr. Vice President—" Meredith was about to contest such deep cuts in her original concept of an integrated and all-inclusive federal health machine.

"No buts, please, Madam Secretary. Wait until you hear what I'm going to ask Charlie to concede.

"Charlie, using the changes I've outlined, your people should be able to make a ball-park extrapolation and arrive at the three-year

355

costs of such a program." The Vice President ignored the protesting hand of the man the agencies and departments called "old skinflint." "Wait, now, Charlie. This idea is here. It has arrived. The votes are there. Sooner or later, you're going to have to cope with it. It's better to do so on pragmatic terms. I'm going to ask Meredith to pledge that she will not try to increase the benefits for a three-year trial period. That will give you time to get your feet under you."

"We can't afford this bill, Mr. Vice President. We'll have a taxpayers' rebellion on our hands." said Voren emphatically.

Canfield smiled patiently. "That same remark was made by fiscal advisors in the past when the Social Security system first began, when Medicare was added and when the initial federal eduation and welfare bills were enacted. Charlie, be reasonable."

Voren thought for several minutes. "Okay. If the secretary will go along, I'll make the effort," he said gloomily. "But personally, I think the bill is a bad idea."

Responding to the Vice President's look, Meredith nodded reluctantly. "I may be tarred and feathered back at the department, but I want to be a team player. I'll accept the cutbacks."

"Good. Then let's get your respective people to firm up the understanding and draft the amendments necessary. I'll talk to the President as soon as we're sure that we're in detailed agreement," said Canfield happily. "Now, let's have a drink to celebrate our accord. Meredith, I have some fine Chablis that I think you'll enjoy." He began to open the chilled wine.

"If it's all right with you, sir, I'll pass," said Voren, looking at his watch. "I promised Margery that I'd pick her up after her bridge game, and it's getting to be about that time."

"Of course, Charlie. You're excused." Then, turning to Meredith, he said in mock severity, "But you aren't, young lady. I have a couple of political matters to take up with you."

Meredith smiled insouciantly. "I hope the price won't be as high as that to my THC."

Canfield closed the door behind Voren, making sure that the night bolt was shot. As he reentered the living room, Meredith was standing with her back to him looking intently at a nude female figure—a Malaysian wood carving he had brought back from his trip. He came up behind her and put his hands on her warm shoulders.

"It's beautiful, Newt," she said, running her fingers over the polished wood.

"Not nearly as beautiful as you." As she turned, he took her in his arms and kissed her. There was no awkwardness, no uncertainty. Passion, released instantly, coursed down the familiar path, but after a minute Meredith said, "Newt, we can't. Not here. It's too dangerous."

He kissed her again, and she pressed against him feverishly, then pulled away. "Don't," she said with a nervous laugh. "You're making me all wet down there."

"Let's go up," he said hoarsely, taking her by the hand and pulling her toward the stairs.

"We can't, not here. What if the agents come in?"

"They won't. It's perfectly safe. Come on." The urgency in his voice was as old as human desire.

Offering only token resistance, she allowed herself to be taken to the bedroom. He sat down on the bed and patted the spot beside him. Hesitantly, looking more like a shy virgin than the very powerful woman she was, she perched primly beside him.

Laughing at her timidity, he pulled her down and began to unfasten the buttons of her blouse. "Relax, Meredith. You weren't nearly so reluctant in San Francisco."

"Newt, I feel funny about it—in this bed. It's like a gratuitous insult to your wife." She put her hand over his, but made no effort to prevent the unbuttoning or the release of her bra.

He laughed harshly. "Forget it," he said, the words sticking oddly because his mouth was dry with passion. "Amy's in her beloved Philadelphia—maybe with someone else. She goes there often enough. Besides, she's too self-centered to notice what I'm doing."

He slipped off her slacks and began to explore her body.

"You are ready, aren't you," he said tenderly as her breath began to come in quick, shallow pants.

"Hurry, Newt." In the two words pulsed an agony of unreleased sexuality.

He got up and quickly undressed. He looked down at the soft curves of her superb suntanned body, framed by the bed and outlined by the white sheet. It struck him at this incongruous moment that his love for this woman went way beyond physical attraction. He would trust her with his life; indeed, he was going to do just that. In the back of his mind, worry stirred at the thought of the last two days' events.

"Newt, please." Her eyes were compelling; he felt lust return and shut the worry out of his mind.

In the rhythmic twisting and pulsing of the next fifteen minutes, he was conscious only of disjointed impressions: the little animal cries from Meredith; the carefully folded brocade bedspread on the side; the slight creaking of the bed as they reached a crescendo. Then his own flurry of endearments and groan of release during the rocketing to a delicious peak before plunging ecstatically into awareness of every vibrating nerve.

When she came out of the bathroom, the oversize towel draped loosely around her youthful body, he was still supine on the bed. His eyes were closed, and, although his body was relaxed, there was a slight frown on his handsome face. She leaned over and kissed him impulsively.

"Cover yourself, you shameless man," she said, laughing. She felt loving and possessive and very relaxed. He smiled and drew her down beside him.

"Here," he said, propping a pillow up for her to lean against and sliding out of the other side of the bed. "Don't go away. I'll be right back."

Meredith desperately wanted a cigarette, but somehow could not bring herself to smoke in Amy's bedroom. She giggled aloud. That was ridiculous. The supreme sin had already been committed. Looking around, she was surprised at the room's impersonality. There were no photographs, no personal mementos, no felt presence either of Amy or Porter Canfield. The decor was aloof— that was the only word that really described the museumlike atmosphere. You could have picked the room up and put it in the middle of the Smithsonian and the sign "Porter Canfield slept here."

Canfield returned and climbed in beside her. He sat upright, his back against the headboard. She snuggled against him, and for several minutes they were content to say nothing.

Finally, she broke the silence: "I love you."

"And I love you."

"Remember when I said we shouldn't worry about where this is going—just let it happen and enjoy it?"

"I remember."

"Well, I'm not sure I can handle it that way." She hesitated, trying to express her feelings accurately. "Oh, I don't mean I'm going to present you with an all-or-nothing-at-all choice. I'm mature enough to recognize the impossibility of that for people in our business—especially for you with the election coming next year." She looked at him plaintively. "I guess I don't know exactly what I mean except that I need to be with you more. It's been a month since San Francisco"—her voice trailed away uncertainly— "and that's a long time."

"It is a long time. We have to figure out some way to be together more. Believe me, Meredith, I can't handle this casually either. I'm in love with you, completely in love with you—but—'' He looked off into space and frowned.

''But what, darling?''

He turned back to her, his face grave. ''We have a very serious problem—or, rather, I have a very serious problem that affects our whole future. There may not be any campaign, or, for that matter, any vice-presidency. I may be forced out of office.''

''Newt, what are you saying? Surely you can't be serious!''

''I'm very serious. I've been set up by our friend, Yoram Halevy, to make it look as though I'm involved in Mark O'Mara's murder.''

''My God, Newt. That's ridiculous! Mark was one of your staunchest supporters. It doesn't make sense.''

''No, it makes no sense at all on its face, but I was tricked into making statements to Halevy—during a conversation that he recorded without my knowing it in my own office—and the statements can be construed to indicate that I agreed that O'Mara should be killed. If Halevy is accused of the murder, he will try to implicate me, and he has a very good chance of doing that with the damned tape available.''

''Halevy accused of murder? I don't understand it at all.''

He took her face gently in both hands and kissed her tenderly. ''Let me explain the whole horrible, complicated mess to you, because I need your help. There's no one else I can trust with my life.''

He told her how, on the subject of the media sellout, he had unwittingly seemed to agree with Halevy that the traitors to the cause should be restrained and, if necessary, prevented by whatever means possible from taking actions so destructive to the security of Israel. Then he somberly related how Halevy had casually reported to him that he murdered O'Mara, as though he had done it with Canfield's approval and at his implicit direction.

''But Newt, who would believe it? The tape doesn't prove that you were involved in anything illegal.''

''Lots of people would believe anything, especially if the President believed it; and Hurley would let them know that he did. But wait. You haven't heard the most fantastic part of this ghastly story.''

Holding himself in tight control, he went on to tell her of Izadi's duplicity and the defection of Sirana Amiri because of her infatuation with Zack Miller.

''Zack knows nothing of the tape or of my discussions with Halevy. He insists that we turn Halevy in to the FBI before he kills others. I suggested that we simply tell Halevy he was duped and there will be no reason for him to kill again. Zack won't go for it. Says it's rationalizing—says that our duty is to turn the O'Mara killer over to the police.'' He swung his legs over the side of the bed and slumped dejectedly. "If the FBI comes in, my whole life is over, and there's a very good chance of my being convicted as a coconspirator in a homicide on the basis of Halevy's testimony and that damned tape.''

"Oh, Newt.'' In the two words she revealed all her compassion and vicarious suffering.

She touched his arm, and after a moment, he turned around to meet her eyes. His face was slack with hopelessness. With an obvious effort, he tried to pull himself together. The agony he was causing her made it difficult for him to regain control. He took a deep breath and smiled weakly. He seemed so tortured that she had to fight down her own emotions.

"Zack is meeting me at nine tomorrow,'' he said, finally getting hold of himself. "He thinks I have agreed to call the FBI but am devising the best way to inform the President. I'm going to try once more to talk him out of his crazy idea of informing, but I have real doubts that there's any chance. He's a zealot about it.''

"But if he understood the magnitude of your problem, wouldn't he be more cooperative?''

"I don't think so. It's a big moral problem for him even to contemplate silence. And anyhow, since the odds of changing his mind are slim, I can't afford to take the chance of telling him. I've got to talk him out of informing or—or in some way keep him quiet until I can figure a way out,'' he finished lamely.

"What are you going to do about Yoram? Suppose he strikes again? He doesn't know he's being used by this Izali?''

"Izadi,'' he corrected. "No, that's a real danger. Somehow I must get word to Yoram that Izadi has deceived him into going after the wrong people. But even if I can devise a way to get a message to him, that doesn't solve the problem with Zack.''

She frowned, utterly perplexed by the problem's apparent insolubility.

He pulled her against him and held her very close. "I guess there's no way out, honey.''

Meredith touched his face lovingly and was startled to find a tear on his cheek. She couldn't restrain her own tears then and wept convulsively. "I'm to blame. I pushed Yoram and INAF on you.'' Each word tumbled out in between sobs.

He let her cry for a few minutes, totally detaching himself from his environment until he became calm again. Finally, her sobbing subsided, and she said with surprising vehemence, "We can't let Zack destroy you for his damned principles! He *has* to listen!"

"Meredith, I have an idea. I hate to involve you, but—"

"Newt, I am involved. I love you."

"I know you do, and it's because keeping Zack quiet is the only way to keep us together that I'm going to ask you to do this for me."

"Anything. Ask anything," she said passionately.

"You're everything any man could want in a woman, Meredith," he said tenderly, with love in his eyes. The feeling that flowed between them was a tangible force—an island of happiness in the center of this ominous sea.

"Here is our only chance," he said, using the plural pronoun without premeditation. "You're going to New York tomorrow about health matters. I'll be with Zack, keeping him under control. I think I can do that for a day or so, at least. Well, you know Yoram and INAF are supporting your health programs. You can get Yoram to visit you at your suite, ostensibly about THC, and then you can give him a sealed, written message from me."

"Why a written message? That's dangerous. Then he'll have absolute proof to blackmail you with."

"I'm going to ask him to be prepared to abduct Zack if I can't handle him. I don't want anyone to know you're involved, dear. Most important, I don't want Halevy to be aware that you know he's a murderer. That's too dangerous for you."

She looked at him, her heart in her eyes.

"You should check with me by phone tomorrow. After you see Halevy. If I can't dissuade Zack, I'll tell you that Charlie Voren is being a problem about the THC budget. You pass that same message to Yoram for me. He won't know that you know it's a signal for him to grab Zack until we can talk some sense into him. Of course, if I can stop Zack, the message will be that the budget looks okay."

Little lines of worry creased her forehead. "But Newt, he could blackmail you with that letter," she repeated anxiously.

He kissed her nose "Don't worry about that. He's got his own tail to protect. And besides, he already has the tape. You see, darling, I'm already a little pregnant—which I hope you're not."

Meredith forced herself to smile. "Okay, boss. I'll follow orders. But now we'd better get dressed and go downstairs. I'm powerful nervous in this bed without any clothes on."

They dressed quickly and put the room in order. No sooner had they gone downstairs than Steve Galdari called on the intercom.

"Sorry to bother you, sir, but Mrs. Canfield called from Greystone. I told her you had left strict instructions not to be disturbed until the meeting was over. She said it wasn't necessary for you to call back, since she was leaving for dinner, but to tell you that the polo match has been canceled and she may be returning tomorrow.''

"Thank you, Steve." The fact that he had forgotten to leave orders not to be disturbed proved that Galdari was thinking. Thank heaven he had the brains to exercise his own initiative when the occasion demanded. And the tact.

He poured Meredith a glass of Chablis and got himself a cold beer. Then he sat down at the living room secretary and wrote a letter to Halevy. "I'm not going to tell you what's in this," he said, sealing it. "I want you to be able to tell Yoram you don't know in case he asks. Just give this to him and relay to me any verbal messages he may have. Let him know where and how to reach you Saturday and Sunday so that you can pass any communications between us that the developing situation may require. They will be in a simple code I've laid out in here." He tapped the envelope and smiled slightly. "You won't have to work too hard to decipher them, knowing what you already do."

Meredith took the letter and put it in her purse. "I feel like I'm carrying a stick of dynamite. Are you absolutely sure you want to do this in writing? I could just tell him."

He shook his head. "No. Yoram's unpredictable. He's not worried about me because of the tape, but he might get to thinking about not having any leverage to keep you quiet. Do it my way."

She reluctantly agreed and they reviewed strategy. Then he took her in his arms and held her very gently and protectively in a sad and tender parting.

For fifteen minutes after she had gone, he sat staring vacantly at the wall. He had made his play, and the wheel would be spinning until the actions of Miller and Halevy determined where the bouncing ball would come to rest. If he won, the game would go on; if he lost, Porter Newton Canfield's career was over.

Shaking himself out of his stupor, he felt excitement stirring within him. Everything worthwhile in life was a magnificent gamble. He drank the rest of his beer, jumped up and began pacing around the room. He would win. He would beat them all—Hurley, Devers and that devil, Dradavov. A manic sense of power ruled him.

Then just as suddenly he calmed down. He buzzed the C.P. and, finding out that the midnighters would be sending out for sandwiches, asked them to pick up a cheeseburger for him. He was hungry as hell.

Going over the bedclothes and the bathroom with a fine-tooth comb made him feel very guilty. He convinced himself only with the greatest effort that crawling around the carpet looking for evidence of misconduct was not demeaning to vice-presidential dignity.

Back downstairs, he wolfed his sandwich and drank another beer. Then, leaving word for the agents to call him at seven-thirty, he turned in and fell into an exhausted sleep.

17

EXCEPT FOR two Secret Service agents on duty outside the Vice President's suite of offices, the second-floor hallways of the Executive Office Building were deserted on this slow late-summer Saturday.

Inside the reception area, the lone secretary handling the phones was talking to the staff duty officer, who had just arrived. "Yes, he's been in since eight-thirty. He's with Dr. Miller and asked not to be disturbed."

"Did he ask for me?" The duty officer was worried about being a half-hour late.

"No, but he did say that if anyone brought the classified material, to send it back. He wants it held over until Monday."

The staffer looked relieved. "Okay, Muriel. I'll be in my office if you need me." The tapping of his heels on the marble floor echoed cavernously up the hallway.

Inside Canfield's private office, there was an uncomfortable silence. Zack Miller's eyes were fixed on the bright light of the Geochron time map over and behind the Vice President's head. The almost imperceptible crawling of the United States across the daylight zone reminded him that time waits for no man, not even an indecisive Vice President. He looked at Canfield, making little effort to mask his irritation.

"We went through all this yesterday," he said sharply. "Whether you agree or not, I consider myself morally obligated to bring Yoram Halevy's crime to the attention of the authorities—and promptly. There is no telling when he may select another victim.

But whether he does or not, he must answer for the death of Mark O'Mara.'' Miller's manner became less harsh. ''Newt, Newt. Yesterday you agreed that it had to be done. When you asked me to delay, it was to give you time to devise a way to tell Hurley. Remember? You said I'd convinced you that there was no other way.''

Canfield's eyes were blue ice. He looked every inch the alienated aristocrat. ''May I remind you that I did not create this monstrous situation that is about to consume me?'' he said coldly. ''Yesterday you came in here and said, and I quote, 'I've gotten you involved in a murder.' And you also wondered why you had let me become identified as a Halevy supporter.'' He cocked his head to one side and examined Miller clinically. ''Really, Zack, aren't you being a little brutal under the circumstances? You led me to this gallows. Can't I even have time for a cigarette before you put the noose around my neck and spring the trapdoor?''

Pain flashed in Zack Miller's eyes. ''I'm disappointed in you, Newt,'' he said sorrowfully. ''Is your career more important than people's lives?''

Canfield sighed heavily. Zack's ignorance of the tape deprived him of his best argument, but he could not afford to play that chip. The fewer people who knew about the tape, the safer he was. Well, the answer was delay—to stall Miller until he could get him out of circulation. He put on a hurt expression. ''No, it's not; and you know me better than that. I honestly disagree with you. I think acting precipitously, in view of the communist threat, is more dangerous than thinking everything out carefully first. You know this will set Israel back ten years, and Dradavov will make a major propaganda coup out of it if it isn't handled properly.''

''That's unfortunate, but I think you're exaggerating the overall effect.'' Zack was firm.

''I am not exaggerating! The Arabs and the Russians will not accept an Iranian as the villain. They will say it was an Israeli plot, and Israel will eventually lose the capacity to defend herself and go down the tube. That would make America vulnerable.''

''You sound like you're still arguing for a cover-up—a cover-up in the interest of national security,'' Zack said acidulously. ''Well, that was tried once before in the White House, and it didn't work very well.''

Canfield sighed again. He leaned back in the big chair and closed his eyes. For a few moments the silence was deafening. Finally, he said quietly, ''Zack, last night I was made aware of certain information held only by President Hurley, his top national security advisor, Josh Devers and the secretary of state. That information is highly relevant to our discussion. I want to get clearance to pass it on to you. Let's recess until I get permission to brief you. It shouldn't take long."

"How long?" Miller was plainly suspicious that this was another delaying tactic, but the lure of sharing a national secret was formidable.

"As soon as I can reach Josh Devers at Camp David," promised Canfield, "I'll call you. I presume you'll be in your office?"

"I'll be there waiting," Miller said in a manner that left no doubt that the waiting would not be patient.

No sooner had the door closed behind him than Canfield picked up his private line. He knew Zack would find a reason to linger at the reception desk long enough to see whether the light went on, indicating that the Vice President's private line was in use.

Canfield laid the receiver on his desk. The dial tone sounded faintly for a while, then clicked off. He had no intention of calling Devers or anyone else at Camp David. Later that day he would tell Zack what he knew—without permission. But it probably would do no good. It would be strictly a delaying tactic.

At one o'clock he called Miller and told him he was having trouble reaching Devers, but expected a call back by two. Meanwhile he was going to the White House Mess for a sandwich. He would take the call there if it came. Would Zack care to join him? Zack said he was not interested in lunch. He would wait in his office and he hoped it wouldn't be much longer.

Canfield buzzed the secretary and learned that there had been no calls of importance. On his way to the Mess, Trent Gilbert told him that Mrs. Canfield was at the residence, having returned from Philadelphia at ten-thirty.

By one-fifty Canfield was back in the office. At two he took his phone off the hook again; and at two-ten he summoned Zack Miller back.

"Zack, I want your solemn oath that what I am now going to tell you will never be repeated to anyone, regardless of what security clearances he might have."

"Of course I make that promise." Miller regarded him curiously. It was amazing, he thought, that one day could so alter the relationship between two people. Canfield was no longer his friend. They were antagonists wholly occupied in protecting their separate interests. For one of the few times in his life, his was an unselfish interest.

"I was able to get permission to fill you in on the big picture," said Canfield ponderously.

God, what an inopportune time for posturing, thought Zack.

Canfield pursed his lips importantly. "Dradavov is threatening to intercept the IRBM ships in the Mediterranean if we try to make delivery to Israel. I think he's bluffing, but Hurley is thoroughly frightened."

Zack was shocked. Brinkmanship had never been one of his favorite pastimes. It was fine to push hard, but always it was best to leave some escape device short of the nuclear trigger.

"That's not all," continued Canfield indignantly. "That pantywaist Hurley didn't put the warheads on the ships as he was supposed to have done! He tricked the Congress and the media."

Thank heaven, thought Zack, that the President turned out to have more common sense than all the rest of us put together.

"As usual, Hurley misread the Russian mentality," Canfield went on contemptuously. "The Russians have let it be known that the absence of the missiles themselves doesn't really alter the situation because the whole world thinks they are on the ships. Therefore, in order not to lose face, the Soviets may have to stop the ships anyhow."

For the second time in as many minutes Zack's heart thumped with fright. "What's the President going to do?" he asked tensely.

"That's what they're trying to decide up at Camp David. There's some hint that Dradavov is going to call him on the hot line soon and make the demand an ultimatum. The press up there is as thick as flies in a horse barn. They don't know exactly what's happening, but they suspect it's something very big internationally." The Vice President got up, walked around his desk and put his hand on Miller's shoulder. "Now you understand my concern, Zack. Dradavov's only bluffing at this point, but if the Halevy thing came out now, he wouldn't hesitate to carry out his threat, blaming Israel for criminal deception of the American people. That's why we have to wait." Canfield squeezed Miller's shoulder, feigning affection. "I knew you'd understand if I could get the facts to you," he added, hoping for a long shot.

"That's not the way I read it, Newt. You and I know that the United States may be on the verge of confronting the Soviet Union on a false issue. The President must be informed that all the hysteria which led to the decision to send provocative and major nuclear weapons to Israel resulted from the deceit of a maniacal Iranian who wants to see the United States at war with the Soviet Union. Given that information, I would expect President Hurley to withdraw the ships and abort delivery, at least until real evidence of Soviet aggression can be provided." Miller rose to his feet to get rid of the hand on his shoulder. "We should go to Camp David right now and tell the President," he said firmly.

The Vice President's face swiftly went through several premeditated changes of expression. First there was incredulity, then disappointment, then patient determination to strike the scales from Zack's eyes.

"Zack, my good friend, we can't do that. If I appear suddenly on the Hurley doorstep at Camp David in the middle of a suspected foreign crisis, those Pulitzer-worshiping gossips will precipitate a national panic. Rumors will fly. They'll even have us under attack from outer space." Canfield began to sweat. "Look, I give in to your insistence that we expose Halevy. But don't send me to Camp David to do it. The harm will be irreparable. I promise you that I will see the President in his office the very first thing Monday morning and tell him all about the whole thing."

"But if they try to stop the ships—"

"That won't happen until Monday. The president will call an emergency NSC meeting and a congressional leadership meeting before he decides what to do. Devers has assured me of that." There was real agony on Canfield's face. "Please, Zack. Listen to me this one time," he begged.

"Let me think a minute," said Miller hesitatingly.

There was a knock at the door, and at Canfield's call to enter, Trent Gilbert put his head in. "Sorry, sir. The receptionist has gone home. Secretary Lord is trying to reach you through Signal. Shall I tell them to put her through?"

"Yes, put her through."

The agent withdrew, and a few moments later, one of the Signal phones rang.

"Excuse me a minute, Zack. Hello, Meredith. Where are you? . . . Great. I assume you're charming all those New York liberals with your expensive ideas on THC? . . . Well, don't count your chickens too early. I'm having some trouble with Charlie Voren about your budget. You're going to have to apply heavy pressure wherever you can. There's not much time left, and I really can't get him to give on the major points. The only way to neutralize him is with maximum outside pressure, understand? . . . Okay, good luck with your lobbying up there. See you next week. . . . Wait a minute. Zack says hi. Oh, we work crazy hours. We're like HEW. . . . Right, Madam Secretary . . . Good luck . . . Bye."

He looked intently at the man whose freedom he had just ordered ended. "Well, how about it, Zack? Will you wait until Monday on

369

my absolute pledge that I will not ask any further delay?''

The advisor's assent was unenthusiastic. "In spite of my instincts, which say no, I'm going to go along because of our long friendship and because I'm partly responsible for the trouble. But I'm warning you now. I intend to hold you to Monday morning.''

"Great! You'll never know how much I appreciate your cooperation, Zack. Now, how about a drink? I think we've earned some transitory happiness, at least.''

"Thanks, but I've got to run along. I've got some stops to make on the way home, and I want to get some rest before this evening if I can. I promised Sirana I'd take her out to dinner and a midnight show afterward. The poor kid is worried sick over this thing. She needs some diversion, and I could sure use some myself.'' He got up awkwardly looking more like the arthritic Devers than the athletic Miller. "You could use some relaxation, too, Newt. Hope you have a pleasant evening.'' Then, saddened by the enormity and finality of the schism, he walked slowly out of the office.

There was a question in Canfield's mind. With the pressure that Zack's conscience had him under, there was no guarantee that he wouldn't crack and go to the police on his own. The girl, Sirana, could have a catalytic effect on his determination to go through with the exposure of Yoram Halevy.

Canfield had the Signal operator get Secretary Lord at her Waldorf Towers suite in New York.

"Mr. Vice President, I'm glad you called.'' Meredith's tone was guarded, but she was eager to talk to him. "I was just getting ready for a magazine interview, and I wanted to be sure I was clear about Charlie Voren's position, because my assistant is standing by for instructions. I assume that Charlie has left your office by now?''

"Yes, he's gone.'' Canfield was pleased that she was handling the conversation so discreetly. For some time he had suspected that Hurley had his lines tapped.

"I was sorry to hear that you couldn't change his mind about THC,'' Meredith said.

"Well, he's agreed to wait until Monday before making the cuts, but his mind seems to be made up.''

"That's too bad. I guess that forces us to make a fight of it from outside.''

"We have to. The program is essential. Meredith?'' He was thinking carefully about how to put it.

"Yes?''

"I think you should have your assistant try once more over the weekend. Have him call on Charlie at his home. He's been there before, so he's familiar with the location. Charlie won't be there tonight, though. He'll be out with his wife until after midnight."

"I understand. What time is he going to be leaving his house?"

"He'll probably be gone by nine, so your assistant should be told that if he gets there after nine, no one will be home."

"I'll see that he's instructed properly," said Meredith. "He's waiting for me to call, so I'd better get that done before my interviewer comes."

"Good. And suggest to him that he include Mrs. Voren in the discussion. She's very strong-willed and could have a lot of weight in the matter."

"I understand. I'll talk to you tomorrow and let you know how things are going up here. Tonight I tape the 'Nancy Davids Show' at seven; and tomorrow I'm the mystery guest on 'The Most Overlooked Issue of the Week.'"

"Good luck, Meredith. I'm going to watch your show tomorrow. Incidentally, how did your assistant take the news that his friend had knowingly passed him bad information?"

She laughed lightly. "He didn't share his reaction with me. Too embarrassed, I guess. But there's no question that it changed his plans. He excused himself and immediately went to make a private phone call."

"At least we saved him from making another mistake."

"Right. Well, I'll talk to you later. Goodbye."

"Take care. Signal can reach me if I'm needed. Goodbye, Meredith."

Canfield hung up and thought about what this phone call would achieve. He would breathe easier when Professor Miller was under close supervision.

To the northwest, an occasional flicker of distant lightning outlined the advancing squall line but did not relieve the darkness of the alley behind C Street. The scattered clouds fleeing before the coming storm hid the half moon and most of the stars. Due to the expert aim of the migratory street urchins of the Capitol Hill area, no man-made illumination provided even a single island of light in the rank-smelling alley's stygian blackness.

Now and then the headlights of a garage-bound car made instant statues of marauding cats busy in toppled garbage cans or seeking a night of casual feline romance. At 11:00 P.M. on an oppressively humid August night, C Street was not much safer than the outskirts of Bastogne in December 1944.

The men moved with the sure and graceful efficiency of the commandos they once had been. In spite of the heat, they wore dark-colored trousers and long-sleeved shirts. Their faces, hands and the backs of their necks had been smeared with lampblack, and they wore black crepe-soled shoes. They came up the alley knowing exactly where they were going, having reconnoitered it by car fifteen minutes before, and then waited in a concealed place until their eyes were well adjusted to the darkness.

The house to the left of the one that was their objective was dark, so they vaulted the low fence on that side and worked their way to the basement door under the back steps, being careful to avoid the patches of light coming from the occupied house on the other side. Three minutes' efficient use of a good glass-cutter and they were in the basement. In five more minutes they were entering the first floor of Dr. Isaac Miller's residence. Using the dim pencil flashlight that they had done without until actually in the house, they quickly went over all three floors upstairs, disturbing nothing. Returning to the first floor, they stationed themselves to await the return of the lawful occupants. One stood at the front living room window and the other one at the window in the dining room, which commanded a view of the alley.

Outside, the lightning flashed more brightly, and the first rumbles of thunder were heard. In the gusts of the strengthening breeze, the old house creaked slightly. The smaller of the two men put an unlighted cigar in his mouth and chewed on it thoughtfully.

By twelve-forty the storm had reached its apex. Rain fell in sheets, and the electrical display was spectacular. Each crack of thunder stepped on the heels of its predecessor.

Suddenly, the big man at the dining room window drew back further into the shadows and hissed a warning. An automobile had stopped in the alley. The driver jumped out hastily and opened the door to the flimsy single-car garage. Then, already soaked, he ran back to the small Datsun and drove it under cover. Through the closed windows, the slamming of car doors and the laughter of a man and a woman penetrated faintly.

Quickly, the smaller man came to the dining room, leaded sap in hand. They calmly hid behind a corner of a large breakfront so that they would be concealed from anyone walking from the kitchen to the dining room. The big man drew a Mauser automatic and eased off the safety.

"Remember to be sure there's no noise; we've got to knock them out together," he said. "And don't hit hard enough to cause a lot of bleeding. You do the talking. He might get desperate and try something stupid if he recognized my voice."

"I got it," replied his companion, who preferred action to talking.

Now the laughing of the man and woman outside could be heard distinctly. Moments later there were running steps on the back porch and the sound of a key in the lock. The intruders pressed back in the corner behind the deep breakfront. Then the kitchen door was flung open, and the couple dashed in out of the rain.

"Zack, your weather is scary," the woman said, taking the kitchen towel he handed her and trying to dry her hair.

He switched on the light and came back to her. "Lots of noise, but it doesn't do much damage," he said, taking her in his arms and breathing in the freshness of her damp hair. "I love you, Sirana. You're my Persian goddess. In my studies of history, I used to favor Alexander, but lately I find myself appreciating Cyrus because the Iranians are such a beautiful people."

She kissed him again. "Oh, darling. I'm so happy—so much in love with you." She sighed. "It will be wonderful when all this trouble is over."

"Don't worry. It will be in a day or so. Now let's go up and get out of these wet clothes. I'll bring a couple of nice cold beers, and we'll drink them in bed. That spicy food really made me thirsty."

He took two bottles of beer from the refrigerator while she got glasses from the cabinet. Then he switched off the kitchen light, and they made their way through the dining room in the dim light cast by the living room lamp he had left burning.

They were almost past the corner of the dining room they had to cross when the shock of a strange voice stopped them in their tracks.

"Don't move. I have a gun. Don't turn around, either of you, or you will be shot to death instantly." The delivery was flat, inflectionless. "That's fine. Now, put the beer and the glasses on the floor in front of you—nice and easy. Don't turn around," the voice snapped, as Zack twisted just a little in straightening up. "Put your hands up high and take two steps backward." The voice was deadly. "Easy now."

Sirana felt that she was going to faint, but somehow did as directed. Zack weighed the chances of resistance and quickly decided it would be futile. This burglar was not kidding. It was best to give him what he wanted and let him escape.

"Good," said the man pleasantly. "Now, keep those hands up high. I'm going to check you for weapons."

The captives could hear muffled movements behind them, but remained perfectly still, their hands stretched toward the ceiling.

Then their world exploded in a bright flash of light when the blunt, leaded instruments struck their heads and sent them into merciful oblivion.

"Excellent," said the large man, as each assailant eased his victim's unconscious body to the floor. "Perfect synchronization and no blood on the carpet in case someone comes in to clean up Monday. Give me a hand, and we'll get them upstairs."

They carried their inert victims one at a time to the third floor. When Zack moaned quietly on the way, he was hit sharply again to insure that he would not regain consciousness while they were getting Sirana.

Working methodically and without haste, they rolled the pair over so that they were face-down on the hardwood floor. The big man placed towels he had brought from the second-floor bathroom under both heads. "Get the bags ready, Sammy," he said to the other man.

Sammy pulled up his shirt and removed two large green lawn bags that were stuck down into his trousers. Carefully, he unfolded them and placed them on the floor.

The big man pulled up his left pant leg and ripped several pieces of adhesive tape from his calf. He put the tape on the floor and kneeled over Zack as though to administer artificial respiration. Sammy directed the pencil flashlight's dim beam at the wicked-looking six-inch needle end of the old-fashioned ice pick that the big man held. Feeling with his left hand along the back of Zack's neck until he located the base of the skull, he placed the sharp point of the pick above the top cervical vertebra and, with a strong thrust, drove the full length of the needle upward under the cerebellum and into the medulla oblongata. Miller's body convulsed as the cardiac, vasoconstrictor and respiratory functions collapsed simultaneously. Calmly, Yoram Halevy withdrew the murder weapon and wiped it on the towel under his victim's head. "Sorry, Zack. Your principles were too high," he said. The venous blood welling slowly in the small puncture hole was concealed by Zack Miller's thick black hair.

The girl stirred slightly, and Sammy reached for his sap, looking at Halevy for consent to hit her again. Halevy watched her for a few moments. Her breathing became regular again, although it was very shallow. Halevy shook his head no. He straddled her in the same way he had done Zack. Through the thin summer dress he could feel the heat of her body against his inner thighs, and desire suddenly coursed through him. What a waste, he thought. He was going to kill this beautiful woman for no reason other than that circumstances had caused her to know his secret. He saw Sammy look at him curiously. Sammy was fully capable of rape under these circumstances, because Sammy could never in his warped little life have a woman like this one.

Halevy's grip tighened on the ice pick. Almost ritualistically, he repeated the preparation, finally driving the needle into the midbrain. He had a fleeting feeling of revulsion as the girl twitched twice and died.

Wearily, he stood up and walked over to the large steamer trunk, which, Zack had bragged, could hold all his worldly possessions. Now it would be his coffin for a while. Three days would be enough, because by then Yoram Halevy would be far away.

They finally succeeded in sliding the cadavers into the lawn bags and taping the bags shut. Before too long someone would discover that the contents of the trunk held something more gruesome than Zack Miller's old clothes, but the airtight plastic bags would contain the odor of death for at least a week before the gases of decomposition exploded them. They had been very careful to exhaust all the air possible when they secured them.

The thunder had died down to an occasional grumble and the torrent to a steady drizzle when the assassins moved quietly out of the alley to their car and began the long drive back to New York. At 6:00 A.M. the two-year-old Chevrolet sedan nosed into the Lincoln Tunnel. The toll-taker paid no particular notice to the men in the dark clothing, for by this time they had cleaned off the lampblack with a weak solution of solvent that they kept in the automobile.

18

NORMALLY, THE secretary of HEW found traveling in the grand style one of the most enjoyable perquisites of Cabinet rank. After a busy evening it was her habit to linger over breakfast in her suite while she read the morning papers. The news always stimulated her natural inventiveness, so she would make a list of the ideas that it suggested. Then she would call in Cynthia Overton, her personal secretary, to see if there were any staff messages and would dictate a few letters. Cynthia would usually place some calls for her before leaving. More often than not, Secretary Lord would bring in the rest of her traveling staff to discuss subjects of current importance before beginning the day's activities—particularly when she was scheduled for a press conference or public appearance.

But this Sunday morning was far from normal. She had hardly touched the excellent breakfast, and the cheerful sunlight pouring through the window of her suite did not ease the torment that had kept her awake most of the night.

Tossing in the darkness of her bedroom, she had envisaged the worst—Porter Canfield's conviction of complicity in the murder of Mark O'Mara, followed by public disgrace and imprisonment— and she had wept. Fear for her own involvement was there too, but it was secondary to her fear for Canfield.

A steaming shower and the bright light of day dulled the panic, but she was still very concerned. How was Halevy handling Zack Miller? How long could Zack be kept silent? Could he be persuaded to abandon his plan to inform the police? If not, they were lost, because the letter she had delivered to Halevy would unquestionably connect Canfield to whatever illegal restraint of Miller had taken or would take place.

She looked at her watch—eight-twenty. Why hadn't Yoram called to let her know what he had done about Zack?

Frustratedly, she threw the front section of "The Greatest Publication That Ever Was" on the floor. Untouched on the chair beside her lay the remaining formidable bulk of the Sunday edition—a montage of fact and fancy, objectivity and prejudice sandwiched in among the thousands of advertisements that gave the paper its querulous life. The dignified black headline of the lead story stared up from the floor at her: ISRAELIS HIT BASES IN PREEMPTIVE STRIKE. Things were moving very fast, perhaps a little too fast. How could Canfield concentrate on what to do about new developments, she wondered, when what he needed most was a breathing spell so that he could devote his entire attention to Zack Miller.

She picked up the paper and read the story for the second time. In what the reporter described as an "action in anticipation of major Arab invasions," substantial elements of the Israeli Air Force had carried out simultaneous surprise attacks on key airfields in Egypt, Iraq and Syria, with results that were called highly successful. At least seventy planes were destroyed on the ground, and only two Israeli F3 supersonics were downed in the engagements. The rest of the story was devoted to attempts by "highly reliable intelligence sources" to justify the attacks. The only opprobrium was aimed at the Arabs, who were accused of "preparing to invade Israel." There was an added-on late bulletin that the Soviet Union was filing a strong protest and had decided to send elements of its Mediterranean fleet to the area "as a protective measure against further unprovoked Israeli aggression."

Meredith was glad that the action was successful, but the prompt Soviet movement of warships worried her. She would feel better when the IRBM's were in place; they would make the Arabs and the Russians think twice before attempting an invasion of Israel.

The intercom buzzed softly. "Mr. Yoram Halevy is on line one. Will you take it?" asked Cynthia Overton.

"Hold him just a moment," said Meredith. She put down the receiver and hurried into the bedroom to pick up the extension; somehow, she felt more secure there.

"Hello," she said guardedly, doing her best to conceal her anxiety. "I've been waiting for your call. How do things look for THC this morning?"

"Much better." Halevy sounded relaxed. "I think we've neutralized the problem so there's no reason to expect bad publicity.

The Vice President shouldn't get any more pressure from the budget director."

Her sigh of relief was audible. "Wonderful. I'll pass that along to the Vice President. He was very much concerned that bad publicity might cause the budget director to make an unfavorable report."

"You can tell him that there is no danger of further trouble." Halevy's voice was cold as steel.

"Thank you very much, Yoram. That's wonderful news." She still felt a vague uneasiness and a need to know more about how Zack had been handled. "Will the, uh, committee call on the Vice President to assure him that it is withdrawing its opposition to THC? It would help to have their commitment so there won't be any chance of the signals being changed again."

After an uncomfortably long silence, Halevy said, a trifle impatiently, "There is no need for such a meeting. The committee has been dissolved. Please give my regards to the Vice President."

The phone clicked in Meredith's ear, foreclosing further interrogation.

Meredith Lord was known for toughness and resilience underlying her delicate beauty. Many a man entering the political lists against her with arrogant condescension had found himself quickly outmaneuvered and defeated while still strutting about the arena. So the tiny knot of dread that worked its way down Meredith's esophagus and lodged in her stomach was an uncommon reaction and one she did not like at all. Slowly recradling the phone, she stood looking out of the window at Park Avenue's Sunday morning traffic, but her mind was contemplating darker corridors than New York's premier thoroughfare. It was as though a door had been slammed shut. "There's no need for such a meeting. The committee has been dissolved." The awful implications of Halevy's words were augmented by her recollection of the flat, robotlike tone in which he had uttered them.

Nervously, she twisted the curled telephone cord in her fingers. Above all, she must not unduly alarm Newt. He had enough to worry about. Besides, she had a television show that rated twenty million viewers to do at noon. THC would get a tremendous boost, and there would be a good opportunity to throw in a few plugs for Porter Newton Canfield. Neither Karen Rankin nor Bradley Barton was averse to a little politicking on "The Most Overlooked Issue of the Week," especially when it was favorable to a candidate they liked—and Canfield was their man.

She dialed the Washington Signal Operator and asked for Steve Galdari. It would be better for Newt to get back to her on his private line rather than take her call when people might be around. She certainly didn't want Amy to know she was calling, especially since the crudely coded conversation might produce some awkward pauses. Galdari could let Newt know she needed to talk to him; he was very discreet. She smiled, remembering San Francisco.

Amy Canfield was a picture of wifely solicitude. "Have some more bacon, Newton," she urged, patiently holding the plate in front of his unseeing eyes. Head bent to the Sunday *Globe*, the Vice President obviously had things on his mind, and Amy knew what. "Newt—" she prodded plaintively.

"Ummm?" He looked up, his eyes clouded for the second it took him to shake loose from his thoughts. The bacon was lean and crisp. Normally he would have attacked it voraciously, but not today. "Oh. No thank you. Just a little more coffee, maybe."

"You're not eating. What's wrong?" What a ridiculous question, she thought, holding back the sleeve of her robe as she poured the hot liquid into his cup.

He smiled feebly, surprised that she noticed. It was rare for Amy to pay attention to what he ate. "Didn't sleep too well."

"Is something bothering you?" she asked, wondering why she was playing this macabre game.

"World problems are on my mind," he said, mimicking the overblown ponderousness of a certain senator they sometimes joked about. "And, little lady"—he continued the charade—"these are not matters for a pretty girl to bother about. These are the rightful concern of men who have accepted public service." Turning his attention back to the newspaper, he said, "This situation with the Russians threatening to stop our ships bound for Israel could be very serious."

"Well, that's not your problem, it's the President's. Thank heaven for that." Had he not already assumed an enfilade position behind the *Globe*'s front pages, he would have been shocked by the look of pure hatred she directed at him.

"Hurley'd better get ready to handle the problem like a President or he'll find the rest of the government in revolt," he muttered. "Everybody's sick and tired of his backing down to Dradavov."

He pushed back his chair. "Excuse me, Amy. I've got a lot of work to do before tomorrow's meetings, so I'd better get down to the office. Some of the staff will be coming in to help. I'll probably be late so don't wait supper."

"All right, dear," she said sweetly. "It's too bad you have to work on Sunday, the only day we get to relax together." The sarcasm was wasted however, as his mind was far away.

Canfield went upstairs and closed the door of the study behind him. Quickly he picked up his private phone and punched out the number Steve Galdari had given him earlier. There were several rings before the Waldorf Towers operator answered.

"Secretary Lord's suite, please," he said.

"Who's calling, please?"

He looked at Galdari's note. "Mr. Newton," he said. Meredith was thinking. She wanted to lessen the possibility of hotel eavesdropping.

"Oh, yes, sir. The secretary is expecting your call. I'll put you right through."

"Hello, Mr. Newton." Meredith waited for the click that announced the departure of the operator. "I was so worried you wouldn't call in time," she said, relief flooding her voice. "I have to leave for the studio in fifteen minutes. I'm on at noon."

"I'll watch you knock them dead," he said. "Now, what's happening?"

"Our friend called me this morning. He said to tell you that they've neutralized the problem and there's no need to expect bad publicity."

"Excellent." He sounded better immediately. "How did they solve the problem?"

"I'm not sure." She did her best not to transmit her alarm. "He just said there is no need for further concern. . . . Newt?" She had to let him know all of it.

"Yes?"

"I asked if the committee which was threatening the bad publicity would meet with you to commit itself to abandoning further opposition."

"Yes?"

"And he said there was no need for that." There was a tremor in her voice as she repeated the statement that frightened her so much: "He said the committee had been dissolved."

There was an instant of silence; then Canfield said calmly, "That doesn't necessarily mean what you think it does, so don't worry. Remember, there would be no way to meet with the committee in either case. The situation required that the committee not be allowed the same freedom of action it had before."

"Newt, I'm worried." A slight choke in the words showed she was near tears.

"Meredith, I tell you you're crossing bridges too soon," he said soothingly. "You're letting your imagination run away with you. Now, everything looks darkest before the dawn. Just leave it all in my hands and let me take care of everything. It'll be all right."

"Oh, I pray that you're right. I'm so worried for you."

"I am right. You get it off your mind, darling. Go do a great show. I'm so proud of you."

"And I'm proud of you. I love you." By a great effort, she suppressed a complete breakdown.

"Goodbye, Meredith. I'll call you after the show. Love you."

Canfield's hand shook as he depressed the button that rang the White House Signal Operator. "Get me Bill Shelby right away," he said.

"Hello, Bill? I'm going to need you and Kathy today. Can you be in the EOB office by one? Good. Notify her, will you? I have a lot of confidential calls to make and I may want you to stay late. Incidentally, Zack Miller will be away for a few days. He said he had some urgent personal business to take care of. Fill in whatever he's working on with someone else for a while, will you? Thanks, Bill."

Forcing himself to abandon any scary speculation of what had happened to Zack Miller, he buzzed Steve Galdari to say he would be leaving for the EOB in fifteen minutes. Throwing off his robe, he hurried into the bathroom for a quick shave and shower.

The big man pushed against the desk leg with his foot, and the old chair gave a familiar creak while slowly spinning him to face the window. In the bright morning sunlight, the artistic deficiencies of the legend INAF on the glass were as starkly revealed as the blemishes on an aging actress's unmade face. Outside, Broadway was full of activity: The Hasidic Jews were returning to work after their Sunday sabbath.

For several years, this building and these people had been his life, but now his usefulness here was at an end. It was hard to believe that it was all over. No more meetings, demonstrations, interviews. No more quarrels with Bea or laughs with Hackenschmidt. Tomorrow he would be halfway around the world, preparing for a new assignment. The years here would be just a memory.

Yoram Halevy stretched. The short nap after the long drive from Washington had not been enough to quash the fatigue deep within him. His muscles ached and his eyes were heavy. He got up and went into the tiny bathroom, rinsed a grimy glass, filled it with water and took two amphetamines. It wouldn't do to be sleepy or sluggish. The final job required full professional competence.

Returning to his office, he quickly reviewed his mental checklist. The phone calls to Iran, Paris and the secretary of HEW had all been made. The vehicles were in position and ready, and so was the driver. His clothing and personal effects were waiting at Charles de Gaulle Airport near Paris. Tickets and passport were in order. Five thousand in cash, partly in his wallet and partly in his money belt. Exterior clothing, beard, gloves, note and tools ready. Dress shoes in truck. Identification card and clip in coveralls. Everything checked out and in order except the weapon. He would do that now because he must leave by ten forty-five. That was only fifteen minutes away.

On his desk was a rectangular metal box—two and a half feet long, one foot wide and nine inches deep—that resembled a portable tool chest. He flipped the catch and opened it. Fitted in cushioned recesses were an Uzi submachine gun and two forty-round clips of 9mm ammunition.

Halevy checked the mechanism and test-fitted each clip. Then he unloaded the clips, round by round, and checked the tension and smoothness of the feeder spring. Satisfied, he reloaded the clips and replaced them along with the weapon in their respective seats in the case. Several times he practiced unlatching the case with one hand while holding it by the handle with the other. Finally satisfied that he could bring the weapon into use within a few seconds, he put the case aside.

It was time to leave. Pulling on the loose coveralls over his business suit, he buckled the wide tool belt from which hung a variety of electrician's supplies, such as wire, pliers and screwdrivers. Then he picked up the tool case and went downstairs. Seeing that the panel truck was there waiting, he checked the street to make certain no one he knew was nearby. Then he stepped out, locked the outer door of the office, walked quickly to the truck and got in. The driver pulled away immediately.

Halevy climbed back into the rear of the truck and propped up a mirror. From a pocket of the coveralls he brought out an adhesive-backed beard. He worked quickly and expertly and returned to the front seat as soon as he had put on the disguise. Taking a forged union identification card with a picture of him in full Castro beard from the upper pocket of his coveralls, he clipped it on where it would be readily visible.

"Let's go right to the place. I'll need a little time to get the feel inside. Diagrams are okay, but they can be deceiving sometimes."

Sammy nodded and looked over at him. "You feel ready? Not tired from yesterday? I can't help you inside on this one."

"I'm fine. Just drive the cars as we've planned, and we'll be in good shape. I took a couple of bennies to keep me sharp."

"Good. We'll go to the West Side. Less Sunday traffic." The little man turned his entire attention to driving the truck, and Halevy began to review the operation in his mind for what seemed like the hundredth time.

"The chairman has agreed not to challenge our ships as long as they are west of Crete." The President squinted in the bright sunlight reflected from his private swimming pool at Camp David. Although dressed in a short-sleeved sport shirt, he still managed to look completely alien to the outdoor setting of the patio.

"And will they be west of Crete until tomorrow morning's meetings are concluded?" asked Joshua Devers, moving his chair so that the morning sun would strike his left shoulder, where much of his arthritic pain was concentrated.

"I have ordered them not to proceed east of the westernmost point of the island without specific and direct authorization from me," the Commander in Chief said. "My experience with Dradavov tells me that his threat to intercept is no idle bluff. It would be idiotic to risk an irreversible confrontation, especially in the midst of the tensions created by yesterday's Israeli air raids."

Devers shook his head slowly. "The raids didn't help, did they?" he said.

The President's voice was bitter. "It was the worst possible timing. A stupid judgment brought on by the encouragement of the Israeli lobby here. And it was due, in no small measure, to irresponsible politics within our own government."

"And within our own administration," added Devers softly.

"Very much so," agreed the President. "We must be realistic. Without the continued prodding of the ambitious Mr. Canfield, we probably wouldn't have two ships heading for Israel with IRBM components. He seems to have stampeded the Congress and even a portion of the Cabinet."

Devers rubbed his hands together nervously. "I have bad news to report on that subject, sir," he said in a sepulchral tone. "Our best judgment, based on intensive Hill checking, is that the leadership is more committed than ever to facing down Dradavov if he challenges our ships—and that includes our own leaders too. Marty Edmonds has been active behind the scenes, and Canfield's tout, that little sneak Bedson, has been buzzing around the senators with all kinds of rumors of imminent attack on Israel. He's even hinting that there's been some kind of preliminary Soviet alert. That isn't true, it it?''

The President looked steadily at Devers for a long moment before replying, ''Josh, I wish I knew. We can't be certain anymore. Since the emasculation of the CIA, we've had to rely totally on satellite surveillance, and that isn't as effective as it used to be. The SALT agreements have allowed them to focus on technological matters and their antisnoop techniques have become so sophisticated that our cameras can't pick up the information anymore.'' He rubbed his face ruefully. ''How I wish we had insisted on on-site inspection at the very beginning.''

Devers did not pursue the subject. In spite of his frank, personal relationship with the President and his duty as a counselor, he saw no need to add to the President's burden by pointing out that the SALT agreements concluded during the Hurley administration had further weakened the United States' position with regard to on-site inspections.

The President got up from the canvas lawn chair, and Devers also stood up painfully. The President put his arm around Devers's shoulders. ''Tomorrow may be one of the most important days in the history of the United States, old friend,'' he said evenly. ''Keep working on the Congress and try to get some of the Cabinet to help instead of worrying about what the press will say. I have a difficult decision to make and it would be good to have a unified team behind me.''

''Yes, Mr. President. I'll do the best I can,'' said Devers. They shook hands solemnly, each aware that the next day's meetings would determine whether or not Walter Hurley could continue to discharge effectively the duties of the President of the United States and each equally aware that the President was in for the fight of his life.

The immediate success of TBS's ''The Most Overlooked Issue of the Week'' was attributed to a fortuitous mix of substance, showmanship and skill. At least, that was the conclusion of the TBS public relations people. Critics were less kind, calling the program a tinsel minor-league version of the other networks' long-established Sunday interview shows. But the fact remained that ''Overlooked Issue,'' in its maiden year, held the cherished number-one spot in the ratings.

The program was the brainchild of a TBS assistant vice-president who, when he showed every intention of taking deserved credit, was kicked upstairs to a sterile vice-presidency with an income guaranteed to seal his lips forever. Disillusioned, he golfed and martinied his way to comfortable obscurity. Meanwhile, Bradley Barton graciously accepted the accolades and installed himself as father and chief moderator of the program. In order to get the direct and indirect assistance of the powerful magazine *Twiceweek,* he had enticed Karen Rankin to cohost on a regular basis.

With Barton and Rankin presumably providing the skill, and the mystery guest of the week presumably providing the substance, the showmanship already built into the format by the show's banished creator made the program interesting enough to attract the attention of the bored Sunday viewer, who needed something to occupy him before the sports event of the day.

There were two major differences between "Overlooked Issue" and the other interview programs. First, the identity of the mystery guest was not announced until he or she was dramatically escorted through a doorway on the set shortly after the show began. And, second, there was a contest, with a substantial prize. Those viewers who had suggested both the issue and the guest for that week qualified as contestants, and the winner was drawn by the guest at the close of the program.

Barton and Rankin kept their weekly secret well. Only the TBS staff directly concerned with the show was informed and even they on a need-to-know basis only. So jealously guarded was the secret that the program was produced live from a secondary TBS studio on the third floor of an old building on Fifty-seventh Street just east of Tenth Avenue.

At precisely the scheduled hour of 11:00 A.M. a limousine drew up in front of this old building and discharged Secretary Meredith Lord into the hands of Bradley Barton, who was waiting to escort her to the studio. She was taken to a small conference room, where Karen Rankin and two senior members of the program staff were waiting. Coffee and sandwiches were served while Barton gave her a preshow briefing.

"At eleven-thirty, we'll send you down to makeup, Madam Secretary. They should take no more than ten minutes." He smiled with what he thought was manly charm. "It's pretty hard to improve on nature in your case. In any event, we'd like to have you in position on the set by eleven-fifty."

Meredith ignored the flattery. "If I understood you, I won't be announced until twelve-eight?"

"Yes, that's right, but we'd like to have you hear what goes on before you're brought out. Then you won't feel like you're coming in cold. There'll be a comfortable chair behind the set and someone there to cue you.''

"We do so appreciate your doing our show," said Karen Rankin. "Health is a vital subject and Total Health Care is not fully understood by the electorate." She watched Meredith carefully. "Even the administration position is cloudy. People find it hard to reconcile your stance with that of Charlie Voren, and no one seems to know where President Hurley stands. He hasn't shown much personal interest."

Meredith laughed comfortably. She was far too experienced to fall prey to the old divide-and-conquer routine. "Oh, the President is very much interested and aware of what's going on," she said. "He appointed the Vice President to assist Mr. Voren and me in reaching a fair administration position, and the Vice President did an outstanding job of mediating.''

Ms. Rankin leaned into the opening. If there was anything she enjoyed, it was dominating a beautiful woman. "Yes, I heard," she said, lust flickering for a moment in her eyes. "It was reported that you and Vice President Canfield worked long hours together to resolve the problem. How are you and Mr. Canfield making out?''

For a moment Meredith was tempted to tell her that they were making out well but not as frequently as she would like. "The Vice President has been able to get us to compromise on a realistic administration position, and President Hurley will soon send a message to the Congress defining it," she said easily. "Everyone is in agreement now.''

"Good. We may ask about that on the air," said Rankin. "Please give us as much of the behind-the-scenes stuff as you can.''

"Certainly." Meredith laughed inwardly, thinking about the behind-the-scenes stuff at the Fairmont in San Francisco.

"Well, I think it's time for our makeup lady to get you ready for camera lighting," broke in Bradley Barton anxiously.

Meredith was led to makeup and then brought back up again ten minutes later to the high-ceilinged studio, which took up two floors of the old building. An unused crane stretched high into the darkness above the lower-level lights. She sat in semidarkness in a comfortable armchair behind the set. In front of her was a door opening on the unraised stage. When Bradley Barton introduced her, she would step through it and be greeted by him and Karen Rankin. And then the questions would begin.

She shivered slightly. The studio was chilly in contrast to the heat outside. She watched the young man with the earphones standing beside her; he would cue her when the time came. He caught her eye and shook his head no. It was not yet time.

In the gloom to her right, the tall scene dock with its stored studio flats looked eerie. Back a little from it, metal steps under a fire escape sign went to the floor below. She looked again at the door in front of her. Out in front of the set, she knew, were several dozen folding metal chairs, now occupied by reporters, studio personnel and members of her own staff—the critics who would evaluate her performance. As always just before an important appearance, her palms felt slightly moist.

The young man beside her moved, drawing her attention back to him. He was looking toward the stairway, his fingers to his lips in the traditional sign for silence. She followed his glance. A workman who had just come up the steps nodded his understanding and disappeared behind the scene dock toward the front of the studio. She could not see him well, but his movements reminded her of someone she knew. Who?

There was a touch on her shoulder—the young man signaled her to get ready. She could hear Bradley Barton announcing the contest finalists and revealing that the most overlooked issue of the week was the crisis over Total Health Care. She started to go to the door, but the cuer stopped her—not yet. It was time for a commercial.

Seventy seconds later, at exactly twelve-eight, Bradley Barton declared that the mystery guest was none other than the secretary of HEW, Dr. Meredith Lord. The young man smiled, pulled open the set door and Meredith walked through, half blinded by the light.

Since all eyes were riveted on the beautiful Cabinet officer, no one paid any attention to the big man in coveralls who walked quickly from behind the scene dock to a position just to the left of the seated observers, and no one noticed that he was shielding something in his left hand with his body as he moved toward the stage.

TBS's celebrated anchor man was smilingly turning his attractive guest toward the cameras, positioning her between Karen Rankin and himself, when the Uzi submachine gun, on full automatic, erupted in vicous ripping snaps. A fraction of a second before the ugly sounds reached the observers' ears, at least twenty-eight 9mm slugs traveling at more than thirteen hundred feet per second slammed into the bodies of the three people on camera, hurling them against the set as though they had been struck by an invisible truck. Fragments of bone and viscera flew against the backdrop, and bright streams of arterial blood poured from the ravaged bodies. Acting out of an involuntary compulsion, the cameraman tracked the mutilated corpses' grotesque ballet, transmitting to twenty million horrified viewers the shocking disintegration of the three murdered celebrities. Seconds later the technician in the control room regained his senses and mercifully broke the circuit.

Halevy swung the smoking machine gun toward the observers in the folding chairs who were paralyzed with fright and certainly no immediate threat. Ejecting the nearly used clip as he ran, he paused behind the scene dock for an instant to snap in the new one before dashing for the fire stairs. As he came from behind the dock, he encountered the young man who had cued Meredith. Without slackening his pace, he shot him down with a short burst, then hurried down the steps. Between the second and ground floors, he ran head-on into the makeup girl, who was carrying a tray of sandwiches and drinks. Her face dissolved in a bloody smear after he rammed the steel butt of the Uzi into her nose. With a horrified gurgle, she toppled over the rail and crashed to the concrete of the basement, a floor and a half below.

Seconds later, Halevy released the nearly full clip from the Uzi and slipped it into his pocket. He took a paper from his other pocket and attached it to the stock of the weapon with a rubber band he had carried around his wrist. Pasted from newsprint in the same crude manner as had been used in the O'Mara case, the message read:

THOSE WHO ENCOURAGE THE ISRAELI ASSASSINS WILL DIE BY VIOLENCE JUST AS OUR BROTHERS DIED YESTERDAY.
DAMN

He then threw the gun down the well to the basement. After listening for a moment to make sure no one was in pursuit, he calmly opened the door, dropped the gloves behind him and stepped out onto Fifty-seventh Street. He walked to the corner of Tenth Avenue, hugging the building line so that he could not be observed from the windows above. There were no pedestrians on the north side of Fifty-seventh Street, and the few strollers on Tenth Avenue paid no attention to him when he turned the corner and walked to the blue panel truck facing north just a short distance away. Unhurriedly, he climbed in next to the driver.

"Let's go," he said. "It's going to be very busy here before long." Only three minutes and forty seconds had elapsed since the Uzi had sung its song of death.

"Did you finish off all three?" Sammy asked eagerly.

"Of course. That's a stupid question."

Sammy sighed. "Seems a shame—a good-looking broad like that. She liked you, too."

"She knew too much. Besides, bumping off a Cabinet officer

will do more for our cause than all the others put together. Now, shut up and get us to the garage. I'm going to change.''

Halevy climbed over the seat to the back, where he was out of view of passing motorists. He stripped off the beard, rubbed a little nail polish remover on the parts of his face that felt sticky and kicked off the Earth Shoes. Then he put on a conservative pair of oxfords, straightened his tie and combed his hair. He stuffed the used clothing into a navy-type duffel bag and, now looking like an ordinary businessman, got back into the front seat.

As Sammy swung the truck into the large parking garage at Broadway and Sixty-third, the faint sound of sirens reached them. He stopped for a moment to take the ticket from the automated meter, and the gate arm swung up.

"C'mon, let's get started. Sounds like the cops have arrived at the studio," Halevy said. "Take this heap down to level three. You know where I parked the Buick."

"Relax, relax, we're home free." Sammy deftly took the panel truck around the sharp angles and down to the third level. There were no more than two dozen scattered vehicles on the acre of parking space. Sammy eased the truck in alongside the late-model Buick sedan with temporary tags over in the corner farthest from the elevator.

Halevy reached around and pulled the duffel bag from the back. "Here you are, sailor," he said with a smile. "See you in Hong Kong."

"Take care, Yoram. Have a good flight." The little man pulled a navy-blue beanie from his back pocket and put it on. Hoisting the duffel bag onto his shoulder, he started for the elevator. In ten minutes he would board a Hong Kong-bound freighter now tied up at a Hudson River dock, and by midnight he would be passing the Statue of Liberty.

Yoram Halevy dropped the keys onto the floor of the truck and then locked it. There was nothing to link him to the truck, which Sammy had rented for the month from an acquaintance.

He slid his overnight parking ticket out from the sun visor of the Buick and presented it to the bored garage attendant. Easing the car into the Broadway flow, he leisurely drove northward.

The inbound postweekend traffic was predictably heavy, but it was hard to understand the creeping paralysis that had stacked up so many suburb-bound cars at the Triborough Bridge. Halevy drummed his fingers on the steering wheel impatiently and glanced at his watch. Four P.M. A late lunch and an uptown movie had dissipated the early afternoon. He would be arriving at Kennedy

International at the proper time for the six-thirty Air France flight to Paris. He would, that is, unless there were some gigantic traffic jam up ahead.

As the Buick eased to a stop at the toll booth, he discovered the reason for the bottleneck. One of New York's finest bent down to take a good look at him.

"May I see your registration and driver's license, sir?"

Halevy fished in his wallet and handed over the license and the temporary registration certificate. "What's going on?" he asked.

"Routine check, sir, that's all." The policeman checked the documents and handed them back. "Okay, you can go ahead," he said signaling the booth attendant to raise the barrier.

Halevy was thankful he hadn't decided to use a stolen vehicle. Buying the Buick had been a lot of bother but it would be little loss to him. The finance company owned most of it and he would never return to the United States of America, at least not as Yoram Halevy.

19

THE DEGREE of tolerance to pain is unpredictable, not only among individuals but even *within* an individual. There are times when a person can stand up under extreme stress and other times when the same stress causes utter collapse. Porter Canfield was fortunate enough to be alone when he went to pieces.

The morning had gone very well for him. Stan Bedson had excellent reports from key congressmen, who apparently were prepared to back him to the hilt in the demands he would make on the President at the next day's meetings. Of course, there was the always churning fear about Zack Miller and Halevy, but he had been told the danger was no longer imminent. And Meredith had delivered his message, which removed any incentive for further bloodshed. Canfield leaned back in his chair, while a delightful vision of an abandoned, passionate Meredith floated across his mind.

Then suddenly he remembered the TBS show. His desk clock told him it had been on three minutes already. Swinging around in his chair, he picked up the remote-control box, clicked on the television and jumped the channel selector to the TBS channel. The pancaked face of the supremely suave Bradley Barton was intoning the names of the contestants who had qualified for the big weekly prize. He concluded, and a commercial came on. Canfield moved to a chair closer to the television set.

Finally the purring lady stopped rubbing the cheek of the meek little man who had just splashed himself with that irresistible manly scent, and the unctuous Barton was back on the screen. Dramatically, he and Karen Rankin went to the set's lighted doorway, where Barton announced that Dr. Meredith Lord, secretary of HEW, was the mystery guest and would, in a moment, step through the portal.

Canfield leaned forward in keen anticipation. The first glimpse of her always sent his heart soaring. Then she was there. What natural beauty, poise and presence she exhibited. He felt proud and very possessive.

Barton and Rankin—mere ordinary mortals defiling a shrine—shook her hand. Barton took her arm and swung her around to face the camera. Why did he have to touch her so aggressively?

Then it happened. It was as though every half-born horror lurking in Porter Canfield's subconscious—all the mind-twisting nightmares of years past—had simultaneously emerged to tug at his sanity. A soft tormented cry came from deep within him when he saw the mortally wounded body of the woman he loved bullet-flung to a spastic twitching death on the studio floor.

He stumbled the few steps to his bathroom, his intestinal muscles convulsing, and began to retch with long, dry gasps.

"Oh, my God . . . my God," he whispered hoarsely, over and over. He sat for some time until exhaustion quieted him. Regaining partial control for a moment, he splashed cold water on his face and went back into the office. He was conscious of the image of Douglas Drake on the screen. There was a slight quaver in Drake's voice, and Canfield caught parts of what he was saying:

". . . one of the most brutal and shocking crimes in history . . . little hope that any survived . . . gunned down by a man in coveralls who appeared to be a workman . . . taken to Roosevelt Hospital."

Canfield slumped down in his chair, only half aware, as the detailing of the few known facts was replaced by speculation.

". . . grievance against TBS over an employee firing . . . mentally ill reactionary who resented HEW spending . . . Arab terrorists."

Someone handed Drake a note. After a moment he looked into the camera and said gravely, "A spokesman for the hospital has issued the following statement." He read from the slip of paper: "Secretary Meredith Lord, Bradley Barton, Karen Rankin, James Whittle, an employee of TBS, and Alice Bellamy, also a TBS employee, were pronounced dead on arrival at Roosevelt Hospital at twelve thirty-five P.M.. The cause of death in each case, except that of Miss Bellamy, whose skull was fractured, was multiple gunshot wounds to vital organs of the body."

Drake accepted another note from an assistant. "The murder

weapon was found at the bottom of a stairwell in the building. Attached to it was a note attributing the killings to DAMN, the same Arab terrorist organization that figured in the unsolved O'Mara case. We expect to have the contents of that note shortly. Please stay tuned. We will return to the air at one o'clock with more on these shocking murders.''

The confirmation of the deaths broke the thin string of Canfield's salvaged control. He slid in anguish to the floor and buried his face in the chair's seat cushion, trying to stifle his wracking sobs. He did not hear the gentle knock at the door.

Steve Galdari waited only a moment before quietly opening the door. A half-hour ago he had heard the radio bulletin on the shooting, and he knew the Vice President was going to watch the program. It was abnormal that there had been only silence from Canfield's office since the tragedy.

''Mr. Vice President?'' Galdari, puzzled that the Vice President was not at his desk, came into the office.

Canfield, past embarrassment, looked up at him tearfully. ''She's gone, Steve,'' he said thickly, tears coursing down his face.

Galdari came over quickly and lifted him back into the chair. He went to the bathroom, dampened a towel and brought it back. ''I'm sorry, sir,'' he said softly as Canfield wiped his face. ''Shall I get Bill? You should issue a statement soon.''

''Don't bring Bill in here now.'' Canfield's voice was shaky. ''Just have him issue a condolence in my name—shocked, et cetera. He'll know what to do.''

''Yes, sir. Now maybe we'd better get you home,'' said Galdari.

The reaction was violent. ''No! I'm not going home now. I'll just rest awhile here. Steve''—he looked imploringly at the agent—''I have to be alone now—you understand, of all people.'' The tears started again.

Galdari felt very sorry for him and for Meredith. He had liked the way she handled herself—particularly her honesty with him. ''I'll be outside if you need me,'' he said gently.

When the heavy door clicked shut behind Galdari, an intense loneliness came over Canfield. The tears had stopped, but now there was a dull ache, a heaviness in his chest. Never in his self-centered life had he known heartache like this—and this monstrous weight that compressed him from all angles, pushing in on his brain until he wished he were dead.

Why, why? Just when he had found someone to share his joys and burdens—why had she been snatched from him?

It was his fault for sending her to Halevy. But what else could he do? The message he sent should have stopped the killing, not caused more. Why had Halevy killed again? Now that he knew he had been deceived by the Iranian, why did this man who was a fervent Zionist execute those who supported his cause? It was inexplicable. He could not in a million years have predicted Halevy's action. No one could. So really it was not his fault. Knowing what he knew then, he would do the same thing again. But an innocent, lovely woman lay dead, murdered. Someone had to be responsible for that. Halevy? The Iranian? Yes, of course, but they were pawns, only tools of another's evil design. Zack? Surely Zack had to bear part of the responsibility, but where was Zack? He had to be dead also. Halevy would not have taken the chance of letting him live—not with this in mind. But even Zack did not cause the conditions which killed Meredith. It was the mewling, crawling condition of the United States that encouraged the arrogant international violence. Hurley. Yes, Hurley—the weak, insecure President was to blame. And Dradavov, the Soviet tyrant. Dradavov. How he hated that smooth-talking Russian hypocrite. Toasting world peace and instigating trouble between the Arabs and Israel. Hurley was the pawn of Dradavov. Under the Soviet leader's influence, Hurley had allowed the United States to be negotiated into a position of nuclear inferiority. Dradavov had brought the whole confrontation about and, essentially, Dradavov must bear the primary responsibility for Meredith's death.

Canfield was overwhelmed by a Messianic passion. He must avenge Meredith. More than that, he must save his country. Dradavov had to be stopped to reverse the tidal wave that soon would engulf the free world. Surely the President of the United States had the power to do that.

But the President was impotent to stop the Russian. He was, in fact, his servant—totally under his influence. Canfield stood up, letting the towel fall unnoticed to the floor. He was oblivious to everything except the silent vow he now took. "I will destroy Walter Hurley tomorrow. As President, I will bring Alexi Dradavov to account for his crimes against the world community."

Twenty minutes later, outwardly calm, the Vice President approved Bill Shelby's draft of a condolence statement and returned to the serious business of telephoning participants in the next day's meetings.

That evening at 5:00 P.M., the White House had passed the word to the news media that President Hurley would speak briefly to the nation at nine o'clock.

All networks carried President Hurley's statement, and commentators remarked later that the President looked grim and very tired. Seated at his desk in the Oval Office, the President read slowly from the pages before him:

"I am shocked and saddened by the brutal and senseless murders at the TBS studio in New York today. I am sure the nation joins me in expressing deepest sympathy to the families of Secretary Lord, Mr. Barton, Miss Rankin, Miss Bellamy and Mr. Whittle. ·

"I knew Miss Bellamy and Mr. Whittle not at all, but I understand they were exemplary employees of TBS who were well liked by their associates and were discharging their duties in a highly satisfactory manner.

"Although I did not know Miss Rankin or Mr. Barton well, I do know that their stature in the journalistic community was such that they will be sorely missed. As for Dr. Meredith Lord, I feel a profound personal sorrow at the loss of this dedicated woman, who carried out the duties of her high office with such skill and devotion. The country will be diminished by her untimely passing.

"My friends, the patterns of confrontation that have emerged in recent months—and these murders are part of it—have brought us to the brink of an international crisis. The political overtones involved in the O'Mara case and in the reports of today's crime have fanned the fires of a long-existing international dispute between the state of Israel and some of her neighbors. As a result, the tranquillity that has for some time existed between the Soviet Union and the United States is threatened because of the pressure on both countries to assist their friends.

"Several weeks ago, the Congress and influential segments of our business and academic communities urged me to respond favorably to Israel's repeatedly expressed desire to have intermediate range ballistic missiles. Against my personal inclination, I dispatched two ships to Israel with preparatory components that would ready Israeli installations to receive those warheads. Mistakenly, the news media announced that those ships contained the actual nuclear weapons themselves.

"Today, Chairman Dradavov of the Soviet Union informed me over the hot line that our ships will be intercepted by the Soviet navy should they attempt to deliver the preparatory IRBM components.

"I have requested the joint leadership of the Congress to meet with me tomorrow morning at eight A.M. to discuss what our response should be. Further, I have called a meeting of the Cabinet for ten A.M. for the same purpose.

"I fully understand that the buck stops here and that the decision as to whether to complete the deliveries of IRBM components rests with the President of the United States. However, I will make that decision only after full consultation with the Congress, the Cabinet and the military leaders.

"You will be informed as soon as the decision has been made.

"Good night."

The nearly full 747 touched down at Charles de Gaulle Airport near Paris at 7:03 A.M., Monday morning, forty-five minutes late. Yoram Halevy was glad to get out of the cramped quarters; flying economy class was not pleasant for a large person when all the seats were occupied. Since the Concorde had begun its expensive high-speed shuttling of the Atlantic, nearly all cost-conscious passengers crowded aboard the old 747's, so the luxury of spreading out across three seats was only infrequently possible.

Halevy showed his passport and inoculation registration to the French official, who let him know for a few Gallic gestures that Halevy was imposing on his good nature when he asked about the location of the Air France freight office.

After riding the automated walkway for about ten minutes, he finally found the freight office and claimed the three bags he had sent earlier. Then he took a cab to Le Bourget Airport. Traffic was very light, and twenty minutes later he struggled, with the three bulky suitcases that contained all of his personal belongings, into the small waiting room at the terminal for private aircraft.

A man rushed up to him. "Let me help you, comrade." With a delighted grin, Anwar Maadi took the largest of the bags.

"Anwar, you old horse," said Halevy, dropping everything to embrace the beaming Iranian. "It's been a long time."

"Six years since we left Aden." Anwar laughed. "Southern Yemen will look good again after the pressures of living with that madman Izadi in Tehran."

"But first we go to Peking to report to the director. Is the plane here yet?" Halevy peered outside, where a silver G2 with Chinese markings waited.

"That's the one," said Anwar. "The mission must have pleased the director. He sent a section chief to escort us. Here he comes now." The Iranian indicated a slim, small Chinese man in a gray military-type tunic without insignia who had left the plane and was coming toward them. He came into the building and walked over to Halevy.

"Comrade Ibrahim Abdullah?" he inquired in a feathery voice, extending his hand.

"At your service, comrade. But for the time being I suggest that you refer to me as Yoram Halevy—until we clear the customs agent. I'm traveling on an American passport to this point."

"Of course," said the Chinese gentleman. "Thoughtless of me, but no harm done." He looked around, making sure again that no strangers were within earshot. "The director has asked me to escort you at once to Peking. Your mission has been highly successful— even more than you realize. Our intelligence reports indicate that there will be an abrasive confrontation between our enemies before the day is over."

"Wonderful," said Yoram. "I hoped that my last project would force the capitalist running dogs to insist on completing the delivery of the nuclear components."

"Exactly what is happening," said the Chinese with a thin smile. "And the barbarians to the north will unquestionably intercept the delivery. The détente will be destroyed and we can reap a propaganda coup by expressing our public shock at the United Nations. We will say that peace is indeed an illusory goal when such aggressive traits show through the veneer of civility displayed in the Tripartite Pact." He picked up one of the bags. "Let's go get you checked through, comrade. There's the customs agent over there."

Ten minutes later the silver jet left the Le Bourget runway and climbed into the morning sun toward Ankara, Turkey. In Peking, a very pleased director of Chinese Intelligence waited for Ibrahim Abdullah, his top Arab agent, to make a complete report on the six-year project just concluded.

The people assigned to the protective forces of the United States Secret Service are accustomed to erratic work hours, so it was not unusual that Steve Galdari had been on duty for twenty-three consecutive hours. Ordinarily, however, the long hours resulted from sudden movements from place to place with insufficient time for advance planning—unlike the present case, in which there wasn't any real reason for the head of the vice-presidential protective detail to remain at the Executive Office Building Command Post overnight.

That Canfield had elected to spend Sunday night and part of Monday morning working in his office, and had slept on a cot set up there, did not bother Galdari. Politicians preparing for critical moments in their careers did strange things. Nor was it the temporary collapse of his protectee, brought on by the shock of Meredith Lord's sudden and violent death, that worried him—such a catharsis was usually helpful. Nevertheless, Galdari had thought it best to remain close to the Vice President. Something strange was happening. Only an hour after his open exhibition of grief, Canfield ordered Shelby to call in additional staff, and until past midnight the office hummed with activity. Calm and cool, the Vice President drove his people unmercifully, preparing for the President's meetings with the congressional leadership and the Cabinet. Over seventy-five phone calls were completed, nearly forty of which Canfield handled personally. Galdari assisted in coordinating the calls because Shelby was short-handed. He was amazed at the detachment of the Vice President when the people he talked to brought up Meredith's death; he might have been discussing the murder of a stranger.

But what concerned Galdari most was the sudden change in Canfield's personality. Instead of the friendliness and warm informality with which he customarily handled his staff, his manner had been cold, almost regal. There was no interpersonal flow; he might as well have been punching the buttons of a machine. As the long night wore on, Canfield became impatient and a rude arrogance crept into his conversations with staff. However, with the dignitaries he telephoned, he was courteous and modest—entirely charming—until he hung up. Then, more often than not, he made some derogatory and completely unsolicited observation about them—their stupidity, big-headedness or two-facedness.

Monday morning had finally come, and in the Cabinet Room of the White House, nine of the most important men in the Senate and House of Representatives now sat around the big table awaiting the entrance of the President of the United States. The secretary of state, the President's national security advisor and the President's chief of staff were also present.

Galdari stayed behind in the hall as the Vice President hurried into the room and took his seat between the Senate and House leaders of the minority party. Directly opposite Canfield was the President's empty chair and flanking it were Senate Majority Leader Roland Gray and Speaker of the House Martin Edmonds. At eight-forty the President entered and took his seat. There were gray circles under his eyes that his glasses could not conceal, and the lines on his forehead seemed deeper than usual. He nodded briefly, forgoing the customary handshakes, and began without apology for his tardiness.

"Gentlemen, you heard or read my remarks last night and you know why you are here. Let me very quickly sketch the situation as it exists at the moment.

"I must caution you that classified information is involved in what I am going to tell you. What takes place during this meeting must not be repeated." He stared hard at Canfield.

"Two of our cargo ships carrying components necessary to the construction of IRBM sites, but no missiles or warheads of any kind, are seventy miles west of Crete and proceeding toward Israel. We have been warned that if they pass Crete they will be intercepted by units of the Soviet Union's Mediterranean fleet, which, our intelligence tells us, are presently just west of Cyprus. Our vessels presently are unescorted, but a powerful segment of our Atlantic fleet is standing by should it be needed. I am hopeful that it will not."

The President's serious eyes moved from one listener to another, seeking their reactions, but the faces remained bland and unrevealing. Tapping his gold pencil on the leather pad in front of him, he continued, "While you were waiting for me here, I telephoned Chairman Dradavov to see whether there could be any softening of his position. He indicated that there could not be, particularly since the provocative statements of Prime Minister Stein. The prime minister threatened immediate and full retaliation against those responsible for encouraging yesterday's terrorist actions that resulted in the deaths of prominent Americans supportive of the Israeli cause."

The President lowered his eyes and his voice faded to a near whisper. "We lost a great lady, gentlemen, but the seriousness of the international situation will not permit eulogies at this point." He looked up at Canfield, who stared back blankly at him. "In recent years, there has been much criticism that our Presidents have exercised their powers too often without consulting the Congress. It is within my executive authority to send those two ships toward their destination or to withdraw them. Before I make that decision, I would like to have whatever recommendations the leadership might care to make. But before I listen to your comments, I think you should know in which direction I am leaning—and why."

The speaker caught the eyes of the House minority leader and raised his eyebrows eloquently, indicating his surprise at the tactic.

"My inclination," continued the President, "is to take Mr. Dradavov's threat very seriously. While we cannot be certain, there are intelligence reports from our allies who still maintain effective clandestine information-gathering organizations that the Soviet strategic forces are now on a secondary-alert status. My long and close observations of the chairman lead me to conclude he is not bluffing and will, in fact, order our vessels intercepted. That would put the ball in our court. If we use force to protect our ships, we have a full-scale confrontation which could begin a chain reaction too horrible to contemplate. On the other hand, temporarily abandoning the delivery while we discuss the situation further will cost us nothing.''

''Nothing but our self-respect and the respect of what's left of the free world,'' said Porter Canfield. There was a rustle of movement as some congressman shifted in their chairs, uneasy because of the Vice President's temerity.

The President's lips set in a narrow line, but he ignored the discourtesy and continued, speaking to the group, ''Perhaps we should ask ourselves whether we were wise in adopting a policy that led to the introduction of major nuclear weapons into the Middle East arms race. IRBM's are not in the same ball park as surface-to-air missiles, even when they have nuclear warheads. It's a question of geographic reach.''

Canfield was not intimidated. ''Mr. President, the United States had a key role in the establishment of a courageous nation called Israel. Without our guardianship and Israeli skill and guts, the communists would have obliterated Israel years ago. The minute we show uncertainty in our support, the Soviets will direct their Arab clients to attack. We would be disastrously wrong to waver in our support of Israel.''

''Thank you for your view, Mr. Vice President,'' said Walter Hurley. Then, turning to the Senate majority leader, he said, ''You've been around a long time, Roland. Would you care to make a recommendation?''

All heads turned toward the majority leader, who had been tracing a design on a pad. The aristocratic silver head came up and the clear blue eyes bored into those of the Vice President. Then, turning toward the President, Gray said with great deference, ''Mr. President, there have been times when I thought we were leaning over backward to make détente work, and, as you know, I have objected to some of the provisions of the agreements limiting strategic arms. However, I am a traditionalist who believes that the proper exercise of foreign policy should rest in the hands of the President. I am a team player, sir, and will support whatever action you determine to be in the best interest of the country.''

Hurley nodded gravely, but relief showed in his expression. He looked over at the Senate minority leader. ''And the man who leads the other side of the Senate?'' he inquired.

The minority leader squirmed uncomfortably. ''I'd like to think about it a little longer, Mr. President. If I may, I'll wait until you hear from the House leadership.''

The President smiled and assented, concealing his disappointment that he did not have Senate unanimity before hearing from the House leaders. He looked at the House minority leader. "How about you, Richard?" he asked.

"Sir, I'll support whatever the speaker recommends in this instance," said Richard Watkins.

"And you, John?" asked the President, turning to the House majority leader.

"The same. The House establishment had decided to follow the speaker in this matter."

The room suddenly became very still, and everyone's attention focused on Martin Edmonds. The President put his hand on the young speaker's arm and said, with an attempt at lightness, "You're pretty young to be in absolute control of the House of Representatives, Marty, but it seems as though you are. Please give me the benefit of your counsel."

Edmonds, not unconscious of the drama of the moment, knew the President had every reason to expect his support because he had called the night before and indirectly asked for it. Edmonds had nearly always been a team player.

Looking Hurley straight in the eye, the speaker spoke up strongly and confidently. "Mr. President, I have followed this developing crisis very carefully, since the Congress overwhelmingly resolved to support the sending of IRBM's to Israel. I think that decision was correct, even though it may have triggered the senseless assassinations that took our colleague from us yesterday." Edmonds glanced past the President at Roland Gray. "We cannot, we must not conduct our foreign policy in fear. Threats from another superpower are not, in my opinion, a good reason to change course in the middle of the stream. Therefore, my counsel is to inform the Russians that we are going to deliver the components and that we will consider interception of the ships an act of piracy on the high seas that must be dealt with immediately."

Hurley's face fell in shocked disbelief. "But, Marty, it could mean war—nuclear holocaust," he said shakily.

"The Russians don't want war at this time. They are afraid the Chinese would use the opportunity to wreak great mischief. Remember, Mr. President, that Kennedy faced them down at Cuba. You can do the same."

"The situation was just the reverse regarding Cuba," said Hurley worriedly. "We would have intercepted *their* ships if they had not backed down. I believe firmly that they will stop ours if we don't back down."

"Sir, I disagree," said Edmonds quietly. "If you let them bluff us here, we're finished."

The President appeared stunned by this major defection. Finally he said, "I must meet with the Cabinet to gain their counsel. Then I will ask that both this group and the Cabinet sit in on my eleven o'clock meeting with the National Security Council. I think we'd better recess now until eleven A.M."

"Wait a minute," Canfield's harsh voice slapped the President as he prepared to rise. "You should take a vote right now to see how many here are with you and how many are with the speaker."

There was a murmur of agreement, but the President paid no heed. He stood up, indicating that the meeting was over.

"How many with the President on this?" asked Canfield, taking charge, his voice full of emotion. Only Roland Gray raised his hand.

The President began to walk out of the room. "How many with the speaker?" Eight hands were raised. "Mr. President, the leadership of Congress of the United States is eight to one against you." Arrogantly, the Vice President flung the words at Hurley's back as the door closed behind him.

Excited by the beginning of a major confrontation between the Vice President and the President, the congressional leaders noisily left the Cabinet Room and went to the Roosevelt Room to wait for the conclusion of the Cabinet meeting. The White House press corps, demanding to know what was happening, buzzed like angry bees around the President's press secretary. He finally managed to quiet them to a degree by promising a presidential press conference later in the afternoon. Inevitably, however, one of the minority leaders slipped out for a few minutes to leak to the media, without attribution, his opinion that Walter Hurley was facing a party revolt unless his response to the Soviet threats stiffened.

At the time the Cabinet meeting was beginning, a red-eyed but resolute Amy Canfield was being driven to the White House by two of the Secret Service agents assigned to her. Earlier she had phoned the President's secretary to say that she would like to talk to the President about a matter of the utmost confidentiality and had been referred to the President's counselor, Mr. Devers, whom she knew slightly. He had invited her to come to his office to discuss the matter, indicating that he would try to work her into the President's schedule, although it would be difficult on such a busy day.

Amy had learned of Meredith Lord's death from one of the Secret

Service agents. She had gone quietly upstairs to her sitting room to think about it. As she sat staring out the window, the icy control she had maintained for two days began to disintegrate. Far from being a relief or satisfaction, Meredith's death frustrated her because it represented the ultimate victory of her rival in a contest never really joined. Just when she had confirmed the existence of her enemy, the enemy disappeared in full victory. Amy was left with one dominant emotion—hatred of her husband. It was more hatred than the sense of civil duty that took her to Josh Devers's office.

Devers received her warmly, and the comfortable informality of his office relaxed her. He was gracious and attentive, making certain that she had a hot cup of tea and assuring her that there was no rush—he had all the time in the world. Of course, the President's time was another matter—she could understand that—and would she be kind enough to tell him as much about her reason for wanting to see the President as she could? He didn't want to pry, but it would be very helpful to the President if he got even a general idea of what this was all about.

Amy wanted so desperately to tell someone her awful secret. Little by little, he cultivated her confidence while describing the time problem of the President. He was such a nice man, so gentle and sympathetic and well-mannered—after ten minutes, Amy decided to tell him everything.

It came in a rush: her gradual estrangement from her husband—her dislike of politics—the separations brought on by his work and her preference for the insulated life in Philadelphia. Then, her burgeoning suspicions of her husband's infidelity, the Andy Jackerson column, the frequent meetings of Canfield and Meredith Lord and the beginnings of Washington gossip about them. Finally, how she learned that Meredith would be at her house for a meeting when she was away, and the servants were too, and how she decided to lay a trap for her husband.

Devers, an excellent listener, made sympathetic sounds and gestures to encourage and reassure her.

Amy explained that in the course of her philanthropic activities, she had participated in a Philadelphia project called "Inner City Articulation." She was one of a group of volunteers sent with tape recorders into the underprivileged areas of the city to record poor people's opinions on social issues. For this purpose, she purchased a good voice-activated machine and learned how to use it. It was while talking to Betsy, the maid, that she remembered that the recorder was in the house. She had loaned it the year before to the Senate wives so that they could record the speech of a renowned woman scientist and had never bothered to take it back to Grey-stone.

Reliving the excitement of laying the trap, Amy animatedly told Devers that after a frantic search, she finally found the machine in an old suitcase in the back-room closet. She took it back to her bedroom and plugged it in. It seemed to be on, but the tape would not turn. She was ready to give up the idea when suddenly she remembered that it was set to voice activation. In a very low voice, she then said, "Porter Newton Canfield, if there's anything besides this on this tape when I get back tomorrow, you are going to be in real trouble." At the first word, the tape began to turn, and her test playback was perfect. She hid the recorder under the bed and left. The next morning she returned after her husband had left for the office and—

Suddenly the weight of what she was about to say crashed down on Amy—the horror of what had happened and the greater horror of what was going to happen.

Tears came to her eyes and her hands tremblingly fumbled in her purse for a handkerchief she could not find. Devers gave her his.

"Just rest a moment," he said kindly. "I can imagine how painful this is for you."

"No, no. I must finish," she said dully. "Please ask the Secret Service man outside to bring in what he's carrying for me."

Devers called his secretary, and the agent was summoned. He entered, handed Amy a black case and went back out to wait.

"I want you to hear the tape," said Amy, fighting back the tears.

Josh Devers was a hard-nosed political operative, an expert user of scandalous information for the destruction of some careers and the advancement of others. Yet, he was essentially a decent man and taking advantage of this heartbroken woman bothered him. "Perhaps that won't be necessary," he said gently. "Why don't you just tell me what you found out and what you are going to do about it." He hesitated, then added, "Since yesterday's tragedy, maybe it won't be necessary to do anything about it."

Amy put the case down on a chair near an outlet and opened it. "You're right in assuming I caught them, but you're wrong in thinking I would want to wash that dirty linen in public," she said, amazingly calm again. "What's on this tape is more important than my marriage, believe me. It involves criminal matters and possibly has a bearing on the crisis the President is dealing with right now."

She plugged in the cord, adjusted the volume and depressed the playback button. In a few moments Amy's voice came on, testing the activator with her half-humorous admonition. Then the recorder clicked off but immediately clicked on again, and the Vice President's bantering voice said, "Relax, Meredith. You weren't nearly so reluctant in San Francisco."

Devers heard Meredith Lord say, "Newt, I feel funny about it—in this bed," and averted his head in embarrassment for Amy.

Later, when Amy Canfield turned off the recorder, Josh Devers had completely forgotten his initial reluctance to eavesdrop. While Amy Canfield watched nervously, he penned a brief note to be handed to President Hurley in the Cabinet Room. Then he called the director of the FBI and told him that the President wanted him to come to the White House immediately on a matter of the utmost urgency. For the first time in his long career, the old counselor was truly shocked.

Every time Walter Hurley looked across the conference table, he encountered his Vice President's self-satisfied smirk. Anger boiled within the President. Not only was his deputy disloyal, but the prestigious group of men he had appointed to run the departments and agencies of the federal government were proving to be either turncoats or gutless ingrates. It was one thing for the elected politicians of the Congress to give way to public pressure and run with the herd, but he expected his Cabinet officers to be made of sterner stuff. It was disappointing to learn that they were not.

Martin Muldrow had the floor. "I've gotta be frank, Mr. President. You knew my background when you appointed me, and you know the AFL-CIO doesn't hold with knuckling under to the commies. The American blue-collar worker has balls and he expects his government to have balls. He's a patriotic guy and he can't stand to see his great country pushed around by the Russians. I say to hell with Dradavov's threats. Deliver those ships to Israel with whatever force it takes. The Reds will back down when it's eyeball-to-eyeball."

Wearily, the President said, "I appreciate your candor, Marty, but don't you understand the need to be careful—the terrible consequences if I'm right and you're wrong about Dradavov's intentions?"

Muldrow shook his head stubbornly. "Kennedy had the same risks during the Cuban crisis, Mr. President. Look, you're the Commander in Chief. You know what the American people want you to do. I say do it." Here was the Kennedy thing again. Hurley didn't bother this time to explain the difference.

One after another, the secretaries were asked for their opinions.

The timid men—West, Abbott, Meadows, Woodhall and Elbrook—were reluctant to advise, but Hurley had no doubt that they would buckle to pressure from Canfield and Muldrow unless he had strong backing from Jendar, Fernandez and Pangborn. He had delayed calling on the latter three, but now it was time to find out whether he or Canfield had them. He decided to go to the young secretary of HUD first.

"Your opinion, Ramon?" Hurley was surprised at how matter-of-fact his own voice sounded.

The bright, young man smiled sympathetically at the President, who had done more to further his career than anyone. He felt very sad about what he had to do. "I'm very sorry, Mr. President, but I must respectfully disagree with you. Unless we stand by our principles and are prepared to defend them against all attacks, this country as we know it cannot long exist. We will be subjected to a wave of bullying, terrorism and abuse that will eventually destroy our pride. Down the road for a nation without self-respect lies revolution." The young man spoke very earnestly, with obvious sincerity. "I must urge you to deliver the components. We must take the risk because the alternative is not acceptable."

Sadly the President turned to Vincent Jendar and nodded silently that he was next.

"I could not say it any better than Ramon, Mr. President," said the attorney general quietly.

Before Hurley could ask Pangborn, the final Cabinet officer, to comment, the President's secretary entered and handed him a note. He opened it, looked up and saw Canfield's curious eye on him. Quickly, the Vice President looked away.

After reading Devers's note quickly, the President shoved it in his pocket and said, "If you will please wait here a little while, I will ask the congressional leaders who are in the Roosevelt Room to join us. The other members of the National Security Council will also attend the final meeting. I will be back shortly."

There was a nervous buzz of conversation as the President departed. In a few minutes the congressmen returned, and little groups gathered to discuss the day's unusual developments. Porter Canfield accepted the congratulations of several participants, who said they admired his courage and wished he were in the position of authority instead of Hurley.

Five minutes after the President had left, the attorney general was suddenly called from the room, but not many noticed that he was gone.

Those assembled in the Cabinet Room were becoming very